NOT MY BLOOD

NOT MY BLOOD

Barbara Cleverly

SOHO CRIME

Published by Soho Press, Inc.
853 Broadway
New York, NY 10003

Library of Congress Cataloging-in-Publication Data

Cleverly, Barbara.
Not my blood / Barbara Cleverly.
p. cm.
ISBN 978-1-61695-154-2
eISBN 978-1-61695-155-9
1. Sandilands, Joe (Fictitious character)—Fiction. 2. Boarding
schools—England—Fiction. I. Title.
PR6103.L48N68 2012
813'.6—dc23
2012012702

Interior design by Janine Agro, Soho Press, Inc.

Printed in the United States of America

10 9 8 7 6 5 4 3 2 1

This book is for
Daniel Joe,
my friend, advisor and grandson.

And for
Polly
whose flash of brilliance lit the way.

CHAPTER 1

Carrying more than a hint of snow, a southwesterly wind gusted up from the Channel, spattering the school's plate glass windows with sleety drops.

Mr. Rapson began to shout. Not a natural disciplinarian, he found he kept better control this way and was gratified by the knowledge that most of the boys at St. Magnus School, Seaford, were frightened of him. He affected a military style that most were familiar with from their own fathers. Peremptory and predictable. "Come along! No footer today, so we're going for a healthy walk. In pairs! Morrison! I said pairs! How many boys go to a pair? Two? That's right. Not three! Drummond? No one to walk with? Walk with Spielman. Come on, Spielman! Get a move on!"

Jackie Drummond didn't want to walk with Spielman. He didn't like Spielman. He had sticking-out teeth, and he never stopped talking, mostly giving rambling accounts of books he'd just read. At least he didn't expect a reply. This left Jackie free to work on his new plan: to run away as soon as possible.

Running away. The biggest sin you could commit, they said. But Jackie had heard of boys escaping from school—the older boys still talked about Peterkin, who'd run away ten years ago and never been brought back. Then there was Renfrew, who'd been in the year above Jackie. They'd said he'd been sacked for bad behaviour and sent to another school, but his best friend had other ideas. "Done a bunk," was his judgement. "Skipped off in the dead of night. Never even told me he was going." The best friend's knowing smirk gave out quite a different message. He'd collaborated. There were things he could tell. And probably had told—to the staff. Jackie learned from this. Even if he'd had a friend, he wouldn't breathe a word of his plans to him. If you're going, just go. Confide in no one.

For the hundredth time he reviewed the possibilities and consulted the list his mother had given him. He'd copied it into an exercise book to be on the safe side, but he carried with him the original in his mother's familiar handwriting. A charm. A talisman to be consulted when life got tough. There were Aunt Florence and Aunt Dorrie in Brighton, only five miles away. This option had the advantage that he could walk there, but the disadvantage that he could swiftly be brought back again. It was the first place they'd look. There were Mr. and Mrs. Masters in Camberley, but he wasn't sure where Camberley was, and he didn't like them very much anyway. His preference was for Uncle Dougal and Auntie Jeannie, his father's Scottish cousins in Perthshire. But Perthshire was a *very* long way away. And traveling on the railways over here was expensive. The fare alone was over two pounds and, even with the best expectations of cash from his birthday, it would be weeks before he had the necessary funds.

Not for the first time he doubted his capacity, but a second look at Mr. Rapson, standing four-square in his college scarf and porkpie hat, ginger-coloured Harris tweed plus-four suit so nearly matching his foam-flecked and bristling moustache, convinced him that he had no tolerable alternative. And Rappo was shouting again.

"Before we set off we're going for a little run. All of you— down to the corner and back again when I say go. Go!"

There was a wailing cry: "I'm cold, sir!"

This was Foster. Foster was recovering from a mastoid, and the biting wind gave him earache.

"Cold?" shouted Mr. Rapson. "Cold? Then run! That's the way to keep warm!"

The run took its predicted course (Smithson fell and scraped his knee and had to go in to Matron), and the walk followed in the teeth of the rising wind, down to the end of Sutton Avenue. Jackie hoped they'd turn right and then with any luck the walk would lead past the station and give him another chance to check his escape route. He liked the phrase "escape route" and said it over to himself. "My escape route!"

"Yes," he decided, "I'll walk down Sutton Avenue, turn right at the bottom, go through that lane beside the biscuit factory. There's not many street lamps here." And if he wore his cycling cape over his uniform no one would know he was from one of the many preparatory schools in the town. As Spielman rambled on, unheeded, Jackie thought to himself, "Three weeks. That should be enough. I'll go in three weeks!"

Back in the school changing rooms, Rappo called a halt to the shuddering, sniffling procession. "All right! Dismiss!"

The boys began to peel off their wet overcoats and hang them on the pegs to drip in dank rows.

"I said, 'Dismiss!' Don't loiter about! Move!"

Spielman stood, looking goofy, as the boys would have said. Mr. Rapson's voice rose and became shrill. His stomach ulcer made him tetchy. He was glad to discharge some of the tension on to a victim: Spielman had sat down—still talking—on a bench. "Blithering idiot! I told you to dismiss. I didn't tell you to sit! Did I? No!" He leapt forwards and seized Spielman by his prominent ears and lifted him bodily to his feet. Spielman screamed in surprise and pain.

Jackie, hardly aware of what he was doing, rushed forwards.

Indignation screwed his voice to a high-pitched squeal. "Leave him alone!" he shouted. *"Pagal!"* The Hindi word of abuse came easily to him. "Leave him alone!"

Mr. Rapson turned towards him in astonishment, and Jackie found his face within a few inches of Mr. Rapson's waistcoat, girt with his watch chain. Rocking back on his heel and using all his small strength, he plunged his fist into Mr. Rapson's midriff. He was crying with rage.

For a moment, time stood still. This was blasphemy of the most extreme kind. Such an outburst was totally without precedent. Masters hit you, you didn't hit them. Rapson was big and powerful, Jackie was small and insignificant. God only knew what would now ensue. The boys unconsciously began to back away, leaving Rapson and Jackie at the centre of a blighted space.

Rapson eyed Jackie, grim with menace. He inflated his tweedy ginger chest like an aggressive robin, and the boys shrank back farther. Smythe 3 hid his face behind a damp coat and whimpered. Finally, with chilling control, Rapson spoke: "I'll see you in my study after tea, Drummond. Six o'clock sharp! The rest of you— how many more times? Dismiss!"

The bell rang for tea. An audience gathered round Jackie. "You hit him! You actually hit him in the bread-basket! Gosh, you'll catch it, Drummond!"

"Did you see Rappo's face!"

"Six of the best," said Spielman, unimpressed by Jackie's intervention on his behalf, "at least. That's what you'll get. Six strokes on the stroke of six!" He began to titter.

Mr. Langhorne, one of the senior staff, was passing by on his way to supervise tea. He'd heard enough to guess what was going on. He gave Jackie a smile, saying jovially, "Take my advice. Fold a copy of the *Daily Sketch* in two and stick it down the back of your pants. I always used to. It helps."

The boys standing by laughed sycophantically, and Jackie went in to tea in total dismay.

He'd thought the day couldn't get worse but—wouldn't it just be his luck?—they'd been given luncheon meat, potatoes and beetroot, and he'd been put to sit next to Matron. Jackie was a well-brought up boy, and his father had taught him that good manners demanded that you make conversation with your neighbour. He did his best: "Do you know, Matron? Until I came to school, I thought that only servants had beetroot." He was aware that the remark had not gone down well, though he could not exactly see why. But then so many things had puzzled him since returning to England from his Indian childhood. The inevitable followed.

"Beetroot may be seen as only fit for servants from your elevated colonial viewpoint, Drummond, but some of us actually enjoy it. Be thankful for what you are given. You will stay here until you've finished what's before you!"

Jackie looked down at the mess on his plate. Beetroot juice seeping into the potato, turning it pink, luncheon meat slices curling at the edge, and a stale glass of water poured out a long time before. Matron went to whisper to Mr. Langhorne, and Mr. Langhorne said, "All dismiss except Drummond." And Jackie was left alone in the empty room, his plate still full before him.

But relief was at hand. Betty Bellefoy, who was in the estimation of the school the prettiest of the three parlour maids, took advantage of Matron's inattention and swept down upon him to whisk his plate away, replacing it with a dish of stewed plums and custard.

"Thanks, Betty," Jackie said, grateful.

"Ah, go on with you," said Betty comfortably.

Jackie spent a long time over his stewed plums. The longer he took, the longer he could postpone his encounter with Rapson. Anything might happen. The school might catch fire. Perhaps his parents would appear in the doorway, or perhaps Uncle Dougal or perhaps the Brighton aunts. (Not impossible. They had once made an unscheduled visit.) But relief did not come. There was no way out. He was Sydney Carton on the scaffold; he was Henry V at Harfleur; he was Brigadier Gerard. What had he said?—"Courage, mon vieux! Piré took Leipzig with fifty hussars!" He passionately wished that fifty sabre-waving hussars would come clattering into the dining room and raze the school to the ground.

One by one the last remaining staff left. Matron went out closely followed by Mr. Langhorne, which was often the case. And Jackie was left alone in the darkening room with Betty. Three plums eaten and the stones carefully arranged on the rim of his dish. *Tinker, tailor, soldier...* He counted them again. That was a good place to stop. He'd settle for soldier today. Jackie had been rather taken with the one in the verse Mr. Langhorne had made them learn last week. The swashbuckling chap who was "full of strange oaths . . . bearded like the pard . . . sudden and quick in quarrel, seeking the bubble reputation even in the cannon's mouth." He wanted desperately to be old enough to swear and have a beard. He'd shown already that he was quick in quarrel. The whole school would be talking about his punch to the Rapson midriff. But, now, in the outfall, he felt much more like the frightened child his father had once hugged and called his "chocolate cream soldier."

He screwed his eyes shut in an attempt to fight back tears. In his imagination his father's big hand tightened around his, rough and reassuring.

Two plums remaining . . . *sailor . . . rich man. . . .* Settle for "rich man"? Money was a good way of getting out of trouble. He would make a lot of it, buy up the whole school and close it down. That wouldn't be bad. Perhaps he should force down the last two plums? Betty looked anxiously at the big school clock and back at Jackie, her eyes wide with appeal. She sighed.

Good manners overcame even the paralysis of terror, and Jackie roused himself. Never keep a lady waiting. He handed his plate up for the maid, and she dashed off into the kitchens in a gust of relief, muttering a word of thanks.

Time to move on and take his medicine.

He got up and put his chair away. What had Lloyd 2 said? "Don't worry too much. It's only a tickle. It'll be over in five minutes. Brace up, Drummond! You're a toff! Everyone's saying so!"

A toff. At least "the bubble reputation" seemed to be coming his way. All he could do was shape up and try to deserve it.

On wobbly legs Jackie crossed the darkened hall, turned into the deserted corridor and began to climb the stairs to Rappo's room. Into the cannon's mouth.

CHAPTER 2

CHELSEA, LONDON. 1933.

J oe Sandilands stood looking down on the restless, steel-grey
surface of the river reflected in the lights of a tugboat and
listened while the bell of Chelsea Old Church struck the hour.
His sister Lydia joined him, handing him a glass of whisky.

"The snow's really coming down now," she said. "Glad I rang
Marcus to say I'd better stay over. Let's hope it's no more than a
flurry and I can get a train in the morning. I don't want to be
snowed up in Chelsea staring at the Thames for a week."

"No fun being marooned in London when you've already
emptied Selfridges of its goodies," Joe agreed. "I can see that. It's
the only time you'll deign to visit me—when you need to go
shopping."

"There are compensations." Lydia grinned. "It's quiet here.
No girls shrieking about the place. No husband asking how much
I've spent. Grown-up conversation. And I thought, since we seem
to be staying in tonight, we could listen to that play on the wire-
less. We'll make a start on the box of chocolates we didn't open
at the theatre."

Joe swished the curtains together, turned on another lamp,
and emptied half a scuttle of coal onto the fire. "I loathe February.
Nothing much happening."

"The calm between the New Year madness and the spring

urges," Lydia said, nodding. She looked at the clock. "Come and settle down. Curtain up in two minutes. I say—you won't be interrupted, will you?"

"That's the big advantage of my new job. Any bodies found floating in the Thames get the attention of one of my superintendents." Joe sank into an armchair. "And no one knows I'm here. Well, go on, then. Switch it on." He eyed the radio console with misgiving. "Warm up its valves, tickle its tubes or whatever you do."

Lydia approached the gleaming black bakelite altar and knelt before it. She began her ministrations, twiddling knobs and whispering encouragement until, after a series of nerve-rending shrieks and bleeps, a station tuned in. Dance music gushed into the room. A reedy tenor was warbling, "A room with a view and you . . . ou . . . ou. . . ."

Joe laughed. "There! Noel Coward agrees with me. *Some* girls would appreciate a river view in Chelsea! No—hold that one—the play's on straight after the Greenwich time signal."

Jack Hylton's band signed off in a smooth crescendo, and they'd counted the first five of nine pips when the telephone rang.

"Ah! Somebody knows where you are," said Lydia.

Warily, Joe went to pick up the receiver. "Flaxman 8891, Joe Sandilands here."

There was a pause and then a hurried and breathless small voice spoke. A boy's voice. "Hullo? Hullo? Is that my Uncle Joe?"

Joe paused, unsure how to reply. He flashed a puzzled glance at Lydia. His sister had two offspring, both at home with their father in Surrey. And both girls.

"Yes, this is Joe," he said carefully, "but who are you?"

"It's Jackie, sir. Jack Drummond. I think I'm in a terrible crisis. This is an emergency."

"Drummond?" Joe tried to make sense of what he was hearing. And, suddenly connecting, whispered, "Drummond."

A recurrent nightmare gripped him, tightening its fingers around his throat. Struggling to find his voice and keep his tone level and reassuring, to sound like the staid old uncle the boy obviously took him for, "Jackie?" he said. "Well, well! Jackie! We've never met! You must be . . . let me think . . . ten years old by now?"

"Nine actually, sir. I'm going to be ten next month."

"And where are your parents?"

"They're in India. They brought me over to school in the summer, stayed for a while, and went back home. I spent Christmas with my aunts in Brighton."

"I see. And this emergency—you're going to tell me you've run out of pocket money, is that it?"

"No sir. This is real trouble I'm in. I was given your telephone number, but they said I wasn't to use it unless I was in a crisis."

"Where are you, Jackie?"

"I'm at Victoria Station. I'm in the stationmaster's office. The lady policeman brought me here. I hadn't got a ticket, you see. She's waiting outside. They're going to arrest me for traveling without a ticket. I'm scared. . . ." The voice, which had been resolute, now had a break in it. "What shall I do, Uncle?"

"Well, what you do," said Joe as calmly as he could, "is three things. First, stop worrying. Second, see if you can get yourself a cup of tea. Third, don't hang up but put the phone down. Go and get the policewoman to come and speak to me. Oh, and fourth, Jackie, I'll be there with you in twenty minutes. Look, it's not the end of the world to be caught traveling without a ticket. I'll bring some cash and bail you out."

The reply was hushed, a voice trying to force down hysteria. "It's not that, it's not that at all, Uncle. You see, I've . . . I'm afraid I've killed my form master."

THE POLICEWOMAN'S VOICE was young, concerned and educated. "Good evening, sir. I take it I'm speaking to

Assistant Commissioner Sandilands? Your nephew had your name and number clutched in his hand when I spotted him trying to creep through the barrier. I ought to have taken him straight to a place of safety, I know, but. . . ."

"You did exactly the right thing, Officer. . . ."

"Huntingdon, sir. Emily Huntingdon, W.P. 955."

"Good, well, listen, Huntingdon, I'm on my way. We have a delicate situation on our hands. I have reason to believe the boy may be a witness to a crime. Keep him safe where he is, will you? And I want you to make sure no one else approaches him, not even the local beat bobby."

There was the slightest pause before Officer Huntingdon replied. "Understood, sir."

"Now who on earth was that?" said his sister. "Who's Jackie?"

Joe was already struggling into a pea-jacket. He picked up a flat cap with a leather peak he'd borrowed from a Thames bargeman and said, "I'm not absolutely certain, Lydia, but there's trouble with a runaway boy. At Victoria Station. They're holding him until I can get there."

Lydia glared in exasperation. "A runaway? But why would you be involved, Joe? They don't call out a grandee like you on a snowy evening to deal with a runaway!" Her expression softened. "Still—on a night like this . . . poor little chap! But I thought you had women police patrols to round up the waifs and strays of London?"

"This is a rather special runaway, Lydia. Pass me those gumboots, will you? Oh, and it's quite likely I shall be bringing him home with me."

WINDING A MUFFLER round his neck, Joe clumped down three flights of stairs to the dimly lit hallway. Inevitably, a door opened, and the hearty voice of his landlord, ex-Inspector Jenkins of the Metropolitan Police greeted him. "Late call, sir?"

"Yeah, late call, Alfred."

"Wrap up warm, then! It's coming cold. Oh—sir! You can use the lift again on the way back. They've been in and fixed it."

"My sister will be glad of that, Alfred. I'll tell her."

Joe stepped out into the street and to his relief there was a light in the cabbies' shelter on the embankment. To his further relief there were two taxis in the rank and he ran across the road to claim one of them.

"Victoria Station," he said. "And get me as near to the stationmaster's office as you can."

"No difficulty, sir," said the cabby, ringing down his flag.

The snow was thickening as they drove the last few yards up Buckingham Palace Road and Joe looked anxiously at his watch. Twenty minutes, he'd said, and twenty minutes it was. He shouldered his way along the platform to the stationmaster's office and saw, standing feet apart, hands behind her back, the reassuring figure of a policewoman.

"Huntingdon?" he asked.

She saluted neatly. Not many of the female officers could do this naturally. She looked bright, efficient, friendly. She did not, beyond a point, look deferential. No one could add grace to the hideous high-crowned, wide-brimmed hat, nobody could look feminine or even female in the uncompromising blue serge skirt and the clumping shoes, but she managed, Joe noticed.

"Where's the miscreant?" he asked, showing his warrant card.

"No miscreant, sir, you'll find," she corrected him with a smile. "No miscreant at all. Just a boy in trouble. Not uncommon around here."

"Thank you for dealing with this. Enter your report. Say that I assumed custody. I'll make it right with your governor, and I'll take the lad in charge for the time being."

"Your nephew, sir?"

"Not even that," said Joe. "He's newly arrived from India, and you know how it is in India—or perhaps you don't? Any family friend becomes an honourary uncle. Or aunt."

"I have one or two of those myself, sir." Huntingdon's smile was gracious, her eyes watchful. "Shall I come in with you?" she asked. "I think what our prisoner needs more than anything is something to eat, if I may suggest, sir. He's had nothing really since breakfast as far as I can work out."

Gently Joe pushed the door of the stationmaster's office open and stood in silence looking in. He saw the stolid figure of the assistant stationmaster doing the crossword on the back of the Evening News, a company of teacups at his elbow and an ashtray brimming with cigarette ends in front of him. The general smell of police stations in the middle of the night greeted Joe, familiar and reassuring.

He tightened his jaw, breathed in, and steeled himself to take his first look at Jackie Drummond.

With legs swinging, a small fair-haired boy clutching a cycling cape about his shoulders looked up anxiously. An Afghan bag with a broad strap lay at his feet.

"Now, what on earth do I say?" Joe asked himself as they stared at each other. What he did finally say, with relief and a rush of recognition, was: "Jackie! I'd have known you anywhere—you're very much like your mother!"

The small face, pinched, pale with bruised circles under the eyes, was suddenly lit by a radiant smile. "And you look quite like my dad!"

Joe held out a hand. "Come on then, Jackie, let's be going. We can talk as we go. I'll take your bag. Say goodbye to the station-master."

"Goodbye, sir," said the boy dutifully, "and thank you for having me."

And, as they left the office, "Say goodbye to Constable Huntingdon."

In the most natural way in the world, the boy shook hands and lifted his face for a kiss. "Thank you, Constable," he said politely, "for looking after me."

"I enjoyed looking after you. See you again soon, Jackie, I hope," said Constable Huntingdon. "Oops! Perhaps I oughtn't to say that!" she added, suddenly self-conscious, and seemed pleased with the swift grin of understanding the boy gave her.

Hand in hand they returned to the waiting taxi and set off once more through the slushy streets, gas lamps flickering in the rising wind and reflecting from the wet pavements.

"Have you been to London before, Jackie?" Joe asked.

"Once. Daddy brought me up for shopping. We went to Hamleys and the Tower and Madame Tussauds."

"Are you hungry?"

"Yes, very."

"Well, come on, we'll find you something. I should think you've drunk enough tea tonight to float the Normandie."

The boy smiled shyly. "Yes," he said, "they kept giving it to me. I don't really like tea very much."

"We'll find something else. Cocoa perhaps? Now, unless I'm wrong about this, you've run away from school?"

"Yes, sir."

"I expect you had a reason?"

"Yes, sir."

"You said you'd killed your housemaster?"

"No, sir. Form master."

"Oh, all right. Form master. Anybody know where you are?"

"No, sir. I don't even know where I am myself."

"Well, I'll tell you what we're going to do. We're going to get you something to eat, and then we're going back to my flat, and then either you're going to bed or you're going to tell me what's been happening. Whatever you've done or *think* you've done, you're safe now. Nobody's following you. Nobody's going to catch up with you."

They dismounted at the cabman's shelter. "What place is this?" said Jackie dubiously, not leaving go of Joe's hand.

"It's a cabman's shelter," said Joe reassuringly. "They have them all over London though not so many as there used to be. It's a place where taxi drivers can get something to eat."

"It looks like a railway carriage."

Long, low, weather-boarded and painted park-bench green, it had a small black projecting iron stovepipe giving out a smell of coal smoke and food, and a notice saying "Licensed Cabman Shelter no. 402."

"Yes, it is like a railway carriage and if the cabbies get to know you, they'll let you eat there. I don't think they're supposed to; it's supposed to be reserved for them. The man who runs this one's an old friend of mine. I sometimes take people here for a quiet chat. Let's go on board and see what we can find."

They stepped from the cold street into a welcoming fug. "Evening, Frank," said Joe to the whiskered man behind the counter. "Something for this gentleman to eat. He's hungry."

"Evening, Captain! Hungry is it? Well, what about shepherd's pie with onion gravy?"

"Oh, I'd like that," Jackie said eagerly.

"And to follow? We've got spotted dick with a dollop of custard?"

Jackie's eyes lit on a basin of steaming pudding studded with dark currants, and he nodded.

"I think that would be entirely appropriate," said Joe. "Make that two of everything, Frank, if you please. We'll sit ourselves down."

The boy settled and looked around him with suspicion. "'Captain?' he asked. "Why did that man call you 'captain,' sir?"

Joe could not hide a smile. Whatever else, this was a true colonial he was entertaining to supper. Death, flight and arrest the child was apparently taking in his stride, but the niceties of rank—that was worthy of question by a child reared in the Indian Civil Service.

"I was a very young captain in the Fusiliers when Frank first knew me.... Early days of the war ... Mons. I was winged manning the barricades—uselessly—against the first German onslaught on France. My rank did improve," he reassured the lad, "but it's the dashing captain image that's stuck with me. I don't mind at all. We all need a reminder of where we've come from. It's a compliment."

There were two other dark figures in the shelter, busy with substantial servings of pease pudding. They greeted Joe. "Evenin', Guv." One looked at Jackie and rolled his eyes in a pantomime of alarm. "Cor! That's a right nasty piece of work you've got under restraint, Guv! If 'e makes a break for it, count on us for back-up!"

To Joe's dismay, the boy began to tremble and look towards the door. Joe leaned forwards and whispered: "Just joking, Jackie. You're safe here. Food'll be up in a minute. No rush, but perhaps you could tell me a little bit about what happened this evening?"

At once the boy's eyes glazed with remembered fear. His hand went to his eyebrow, and he began to rub at it with the knuckle of his forefinger. Accustomed as he was to interrogating suspects to cracking point, Joe recognised the gesture as a sign of acute distress and cursed himself for an insensitive fool. He reached over, seized the little hand, and gave it a squeeze. "There's no hurry," he said once more. "Just take your time."

The boy took a while to pull his thoughts together and then burst out: "Well, it's Mr. Rapson! I hate him," he added almost apologetically. "Everybody knows I hate him, and when they find he's dead they'll know it's me that did it."

"I'm not sure of that," said Joe, "but go on."

"Well, they will know because I've attacked him before."

"Great heavens!" Joe said lightly. "Are you telling me you've got previous? I mean . . . that you're a seasoned beater-up of form masters?"

Jackie gave him a pained smile. "Just once, sir." And then he burst out: "I hit him! I went for him! Perhaps I shouldn't have done. But I don't think I was wrong. There's a boy in my class called Spielman, and he's not . . . not really all there, you know. He makes silly faces. He can't help it."

"Silly faces?"

"Yes. Like this." He gave a demonstration. "And he looks—well—loopy. He's got big ears—great big ears and sticking-out teeth and everybody teases him. And Rappo's the worst of all. He's always going for him, making him stand out in front of the class, and this afternoon he pulled Spielman up by his ears. By his ears! Spielman started crying. It must have really hurt him. He's only just got over a mastoid. I lost my rag, and I went and hit Rappo."

"Hit him?"

"Hit him in the stomach. With my fist. As hard as I could manage. That hard, sir." He held out for inspection a small hand whose knuckles were skinned and swollen. "I got him in his watch chain. And then he went into the usual Rappo Rant. 'See you in my study after supper, Drummond!' and all that." Jackie shuddered and fell silent. "Pretty scary!"

With a flick of a teacloth, plates of shepherd's pie appeared on the table.

"Mustard, sonny? Ketchup? Cupper tea?"

"No, no cupper tea, thank you, but everything else, please."

Between mouthfuls, Jackie resumed. "Perhaps I shouldn't have hit him, but I didn't think Dad would have minded. Once, he saw a soldier, a private in the East Yorks, hitting a little Indian man, and Dad really let him have it! Felled him to the ground,' he added with relish. 'And my father's a . . . well, you know my father. He said you always ought to stand up to bullies, and this seemed to be the same. Don't you think?"

"Yes," said Joe, "I do think. And I know Andrew would have done just the same. He's not a man to stand by and see injustice done."

"That's right, sir!" Jackie nodded with pride. "He's not strong, my dad, but he never lets a game leg hold him back."

"No indeed," said Joe softly. "I've stood shoulder to shoulder with Andrew in—er—difficult circumstances and been glad of his strength."

The pie disappeared at surprising speed. The pudding followed. Jackie's face acquired some colour, but his speech began to slur and his eyelids began to droop.

"You don't have to finish," said Joe comfortingly.

"I want to finish."

Tea-towel round his stomach, the proprietor walked over to them. "You all right, son? Had enough have you? There's more if you want it." And then to Joe, "Time this one was in bed, I think, Captain?"

Joe had come to the same conclusion. He'd decided that Jackie was the type of witness whom you couldn't hurry, but who, if left to himself, would produce, by degrees, an accurate statement. "Just one thing," he said, "and then we'll go home. After this confrontation with Rappo you decided to run away?"

"Oh, no. I decided to run away a long time ago. I was only waiting until I'd collected enough money to get to Uncle Dougal in Scotland. But I had to, well, bring my plans forwards a bit and go for it tonight. I was ready. I had my running away bag all packed." He gestured towards his shoulder bag. "I knew I had to get away before anyone found me, and then I thought, I'll use the number Mum gave me. Killing someone's an emergency all right, isn't it?"

"Yes," said Joe, "you did the right thing."

While they'd been in the shelter the snow had begun to lie and wind-blown snow was sticking to the southerly face of the power station chimney stacks. Slated roofs were turning from grey-blue to white.

"That's where we're going," said Joe, pointing, "that lighted up window there. That's my flat. My sister—your Aunt Lydia, I suppose—is at home and still up, you see. People sometimes think it's a funny place to live, but I like it."

A reassuring figure in dressing gown and slippers, Lydia was standing in the hall as Joe unlocked the door.

"Hullo!" she said. "And who's this?"

"Jackie Drummond, Aunt Lydia. I'm sorry to be arriving so late."

Though clearly puzzled, Lydia moved smoothly into action. "That's quite all right, Jackie. I took the opportunity of making up a camp bed in the box room. You must be exhausted! What about a nice hot bath and then bed? Here, let me take your cape."

Lydia put out a motherly hand to unbutton his cycling cape and the boy abruptly pulled away from her in alarm, clutching it tightly round his shoulders.

"What's the matter, Jackie?" said Joe.

Jackie looked from one to the other and then, apparently coming to a decision, took off his cape and handed it to Lydia. Lydia gasped. Joe swallowed. The front of the boy's uniform, white shirt, grey shorts and grey blazer were covered in rusty-red stains.

"It's not my blood, sir," whispered Jackie. "It's Mr. Rapson's."

JOE AND LYDIA stared at each other and then at Jackie in silence for a moment until Joe collected himself.

"Well," he said, "first things first. And the first thing is to get out of those clothes and into a bath. Have you got pyjamas in your exit bag? Good. Lydia, why don't you take him? Put his clothes in a bag and keep them together. They just might be evidence. Of something or other. . . . Go with Aunt Lydia, Jackie."

Lydia slipped an arm round Jackie. "Come on then," she said, "let's posh you up a bit. And we'll see if we can find a plaster for that hand. You look as though you've gone five rounds with Jack Dempsey." They left the room together.

When Lydia returned Joe was staring out of the window at the dark river and the fluttering snow. He turned, and brother and sister looked at each other in amazement.

"It's all right," said Lydia, breaking the awkward silence, "he's enjoying his hot bath. I gave him your model battleship to play with. Tell me, Joe—what is all this? You look absolutely shattered! You've looked as though you've seen a ghost ever since you came back with that boy. Just what *is* going on? What *has* happened to him? Who's Mr. Rapson? And, for heaven's sake—who is *he?*"

"Lydia," said Joe, "you're not going to believe this—I'm not sure I believe it myself but . . . oh, God, could I be wrong about this? I think . . . I'm almost certain . . . that boy is my son!"

CHAPTER 3

"Joe! For goodness sake! You haven't got a son!"

Lydia was silent for a moment and then went on more thoughtfully, "Sorry. I suppose I have to say—is it possible? I mean, *could* he be your son?"

"Not only possible," said Joe slowly, "but I'd have to say probable."

"But who? How? Did you know he was coming?"

"Know he was coming? I didn't even know he existed! His mother gave him this address but more than that I really don't know."

"His mother! Who *is* his mother? And *where* is his mother? She's not on the next train, is she?" Lydia looked about her in mock alarm. "This place is hardly big enough to accommodate a growing family. Any more to declare?"

"No, Lyd. I'm reasonably certain of that. And the lady's name is Nancy Drummond. She's in India."

"Oh! India!" Her relief was clear. "Yes, come to think of it, that fits. Ten years ago you were in Bengal." She smiled. "I always thought there must have been more to your Indian interlude than multiple murders and man-eating tigers. Rather glad to hear there were lighter moments."

"Yes. Well, his mother is still apparently in Bengal. So is his father . . . well, you know what I mean. Andrew Drummond, her husband. The man the world—and the boy—thinks is his father. The Collector of Panikhat."

"Oh. A husband? Tell me, Joe, was he—Andrew, the Collector—aware that. . . ?"

Joe nodded silently, thoughts and memories suppressed for years flashing painfully to mind. "Oh, he was aware, all right," he murmured.

"Did it come to fisticuffs, pistols at dawn, perhaps?" Lydia asked hesitantly, her intense curiosity pushing her to ask questions she sensed would be unwelcome.

"No!" Joe's sudden grin punctured the tension between them. "I knew Andrew for just a short time, but I count him one of my dearest friends. And I know he liked me. Well, you'd have to have some pretty positive feelings for the chap you've chosen to father your wife's child, wouldn't you?"

"Chosen?" said Lydia faintly and she sank down onto the sofa. "Are you going to explain all this? And can you really be so certain that the boy's yours? I mean. . . ." Her eyes strayed to the bathroom door, and they listened for a moment to sounds of contented splashing and the 'whoop, whoop, whoop' of a Dreadnought siren. ". . . I have to say this and perhaps you've already noticed—that child doesn't look in the slightest bit like *you*."

"That's the irony!" Joe gave a bitter laugh. "*I* was selected to be the father of Nancy Drummond's child quite deliberately, I believe, because physically Andrew and I are very similar. Tall, dark thick hair, a bit bony. . . ."

"Emphatic features?"

"Those too. The first thing that boy said to me was 'You look like my father.' He saw it straight away! The vital *difference* between us is that Andrew was badly injured in the war. The medical report—oh, yes, I did a bit of snooping, once I'd caught on to what was going on—mentioned, as well as a badly shot-up leg, something the military doctors delicately termed 'intestinal chaos.' Careful chaps, those medics—they went in for euphemism of the most ingenious kind to avoid blotting a chap's record forever more. You can read what you like into 'intestinal chaos,' but I think, as well as a probably quite appalling stomach wound, it means Andrew had some essential equipment damaged and was rendered unable to have children. Her uncle hinted as much to me, but I wasn't quick enough to catch his meaning. Nancy desperately wanted a child. And what Nancy wanted, Andrew was going to ensure that she had, whatever the practical difficulties. Or the heartache."

"Not the easiest thing to supply to order, I'd guess—in India. A child. You don't find offspring in the Gamages catalogue, colonial edition. Wide choice of colour and size," Lydia said thoughtfully.

"No indeed! And you know what India's like! Worse than Wimbledon! Tight community, and the memsahibs have eagle eyes, suspicious minds and tongues like razors. Now, if a dark-haired policeman passing through the province on duty were to get close to the Collector's wife—and they were discreet about their closeness—it might just go unremarked if, nine months later, she has a dark-haired child—because her husband also has those same dark looks. Careful girl, Nancy. I have to say. She made apparently innocent but—I realised later—precisely targeted enquiries into my pedigree. A Lowland Scots gentleman with a law degree from Edinburgh and a chestful of medals seemed to be entirely satisfactory for her purposes. But I'll tell you, Lyd, if I'd spent my war years behind a desk or—even worse—had curly red hair, I wouldn't have stood a chance with Nancy Drummond!"

Lydia risked a smile. "Good old Fate! I'd guess then that the child looks like his mother. And she went to all that trouble for nothing!"

"Not for nothing. And whatever it was, it was no trouble," Joe said with a fleeting grin. "At the time. Though after I found out what they'd been scheming towards I was a bit miffed. I loved her, Lydia."

"A bit miffed!" Lydia was reddening with anger, a sisterly outrage gathering to pick up and counteract his understatement. "This pair used you for breeding purposes—that's what it amounts to—like a Black Angus bull! Except that, unlike a good Scottish stockman, Drummond didn't pay a stud fee before he let you loose in his paddock, I'll bet!"

"Lydia!"

"Sorry. But, Joe, are you quite sure you had no idea . . . they didn't ask your permission or drop a hint they were about to steal. . . ." In her emotion, Lydia groped for an acceptable word. ". . . your essence?"

Joe fought down an untimely rush of hilarity. He shrugged and answered seriously. "No, not a clue. I put it all down to my manly allure. By the time I caught on it was—evidently—too late, and no amount of indignant spluttering was going to affect the issue."

"Ah, yes. The issue." Lydia's voice softened as she nodded towards the bathroom door. "Wherever he came from and who-ever's issue he is—I'll tell you something, Joe: that's a fine boy. Plucky. Resourceful. Handsome. A worthwhile addition to the human race, you'd say. And one can hardly unwish him. But I can imagine your feelings. Poor Joe! I knew you'd changed when you got back but then, I told myself, India does change people. I never guessed about the broken heart. Wouldn't it have helped to talk about it?"

"Lord no! Hard to talk about the event without sounding self-pitying—or, worse, comical. Why burden others with my tales of woe? My mates would have grinned, dug an elbow in my ribs and said, 'Lucky old bugger, eh, what!' No. Some things are better kept out of view. I thought I'd buried it all until I saw the little chap sitting there looking so like his mother. Same coppery hair and light frame. . . ." He broke off, hearing the bath plug pulled. "Look, Lydia, what's happened to him—Jackie, that is—I have no idea. But obviously, whatever it is, I must look after him."

"*We* must look after him. If you think about it, Joe, and your calculation is correct, well, then, he has an aunt now. A real one! That's a role I can take on and play openly. Besides, I've had plenty of experience—there's always some waif or stray of yours hogging my spare room. But what are we going to *do* with him?"

"I can't tell. But I'll tell you what I'm *not* going to do and that's send him back to that school. Whatever happened this evening, it was something damned dangerous. That was blood all over the front of his uniform. A large quantity of blood, I'd say."

So they talked on in hushed and urgent voices until Jackie, scrubbed and cleaned in pyjamas and an old shirt of Joe's, came back through the door.

"There are things," said Joe, "that I need to know, Jackie. Lyd, see if you can find a cup of cocoa. One for me too while you're at it. Suit you?"

"Yes please, sir. Two sugars, if I may."

Joe took Jackie's hand and sat him down on the sofa. He plumped up a cushion and poked up the fire. "You told me you were on your way to see this Rappo. Is that right? Tell me some more. Pick it up from there. What happened when you got to him?"

"Well, I went up to his room and banged on the door. No answer. I banged again. Still no answer. I opened the door and looked in. As far as I could see, Rappo wasn't there so I went in and looked round the room. I was right—he wasn't there, and I began to think 'Oh, crikey, he's forgotten!' I didn't quite know what to do. I just walked round the room a bit and then I saw my running away bag. It was up on a high shelf. He'd taken my running away bag from my locker in the dorm! He shouldn't have done that, should he? It wasn't anything to do with him and I couldn't think why he'd taken it. The strap was hanging down and I could reach that so I gave it a pull. Then something awful happened! My bag tipped over and fell and everything spilled out onto Rappo's desk. I was afraid Rappo would come back before I'd put everything together, but he didn't. I stuffed everything in. Not neatly as I'd done it before, but at least I got it all back in. I mean there was clothes, spare shirts, spare pants, spare socks, *Treasure Island* to read, my map of London. But Rappo still didn't come back. So I wrote him a note."

"What did you say, Jackie?"

"Can't remember exactly but something like: 'Came to see you at six and waited for a bit. Sorry about the mess. Signed, J. Drummond.' Something like that. I left it in the middle of his desk and weighed it down with a paperweight so he'd be sure to see it. Well then I went out onto the landing, and there were people standing about, talking, on the front stairs. I didn't want anyone to see me in case they thought I was sneaking off . . . you know . . . in a funk. Then I remembered the back stairs. They go down to the changing room and the kitchen and the back door and places like that. I don't know what I was going to do. Perhaps I was going to hide a bit but well anyway I set off down the back way and . . . oh . . . Uncle Joe, it was terrible! There was Rappo standing halfway up the stairs. He was standing there just staring at me. He was holding onto the banisters with both hands and he looked all funny. He had poppy eyes and his mouth open . . . like this. . . ."

"What did he say?"

"He didn't say anything except, 'Ah, ah, grrr. . . .' Like that. Growling and spluttering. I think he hardly saw me. He was panting for breath—I thought he'd been running, though Rapson never runs anywhere. He held out his hand as if he wanted to catch hold of me. I wasn't going to let him touch me! I tried to duck past him on the stairs but he grabbed me and held on to me, sort of groaning and trying to say something. I was ever so scared! He looked so mad! I gave him a push. Only to get away from him! I didn't mean to hurt him! I gave him a push and...." Jackie began to sniffle.

"Jackie," said Joe, "it's all right. I'm here. You're safe. Of course you gave him a push. It sounds as if it was very frightening. So what happened?"

"He fell! He fell backwards down the stairs all the way to the bottom and he sort of crumpled and rolled over. He landed on his front. He looked broken up. Like Humpty Dumpty. All his arms and legs were sticking out. I knew I ought to go to him and I made myself climb down the stairs after him. I tried to turn him over to see if he was still breathing. But he was too heavy. I couldn't move him. I couldn't hear anything so I put my ear to his chest to see if his heart was still beating but ... Uncle Joe, he was dead! When I touched his jacket my hands got all sticky!"

Jackie held his hands out, his eyes wide with horror at the memory. "His front was sopping wet. I thought he'd been out in the snow and got wet through but it was blood! He was dead and all bloody! I'd killed him! I'd pushed him down the stairs and killed him! Broken his neck? I don't know. People do break their necks when they fall downstairs, don't they?"

"Well, yes, they do," said Joe, "but I don't think that can be what happened to Rappo."

Lydia edged back into the room with a tray. "Here we are!" she said in the cheery tone of one bearing cocoa and ginger biscuits. "I floated some cream on top as they do in Vienna. Thought we all deserved a treat. Do go on. I heard what you were saying, Jackie. Poor old thing! What a dreadful experience!"

"Thank you, Auntie Lydia." He sipped and gave a shaky smile. "Well you see, then I thought: Now I really am in trouble! They'll all know I've killed Rappo! I must run way. Bring my plans forwards, you could say. So I ran to the cloakroom and washed my hands, then I got my cycling cape and put my bag round my shoulder. It was about a quarter to seven and I thought if I hurried I could catch the seven o'clock train—the train to London—and come to you."

"Jackie, I'm very glad you're here, but why me?"

"Well," said Jackie, "There was Uncle Dougal in Scotland but I hadn't enough money for the fare, and the aunts in Brighton but they'd soon catch up with me in Brighton. And there are people in Camberley but I don't really know them and then at the end of the letter Mum gave me—I've got it here...." he said and went to feel in the pocket of his cycling cape. "Here you are, you see, here are the telephone numbers and addresses and at the end—look...."

He handed the much crumpled paper list to Joe, who read it and passed it on to Lydia. The list of names concluded: *In emergency only, Joe Sandilands, 2, Reach House, Chelsea, London. Flaxman 8891. Uncle Joe is a policeman. He will take care of you.*

"That's not Mummy's writing," said Joe, puzzled.

"No," said Jackie, "it's Dad's. He added you just when I was saying goodbye to him. I'm glad he did!"

"Yes, by God!" said Joe. "I'm glad he did too! I don't like to think of you loose in London without a bean."

Jackie sat between them on the sofa, empty mug in his hand, blinking owlishly from one to the other.

"I think that's enough," said Lydia. "Come and see the bed I've made up for you. Quite cozy, you'll find. I'll tuck you in."

"Will I be by myself, Auntie?"

"Yes. In splendour and state. Well, not much splendour—it's only a box room. But there won't be twenty other boys fussing about to keep you awake."

"Lydia," Joe called after her, and then, hesitantly: "I think you've misunderstood. He mightn't *want* to be alone . . . nightmares and all that. If you look in the bottom drawer of the pine chest, you'll find something you'll recognise. You can offer it to Jackie. It may help."

"Go and climb into bed, Jackie. I'll be with you in a minute. . . . What are you on about, Joe?"

"Hector. You can give him Hector." He frowned to hear her peal of laughter.

"Your disgusting old horse? He was declared unhygienic and mother threw him out years ago. Anyway," she whispered, "the boy's nearly *ten*. I don't want to insult him."

"Do it anyway, Lydia."

Joe sat and listened for a while to the soft voices coming through from the box room, first Lydia then Jackie in reply. There was a shared laugh. Probably greeting Hector's appearance. These were the most natural of sounds, friendly and domestic. Impossible to believe that there was a bloody background to these moments of peace, hard to believe that they sat in the outfall of manslaughter at the very least.

"Well, Joe," said Lydia when she returned, "what now? Worked out your next move, have you?"

"Yes, my immediate next move, said Joe, "but beyond that I can't see. My next move has to be to ring up this wretched school. I should have done it hours ago but this has been rather a precious moment for me and I didn't want policemen clumping all over the place. Or headmasters. I didn't want Jackie to be in any kind of trouble whatever and we can keep him safe and warm and fed here. I even had a sort of mad idea that he might go back home with you for a bit at least. Was that so daft?"

"Well I have to say I think it was a bit daft. Of course he'd be totally welcome and for as long as you can manage—you know that. But there are others involved, aren't there?"

"Quite a few," said Joe. "Quite a few."

He picked up the phone and dialled directory enquiries.

Lydia heard him say in a very police voice, "St. Magnus School, Sussex please." And after the delay, "St. Magnus School? Please put me through to someone in authority." And then, "My name is Sandilands. I'd like to know to whom I am speaking.... This is important and confidential. I would prefer to speak to the headmaster. You may tell him it concerns a boy of his. Jack Drummond."

Almost at once a worried and angry voice: "Hullo? Hullo? You have something to tell me about Drummond? Do you know where he is? I say, do you know where he is? And, incidentally, who are you? Are you saying you've got Jack Drummond *there*? How did this happen?" The voice was anxious, hostile. "The police are looking for him you know."

"I didn't know but I thought it was possible. But I need to know who I'm speaking to—is that the headmaster?"

"Yes. Farman here. Where are you speaking from?"

Carefully and succinctly Joe gave his name, address and telephone number.

"London! How the hell did he get there?" said Farman, clearly not in any way reassured. "Who's holding him?"

"No one's *holding* him," said Joe. "He's in my care."

"What's it got to do with you? How did you get in on this?"

Patiently Joe explained. "Mr. and Mrs. Drummond gave Jackie my name and address as a contact if he was in any sort of trouble. I met him at Victoria Station and brought him back to my flat here. I've fed him and he's now in bed. I do not want him disturbed or worried in any way tonight. He's obviously been through an alarming experience. Now—you said the police were looking for him. Can you explain to me why?"

"There's been a bit of ... an accident here. It is apparent that Drummond was in some way involved. The police need to interview him. Perhaps you'd better speak to them. Come back to me when you've finished—we must arrange for Drummond's return as soon as possible. I consider that of paramount importance. I am, after all, *in loco parentis*."

"And, by the same token," said Joe, "I find myself *in loco* patris." He delivered the invention with all the gravitas of a lawyer. "Which is to say, the boy has been transferred to my care, in writing, by Andrew Drummond. I have the document to hand. I have assumed paternal responsibility for him."

"I shall need to see your proof. I have a list here that his parents gave me of relations and friends he might contact and I don't see your name on it."

"I don't think I'm going to like this man," Joe thought. "Do I play my trump card now? Yes, I think I do."

"Before we say any more or make any plans for the immediate future," he said frostily, "I want to speak to the officer presently in charge of this case."

And Farman's voice distantly, "He wants to speak to you. Some interfering blighter called Sandilands. I'm not getting much sense out of him myself. Will you take this? That might be best."

An efficient police voice took over. "Detective Inspector Martin."

"Good evening, Martin," said Joe. "My name is Sandilands. You may possibly have heard of me. Assistant Commissioner Sandilands, Scotland Yard."

There was a grunt at the other end. "Would you mind saying that again?"

Joe did so.

"And may I ask what has been your involvement so far, sir? This is a complicated case, as you probably gather, but I wouldn't have thought it warranted the full attention of. . . ."

In the background Joe heard Farman's voice: "Go on, Martin, tell him to mind his own bloody business! Tell him to get off the line and bring the boy back here. Or can we send a car for him?"

Then Martin's voice: "Just a minute, Mr. Farman. Now, say

again—this has come to the attention of the *Metropolitan Police?* What, may I ask, is precisely your involvement, *Assistant Commissioner?*"

Joe smiled as he heard the emphasis, emphasis no doubt for Farman's benefit.

"The boy was committed to my care by his parents. I expect you're making notes? You may pencil in: 'uncle' and add: 'Indian connections . . . diplomatic interest. . . .'"

"I don't care if he's the Mahatma's grandson, we want him here as soon as possible." Martin was clearly irritated by the suggestion of influence. Irritated to the point of rudeness. "He may be a witness in a murder enquiry. Do you know anything about this? Are you acting in an official capacity?"

"I know only what the boy's told me. But may I make one thing quite clear? That boy is going nowhere tonight. If you want to interview him you can speak to him here in my presence or, if you can persuade me that it's absolutely necessary, I will bring him down to you. Starting out tomorrow. It's snowing heavily here in London and I expect it's even worse down there in Sussex. It may not even be possible to undertake the journey. The best I can offer is to start out in the morning and spend the night at the boy's aunt's house in Surrey, thus breaking halfway what looks like being a difficult bit of motoring. In the meantime, believe me, I have no desire whatever to interfere, though I own to an interest."

"Yes. . . ." said Martin more calmly. "It's an interesting situation to say the least. Look here, sir—confidentially, the boy is a murder *suspect* and I'd sooner he was in police custody."

"That," said Joe, "is precisely what I am anxious to avoid. Would I be forcing a confidence if I were to ask what is the present situation of Mr. Rapson, master at St. Magnus School?"

There was a long pause at the other end. "I have no reason to doubt what you say but please recall that I have no proof of your identity. I release information in respect of Mr. Rapson only because it will very shortly become public knowledge. His present situation is not a happy one. He is, in fact, dead. He is the victim of multiple stab wounds. As far as we can see, the last person to see him alive was Jack Drummond. So we have this situation—at the very least, Jack Drummond is a material witness in a murder enquiry, or—and I'm sure I don't have to spell this out—is a suspect. You will understand why I want to interview him, why I want him here, in Sussex, where the crime occurred and where it must be resolved."

"A witness, obviously, but are you telling me the injuries you describe could have been inflicted by a small ten-year-old boy?"

"You're going rather too fast for me, sir. I repeat: I need to interview the boy. I want him down here without delay. Can I rely on your cooperation?"

"Yes, of course," said Joe impatiently, "and I will make arrangements accordingly. But don't expect us too early. Quite apart from anything else, the boy has no clothes other than pyjamas."

"No clothes other than pyjamas?" Martin repeated incredulously. "How did that happen? He left here wearing his uniform."

"There's a lot of questions to answer," said Joe, "and we could waste a great deal of each other's time trying to deal with them over the telephone. If I say I'll bring the boy to you as soon as I conveniently can, then let's leave it there, Inspector—was it Inspector?—Martin."

"Very well. I suppose I shall have to leave it there." Frustration pushed him to the edge of insubordination. "And, not for the first time in my police career, I defer, against my better judgement, to superior rank . . . Sir."

Joe turned away from the telephone as Lydia came through the door. She put her arm over his shoulder. "You look absolutely done in, old boy," she said.

"I feel as if I've been through the wringer! And a hoity-toity

D.I. who is well aware of his rights down in Sussex is the last thing I need. Chap shows some spirit though. He'll need it. Well—this has been quite an evening one way and another!"

"Can you stop? Can you stop and go to bed?"

"Bless you, Lyd," said Joe, "but no. Soon perhaps but not now. Things to do. Don't worry! Go to bed yourself. I have to notify the boy's parents."

"The boy's parents!" said Lydia. "Yes, of course."

Joe began to draught a long cable to distant Panikhat. Panikhat! For him, of so many memories. Panikhat. He would never have expected it to come into his life again. He thought of Andrew Drummond, who had been his friend, and Nancy Drummond, who had been—so briefly—his lover.

CHAPTER 4

Curtains of snow were falling across the river when Joe awoke in the morning. Woke! He had hardly slept. But there were voices from the kitchen and a reassuring smell of coffee. Lydia and Jackie were sitting side by side.

"I found a ham and some eggs," said Lydia, "and I've fed the hero of last night's entertainment and here he is!"

"Good morning, Uncle Joe," said Jackie politely.

"Good morning, Jackie," said Joe. "Do you never stop eating?"

"I like breakfast," said Jackie. "I think it's my favourite meal."

"Got some for me?" Joe asked, and then, "There are things we've got to do. Lyd, can you do something about Jackie's clothes?"

"That's not difficult. I've had a look at the labels. I'll ring up Derry and Tom's, give them his size. They'll have a commission-aire or a messenger of some sort they can send round, I expect. They should be open by now—I'll give it a go."

They heard her speak with crisp authority into the telephone. ". . . put me through to the school outfitting department please. . . . Oh, good morning. Mrs. Marcus Dunsford here. May I know to whom I am speaking? Mr. Partridge? Mr. Partridge, I have an urgent commission for you. . . ."

Joe listened while she steered the conversation through to a successful conclusion. "You can do that? Excellent! You may send it to me here at Reach House, Chelsea. . . . And when shall we look for you? . . . Before noon? . . . *So* grateful, Mr. Partridge!"

"While we're waiting for Mr. Partridge to produce the goods," said Joe, "we have things to do."

"I'll make a start. I'll pack up Jackie's bag for him. And make a few sandwiches. A flask of something hot for the journey. . . ." Lydia bustled out, leaving Joe with the boy.

"There's things we ought to talk about, Jackie. Sorry, but—firstly, I sent a cable off last night to your parents to say what has happened."

"Will they be cross with me for running away?" said Jackie anxiously.

"Worried, I expect, but not cross," said Joe. "It was difficult to explain what had happened but I did my best. Now, you and I have to go down to the school and talk to the Sussex police about Rappo."

"I don't want to go anywhere near the school," said Jackie almost in a wail. "I really don't! Would I have to see The Fatman?"

"The fat man?" said Joe.

"It's what we call Farman. He put up a notice and somebody changed the 'r' to a 't' in his signature and now everybody—even some of the masters—call him The Fatman."

"Well, the best I can offer is a slight delay." Joe smiled. "I used the weather as an excuse for putting it off until your dad has had a chance to reply to the telegram I sent last night. We'll set off from here when you've got your uniform and the streets have been cleared. Then we'll thrash on down to Surrey to your Aunt Lydia's house where we'll break the journey. You'll be comfortable there and you can meet your new cousins. We'll spend the rest of the day and the night there before doing the final leg down into Sussex. I asked Andrew to send his reply straight to me down at Aunt Lydia's. St. Magnus can wait another day."

~

GEORGE GOSLING PUSHED his way through the crowds of boys milling about in the entrance to the hall on his way to the staffroom. An early and unscheduled meeting had been called by the headmaster for the whole of the teaching staff. It would be left to Matron and a couple of helpers to contain more than one hundred excited boys in the hall until normal classes could be resumed. He didn't envy Matron her task. The boys had got wind of the event of yesterday and their awful unbroken voices screeched and yammered around him as he made his way along the corridor. Some of the little brutes even tried to accost him for information.

"Sir! Sir! Is it true?" This was Spielman, whose mastoid-infected ears had triggered the whole nasty business. "Was it Drummond who killed Rappo? They're saying he'll swing for it. Is it true? Will he swing? Sir? Sir?"

Gosling clenched his hands behind his back. The impulse to wipe the ghoulish fervour from the ugly little face was almost overwhelming.

"Oh, I doubt it," he said dismissively. "Down here in Sussex they tend to go in for penal servitude for life for youngsters these days." Masterson's brief came back to him: *Ingratiate yourself with both boys and staff. Make sure that they trust you.* Gosling leaned over and smiled his crooked, boyish, all-pals-together-in-adversity smile. "But you seem to know more about this than I do, Spielman. Why is it that the sports master's always the last to find out what's going on? Hey! Foster! Tonsils giving you any trouble today? No? Good man!"

He was the last to enter the staffroom. He slid in quietly but he'd been noticed. The head looked pointedly at his watch and the other twelve teachers, gowned and huddled in their usual groups, smiled, gratified that they were not the target of all eyes. Unconcerned, Gosling gave a formal nod to the headmaster and said in a cheerful voice, "I'm two minutes late—frightfully sorry, sir. Matron needed a little help marshaling the mob and I happened to be passing. . . ."

"I'll hear your apologies later, Gosling. We have more important matters than staff punctuality on our agenda this morning." The voice, icy and dismissive, was at odds with the Pickwickian corpulence.

George chose a seat, as he always did, near the door and to the side of the gathering. From here he had a clear view of his colleagues and could come and go attracting the least attention. One of the staff, more observant than the rest, had once jokingly remarked on this ability of his to disappear or materialise at their elbows: "Remind me, if you can, Gosling—who was it Macbeth described as 'moving like a ghost'?" And after a token pause to allow for a response: "Ah, yes, of course, I believe it was the wolf. A creature with which, I suspect, you have much in common." He'd turned to enjoy the smirking appreciation of his colleagues.

George had regretted his automatic riposte: "No. I'm sure the mysterious mover you're thinking of was 'Murder' himself, not his watchdog, sir." Bloody stupid! Always a mistake to indulge in arm-wrestling with the Head of English Lit. And particularly when you'd accepted a skirmish using your opponent's choice of weapon. Edmund Langhorne. King of the Quotation. Arrogant tosspot. And now—quite unnecessarily—his enemy.

George's sports shirt and slacks were the most unremarkable Lillywhite's had to offer but they marked him out as an alien element amongst the swirls of custard-stained heavy black repp worn by his academic colleagues. His insouciance signalled that he didn't much care if he was viewed by the rest as a form of pond life. A sports master filling in with the odd geography lesson or two could only survive the condescension of his fellows by affecting a jolly ignorance of their scorn. He could only know his place, do his lowly job well and bite his tongue. George reckoned his rowing blue, his boxing medals and his broken nose gained him respect from the pupils, though with the staff he'd swiftly acquired the reputation of a pugilist and, inevitably, the nickname of "Gentleman George."

George settled to listen to the official account of the fiasco on the back stairs yesterday. It was going to be interesting to hear what version of the story the Head would expect them to swallow.

Farman flipped a finger right and left under his nose, checking his moustache was standing at the ready, and cast an eye over the staff, gathering attention. "Gentlemen!" He tucked up the trailing sleeves of his academic gown and clamped them to his sides. He rocked forwards and back on creaking shoes for a moment. He harrumphed noisily. Like a lumbering flying boat scrambling to take off, Gosling always thought.

"Gentlemen! Good morning! You'll know why we're here. You'll all have heard the tragic news. You'll be aware of Edgar Rapson's death in mysterious circumstances." At last airborne, he began a steady ascent: "I won't say more than that for the moment. It would be inconsiderate of me ... nay ... possibly unlawful if I were to enlarge on those circumstances at this time. But I think it would be appropriate if we were to pause now in order to remember a valued colleague. All stand."

Valued colleague! George Gosling sighed. He sprang to his feet, adopted a suitably grave expression and lowered his eyes.

The eulogy winged its duplicitous way over bowed heads, faces fixedly sober for the meagre two minutes it took to remind them all of Rapson's achievements, character and skills. They looked up with more interest when Farman got on to his outline of the previous night's events. In death Rapson cut a far more dashing figure. Gosling ran a discreet eye over the company, on the alert for any off-key reaction to the circumstances of their colleague's death.

"... body discovered late last evening at the bottom of the back stairs ... heavy snowfall ... any traces of an incursion from outside the school obliterated, but we're not discounting the possibility ... indeed—*probability*—of aggression by intruders. Cause of death? As yet unknown...." The lift of his eyes to the ceiling signalled a lie to his audience. "Pathologists still at work...." The excuse swiftly followed. "All safely in the hands of the Sussex police. You may refer yourselves to Inspector Martin if you have information," he added. "And I must ask you to prepare to be interviewed individually. School goes on as normal, and when you are called on to make your statement I will ensure you are relieved by another member of staff. And—there is one vital substitution to be made—Rapson was a form master, and his flock is left without a shepherd. Who will replace him?"

Farman surveyed the gathering, taking his time to indicate that the question had been carefully considered by him. "Gosling! I'm going to ask you to take his place. You will not have an easy task. The boys will be much exercised, not only by the death of their master, but also by the regrettable absence of one of their number."

He put out a hand to deflect questions from the audience who seemed suddenly galvanised. "Drummond is the boy who disappeared at about the same time. Drummond, who came to us from Bengal last year. This boy is a possible witness of Rapson's last moments. I'm pleased to say he has been located and is being returned to us this very day. You will have further information when I have it myself. You may dismiss, gentlemen. Oh, Gosling? Not so fast! A word if you wouldn't mind...."

The other men grinned as they passed him on their way out. "Late again, m'boy? Tut, tut!" The supercilious Langhorne even cocked an eyebrow and without a word slid a copy of the Daily Sketch into the young man's hand as he filed out.

～

FARMAN CLOSED THE door when the last master had left. He wiped his forehead on the sleeve of his gown. "Well?" he asked. "And what have you to say?"

"Quite a bit, Farman. Quite a bit! But first—that was rather well handled. You said just enough to satisfy their curiosity and managed to give nothing away. Now, I contacted London. There's a further problem I'm afraid. They were full of information we'd rather not have on this Sandilands fellow. This self-styled uncle. Had you any idea?"

Farman shook his head. "I told you! Not a hint! Who the hell is he?"

"The last man you'd want poking about down here in the circs. He is what he claims to be—recently appointed Assistant Commissioner. Young. Quite a star. And well connected. You'd have to be to reach those heights by his age. Just the sort of military, ramrod-up-the-backside bloke Commissioner Trenchard *would* promote." Gosling sighed. "And you know what the rank of Assistant Commissioner brings with it?" The young man eyed the older with weary scorn. "No, why would you? Well, this one's C1. 'C' for 'Central.' He doesn't concern himself with traffic offences and administration and bureaucracy like the others. His department has authority over the Detective Branch and usually over the Special Branch as well. As far as anyone's ever allowed to cut any ice with the Branch. . . . Now, how do you fancy a pack of those smart alecks in knuckle-dusters sticking their patriotic noses in?"

He shot a grin devoid of humour at the headmaster. "Sorry! But, Farman, if this chap is who I think he is, he could have the whole school turned inside out and shaken all about before you could say *knife*."

The headmaster cringed. "Can't have that, Gosling. Can't allow it."

"You've brought it on yourself, Farman. Should have run a tighter ship. Not given Rapson so much rope."

"That's easy enough to say. And what do I do when this gets out? When the daily rags start clamouring for interviews?" He wiped his shining forehead again. "When the parents get wind of it and start withdrawing their sons? They will do, you know!"

"I'll tell you what you *don't* do. You don't look to me for help. If the lid comes off there's nothing I can do. I have my orders. The moment the sun shines on this can of worms I withdraw and leave you carrying it."

"You're maltreating your metaphors again, Gosling! Thank God I didn't entrust you with Year Three English!"

"I only do it to annoy. Now—brace up and tell me where this joker's sprung from, Farman."

"I've searched the boy's records, and there's no mention of a Sandilands. Someone's pulling a fast one. The only connection that occurs to me is—India. He mentioned it himself. Oh—and he bandied the word 'diplomacy' about in a menacing way. Reeks of—er—influence, I'd say."

"Damn it! Look, whoever he is—we don't want him anywhere near this. The whole thing is supposed to be kept under wraps. Fat chance of that with the Met and the Branch swarming all over it." Gosling spoke firmly. "Get rid of him. Tell him that you're happy with Martin's coverage. The good old Sussex Constabulary can cope. Keep it local. Stress your total confidence in them. You'd be quite right to do that—Martin's an impressive officer. Be polite but make sure of two things—one: that he's left the boy behind and two: that he's buggered off himself by the end of the day."

He turned to leave, paused and grumbled over his shoulder: "Oh, and thanks a bundle for handing me charge of the Crazy Gang! Yes, a hideous thought, but—I have to say—good tactics, Farman. I think I shall have to make a friend of young Drummond. Offer a sympathetic ear for his confidences. Listen to his adventures in the Big Smoke. . . . Now, if you'll excuse me, I'll fix on a suitably chastised expression and nip off to—where is it they have their awful rookery?—room 10, is it? I'll take the roll call and dodge the ink gobbets. Oh, and, this copper, call me when he gets here, will you? I'd like to meet him."

CHAPTER 5

Joe paused on his way out into the still dark street, hesitated, then came to a decision. Better safe than sorry. With the boy's sudden appearance last evening, there had gusted into his home an unease as menacing as the snow-bearing wind. Joe had learned over the years to conceal these presentiments under a cover of bluff normality, but he never disregarded them. He picked up the two bottles of milk from the step, smiling to see that the frozen liquid had forced its way up through the cap and was sitting like a penny-lick of ice cream at the neck. He stepped back into the hall and tapped on the door to his landlord's ground floor apartment.

Alfred Jenkins didn't keep him waiting. His door was flung open, revealing a stocky, shirt-sleeved figure against a glare of bright electric light. A blast of air lightly scented with smoke and coffee gushed out, and Joe heard in the background the friendly domestic sound of electric trains rattling their way around a circuit.

"You're a bit late this morning, sir? Oh, thanks for that. Just in time. Glad you got to it before the sparrers! I'll chisel a bit off the top for my cuppa. Join me?" The china mug of coffee raised invitingly at him and the sight of the morning's *Daily Mirror* spread out over the kitchen table very nearly lured Joe inside to spend a happy half hour with Alfred setting the world to rights.

"Morning, Alfred. Something of an emergency on, I'm afraid. I have to go out for an hour or so. Look—I'm leaving my sister up there and she has someone with her. It's my nine-year-old nephew from India. Name's Jack. He's in a spot of bother. They won't be leaving until I come back to pick them up and—I feel a bit over-dramatic saying this. . . ." Joe shuffled his feet but, encouraged by an alert and enquiring face, hurried on: "Could you keep an eye out. . . . My nephew may possibly find himself the subject of unwanted attention. No one should be allowed in to visit them." He grinned. "Especially not our flat-footed chums. It's quite possible that a contingent of the provincial Plod may come calling and try to pick him up while my back's turned. You'll have no trouble identifying them—they'll be a pair of florid six-footers with a Sussex accent. Oh—one exception—there's a delivery expected in the name of Mrs. Dunsford. A Mr. Partridge of the outfitting department is sending out some things from Derry and Tom's but no one else should go up. Just tell anyone showing an interest that the flat's empty, will you? Not that I'm expecting anyone will call." His rambling speech was betraying his anxiety and he stopped himself.

"The lady's safe with me. And the young gent," Jenkins replied briefly. "I've cleared the pavement out front, but watch your step. It's come down thick in the night and it's frozen over. Nasty."

IN HIS LONELIER moments Alfred Jenkins, retired Metropolitan Police Inspector, told himself that he lived a full and rewarding life. His wife Mavis had died just after the war, but she'd left him with a good son. And now that son had sons himself, and Alfred was blessed with their frequent company. Their ma was a hard-working woman and left the lads with him while she got on with her jobs. Early severance from the Force due to injury some twelve years ago had left him a promising officer with a police medal for gallantry but with ambitions unfulfilled and a minuscule pension. Jenkins' optimistic nature scorned to dwell on the disappointments. He reckoned he was a lucky bloke. Thank God he'd inherited his old uncle's house at a dark moment. A bit of a ruin and out here in mucky old Chelsea down by Lots Road power station. All the advice had been: "Get rid of it, Fred. It'll be a millstone round your neck. Shift it quick." But he'd seen the possibilities. Georgian building. Good structure. Spacious. Just a bit faded. He'd taken a chance and spent his severance pay on refurbishing the top floor and having electricity put in. And a lift. In the end, he'd been able to pin a notice on the board at the Yard offering superior modern accommodation to a single professional gentleman. He'd been delighted when Sandilands had turned up holding the notice in his hand. His price and terms had been agreed without a quibble.

He hadn't expected the young officer to spend many months under his roof. He was a professional all right, meticulous and driven you might say, but—single? Sandilands didn't have the look of a bloke who'd stay unmarried for long. Yet twelve years down the road, and here he still was. Odd that, Jenkins always thought. It wasn't as though he was uninterested in females. He never brought a floozie back, of course. The man was a gent, after all, but he did sometimes come rolling home late smelling of brandy and exotic perfume, collar melting and tie askew. Late? Sometimes early. Dumping the milk bottles at his door with a cheeky grin. Plenty of time though. Most men with a career to build waited until they were into their forties before they settled down. And the Captain, as his oldest mates who'd known him in the war years still called him, was on the right side of forty. Still looking around. Plenty of time.

Alfred decided he'd wait until ten o'clock before he went upstairs to check with Miss Lydia that all was well.

THE DERRY AND Tom's van passed his parlour window just after eleven, and Alfred made his way into the hall to greet the messenger.

The smart young man was holding a package and looking around him, getting his bearings. "Delivery. It's for Sandilands. Top floor? I'll take it up. That lift working is it?"

Cockney accent, Alfred noted. "Hold your horses, mate! Deliveries have to be recorded. Give me a minute to get the book, will you?" Alfred made his way back into his parlour, and found his record book on the sideboard. When he emerged, he found the man had followed him and was looking eagerly over his shoulder into the room. Pushy blighter.

"Train set is that? Electric? Cor! Gentleman's hobby, would that be? Bet the kids love it!"

Alfred understood his interest and responded warmly to a fellow enthusiast. He smiled his pleasure and opened the door wider to allow the friendly young man a view of the room. "I keep it here for my three grandsons. Their ma leaves them with me every morning while she does her charring."

Three small boys in check pinafores were squabbling gently over the train track. They all looked up on hearing the stranger's voice at the door but turned back at once to the railway. A delivery man was no distraction from a derailed Flying Scotsman.

"Now then, Sid and Ian—you little 'uns better listen to your big brother," Jenkins directed firmly. "Do what Andy says while I deal with this gentleman, will you? I don't want to hear any quarreling when I've got my back turned. Or I'll pull the plugs," he finished with cheerful menace.

He waited for the automatic acknowledgements of "Yes, Grandpa" before turning back to the visitor. "Now, if you wouldn't mind signing just here? Oh, and thank your Mr. Peacock for being so prompt with the order, will you? It *is* still old Peacock in outfitting, is it? Or has he retired by now?"

"Still there, sir. Bit doddery but he gets by."

"Know the feeling! You can leave it down here with me, if you like."

"Naw! Thanks, but I have to make sure it's got into the right hands. I'll use the lift."

"Right-oh, then. Oh, Sandilands has nipped out, but it's all right—his sister's up there. She'll see to you. Watch out for the lift—it can be a bit temperamental. Well, if you're sure. . . ." And, as the Derry and Tom's man walked off with jaunty stride towards the lift, he called after him helpfully: "Just press button 3, mate."

CHAPTER 6

Joe took a taxi to the government offices at Whitehall. He got out on King Charles Street and turned in to a courtyard lined by architecture of an Italianate flavour. Sir Gilbert Scott was responsible for the ornate Victorian grandeur, Joe remembered, and he paused to get his bearings and admire. There could be no doubt that he was approaching a temple to Britannia.

Chilly and echoing, the building Joe entered had the feeling of a busy space suddenly deserted. Without the animation of the usual swarms of bowler-hatted men jousting about with briefcase and brolly, he was feeling more keenly conscious of the grandeur of the surroundings. And more out of place. He looked down at his feet. Gumboots had seemed the obvious choice this snowy morning, looking purposeful and proper with the ancient tweed suit he'd put on, mindful of the journey into the country.

Lydia had thought to question his choice of get-up. "Is that going to be quite right for Whitehall, Joe? Will they let you in or hand you a spade and send you off to clear the pavement?" The kind of comment that roused a growling contrariness in Joe. Now he watched regretfully as dirty gobbets of melting snow oozed from the runnels of his boots and settled on the Minton tiles. Gold fleurs-de-lis, he noted, on a background of magenta and blue. Tiles so sumptuously heraldic deserved to be dripped on by nothing less than a pair of Lobb's best, he thought guiltily.

The civil servant in attendance cut short his anxiety. He was expecting Joe and with one stately finger directed a footman to take his hat and overcoat. Joe was reassured to be greeted by title. "Assistant Commissioner? We'll go straight up. Sir James fought his way through from Albany half an hour ago and is waiting. Commissioner Trenchard is with him. And one or two others. This way."

Sir James? The Commissioner? One or two others?

Joe kept his surprise to himself and followed his guide in silence. In his flurry of calls and returned calls after breakfast he'd simply tried to set up an informal meeting with his chief superintendent, Ralph Cottingham, and one other: "any bright bloke from the Department of Education, if that's not an impossible request . . . and if there's anyone at home. . . ." he remembered saying. The final message had come through an hour ago, fixing "a meeting with interested parties" in one of the government offices in Whitehall. A courtesy to the Education bloke, Joe surmised. Statesmen of any rank in the rumour-mill that was Whitehall preferred to avoid the indignity and possible stigma of a trip down the corridors of Scotland Yard. But why such a gathering? Early in February grandees of this political type ought to be away holed up on their wide country acres or skiing in Zermatt. Had Ralph overreacted?

Mind racing, Joe was chilled by the thought that the series of phone calls he'd instigated must have got out of hand, rolling along gathering substance like a snowball. And who the hell was Sir James, anyway? He could think of at least five Sir Jameses in the upper ranks of public life.

He was ushered into a carpeted and well-lit first floor reception room that was already occupied by some half dozen people sitting, it seemed casually, around a low table. His first glance took in a preponderance of sober grey pinstripe and even a uniform. All eyes lifted to him as he approached.

"Thank you, Spencer. That'll be all." The voice that dismissed Joe's guide was unknown to him. It was low, authoritative. The speaker rose to greet Joe, indicating with a crisp movement of the hand that the others were to remain seated. "We've kept you a place over there at the end opposite me, Sandilands. Help yourself to coffee, will you? We're all enjoying a certain informality this morning, you see. No clerks, no tea-ladies. Glad to note you've dressed—like me—in keeping with the weather. Harris tweed and galoshes! The only possible riposte to an unscheduled summons to the work place in the middle of a blizzard. Good man!" His voice dropped to a level of confidence: "Now, your boss will never admit it, but I do believe Trenchard still has his pyjamas on under that Savile Row outer layer."

This must be "Sir James," Joe guessed. Talking lightly to put him at his ease? Disturbing, perhaps, to think that he needed to be put at ease, but Joe rather liked the aplomb with which the man dared to tease the austere Lord Trenchard. The Commissioner appeared less diverted, and Joe avoided meeting the basilisk stare.

Alarmingly, they all waited until Joe had settled and taken his first sip of coffee before his host continued. "Now, we all know who *you* are, Sandilands—indeed, your ears must have been burning for the last half hour as we all heard your praises sung— but you may not know all of *us*. I'll go round the table. Where shall I start? With the prettiest . . . why not? Miss Peto I think you are acquainted with?"

Dorothy Peto, the newly appointed Superintendent of Women Police, was managing to sit to attention, spruce in her blue serge. No one had ever seen her in civilian clothes—indeed, the word was that she slept in her uniform. She dimpled at Sir James, acknowledging his gallantry, then nodded and smiled at Joe. One ally then at least in this company. Miss Peto and Joe had done a lot of agreeing over the employment of women in the force over the years, though he would never have had the gall to call this undeniably attractive but formidable woman "pretty." Effective, clever, tough, principled, redoubtable—many adjectives would have sprung to Joe's lips before "pretty." But, by God, here she sat, turning a tender gaze on Sir James instead of a frosty set-down.

"And here you see, we have your boss, Lord Trenchard, and, on his right hand—for where else would you find him?—his Right Hand: Howgrave-Graham, whom you know." Joe nodded with pleased recognition at the grey-suited Secretary of Scotland Yard. A civilian but much admired by the officers of the Met, he was known to be the trusty backstop for the Commissioner. "And Superintendent Cottingham, who issued the invitations."

Ralph twitched his shoulders and grunted. Joe detected the signs of rising irritation in his normally equable colleague.

"And now for the non-police handout—the other chap armed with a notebook is my own private secretary Christopher Gledhill and, on his left—the man you really wanted to see—a minister in the Department of Education. A junior minister but word has it not junior for much longer: Aidan Anderson."

Joe rose and reached over to shake the hands of the men he had not met before. As he murmured pleasantly, he cobbled together a swift inventory. This double quadrille seemed to him to consist of four specialists in their field (the head of the Met and the head of the women's police plus two politicians), balanced on the other side by four work horses: two secretaries and two coppers.

"And our *convener*, Sandilands," Trenchard's dry voice broke in, "who assumes that everyone knows *him*, I will introduce myself. With proper regard for procedure. And to spare you, Truelove, the embarrassment of blowing your own trumpet. You wouldn't want that! Sir James, may I present to you: Joseph

Sandilands, one of my assistant commissioners? Sandilands, I'd like you to meet Sir James Truelove, the Secretary of State for Reform."

Everyone was uneasily conscious of the set-down, with the exception of Truelove himself, who genially extended a hand. Joe was expecting the token squeeze dished out by an elegantly manicured politician and was surprised by a vigorous shake from a square and rather rugged hand. Joe had encountered similar callouses before. On men who handled oar, ax or spade. Truelove! Joe's consternation grew. The rising star of the government by all accounts; next prime minister but one, it was whispered by those who claimed to know these things.

Joe had seen photographs of him in the newspapers but would not have recognised him from their evidence. The black and white prints gave emphasis to the smooth, lofty forehead, the neatly barbered, brilliantined hair, the commanding nose and the cold intellectual stare that brought reassuringly to mind the face of the young Duke of Wellington. The pressmen's flash bulbs turned him into a sleek assembly of planes in light and shade, from any angle a challenging face, a modern face. A face often photo- graphed above a white tie and stiff collar, leaving the Savoy or the Ritz. But the flesh and blood reality in front of Joe this chilly morning was less the impeccably groomed hero of a Hollywood movie, more the backwoodsman. He was much younger looking than his forty odd years. His hair had received only cursory atten- tion; the rough jacket and trousers were more suited to a grouse moor than the city. A man who'd dodged the attentions of his valet this morning, Joe thought with approval.

The minister smiled at the group and the smile reached his dark eyes, sparking them with complicitous humour. An intelli- gent man, Joe knew that much. Details from his Special Branch record were coming swiftly to mind. Eton and Cambridge. Rowing blue. Stroke in a winning pre-war Boat Race eight.

Scientific and philanthropic family background. Wealthy. And—a progressive.

The best England had to offer had dashed out in tweeds on a chill morning to attend a meeting with him. Why?

Joe swallowed. "I'm honoured to meet you, sir," he managed and resumed his seat.

"The honour is all ours, Sandilands, if we're to believe what we hear." The minister stopped short and looked at him expectantly. All eyes turned on Joe.

So, there it was: The first exploratory ball had been bowled. The crowd was waiting to see how he dispatched it.

"Honoured, sir," Joe repeated, "but puzzled! My message to Cottingham was simplicity itself, I had thought."

Ralph Cottingham looked down and examined his cuff-links.

"What's been going on? Shall I tell you what I *think's* been going on?"

The concentrated attention of his audience fed the performer in Joe. He decided to go for a boundary shot. He leaned forwards and caught each questioning face in a conspiratorial glance. "You've all been playing the Telephone Game!" His tone was one of playful accusation. "Or 'Chinese Whispers' as we used to call it in the trenches. I ring Cottingham at six this morning with a swift plea for access to certain files: *Arrange for an expert to be on hand.* It passes down the line and comes out at ten as: *A range of four experts and a brass band.*"

It was Trenchard, notorious for his lack of humour, who gave a snort of laughter. The rest eyed each other uncertainly. Shoulders still shaking with amusement, the Commissioner took up the tale. "Rest assured, Sandilands, there's nothing wrong with Cottingham's ears or the brain between them. It was I who intercepted your message and took the matter out of his hands. Your request hoisted a signal, d'you see? Or do I mean, sprang a trap? It was Cottingham who, questing about, unwittingly got his fingers chopped off. Anyhow, the name of this school you're interested in—St. Magnus—its file is stickered." He sat back, content with his announcement.

The questioning lift of eyebrows directed at him by Cottingham encouraged Joe to ask: "Stickered, sir?"

"That's what I said. A purple sticker. Anyone enquiring would be finding himself looked at carefully. It signifies that the contents are currently of interest at the highest level. MI5 would designate such material 'Top Secret' in their dramatic way. In fact—there's not much to catch the attention in there. The interest lies in who precisely wishes to avail himself of it. What a surprise to find we've caught two of our own with sticky fingers—the Assistant Commissioner and his assistant!"

"May I ask, sir, at whose request the file was stickered? By the department itself?"

"No. As a matter of fact, by Military Intelligence initially." Truelove admitted this reluctantly and added swiftly, "Though they had the sense to realise it had little to do with military or state security. Just for once, they agreed to pass it on to the Met."

Trenchard stepped in to clear up Joe's evident mystification. "Your predecessor it was, Sandilands, who picked this up and decided there was nothing to it. Rumours passing between armchairs in clubs ... yarning over the whisky ... hysterical women demanding favours—you know the sort of thing."

Joe frowned and waited for more clarity. It was his experience that if you left a puzzled silence the commissioner often obligingly filled it.

Trenchard went on: "Upshot was—the Met had the file marked. With much grumbling from the Education Department, if I remember correctly, hey, what, Anderson?"

The education man winced and smiled politely. He directed a glance full of meaning at Joe and sighed. Joe did not respond. He might disagree with his boss occasionally, but he would always support him in public. "You resisted an application, minister?" he asked. "I'm wondering why?"

Put on the spot, Anderson shrugged. "Nothing whatsoever in the allegations. St. Magnus is an excellent educational establishment. Its boys go on to the very best public schools and then on to Oxford or Cambridge as like as not. I ought to declare an interest—I was a boy myself there. My own sons have been pupils and speak highly of it. Malicious gossip—no more than that. But—harmful, I agree. And, no doubt, a stop must be put to it."

Commissioner Trenchard waited for the exchanges to be over, then allowed himself an acid smile and continued as though oblivious of the interruption. "But, ironically, the poor blighter to whom I was about to assign the investigation of this ants' nest is your good self anyway, Sandilands. And you won't thank me! So. You might say this business has been short-circuited by your convenient personal interest. I hope I make myself clear?"

Sir James Truelove assumed that this was anything but clear and added helpfully: "It's all working out rather well, sure you'll agree? Sensitive issue. Concerned parents who have the ear of the top level of government, and who have *my* ear, need elucidation and reassurance. Needs careful handling. We're sending you down there to infiltrate the suspicious area—as our Trojan Horse. A wonderfully crafted and entirely convincing interloper! They'll drag you in and form a line to tell you all, you'll find. But first, you'll have to be briefed . . . you'll need to know the truth . . . the reason why this school has come to our attention. I warn you— you may find what we have to reveal, in view of your close familial association with one of its boys, er. . . ." He hesitated and, sending a propitiating glance towards Dorothy Peto, the one female presence in the room, finished limply, "somewhat disquieting."

"Is that what you'd say, Sir James?" Miss Peto fixed him with a quizzical smile. "I'd call it damned alarming!"

〰

AS HE STOOD on the pavement squinting through the snow to spot a taxi, a hand grasped his elbow. Joe turned to find the education minister standing beside him. With an effort he remembered the man's quite ordinary name: Aidan Anderson.

"We'll share a taxi if we can catch one of the blighters out and about," the minister said. "Ah! Here we are!" He stepped boldly into the road, umbrella extended, fingers to mouth, uttering a peremptory whistle. The taxi skidded to a halt. "Chelsea, cabby," Anderson said.

"Are we going in the same direction?" Joe asked.

"No. You're going west. I'll drop you off and return to my club in St. Jameses. Well, I thought, as *briefings* go, Sandilands, that's exactly what we were handed. Unsatisfactory amounts of information. Unfair that you should be caught up in what is no more than a personal struggle for power and notoriety. I thought I'd tell you."

Joe looked with greater attention at the austere features as the man settled back in the cab. A cadaverous, academic face echoed the long, spare limbs. Large nose, large feet, large hands, Joe noted. A man a good bit older than himself, he calculated. With—what had he said?—two sons having passed through St. Magnus, he must be approaching fifty and Joe wondered, as he automatically did, what Anderson had done in the war.

"I have the advantage of you, Sandilands," he confided with a tight smile. "I've seen your file. Splendid. Quite splendid! Complete misuse of your time—that's what we're looking at. They're loading up a Holland & Holland to shoot a squirrel! But you know nothing of me. Briefly: Oxford man, Cavalry, wartime Military Intelligence turned politician. If you can be bothered to ask about they'll tell you—a fanatic about education. And I won't deny it. I can think of no more urgent cause. It is the duty of our country to produce a generation of scientists and thinkers. The only way we shall uphold our position in the world to come."

Joe thought uneasily that he could only wait for the revelation that was undoubtedly hovering in the air. Into the space he had been left for comment, he muttered disjointed phrases including the words: "Patriot? Of course. Aren't we all? See what you mean. . . . Cause for concern. . . ."

"I thought as much. I thought I recognised a man who would put his country before the personal aspirations of a single renegade."

Joe guessed he was talking of Truelove and waited for more.

"Truelove! Minister for Reform? Minister for Mischief, more like! The man's eyes gleam with naked ambition—did you see it? He's a man who'll use anything and anybody to further his own career. He doesn't care much whose reputation he smirches in his climb to the top. He's using this new free-wheeling post of his to snatch at and absorb areas of interest that should rightly be the preserve of other departments. Education, as you've just seen demonstrated, is one. Watch out—he may next have his sights on law and order. Indeed, I know that he has."

"One small prep school on the southern coast of the country would seem to be a very small target, Anderson. I can't see how a scandal there might advance his assault on the premiership," Joe said bluntly.

"Truelove wants to make his mark with a root and branch reform of the English school system, both fee-paying and state establishments, and—am I being fanciful here?—I'm guessing that if he can hold up one rotten apple as an example it will justify his case. He's obviously not going to take on—say—Rugby or Eton, but a tiddler amongst schools, a small country prep school—that's a much more likely candidate. This man has a nose for publicity. He frequently stoops to manipulating the press. He has the barons in the palm of his hand already."

"What headlines are you imagining in the *Daily Mirror* if his plans come to fruition?"

"Oh, something on the lines of: *Murder and corruption rife in*

English schools. Are our children safe? The article worded so as to make tongues wag and voices call out demanding to know how widespread the problem is. The next thing will be an impassioned speech to Parliament. Truelove is an inspired orator. He'll make use of any scandal you can uncover to fuel public outrage. To put out a fire in a heroic way, Sandilands, you first have to start your fire. He's set it, I do believe, and you are being sent in to locate the blue touch paper and put a match to it for him. Mind you don't get your fingers burnt."

WHEN JOE RETURNED at noon, he answered a bellow from Alfred's room.

"We're all in here!"

"Great Heavens! You're throwing a party, Alfred?"

The room was humming with heat and noise. Three small boys were scrambling about on their stomachs on the carpet, organising the railway. His sister Lydia, watching their antics, rolled her eyes at Joe from over their heads, conveying acute boredom.

"If you wouldn't mind stepping into the hall, sir?"

Puzzled, Joe followed him.

"Seemed the safest way—keeping them all together under my eye. Your Jackie. . . ." He grinned. ". . . or 'Andy,' as we're calling him for the duration, is getting on well with my two. I popped a pinny on him, seeing as he was a bit lacking in the clothes department like. And they can get a bit mucky rolling about on the rug. Hard to tell one from t'other. Peas in a pod. But you were right to be concerned, sir. Someone did try to get at your sister—or your lad."

Joe stiffened. "I see that all's well but—Alfred—who? How?"

"No idea. I thought I'd better keep hold of him for you to take a look at."

Jenkins took a small fuse from his pocket and said carefully:

"Sudden power failure. Poor young gentleman got himself trapped in the lift. Right between floors 2 and 3. I'll have to call the engineers back again. Unless I can fix it myself. You never know."

"What! He's still up there? In the lift?"

"Yes. Top half on your floor and available for interview, you'll find. You can go up and talk to him through the safety bars."

"Ah! He's talking is he?"

"Hardly. Cussing a lot. Must say I can't get much sense out of him. Though Miss Lydia did manage to get the package off him. Just asked him nicely to pass it through to her when she handed him a cup of coffee. That was before he began to get suspicious, and he didn't quibble. I don't think Miss Lydia's twigged yet. Thought I'd better leave it to you to explain. Anyway, I've told the feller we've been having problems with the lift. Not sure he believes me. Not sure I believe *him* if it comes to that. He's no Derry and Tom's boy."

"What makes you so certain of that, Alfred?"

"Didn't know the name of his department head. Doesn't know a Partridge from a Peacock apparently. And he tried to tell me the package was for someone name of Sandilands. You'd told me it was for Mrs. Dunsford. It wasn't much, but enough of a discrepancy to sound the alarm for me. You never lose that ear for a wrong note even when it's coming from a smiling face. He could have waylaid the genuine delivery boy on the doorstep, offered to carry it in. . . . It's an old trick. Anyway, I thought he'd better be detained for your inspection."

Joe grinned. "A good thought. And a good maneuver. If our chap proves to be who he claims to be—and of a mind to sue for unlawful detention—we can offer our sincere apologies, along with a lot of convincing guff about lift mechanisms. Your contraption has got previous, after all, Alfred. I'll go and have a chat with him. But first, a phone call to the Yard, I think!"

"MY DEAR CHAP! How can I apologise?" Joe sank to his knees on a level with a sullen face. "Damn lift! It caught me last week. I was stuck for twenty minutes. Let me assure you we're doing all we can. Engineer fighting his way through the snow as we speak. I can report that the municipal ploughs and gritters are out on the highways and doing a dashed good job. Won't be long now! Can I pass you a drink through the bars? Oh, I see my sister's already obliged. . . . Banana then?"

A growl and a furious shaking of the grille gripped between large fists betrayed contempt for Joe's levity. The narrowed eyes directed a violent rage at him, but Joe detected something more—perhaps also a fear amounting, he guessed, or desperation barely under control. It was more than an attack of—what had Lydia called this unreasonable fear of lifts? Claustrophobia? Vertigo? Joe didn't think a ticking off from Mr. Partridge was the consequence exercising the prisoner's mind. The man had a feral aura, giving off a sense of danger caged, the whiff of a wolf at bay. Joe was, for a moment, glad of the protection of the creaking metal barrier between them.

He decided to take the tension down a peg. "Hang on, old man! We've rung your store to tell them you'll be delayed. But—wouldn't you know it!—they haven't missed you yet. Look, I'm afraid I have to go now." Joe got to his feet and dusted off his knees. "I shall have to leave you in suspense, hey, what! I'm taking my family away for a week. Weather permitting, of course. Best of luck!"

"Not known to me," Joe commented to Jenkins. "Nasty piece of work, I'd say. Well kitted out, did you notice? Good silk tie, expensive fedora. Nothing showy—but good. I couldn't detect a hidden weapon. Though you can hide a knife easily enough under good tailoring. Even a gun. Well-muscled type too. I wouldn't like to try conclusions with him."

"Wonder what he was after in your flat, sir?"

Joe shrugged. "I think you know. Something that wasn't there yesterday morning. The boy. But why? No idea, Alfred! We'll leave him where he is for a bit. I've summoned the two best shadows we have at the Yard. When they've checked in and got themselves in position you can put the fuse back in and let him loose. I'd like to know where he goes and whom he contacts. I'll ask the boys to let him run and get what they can from surveillance before he goes to ground and—if they can judge the moment—jump on him!"

"Frog march him to the Yard on some pretext," Jenkins said with satisfaction. "I'm sure they'll find he's tied his shoelaces the wrong way. Leave it to me, sir. Your luggage is by the door ready for off. I'll give you a hand while Miss Lydia gets your nephew into his new uniform. She says she's packed what you need." He smiled. "And a fair bit more, I'd say. I put the lad's fancy bag on top of the pile."

Joe was struggling to push the last of the suitcases into the back of the car when a passing businessman in dark overcoat and bowler stopped to lend a hand then went on his way. Joe barely caught the "Reporting for duty, sir," as they bent together over the back seat. A discreet glance around gave him no sight of a second presence in the eerily deserted street. Overcast skies, chilly wind. The few pedestrians braving the weather were hurrying, heads down, through the snow, their outlines blurred by overcoats, mufflers and umbrellas. Perfect stalking weather. Joe felt for a moment an ancient stab of excitement, the hot impulse to pursue his quarry on his own two feet.

He wouldn't keep his men hanging about. He hurried back inside and herded Lydia and Jack into the car, murmuring good-byes to his landlord and a casual, "Well, there we are at last. Thanks for your help, Alfred. All arrangements in place, I think."

CHAPTER 7

"He's fallen asleep, Joe," Lydia reported as they chugged their way through the last of the London suburbs. "Thought he might. He went to bed very late last night and was up and about early, and then there was all the excitement of playing railways."

"To say nothing of the snug little nest you made up for him in the back there."

"Are you ever going to tell me what this is all about?"

"If I knew myself I certainly would."

"Do you mean to tell me you gleaned nothing from your hastily arranged meeting at the Yard? I don't believe you. Who did you manage to drum up to see you? Anyone available, or did you have to consult the tea-lady?"

"Oh, there were people there. An Education minister, two private secretaries, Miss Peto, the Commissioner himself. . . . Will that do to be going on with?"

"Big guns! But what was Miss Peto doing there?"

"There's a child involved. Waifs, strays, children and tarts— they all trigger a female presence. I was offered the flower of the Force to escort young Jackie back into the lions' den. I turned down the offer for the time being since I have you on hand, Lyd. I'd rather handle this school with discretion and walking in escorted by a female policeman in full kit would not be the way to do it. A concerned family member—that's fine. But all these characters played walk-on roles—the star of the show was the Secretary of State for Reform."

"James Truelove?"

"That's the man."

"But what could he possibly have to say to *you*, Joe? Do you need reforming? Why is he meddling in police business?"

"Well, of course, he oughtn't to be. And, as far as I can see to it, he won't. The police force isn't at the beck and call of the government. We need to remind them occasionally that it's the *country* we serve, not ministers. This new office of state someone's thought fit to endow him with worries me. It's a bit nebulous, a bit embryonic. I mean—name *anything* that couldn't do with a bit of reforming! Where do you start?"

"You could start with the Met, if you think about it."

Joe snorted with laughter. "We may well be on his list! But after a punishing war and a financial collapse, the whole country's in desperate need of rebuilding . . . a change of direction, heaven knows! But, all the same, I'm wary of such unspecific, all-encompassing titles. He seems to have been given a roving brief to stick his aristocratic nose into anything that he considers smells less than rosy. And with a background of scientific knowledge—his degree's in Natural Sciences I think—and all that philanthropic family tradition behind him. . . . Well, it's very compelling."

"Know what you mean," Lydia said thoughtfully. "We do like our heroes! The Darwins, the Huxleys, the Galtons and the Trueloves—they're all bound up with our national identity. And they have the advantage of having no whiff of militarism about them."

"People hear the name, listen, believe and obey."

"Ah—is that what you're seeing? The messianic type? That wouldn't appeal to you! Not sure it appeals to Marcus either. I've never met him so I can't really give an opinion but . . . but . . . the man is not unknown in our house." Lydia seemed about to add more and Joe waited to hear it. Finally: "I think Marcus knew his late father, Sir Sidney, rather better. He talks of James as a man who's being groomed for performance at the highest level in government."

"Sounds likely. He's learning his political trade, Lydia. In a position powerful enough to bring him into contact with the nation's most influential men."

"So what's he doing spending the morning with you?"

"It's that school, Lyd, that's sparked his interest. He said he was acting in response to the concerns of parents but . . . oh, I don't know . . . he appears to have turned his reforming zeal on a very large target. Nothing less than the education system itself. Unchanged from Victorian days, he maintains. The public schools are backwards, reclusive, badly managed. And who will disagree with him on that point? He's proposing a scheme to introduce compulsory inspection and reform. And the state-run establishments don't escape his attention either. Academic achievement must rise, bodily fitness must be improved. Every school to have its football pitch, gymnasium and swimming pool. Lyd, he'd got with him a secretary holding a sheaf of statistics that (amongst other things) show just how miserable and unfit for anything the average recruit was at the time of the war. And he says, more than a decade on, things haven't improved—they're getting worse. Oh, yes, he's putting the boot in with the Department of Health too. *Mens sana in corpore sano* would seem to be his motto."

"*In patria sana*, could you add?" Lydia gave a comic shudder. "The man's not newly returned from Germany with a few ideas, is he? You know what they're like over there for building bodies and improving minds."

Joe was silent for a moment. "I'll check," he said. "I'll put Special Branch up that drainpipe. I wouldn't think 'National

Socialism' would be Truelove's cup of tea but they'll know. He *is* very patriotic. Not a sin, so am I. So are you. But he dares to voice harsh criticism bluntly. The country's suffering, he declares, from the existence of what he calls a 'social problem group,' a section of society which is threatening to drag us all into the mire."

"All very laudable. I had wondered myself. But I still don't see what Truelove's search for Utopia has to do with you."

"This so-called group . . . no, *legion* of sickly degenerates he's got in his sights is responsible for much turpitude, including the increase in the crime figures, according to Sir James. We're all about to sink under a tide of lawlessness and public disorder, did you know?"

Lydia gave a gurgle of laughter. "So—he's taking a poke at Health, Education and The Law all at once? I'd like to meet this modern-day Don Quixote! He sounds just my type. I can't imagine he went down well with old Trenchard though."

Joe gave an exaggerated shudder at the memory. "He didn't! Truelove delivered his awful warning—nothing less than a finger-wagging rebuke—to the Commissioner's face! What a nerve! I mean, you don't talk to the ex-Marshal of the Royal Air Force and a war hero like that. It all seemed a bit ill-judged even for someone bent on establishing a reputation for innovation."

"Ouch! Did Trenchard defend himself?"

Joe grinned. "Didn't need to! Howgrave-Graham and I, with one mind, decided to preserve our boss's dignity. We came galloping up, sabres drawn and attacked from two sides. First, we unseated his Sancho Panza and then disarmed the minister. We made a good double act. You'd have thought we'd rehearsed it! We took it in turns to bludgeon them with statistics. 'Only twenty-nine murders in the Metropolis last year, burglary down eleven percent, grievous bodily harm down thirteen. . . .' I pelted them with figures. 'Recruitment to the Force up thirty percent. . . . Levels of fitness for entry raised,' Howgrave-Graham assured them. Neither of us needed to refer to notes. I invented some of the figures, and we both managed to keep a straight face. Sir James had the grace to back down and come off it, and then he started to tell us what I'd really come to hear."

Lydia put a warning finger over her lips. She reached over into the back seat, pulling a rug up to the boy's chin and gently stroking his hair.

"It's all right. He's gone out like a light."

"That school. He wasn't forthcoming about his information sources but he seems to have concluded that there's something not quite right with it. Fact is, Lydia—boys have been disappearing from it over the years. Complaints have been made 'to the highest authorities,' he told us mysteriously. No action by the local Sussex police and, of course, under the present system, no one's responsible for checking it over. Truelove wants to make his mark with a root and branch reform of the English public school, I'm told."

"And how is he going to use you in his schemes? I expect that this is what it's coming to."

"Operation Trojan Horse. I'm being sent in to sleuth about, looking every inch the concerned uncle, and deliver whatever mud I can stir up into his hands."

"I suppose there's something wrong with all this because you sound so cross, but can that be bad, Joe?—finding out what's really been going on? Who are these parents who've raised storm warnings? And if Jackie's in a dangerous place, we want to know about it, don't we? Is the child in danger?"

"I think he is. I think he's being pursued. The man Alfred trapped in the lift had come to do him harm in some way, though I don't know why. We must think there's a connection with the school and the murder of Mr. Rapson. Now, this Rapson may well have been all kinds of a villain—though we only have Jackie's evidence for this—but the sudden appearance in our midst of what could be a hit-man tells us he wasn't a *single* villain. He wasn't working alone. And a network—that's always more disturbing. But you'd already got that far, I shouldn't wonder?"

"Oh, further. I haven't had chance to tell you in all the stirabout. . . ."

"Tell me now."

"I think that man *could* have come to do Jackie harm . . . kidnap, kill him. . . . Certainly capable of roguery of that nature, don't you think? Did you notice his eyes?" Lydia shuddered. "More menacing than a cobra's. But, no, I think he was after something else."

"Go on."

"When I was packing Jackie's bag for him—that red and blue patterned Afghan thing he calls his 'escape bag,' I shoveled in his *Treasure Island*, his map, his humbugs and all the rest of it. Amongst his stuff was something that clearly didn't belong to him. Something that wouldn't belong to any small boy. A black leather-backed moleskine book—you know—the deluxe sort gentlemen travelers spend an awful lot of money on when they've decided to go to Greece and they feel the urge to note down and keep for posterity their timeless impressions of foreign parts."

"Filled several of those myself," Joe admitted. "But I agree—unless you're Edward Lear, the receptacle always outshines the contents. Get on, Lyd."

"Not the sort of thing that would appeal to a boy, I thought. Too grand. Too sober. You couldn't possibly do noughts and crosses or a game of battleships on those pages. And then I remembered Jackie saying last night that he'd spilled the contents of his bag all over Rappo's desk, scooped them back in a hurry and made off."

"Yes, he did say that. So the book came from Rappo's desk. What was in it?"

"You assume I'd look inside, Joe? Me? I couldn't make much

of it. Letters and numbers is all I could see. In rows. Possibly code. I wouldn't know. Then I noticed there were some photos stuffed into that useful pocket arrangement those books have inside the back cover."

"Photos? Of whom?"

"Look, I only had a few seconds to rootle about in there before I heard the commotion down below. I think that chap in the lift had come to retrieve the book. I think he'd been sent to snatch Jackie's *bag*, not necessarily Jackie." She snorted. "Huh! If you and Alfred hadn't decided to behave like Bulldog Drummond and Algy, pulling fuses and poking sticks through bars, I could have just handed the bag over and let the villain trot off with it. Or turned a blind eye while he pinched it. That way he'd never have known we'd guessed what he was up to. And he'd have been very disappointed! Nothing more sensational in there than a limp copy of last month's *Boy's Own Paper*. I'd already put the Rapson book away in my handbag. I've got it right here on my knee."

Joe controlled the skid the sharp movement his foot had produced. "Well what are you waiting for? Rootle some more! Find out what is of such urgency it can bring out a hit squad in hours on a snowy winter's day."

Lydia produced the black book and began to turn the pages in total absorption.

"We're in no position to start wrestling with code, driving a few feet behind a gritting lorry," Joe said. "Just go to the back and take another look at those loose sheets."

He waited as she leafed silently through snippets of paper and photographs.

"Well, come on! What have we got? Coordinates for the last resting place of the Grail? Photos of The Fatman in flagrante?"

"Why do you assume it's something reprehensible? Even toads like Rapson have a private life. Aren't we more likely to find a photo of his spaniel or his mother or a love letter from Matron?"

Lydia sighed and silently shuffled through the contents of Rapson's back flap.

"No, Joe," she said eventually, "I concede that your suspicions were well founded." Her voice lost its touch of gaiety and took on icy deliberation as she added: "Look, you must tell me if I'm making too much of this. . . . All those hours I've spent succouring the disadvantaged, listening to rather hellish stories, may well have made me a party to information on the world other women just do not have. Once you know what men are capable of, you see evidence of their depravities everywhere."

"You're a saint—as all agree, Lyd—but a *knowing* one. Which in my book makes your opinions twice as valuable as those of any other charitable lady. Get on, will you. But just wait until I've got past this lorry."

Her silence was more unsettling than the voluble comments he'd been expecting. Finally, she gathered all the loose bits together, tucked them back into the pocket of the book and closed it firmly.

"It may be worse than we thought, Joe. And, if I'm right, I shudder to think that little Jackie was anywhere near this man. Or under the influence of an establishment that must be either criminally careless or carelessly criminal. Joe! You have to get hold of this Farman and fillet him! When you've had a chance to kick a confession out of him, of course."

Joe's voice was bleak. "Confession to what exactly, Lyd?"

CHAPTER 8

"Almost there! Look, I think we won't refer to this business in front of the family. Anyone who wants to know can hear that Jackie's been spending some time up in London with me and I'm delivering him back—a bit late—to his school. Better tell me who you've got in the house at the moment."

"Oh, just the usual hand-out."

"A long-suffering husband and a gaggle of left-over-from-Christmas orphans?"

"No. We're remarkably un-busy as a matter of fact. Close family, that's all. It's why I was able to get up to London for a couple of days. I left Marcus and the girls in capable hands." She added carefully: "We've got Dorcas staying with us. Perhaps I should have mentioned it earlier."

"Dorcas? Heavens! I haven't seen the child for ages." Joe spoke heartily to cover his surprise. "Now, *she* won't be pleased to see me turning up unexpectedly. You can't have failed to notice, Lyd, that she's been avoiding me like the plague for years. And she's never taken the trouble to tell me why. But I do notice that when I spend any part of any holiday with you, she's not there. And she descends on you the minute I've gone back to London."

Joe left a space in the hope of an explanation. He realised he would even have settled for a polite denial. But Lydia wasn't hurrying to allay his fears. "It's mystifying, insulting and—dashed annoying," he finished in a spurt of disappointment.

"It's tedious for the hostess. And saddening that two people I love dearly behave like the figures on an Alpine weather clock. You know—those wooden contraptions people will bring back from skiing trips. When the sun shines a lady comes out of her little chalet, smiling. When the rain starts, she goes inside again and a gentleman in lederhosen pops out yodeling. Rather unseemly behaviour, I've always thought."

"One in, one out, never seen together. That's me and Dorcas, all right."

"And you used to be as thick as thieves. She trailed after you wherever you went, whenever she could, and you were always patient—no, you were more than that, you were—jolly *kind* to her. I know you can be as hard as nails. I've seen you beat a man half to death." Lydia grinned and patted her brother's knee. "I don't forget that in your blood you're a moss-trooper, a sheep-stealing, hot-tempered Borderer. And the war turned you into a killer. You still keep the visible evidence of it right there on your face as a warning, I do believe. That scar! 'Keep your distance!' it says."

"There are those who admire a tough exterior."

"But Dorcas saw what I've always seen. The lovely man underneath. We all thought—don't laugh—that she had a crush on you. You know, like the passion I had for father's steward when I was that age. I *grew* out of my obsession but Dorcas seemed to *snap* out of hers. Whatever did you do, Joe? Or was it something you said?" Lydia hesitated. "I've never liked to ask, always expecting it would blow over. . . . And then, somehow, it was too late to bring it up. Do you think you could tell me?"

Joe allowed his truculent silence to stretch on, testing the boundaries of sisterly patience and, a moment before she boxed his ears, said brusquely: "Watch it, Lydia! You risk adding insult to Dorcas's injury. Not quite sure what you're implying. If I were, I'd probably chuck you out into the snow. I'll just say: No fault of mine. Honestly. It's worried me, too, and I've given it serious thought. I've absolved myself of any possible misdemeanour, intended or otherwise. Sorry! How pompous." He added lightly: "She was never the same after she got that French haircut."

Lydia smiled. "Well, I did notice she'd changed when her father brought them all back from France. I put it down to Nature. Growing up."

Joe snorted. "Growing up? The child had found her long-lost mother and the French family she didn't know she had. She'd fallen in love with an entirely worthy scion of a noble Champagne family. Affection reciprocated to all appearances. And been closely involved with two murder cases. All in the space of a summer. Bound to have an effect."

"But no reason there for dropping *you* like a soiled glove."

"She made use of me, Lydia. I've realised she always did. The 'crush' you mention would have been more acceptable. Flattering even! And I could have handled it." His swift smile faded. "No, it was the hard man that she saw and was intrigued by. Dorcas had no time for gallantry. She had a heap of troubles on her plate seven years ago. The day I first clapped eyes on her, she watched me deliver a shot amidships to her appalling grandmother who was making her life hell and she decided there and then to recruit me to sort out her remaining problems. That's her father's theory, and it's mine too. She's quite unscrupulous, you know. She cracked her whip, and I performed my circus tricks. Did what she asked. Took her where she wanted to go. And then, when she was entirely satisfied: 'Thank you so much, Joe, that'll be all' is what I heard. And, having found her wings, away she flew."

"Well, she didn't fly far. She still spends as much time with *us* as she does with her scoundrelly father. And we're delighted to have her. The house comes alive when she's here. And the food improves no end! Did you know the girl can cook, Joe? I mean *really* cook?"

"It runs in the family. Her mother's the best I've ever encountered. I expect she's been learning at her apron strings."

"It's a talent but it can be inconvenient. It doesn't go down well with the staff. Dorcas gets very bossy in the kitchen. I've had two cooks hang up their pinnies, put their hat on, and stomp off in high dudgeon when her suggestions got a bit—er—fanciful."

"You're about to give me some sisterly advice, Lyd?"

"No. An ultimatum. Brother, I insist that you come to some socially acceptable arrangement for as long as you stay under the same roof. I won't put up with bickering. It might not be easy. Dorcas has never asked for your news and *you* have never tried to catch up on her. You might as well be strangers. Oh, and let me tell you . . . she's certainly not a child any more. She's twenty-one—that's practically an old maid these days—and she graduates this year. In psychology, in case you'd forgotten. And that's *psychology,* not *psychiatry.* She gets angry if you confuse them. So. I want you to treat her with some respect, Joe."

"I always did, Lydia."

IT WAS ALREADY growing dark as they passed through a quiet village and turned off the High Street between the two stone pillars that marked out Dunsford House. Sensing the change in speed and the crunch of gravel under the tires, Jackie began to stir and yawn.

"Well, here we are, old man!" Joe announced and, parking the car by the front door, spent a moment gently reminding the disoriented boy of who he could expect to see greeting him in the next few minutes. "Your Uncle Marcus. Your two girl cousins—remember their names? That's right. Big girls now . . . they'll take good care of you. Oh, and a friend of the family, Dorcas Joliffe. She's a grown-up. A student at the university."

He gave a toot on the horn, and the door was flung open to reveal the cast list. A manservant struggled through the flurry of welcoming laughter and kisses to take Joe's hat and see to the luggage. Lydia put up a hand for calm and reached into the back seat to draw Jackie forwards.

"Girls! This is your cousin from India. Jack Drummond. I say 'cousin' because he's the son of two of your Uncle Joe's dearest friends: Andrew and Nancy Drummond. Andrew is something big in Bengal. He fought in the same regiment as Joe in the war and was wounded at Mons," Lydia said airily. "Jackie, this is Vanessa and this is Juliet." Her two fair-haired daughters came forwards to shake his hand and then give him a hug, murmuring a welcome.

"And here's your Uncle Marcus."

"Drummond! Delighted you could come!" said Marcus, responding to the child's formal stance and outstretched hand. "Now, what about a spot of tea?"

Joe's eyes were seeking out the dark girl standing a little behind the family group. "I can see you, Dorcas! Come and meet Jackie. Jackie, this is Dorcas, the daughter of Orlando Joliffe, a friend and neighbour."

Joe watched anxiously as they shook hands and eyed each other warily. As a girl, Dorcas had always had a way with younger children, showing an interest and an instinctive understanding. Could this skill have survived maturity and still be there under the layers of sophistication she had no doubt built up over the years? Joe wondered.

In appearance, she'd hardly changed. The inches she'd put on since his first sighting seven years ago had brought her up to average height for a woman, but she still had the slender, whippet-like figure, the same glossy, dark bobbed hair. Long gone and unregretted were the hand-me-down clothes and worn sandals Joe remembered. The thick red sweater she was wearing suited her but Joe wasn't so certain about the black cord trousers of mannish cut. Jackie, of course, with his Indian background, would be completely at ease with the sight of women in trousers, from whipcord jodhpurs to silken harem pants.

"Tea? Oh, I think we can do better than that, Uncle Marcus. I saved you some lunch, Jackie," she told the boy. "Just in case you didn't find time to stop anywhere on the way down. Did you?" Her voice was lower than he remembered with no trace of the country accent she'd had seven years before.

"I don't know if we stopped. I've been asleep. But I know I'm hungry."

"Good. Then what do you say to some fish pie? And then cherry trifle—bottled cherries, but delicious—with cream from the home farm. It's as yellow as a buttercup."

"Oooh, ahh. . . ." Jackie turned to Joe for help.

"Well, I don't know about Jackie, but I'm growing faint at the very thought. Shall I speak for both of us? Lead us to it!"

She smiled and, tucking the child's arm under hers, led him into the hallway, leaning towards him and talking confidentially. Hurrying to follow behind, Joe thought he caught ". . . regiment . . . wounds . . . hero . . . ." and an amused look thrown back at him over her shoulder. He was touched by Jackie's emphatic response to her comments: "No, Dorcas. Uncle Joe was a Northumberland Fusilier. . . . he told me so. . . . Daddy was an officer in the *Indian* Army. And he was wounded at Ypres. Auntie Lydia got that wrong." Dorcas accepted the correction without demur and took down the tension with a joking remark. Jackie was emboldened to pour more military details into the ready ear.

For the second time, Joe noted that the boy was a stickler for detail. Well brought up, he apparently was uneasy with anything less than the truth. Wherever else, he didn't get *that* from his mother! Joe crushed the unworthy thought. This was a quality that could prove awkward over the next few days. But, again, it could be an asset—if carefully managed.

"UGLY LITTLE BRUTES!" Marcus's voice was gruff. "What a collection!"

He poked at the photographs Lydia had spread at random on the table in the drawing room after supper, not comfortable until he had them in a straight line and equidistant from each other. Sensing his companions' disapproval, he tried to explain himself. "I mean—look at them! Seven . . . eight . . . *nine* of 'em and *all* dashed unattractive . . . Spotty . . . Skinny . . . Goofy . . . Tubby and Big Ears. I know who they are—saw them playing Snow White's little helpers in the panto at the Lyceum the other day. And will someone tell me why boys of this age always have such big teeth? Looking at this line-up I'm happy I've been blessed with girls. Bonny from the day they were born!"

He looked to his wife for approval, but Lydia glared at him and he plunged deeper into the mire: "You have to take your hats off to these schoolmaster chappies—facing up to serried ranks of brats like this just to earn a crust. Imagine being greeted by this lot on the front row on a Monday morning!" Something in his arrangement caught his attention and he picked out one face and thoughtfully placed it on the extreme left of the line.

"Marcus! You're being facetious! I thought you'd understood! We don't know who they are or where they are. These poor little sausages could well be victims of some unspeakable crime. These photos were secreted away in the pocket of a notebook of a dubious character violently done to death almost under the eyes of our Jackie!"

"If you say so, my dear," Marcus batted on. "Though I don't see what his death has to do with his photo album. Perhaps he owes the racecourse bookies a bundle? The Brighton gangs are notoriously strict about payment of debts. Leg-breaking and worse goes on! I get some of these cases up before me in the Magistrate's Court after every big race. Or—more likely—he's got Matron into trouble and she's wreaked vengeance on him. Grabbed a tongue depressor and inserted it into a soft part? Something on those lines? I can't see why you and Joe are making such a song and dance over these. Am I the only one to notice the obvious?"

Marcus collected their enquiring glances and shrugged his shoulders. "The tenth photograph!"

They looked again and counted silently.

"Conspicuous by its absence, you'd say. Hey? No sign here of Joe's nephew, is there? I search for but I don't find *his* handsome features in the gallery! If there's anything going on, your Jackie has nothing to do with it. Not on the menu, I'd say."

Lydia and Joe exchanged looks.

Married couples, Joe had observed, soon fell into a mutually agreed role-playing arrangement. In this marriage, Lydia was always presented as the clever one, the undervalued mainspring of the family and Marcus her largely ineffectual but indulgent and loving husband. Not all true, Joe considered. He turned to the comfortable figure of Marcus, fair hair glittering with silver in the lamp light, florid features beginning to show the effects of a second brandy. Joe resisted any invitation to patronise or under-estimate his brother-in-law. The sharp eyes missed little, the good humour in his remarks often masked a fund of cool common sense.

"So how then, Marcus, would you account for this unusual collection in our victim's private journal?" Joe appealed to him. "Any theories? Help us out!"

Marcus turned over one of the images. "Oh, right-o. If you like. For a start, they've been roughly cut with scissors from a larger print, see here. . . . And we're all familiar with this size of head shot. Been taken from the annual class photograph. You know—line them up on the first day of term . . . shoot 'em . . . and there they are preserved in the amber glow of happy schooldays forever more. The girls have both got their own class photos in their rooms. Compare them for size in the morning if you like."

Joe nodded encouragement.

"And, if you look on the back, as I just did," Marcus went on, gaining confidence, "you'll see something remarkable, which is to say, nothing at all! The girls—and all the children I know—write the name of their classmates on the back. But as you see, nothing here to identify these fellows. I dare say this Rapson knew exactly who was in his collection but was too discreet to record it. You'll just have to find other means of identifying them. If you think it will help. Mightn't be easy. Some of these are much older than the others. The photos I mean. This one here's in sepia." He pointed to the one he'd moved to the end of his row. "Pre-war, would you say?"

Joe nodded again.

"I know you detectives look for links and, apart from the obvious ones like uniform, I'd say there's just one."

"Which is?"

"Age."

"Age? They're all prep-school boys. *Between the ages of seven and thirteen. Colonial and foreign pupils a speciality. All dietary requirements catered for. . . .*" Joe quoted from the brochure he'd been handed.

"I'd judge first year of prep school. Not much older. None post-pubertal. One of them, you see, is very young—he still has a gap where his second teeth should be. Late developer? Early entrant? And if you think about it, that would put Jack into a different space, wouldn't it? Didn't someone tell me he was a late arrival at St. Magnus?"

"Yes. That hadn't occurred to me," Joe said. "He was sent up a year or so after the normal entry. He tells me his mother hung on to him as long as she could. It was his father who insisted on sending him to his own old prep school. They came over and stayed with him in the neighbourhood and visited the school before the start of the school year last summer. It would seem to have passed muster as the boy stayed and they went back to India."

"But they would have had no way of knowing that this establishment is the subject of an enquiry at the highest and most secret level of government," Lydia said. "Go on! Tell him about Truelove's interest, Joe!"

"Truelove? James Truelove?"

"Ah, yes, I believe you know the man, Marcus. . . ."

"Shall we say he's known in this house?" He exchanged looks with his wife.

Marcus was fascinated to hear of Joe's encounter with the Secretary of State but confessed himself nonplussed. Finally he gave his verdict: "Politicians! They're a mystery to us all! Never trust 'em! Though if you had to take one seriously, you could do worse than pick this one. At least he's consistent. He's clever . . . wonderful orator—go and hear him in the House one day, Joe. He's got the most solid of backgrounds and he's charming. He'll need all of those assets if he's going to win round the crusty old buffers in his party. He's a Tory, of course, but . . . um . . . rather of the left wing, it's whispered. The words 'socialist leanings' have been mentioned."

"Perhaps the day will come when we no longer have to whisper them," Lydia commented sweetly. "Whatever his politics, I'm glad to hear there's a man of strength and principle in this ragbag of assorted egotists you men call a government."

"Is that quite fair, my love?" Marcus protested mildly.

"Oh, I don't know," said Joe. "How else do you describe a Tory majority run by a Labour prime minister with the fickle support of the Liberals? A coalition? That is to imply some sort of working together, perhaps even with a plan in mind to advance the general good. This mob is uncontrollable. Ever tried to herd mountain sheep without a good dog at your beck and call? You can't. They scatter and run in all directions. Ramsay MacDonald will need to call on all his ancient farming skills if he's to shepherd this bunch to a safe place. No—I prefer Lydia's label."

"They style themselves the 'National Government,' and who can argue with that? It will do for the moment. But there are those who've concluded that the head of our government is quite unqualified for the job: He's self-educated, the illegitimate son of a Scottish farm-labourer and house-maid, he's an advocate of Scottish home rule and seemingly over-indulgent towards our enemies, the Germans. That sort of thing doesn't go down well in the Shires, you know."

"It goes down well in the cities where he's tackling unemployment, alleviating poverty and improving schooling," Lydia said. "And besides, you've got to admire a man who dares to appoint a woman to a cabinet post."

"A good move, Lydia, as all agree, but—he also appointed that scallywag young fascist Mosley to the Privy Seal's office," Marcus countered equably. "That alone makes the old man's judgement questionable in my book. Tired? Ill? Too many lavish suppers chez Lady Londonderry? So—the jury's out, I'd say, on his latest appointee—the holder of this new Office of State. Reform, eh? A broad canvas. I expect he's treading on a lot of toes while he sets about marking out his territory."

"And *I'm* thinking that perhaps the shepherd has found his dog," Joe said. "In which case we should all be heaving a sigh of relief that it's not Oswald Mosley he's chosen to go haring about biting bums on his behalf! Do you think that could be so, Marcus? That what we're looking at is no more than the tip of an iceberg? The visible bit of a political power struggle. How dull!"

"Dull for you and dull for me," Marcus said thoughtfully. He began to rearrange the photographs to his further satisfaction.

"Perhaps not for these poor little tiddlers. How do they come to be caught in the net? I'm thinking you'll be needing all your nifty footwork to sort this lot out, Joe!"

"No nifty footwork expected. I find myself once again the tiniest cog in the affairs of state. I'm just required to do my job without snarling up the works. Insignificant."

"Below the horizon isn't a bad place to lurk in dangerous times," Marcus commented. "It worked for Lord Nelson. Be insignificant but—make sure your cannon are primed and ready to go. Now tell me why young Truelove's poaching on police preserves."

He grinned and added: "And how you're planning to confound him!"

CHAPTER 9

"With low cunning and a crunching right fist!" Dorcas answered for him. "His usual technique."

She had entered unnoticed. She put down a glass of whisky in front of Joe, murmuring: "Glenmorangie with a teaspoon of chilled water," and squeezed herself in beside him, smelling deliciously of something he thought he recognised. Roses and sandalwood. He'd left a bottle of expensive scent under Lydia's tree for her Christmas present.

"Lydia—before we get on to plotting the downfall of the government, may I just report a small domestic detail? I've exceeded orders upstairs. Everyone is happily bedded down, though not necessarily in their own bed or their own room. The girls are completely besotted by Jackie—insisted on taking him in with them for the night. He was playing up to this no end— told them he'd never spent a night in a room on his own until last night at Uncle Joe's."

"True enough," Joe supported the boy's assertion. "In India he would have been in the constant company of his Ayah. And then twenty-nine other boys in the dormitory at school."

He hardly knew what he was saying. He was dealing with a blinding flash of memory that took him back through the years to a château crowded with children and showed him again the skinny girl struggling to appear grown up, all eyes and elbows and determination. She'd always known what to say to children when he'd been left mumbling.

"And the girls took pity on him?" Lydia nodded.

"Who wouldn't? With those innocent blue eyes and that golden hair, he's a baby Apollo! And can he ever tell a story!"

"But where have they settled?"

"All three are in Vanessa's room. There's a good fire in there and a big bed which Juliet has agreed to share with her sister. We all dragged the guest bed in for Jackie and put it next to them. I left him telling them an Indian ghost story. He doesn't seem at all sleepy. Now, I overheard that last bit. Why, Joe, would you be thinking of locking antlers with my hero? It *was* my Sir James you were talking about, wasn't it?"

"Dorcas! You know him?"

"Of course. He's a huge supporter of the sciences. He's donated vast amounts to my own department at the university. He funded a project I was involved with myself last year and that's how I met him. We're all required to take a term out 'in the field,' doing research."

"Into what?" Joe interrupted. "You must excuse my ignorance, Dorcas, but no one has thought fit to tell me exactly what you've been up to these past seven years." A look from Lydia confirmed that his tone had been aggrieved, and he lapsed into an awkward silence.

Dorcas appeared not to notice his discomfort. "Research into genetics, Joe. Inheritance of physical and intellectual qualities. That's my special interest. 'Psychology' is a bit of an umbrella subject and they're still trying to define its borders. Sir James is keen on exploring and expanding them. We're encouraged to study widely for our first degree and then, if there's any prospect of continuing, specialise after that. That's when the real work starts."

"And where did you spend your term out?"

"Not far from here. In Sussex. I was based at St. Raphael's Clinic in the North Downs. A lovely spot. A wonderful establishment. I was lucky to get the placement. I'm writing up my findings at the moment—getting together my thesis for finals. That's why I'm down here at the moment—we're all on home leave until Easter."

Joe sipped his whisky with pleasure. She'd remembered the drop of iced water. Should he feel flattered? He was sure he was meant to, as he was meant to notice she was using the perfume he'd given her. He was uneasy that he still fell for it. He told himself that this was ever her way—she'd deliver a pat on the head which would be followed by a kick in the shins. He took a discreet look at the confident and beautiful young woman at his side. He noted the purity of the profile, the brilliance of the dark eyes, the slenderness of the neck with its simple decoration of a single strand of tiny pearls and swallowed uneasily. He told himself that the annoying child he'd known was probably still there under the silk dinner gown, waiting to make use of him.

"So, I won't hear of any attempt to do him down. Sir James is very . . . caring . . . Joe. He came out several times to supervise the work I was doing at the hospital. He's a busy man; he didn't have to do that—he was just interested. And knowledgeable. He made some rather useful suggestions which put me right on track for a good result. Well he would know, wouldn't he? His father did some splendid work with peas. You know—verifying and expanding on Mendel's experiments. If I'm to declare an interest here I ought to add that. . . ." Dorcas's firm tone faltered for a moment and, to cover her sudden loss of confidence, she took a defiant gulp of Joe's whisky. ". . . to add that . . . he did hint . . . and at this stage of course it could never be more than a hint . . . that . . . I'm just the kind of researcher he would think of employing in the family concerns when I graduate."

Marcus hurried to support her. "Well, there is life beyond the degree ceremony, you know, Joe. Doesn't all end with a mortarboard and a scroll. What's her father going to do about her once she's graduated and at large again, eh? Orlando doesn't have a clue! She's not the marrying kind, she tells us. And I, for one, believe her," he said thoughtfully. "No—the openings for a woman are not many and not good. With Truelove's backing she could get somewhere."

"So, on the whole, Joe, I'd be obliged if you could hold off confounding him." Her smile was dazzling but was swiftly followed by a frown as she turned her attention to the table. "Now, who've we got here? Will someone tell me why the table's spread with photographs of small boys?"

"Better tell her, Joe," Lydia said.

"I'M KEEPING AN open mind."

Joe remembered that these words always prefaced a decided personal opinion from Dorcas.

"But I think I can reassure you that if molestation of a sexual nature is clouding your minds, you can forget it. At least as far as Jackie's concerned. For these others," She gestured to the photographs, "who can say?"

"Dorcas, how would you know?"

"Come off it, Joe! Sexual exploitation is probably the first suspicion that came to mind. Everyone's mind. But especially a policeman's. After that ghastly business the Yard had to deal with a couple of years ago! And when a boy is so unhappy he runs away from school it's something you have to consider. So I asked him."

"Good Lord! How on earth did you find the words? Did he understand what you were getting at?" Joe wanted to know.

"I try not to be deliberately mystifying. I used words a nine-year-old uses. And they have a surprisingly wide vocabulary. Jackie's no fool. And he's honest. He gives you a straight answer.

If he doesn't understand, he expects an explanation." She smiled. "Come to think of it, he probably learned more from *me* than I did from him in our little chat."

"Dorcas, have you been trained to. . . ."

A scathing look cut him off. "No. I'm not concerned with psychiatry. I'm not and never intend to be a meddler with people's minds. I use my common sense to find out what they're thinking. That's all."

"So you established that no master laid an evil hand on him?"

"Yes. Sexually speaking, no advances whatsoever. There's the usual skirmishings between pupils in the dorm after lights out, but Jackie didn't seem to be worried by this. He puts it down to the temperature."

"What do you mean?"

"It's been very cold. You must have noticed. Joe, their dormitory would have challenged Captain Scott of the Antarctic! The radiators go off in the afternoon and they have to sleep under quite inadequate bedding. Do you know what they're reduced to? They pick up their bedside mats from the floor and put them on top of their coverlets to keep the cold out. Sometimes the littlest ones cry all night and can't get to sleep for shivering. Often a boy will creep into his friend's bed and snuggle up for warmth. Jackie hasn't got a best friend. And he arrived late at the school, so he got the last vacant bed. You can guess where that is! Right at the end under the window. And Matron makes them keep the window open all day and all night."

"If I'd thought about it I might well have guessed as much, Dorcas. That's the usual practice in English schools," Joe said. "Jackie hadn't brought it up as a reason for flight. He was rather more concerned with the bleeding corpse that he found he had on his hands."

"Well, he wouldn't complain—not for himself. He may look as soft as a marshmallow, but I suspect young Jackie is made of stern stuff. He's more worried about the lads less able than he is to withstand the rigours. They seem to go down like ninepins with flu, measles, ear infections and even pneumonia. And he assumes, like all the other poor mites—because that's what his elders and betters have always told him—that this bad treatment will toughen him up . . . make a man of him, don't you know." Dorcas shuddered. "The last goal any reasonable human being would be working towards!"

"Dorcas, we've all survived such schooldays," Marcus began to say gently. "Joe and I have, each in our own time, been the new bug under the window."

"Marcus, if you say 'It didn't do *me* any harm,' I shall be obliged to reveal exactly what harm it *did* do!" Lydia threatened.

"I agree with Dorcas for once," Joe broke in to avert the revelations and to keep his promise to strive for a peaceful household. "The British public school can be a bit Spartan. But most survive. Those who don't go about shoving stolen foxes up their jumpers, that is."

"Well, I mention it because Jackie tells me you're going down to St. Magnus with him and you're staying on to sort things out. While you're down there, you might be able to work your way through to acquiring a position of leverage with the Headmaster and you might be able to use your weight to do some good."

"Oh, a little moral and physical coercion you mean? 'Look here Farman, old chum,' I snarl in a sinister way as I twist his arm a further inch up his back. 'Which is it to be? Either I reveal you've been caught with your left hand in the till and your right up Matron's skirt or you turn on the heating in the junior dorm'?"

"I think that's blackmail but it will do very well." Dorcas beamed over the table at Lydia. "So good to hear the old bruiser's not lost his edge. I wouldn't want to be letting myself in for a week of boredom down in Sussex."

LYDIA'S SUDDEN NEED to bustle off and attend to the drinks tray alerted Joe to the conspiracy that had gone on behind his back, though a glance at Marcus's astonished face exonerated him at least.

"Hang on, Dorcas!" Joe managed to say lightly. "You've turned over two pages at once. In fact I think you're reading from a different script altogether. The wrong script, if I understand what you're saying."

"No she's not, Joe." Lydia, returning, had refreshed her gin and tonic and recovered her aplomb. "A sensible arrangement for all concerned. I'm frightfully busy at the moment. I can hardly spare the time to trim my nails, let alone go swanning off down into Sussex to sit by you while you interview schoolmasters." She blushed as she told the lie, knowing she was deceiving no one. "Dorcas is free for the coming week, and she'll agree to accompany you if you ask her nicely. It's just her sort of thing."

"That at least I will accept. Though these days what I used to call 'meddling' is dignified with the word 'research.' No! I'm sorry you're suddenly not available, Lydia, but. . . ." He looked at the clock. "Not too late. I'll ring Cottingham at the Yard and tell him to send down a lady policeman which is what I ought to have done in the first place." Joe searched his memory. "Constable Huntingdon! Efficient officer and known to Jackie. I'll request her."

"A uniformed presence? An overtly *Metropolitan* presence? Is that a good idea?" Dorcas asked. "I can't imagine the local Plod will be pleased. Out of uniform, you can pass very well as a concerned uncle, Joe, but a lady in blue serge with a bowler hat and boots trotting two paces behind you with a notebook might just give the game away."

"She would arrive with some authority at least. And she'd take her orders without quibble. A young, female, bolshy non-relative, on the other hand, would be harder to account for."

"We've thought about that." Dorcas and Lydia exchanged looks. "Dorcas doesn't want the indignity of pretending to be someone she's not."

A thing Dorcas had been doing for the whole of her life. The child had been a consummate actress. Joe hoped his features hadn't expressed the sour thought.

"We had the notion that she could be parachuted in from on high—isn't that the phrase? Sent in to the school on the highest authority for the most respectable of motives. It occurred to us that she could be welcomed with open arms by the headmaster if. . . ."

As Lydia ran into the buffer of Joe's stony glower, Dorcas took over. "I could ask Sir James to telephone the head and tell him he's to accommodate me as his representative. A psychologist interested in child welfare. An emissary from his government department if you like."

"The Ministry for Mischief?" Joe's exasperation was evident. "The man's found a girl after his own heart, I think."

Dorcas grinned.

"And how were you proposing to set this up? Busy man, as you point out. He's promised me full cooperation in this affair, but I'm not sure I could find the words to plead for the inessential presence of an unconnected busy-body."

She shrugged at the slight and sighed. "I wouldn't expect you to try. Look, it's not late. I'll ring him up and speak to him myself. I think *I* can find the words."

Joe groaned. He took out his notecase and selected a card. "Eight o'clock. He'll be just going in to dinner. If they pick up at all, you'll get a cross butler. Tell him to ask Sir James to ring you back in the morning. His home telephone number is the one written in pencil on the back."

Dorcas held up a hand, smiling gently, and waved the card away. "That's quite all right, Joe. I've got his number."

SHE'D BEEN GONE for twenty minutes behind the closed door of the front study where Marcus kept his telephone. Joe began to pace about the drawing room straightening the pictures.

"It looks as though she's got through," Marcus commented. "She usually does."

They heard Dorcas's swift footsteps scurrying down the corridor from Marcus's study and she came through the door looking pink and pleased. "Hurry, Joe! He wants to have a word with you. I left it off the hook."

With sinking heart, Joe picked up the earpiece Dorcas had left on the desk and spoke crisply. "Sandilands here."

"Sandilands! Well, this is a surprise! I wasn't aware! No, honestly! Miss Joliffe never mentioned the relationship."

"No reason why she should, sir. We haven't met since she was a child, and the relationship you speak of is a rather obscure one. My sister is the one who has the connection, and it's one of friendship, not a blood tie," Joe heard himself saying repressively.

"I'd say any connection with Miss Joliffe is one to be valued, Sandilands," came the mild reproof. "Lucky chap! She tells me you were instrumental in clearing up the unfortunate demise of her aunt, her German aunt, Dame Beatrice Joliffe, some years ago?"

"Sir. Dame Beatrice was half German—on her mother's side—and her demise, as I'm sure you know, was rather fortunate for some. Not least the prime minister of the day."

"Ah, yes!" The voice was amused, leisurely, conspiratorial. "Know what you mean! The old girl made off with the family emeralds and then bashed her own skull in with a poker, all in the comfort of a suite at the Ritz, of course. Thereby saving some blushes in Intelligence circles. Am I getting this right?" He broke off. "What's that, Charles?" he called impatiently. "No—tell Lord Meldreth I'll be there directly. Something urgent's come up.

"Now, Sandilands, Miss Joliffe seems to endorse the high opinion I hear from everyone else and expresses great faith in your investigative abilities. So go to it, man! Take her along with you by all means. I'll smooth your path with the school authorities. Leave that to me. You'll find your companion very . . . insightful. But—a word of advice—don't try to run her in blinkers and don't patronise her if you want to get the best from Dorcas . . . Miss Joliffe."

The suave voice took on a rough edge as he added uncertainly: "Don't let her run into danger, Sandilands. I won't have it! She's a spirited girl and she speaks her mind without fear or favour. You may be unaware. . . . I ought to say. . . . She is very highly valued in some circles. . . . Look here, I hold you responsible for her welfare."

Joe gave him a curt goodbye and slammed down the receiver. "Bloody cheek!" he muttered. And, suddenly perceptive of a presence close by—was it a suppressed snort of laughter or a waft of *Arpège* through the open door?—he grimaced, picked up the receiver again and slammed it down more emphatically, exclaiming loudly: "What an arsehole!"

HE RESISTED THE impulse to drag her in and box her ears. He didn't go to join the others.

Joe closed the door firmly and went to collapse into an armchair, holding his head between his hands as though to catch and calm the whirling thoughts and confused emotions.

He—Joe—was responsible for her welfare. And none other. That much was blindingly clear to him. Not even her feckless father, certainly not this smooth politician with his over-warm interest. And Joe had always known it. He'd struggled with the notion, denied it, ridiculed it, rationalised it and finally accepted that, like a good Christmas pudding made with the very best raisins and French brandy, it simply had to be put away in the darkest recesses of a cool pantry and left to mature.

Had she seen that? Of course she had! More clearly than he had himself. The distancing had been all her idea. She'd enclosed herself in an impenetrable cocoon of learning. With many years of educational neglect to make up for, she'd kept at it through term time and vacations alike and used her studies as an excuse to avoid his company. And, despite his protests of ignorance to Lydia, he thought he understood why. She'd felt she needed the time to grow into someone he might look at eye to eye.

Silly girl! Quite unnecessary self-inflicted discomfort. They had always reverberated on the same note. She could have trusted him. The retreat had been well understood by him but none the less hurtful. And now, suddenly, it seemed she no longer needed to maintain her distance. With foreboding, he wondered why.

This interest from Truelove? What had the man been trying to say to Joe? Or trying to avoid saying?

He remembered with a flash of insight a comment Dorcas had made—lightly—when they'd been caught up in an unpleasant and murderous situation in a château in Champagne. She'd enslaved the family's fierce old boar-hound by dropping a few honeyed if outlandish words into his ear, one of the many skills she'd acquired at gypsy fire-sides where her father liked to spend his unbuttoned moments. Noting that the young son of the house was becoming as smitten with Dorcas as his dog, Joe had jokingly asked: "That trick of whispering magic into dogs' ears, miss—does it work on boys?"

She'd given him a strange look and replied: "Oh yes, it does. Trouble is—you can only use it once on a human. I'm saving it up."

Oh God! If the girl had been whispering in Truelove's ears, Joe knew with certainty that he would tear them off and feed them to Marcus's hounds. Seven years? What entanglements might she have got into during that time without his knowledge and direction?

His dejection was not lightened by the memory of the wailing and yelling from the pantry one disastrous Christmas Eve when his mother, retrieving the pudding in preparation for dinner on the morrow, had discovered that the mice had got in and feasted before them.

CHAPTER 10

COOMBHAVEN. SUSSEX.

N ine o'clock chimed on the mantel clock and, seemingly at the signal, the dying fire below slumped and darkened in the grate, giving up the struggle. Molly Weston shuddered with foreboding and turned up the wick of the oil lamp to cheer up the mean little room.

If they're not back with him by nine, it's all over.

She'd set herself a limit. Now that limit was passed; what could she do next?

She strained to listen for sounds outside in the lane but heard only the quiet sobs and desultory talk of the two girls filtering through the ill-fitting floorboards and thin layer of linoleum in the bedroom above. The baby in his cot by the fireside mewed and fretted and punched the air with his tiny fists. Molly held her breath. *Please, God, let him not wake up!* She couldn't cope with his screams and his hunger. A moment later he settled back into sleep.

Her eyes went again to the one photograph the sparsely furnished parlour of the brick and flint cottage contained and focussed on it with the pleading gaze of one worshipping an icon. The family group. No baby Billie when that was taken last year. She'd been two months pregnant and nothing showed as she stood looking small and quenched next to her burly husband. A fine figure of a man, Jem. Everyone said. There he stood, smiling with paternal pride. The children were ranged up in front in height order, the girls neat in their best dresses and plaited hair and their younger brother, left sock drooping, head on one side, gormlessly peering at the photographer.

Jem had wanted to leave the boy at home. *He'll only show us up! I'm not risking it.* But just for once, Molly had prevailed. It had taken less than a second for the shutter to click, but in that short time the camera had recorded an undeniable fact. Plain as day: Walter wasn't quite right in the head. He'd never be able to look after himself.

Now he was out there in the snow on a pitch-dark night. Eight years old. Molly's daft lad.

In a sudden urge to follow him, get him back and hug his cold little body to her, Molly got up from the wooden armchair and made for the door. *Stay put!* Jem had told her. *Don't leave the children. The constables'll find him.*

That had been four hours ago. She lifted the sneck and opened the door an inch, just enough to peer through onto the lane, not enough to let the cold air in. At least the clouds had lifted and the moon had come out. By its light she could just make out the single line of small footprints heading for the road. The last signs of her son. The policemen had had the wit to keep their big boots well to one side so they could see the direction he'd made off in. She'd told them: *He'll be off to the old forge across the road and into the woods. He usually hides up there.*

And, of course, they'd asked: *Why would he be making off at this hour in the snow, Missis?*

They had to ask. But their closed faces told her they already knew the answer. Jem Weston and his bloody belt. *His dad were goin' to give him a thrashing.* There. She'd said it. It had been easier than she expected.

Jem just stuck his nose in the air and defied them. *Not that it's any of your business . . . but I'll tell you anyway.* He'd broken a milk *jug, clumsy bugger, and pissed his britches. He's a kid who just won't learn. Now are you going to stand about gassing to my wife all night, or are you going to lend a hand?*

The senior bobby, PC Snipe, had tried to reassure her. *We'll get him, don't you fret. He won't have gone far on a night like this. If he's still missing in the morning we'll send to Brighton for the tracker dogs.*

A torch was wobbling down the lane. Molly shot back into her seat and looked up as Jem came in, stamping the snow from his boots in the porch.

"Don't get excited. Nothing. No sign of him in the forge. Can't search the woods just like that. Trail ran out straight away when he hit the main road. Must have followed along the car tracks . . . easier walking. No idea whether he turned left or right."

"What about the coppers?"

"They've gone home. Nothing more they can do."

"Did you see the doctor?"

"You set too much store by the doctor! Thick as thieves with the doctor you are. I don't know what the bloody hell you think Doc Carter could do!"

Savagely Molly answered back: "More of the same! Put back together what you've smashed over the years with your great fists, Jem Weston! He's a good man!"

"Watch it! He weren't there anyway. I had to leave a message. He's out delivering Mrs. Cumming's fourth brat."

Molly flinched, expecting the usual back-hander as he came and towered over her, pushing his face up close and talking slowly as though she were an idiot. "You're going to have to get used to the idea—the kid's not coming back alive. It's bloody freezing out there, and he's hardly got the wits to find his way across the yard to the jerry on a good day. Some bugger'll find his remains in a ditch come spring, you'll see. Then we'll know for sure." And, a note of conciliation creeping in: "Look at it this way, love—it might be a blessing in disguise. One of the Lord's funny little ways. He were running you ragged, Molly. And never likely to get any better—you heard Doc Carter. Worse, in fact. Didn't know his own strength. I've tried to train him . . . he'll have to work in the forge one day, and he'll have the muscle power, but it's the head, Molly. . . . He's weak in the head. Always will be. It could turn out better for the girls in the long run, better for little Billie, better for you. We couldn't pay for any more doctoring."

"You didn't pay for the last lot . . . or the one before that," Molly muttered.

"Cos the doc's a generous bloke! But he can't go on dishing out welfare just like that. I don't much like the idea of taking someone's charity, neither. You know me. . . . Never be beholden to nobody I were always taught."

"Then perhaps you could drink less and have more to spend on the kids," Molly thought to herself, but she dared not say it aloud. He still caught the silent message and his hand twitched.

Throat thick with hatred, Molly went to the cradle and snatched up the sleeping baby. She pinched his leg until he wailed. "Thought so. He's just coming round. Time for his evening feed. You go on up to bed. I'll see to Billie and maybe sleep down here in the chair. Just in case Walter comes back home."

"Well, all right, then." Jem cast his master-of-the-house look around the room. "I see you haven't laid for breakfast yet? Get it on early. We're off again come first light."

CHAPTER 11

Joe eased his salt-spattered Morris off the main road and up
the drive of St. Magnus school. What was the quality of school
driveways that gave them the power to rouse such dread in anyone
approaching? The gloom of laurels lining the route set the mood,
he decided, as they ushered the visitor onwards. Unnaturally
glossy at this dead time of the year, they stood in ranks, deferential but foreboding, like undertakers' well-drilled assistants. Joe
shuddered. He'd spoken once to an old schoolmaster he much
admired, a sanguine and rational man who confided that this
terror of approaching a school had never left him in half a century.
What must young Jackie be feeling?

Joe glanced in the mirror at the anxious little face on the back
seat and, for a reckless moment, he contemplated turning round
and making off for the chalk uplands. Striding out in an open and
treeless space for a good long tramp and a talk.

At least the sun had made an appearance to cheer up what
promised to be a difficult day. A change in the wind overnight
had bundled the snow clouds off to trouble the west and left the
south country lightly dusted with the glamour of a Christmas
card. Another of old Mother Nature's jokes. "Oops! I'm a bit late
with the snow . . . so sorry I missed December!" Like an adored
actress who always arrived late for a party, said the wrong thing

and got drunk, she was always forgiven, always a lively topic of conversation. Well, Joe was glad enough for the sunshine, glad to be seeing the school, for the moment at any rate, in the best possible light.

The carriage-drive had been neatly cleared of snow, he noticed. Murder and mayhem might reign indoors, but the maintenance work on the exterior was faultless. One or two cedar trees stood about in ducal dignity; already stately, they were further ennobled by the ruffles of snow they shouldered. They signalled, by their maturity, that a building of some distinction might be anticipated around the next bend.

Joe tried to estimate what would be the feelings of a parent on delivering his son and heir into the care of this establishment, and he decided that he was, so far, very favourably impressed. The spacious grounds the brochure had promised were certainly there, resisting the encroachment of the sprawling modern town. But even the proximity of the unattractive development on its doorstep was presented as an advantage: *Railway station delivering speedy service to the capital a few minutes' walk away. . . . Local amenities: theatre, golf course, tea-rooms, cinema, swimming pool, hostelry, cliff-top walks. . . .* Joe doubted that the boys would be allowed to enjoy many of these. Apart of course from the visits to the *Lavender Lady* for a cream bun followed by a three-reeler at the Odeon on a wet weekend when the parents put in an appearance.

The escorting laurel bushes gave out dramatically, in good time to grant an unencumbered view of the school. It was grand but not grandiose, solid but not forbidding. An elegant example of late Georgian architecture, though it could just be early Victorian. If he ever had the opportunity, he'd check. Joe slowed to scan other details more revealing than the well-kept drive and the stout front door. His eye ranged upwards over the chimney pots, the roof tiles and the window frames on the topmost floor.

He was looking for signs of decay, and this is where it would show itself first, up here above eye level. Years of war and financial collapse had worn down many a thriving concern and reduced it to rubble within a decade. But here was a different story: Like the grounds, the fabric of the house seemed to be in prime condition. Even the weathercock atop the pinnacle of what must be the chapel appeared freshly gilded and jauntily catching the sun.

"Andrew's old school, eh?" Joe addressed the remark to his two passengers sharing the back seat. "I think he must have been well pleased with it."

"Oh, yes," said Jackie dimly. "Daddy liked it here. Before he went up to Haileybury. He has lots of stories."

Dorcas leaned forwards and put a paper into Joe's hand. "You'll be needing this. Andrew's telegram."

"Oh, yes. Thank you." He put the insignificant folded sheet of brown paper carefully into his inside pocket. "I'll give it back to you, Jackie, when it's worked its magic. For your scrapbook."

The telegram had been delivered while they were still at the breakfast table. With all eyes on him, Joe had opened it, read, and summarized the contents for his audience. "It's from India. From Andrew Drummond. He's conferring temporary parental powers to me (to be confirmed by his London lawyer who is receiving instructions) until such time as Jackie's mother can arrive in England to assume control. He's sent a similar statement to the head at St. Magnus. Nancy is on her way and is expected to arrive early next month. In three weeks' time. . . . Three weeks. Good Lord! Oh, and at the end he says they both send their love to you, Jackie. Well, that's all right then! This gives us the edge we need!" Deep in thought, he began to fold the sheet.

Dorcas had deftly plucked it from his hand and passed it to Jackie, who was sitting next to her. The boy clutched it and read with trembling lips, running a finger under the printed words. An arm around his shoulders, Dorcas bent to whisper the meanings of the long words and the Latin legal phrases as he struggled through. Joe reached for the marmalade and held it up to the light, making distracting remarks about the sun shining through the Cooper's Oxford, pretending he hadn't seen Dorcas hurriedly dabbing up with her napkin the teardrops that splashed onto the flimsy sheet as Jackie neared the end. At a look from Dorcas, Joe had made no attempt to take it back.

He parked neatly by the front door of the school and turned to speak. "Ten o'clock. We made good time, and we got here an hour before our advertised arrival. We may catch them on the hop. What's likely to be happening in there at the moment, Jackie?"

"They'll be nearly at the end of the first lesson. Ten minutes to go."

"Good. A moment of calm, then. Look, stay here with Dorcas for a minute, will you, while I go and alert the head master."

As he got out of the car a young man flung the door wide and came forwards with an air of enquiry. He stopped in his tracks, stared at the car, then started forwards again, holding out a hand. "Sandilands? You must be Assistant Commissioner Sandilands? Sir, you are expected . . . but you arrive a little earlier than we looked for you. No matter—Mr. Farman is in his study and will see you straight away." The man's attention was immediately switched to Jackie, and he bustled over to the car door to help him out. "Hullo there, Drummond! Good to see you. Look, before we go any further, you ought to hear that I'm your new form master."

Jackie greeted this news with a squeak of pleasure, and Joe looked with increased interest at the man the school had chosen to go out in front bearing the standard. A good choice, he decided. Impeccably suited and confident, yet having an edge of modern informality. And, a feature of instant appeal to small boys—and to Joe himself, he admitted with amusement—the man had the intriguingly battered features of a boxer.

"Mr. Gosling! Oh, good! Uncle Joe, this is Mr. Gosling who teaches games. Mr. Gosling, this is my cousin Dorcas who's been looking after me."

"Ah, yes. Miss Joliffe, would that be?" The master shook her hand. "Delighted! We were told you were coming. If you'll give me your keys, sir, I'll see to your motor. No, no! Let me take Drummond's things. Now, what's he got? Ah. I see he's acquired a suitcase in the interval? And the old Afghan bag, I think I recognise."

Gosling heaved the luggage out of the car and placed it without further comment a careful distance away from a second, much larger, collection. A trunk with two further suitcases and a pile of books tied together with string sat waiting by the side of the carriage sweep.

Dorcas eyed this arrangement casually. "Comings and goings this morning, Mr. Gosling?"

"Always comings and goings in a school this size," was the noncommittal response.

He seemed eager to bustle them straight inside, but Jackie with a sharp cry went over to the pile of luggage and was staring at the books. He bent and turned over a luggage label. "Spielman! These are Spielman's things!"

Gosling stopped in his tracks and, with a sigh, went over to Jackie and exchanged a few quiet words. Turning to Joe he spoke with an air of resignation: "Only to be expected, of course. The first of many abrupt withdrawals, I'd calculate. News spreads fast up at that level. Our parents are ... of a certain status in society, if you understand. Diplomats, politicians, Civil Service posted abroad—that sort of thing. The kind of people who can't be doing with the slightest whiff of scandal. Spielman's father is a diplomat so we're not surprised that he's the first to get wind of the—er— sad occurrence. And—worse—he's got a very fussy mother. It's Madame Spielman who'll be the instigator of this panicking rush for the exit."

He turned again to Jackie. "I think you knew him better than most," he said gently. "Look, he's sitting waiting in the trunk room just inside. Would you like to say goodbye?"

At that moment, a Daimler purred in stately fashion up the drive and braked behind the Morris. A chauffeur in grey uniform stepped out and saluted Gosling. "I'm here for Master Spielman," he announced. He glanced at Jackie. "Is this him?"

"No, no! Wait a moment, will you? If you'd like to start loading these things, I'll just go and get the young gentleman."

He went inside and reappeared a moment later with a small boy.

"Spielman!"

"Oh, hullo, Drummond," the child said warily. "You got away with it, then?"

"Can't say. I don't know what 'it' was, Spielman! They've brought me back to have it out. But where are you going?"

"My people have sent for me. Mama doesn't want me staying in a place infested with murderers and such riff-raff."

"Oh. We'd better say goodbye then," said Jackie politely.

The chauffeur had finished his loading and jangled his keys in a marked manner. Spielman stepped forwards, eager to be off.

"Look—I'll miss our talks about books," Jackie said, grabbing him by the sleeve. "Wait a minute!" He dashed to his Afghan bag and took out his copy of *Treasure Island*. "Here, take this. I've finished it."

"Oh, I say. Are you sure? Can I put my name in it? Thank you very much, Drummond. I'll say goodbye then."

The chauffeur held the door for him and the small figure, clutching his book, scrambled into the back seat. He didn't look around as they drove off.

Joe noted the swift pat on the head Jackie received from his new form master.

As he led them down the corridor, Gosling leaned to Joe out

of earshot of Dorcas and Jackie and muttered, "Sorry about that, sir. You weren't supposed to witness the departure. Bad for morale. They tried to schedule it discreetly."

"At least the two friends had time to say their goodbyes," Joe remarked.

"Not sure 'friends' would be the right word for that relationship," Gosling said. "I don't think Drummond will be heartbroken. Spielman didn't fit in here. Made no effort to fit in. Not a sporting type. Only happy when his nose was in a book. And he had certain physical problems which are not best catered for in general schooling. It was all getting too much for Matron, I'm afraid. He wrote every week to his parents asking to be taken away, so, at last, he's got his own way."

"You fear a similar panic amongst the other pupils? More letters home begging a swift removal?"

"You've got it. It would be a disaster. But there are two things that could avert it."

Joe looked at him questioningly.

"First—the behaviour of your nephew, sir. He's a steady lad, I've observed. If he can settle down again as though nothing's happened, it would help to calm nerves and silence tongues. As his form master, I can help with that. I've already been preparing the ground. Drummond should find he has no difficulties as far as his classmates are concerned."

"And the second palliative action?"

"Would be initiated by you, sir. Top policeman? That's what they're saying. The very best outcome—speaking for St. Magnus, naturally—would result if you were to acknowledge that the crime has nothing to do with the school."

"Apart from the uncomfortable fact that a killing occurred on school premises and deprived you of one of your senior masters?" Joe was taking exception to being steered into any premature conclusions by this young squirt. "Bit difficult to brush a bleeding corpse under the axminster, I would have thought?"

Gosling gave one of his conciliatory grins. "Both incontrovertible facts, as you say, sir. But then, easier to account for and dismiss when you understand that the crime has, in fact, been solved to the satisfaction of us all and—more importantly—to the satisfaction of the Sussex Constabulary."

"Solved?"

"Yes. Inspector Martin has a man in custody in the local jail. A man *known* to the school, indeed known to the whole town and the county but totally unconnected with us as an educational establishment. An itinerant knife-grinder."

The affable features hardened into something more knowing, more sardonic as he confided, "It was he who put the fine edge on the weapon that skewered poor old Rapson."

THE HEADMASTER HAD chosen the sensible route, Joe estimated, in the preliminary social skirmishing and had decided to address him as an equal. His tone was neither lofty nor unctuous. Joe's was civil and direct. They established that Joe would be referred to as "Commissioner Sandilands" and the head would be "Headmaster" or "Mr. Farman."

Dorcas had been greeted politely, the Sir James connection acknowledged, and immediately assigned the suitably female task of escorting Jackie and his luggage to Matron's room for what the head called "the usual inspections." A quick search for head lice, Woodbines, smuggled comics, and any other contaminants from the capital, Joe guessed. To his relief, Dorcas had gone quietly.

"Delighted you could find the time to come down, Commissioner!" Left alone with Joe, the headmaster appeared to relax, and his knowing smile indicated that the irony was deliberate. His features instantly took on an earnestness as he continued: "I'm not going to make light of this—it could have been a serious matter . . . a runaway boy, at large in London . . . recipe for disaster! I expect you're only too well aware of the dangers. Thank God you were there to pick up the pieces."

Joe noted that a certain evolution in the head's thinking had taken place over the past thirty-six hours. He made no comment but wondered if he detected the pervasive influence of Sir James Truelove in this development. He'd wait to see the opposition's cards on the table before he made his own play.

"Indeed. And thanks also to Andrew Drummond's clear instructions regarding his son. You will have received. . . ?" Joe's hand went to his pocket.

Farman waved away his search for documentation. "All that is in order, I assure you. The boy's mother will be here in a few weeks and will doubtless make her own arrangements at that time. Meanwhile, it's *you* we have to deal with, *your* requirements and *your* decisions we have to hear."

At last a flash of irritation. Joe was glad to hear it. He never walked comfortably along a path too thickly strewn with rose petals. He smiled affably. "My first concern is for the boy's well-being, Mr. Farman. I'm confident that, together, we can decide on a course of action that will ensure it."

Placated, the head was encouraged to play another card. "Continuity, that's the key, Sandilands. Sure you'll agree. Enough disruption in the boy's life already, you know. He was bedding down nicely. Beginning to make friends. Scored a try at rugger the week before he bunked off. The other boys were noticing him and appreciating his qualities. Best I think for all concerned if he were to resume his place in school with the least possible fuss and bother."

"Is that option available to us?" Joe asked. "In the circumstances? Blood spilled and all that?"

This was exactly the cue Farman had been waiting for. He sat back in his leather chair and a smile spread across his chubby features. "Ah, yes. Only good news on that front, Sandilands. We understand now that Drummond was the accidental witness of Rapson's last seconds of life. Fingerprints establish that they met on the back stairs. The sight of his form master bleeding and expiring right in front of his eyes would have been enough to send any youngster into a tailspin. As a witness, he will, of course, be required to give his evidence to Detective Inspector Martin, who is in charge of the case." His smile widened. "Evidence of academic interest only now, I may add. Now that Martin has established the boy's innocence of any direct involvement with the killing. A stabbing occurred, Sandilands, no one's denying it. But it didn't occur on school premises."

"Not on school premises?" Joe repeated in surprise.

"No. At least, not in the school buildings as far as we can ascertain. Martin's men have tracked him back from the place where he—er—succumbed. Thanks to an overnight three-inch covering of snow, things have rather ground to a halt. But we'll get there."

"You're saying Rapson managed to travel some distance in his wounded condition before he fell dead down the back stairs?"

"Exactly that."

"With a bit of luck and a long measuring tape, you may manage to track the unpleasantness all the way back to the chip shop in the High Street?"

Farman weathered the sarcasm, smirked, and ran with it. "Ah, yes! An undignified spat with a townie? Some argument over the cod and mushy peas? We should have given it some thought perhaps." His smile faded as he uncovered his big gun and fired his shot. "But no need for fancies of that nature. Inspector Martin, whom you will shortly meet, has the perpetrator under lock and key in the town jail."

"Enter the gypsy suspect?" Joe asked mildly.

Farman frowned. "No. An itinerant workman, but not, it

appears, a gypsy. 'The *usual* gypsy suspect,' I imagine you were thinking."

Again Joe had provoked a burst of antagonism. Farman heard it and adjusted his tone. "But this has little to do with me. It's Martin's business. *Police* business. You will be able to chew it over to your heart's content with your colleague." He got to his feet. "Two things to do before you set off back to the metropolis. So we'd better get on with it. It gets dark so early these days and the roads are very uncertain, don't you find? You'll want to see your nephew happily established in his routine, and you'll want to confer with Martin. Shall we start with Martin?"

Sensing that the curtain was about to go up on the second act of a well-choreographed performance, Joe tilted his head politely and headed for the door.

CHAPTER 12

"Well, here you are," Farman announced. "Temporary police HQ. The old sports-kit storage room. Not what you're used to, I'm sure, but the best we can do. Martin's already in there at work. Early bird. Good man. I'll introduce you."

As he flung the door open and walked in, he said as an afterthought: "By the way, Commissioner, we'll lay a place for you—and Miss Joliffe of course—at the top table for lunch. Twelve o'clock sharp. Martin shuns our company and chooses to bring his own sandwiches. Now, Sandilands, may I present—"

The two officers fixed each other with a calm police stare. They went through the ritual of introduction, waiting for Farman to leave, each taking the other's measure. As Joe had feared, the Sussex Detective Inspector looked unfriendly, irritated at being disturbed earlier than anticipated. He was as tall as Joe and handsome in the fair, corpulent way of Sussex men. Large parts of his ruddy cheeks were covered by a luxuriant mustache to rival that of Ramsay MacDonald. Smartly suited, wedding ring. A pipe smoker, judging by the thick atmosphere.

It was Martin who jumped in first to break the silence that followed the welcome closing of the door behind Farman's billowing black gown. "I don't know if you're a man who takes advice when it's given with good intent, sir, but I have some to offer."

Portentous. Unsmiling. Joe braced himself for the ritual clearing of the decks, the assigning of roles, the growling warnings about territory.

"Avoid the meat pie. The pastry's made with lard, and the meat's made with something I'll swear never mooed."

"I always listen to advice," Joe replied carefully. "Sometimes I take it. I'll fill up on the rice pudding," he finished with a grin.

"Sensible course, sir. That's actually good. They keep a couple of Jersey milk cows somewhere in the vicinity and likewise ponies for drawing the grass-cutter and the snowplough. They've got chickens and such-like. A sort of school farm or menagerie. Out the back. I'll show you when we go on our mystery tour—the Last Reeling Steps of Rapson. Any idea, sir, how far a man who's just been stabbed in the heart can travel? You're going to be surprised!"

"Oh, I don't know," Joe said. "In London our record's a hundred yards. Knife still in the wound. But then we breed them tough in The Smoke."

Martin stepped forwards to pull up a chair for Joe on the other side, the visitor's side of the desk. "Sorry, sir, for the accommodation. What space I could make I've already filled, I'm afraid. And there's as much again down at the station." He moved a few files and piles of paper around on the dust-covered desktop and settled himself again. "Do sit down, and don't worry, sir. I've chucked out the field mice and the spiders."

It was more than Joe could bear to sit with his back to a door. It was a phobia, he supposed, one he shared with other fighting men, and, like a fear of snakes, there was no reasoning it away. But he'd learned to live with it. He took the chair that had been set for him and moved it, placing it at one side of the desk, angled towards the doorway. He sat down casually and slipped one leg over the other, relaxed and friendly. "Not taking up residence, Inspector. Quite happy to perch here. And if some fiend bursts through the door wielding a cricket bat, I'll 'ave 'im!"

Martin smiled, understanding the reason behind the defensive stance. "Ah!" he said and looked more closely at Joe's face. "The commissioner had a Good War?"

"No such thing as a good war, Martin!"

"You were clearly in the war, and you survived," Martin commented drily. "As good as it gets, wouldn't you say?"

Joe nodded. "Yourself?" he ventured. To talk about the war and one's part in it was bad form, but he sensed that Detective Inspector Martin was set on discovering or revealing information—or perhaps prejudices—that had to be taken out of the way. He would have guessed that the Sussex man was about his own age—late thirties, early forties at a stretch. Certainly a young age to have reached his current position in a county force where promotion tended to go by years of service and not on ability or social contacts. A bright man, Joe guessed, but one with a chip on his shoulder most probably, when faced with a rising star in the Metropolitan force. The barely concealed resentment betrayed by the war comment indicated as much. For years, Joe had dealt with the suspicion and criticism that came his way at each promotion, bad feeling largely spilling over from the continuous appointments of retired military grandees to the all-powerful position of commissioner: Field Marshal Lord This. General Sir That. Marshal Viscount The Other. Aristocratic old warriors, sent in to bat at the end of the day, to play out the over as twilight fell. The Nightwatchmen.

With a quiet show of spirit and acuity, the Nightwatchmen, one after another, had calmly seen what was required, had listened to good advice and implemented improvements before hanging up their bats. Each had valued and rewarded the input of an officer like Sandilands. "Clever man. Effective. A patriot (something of a war hero) but watch it—he has his bolshy side," seemed to be the opinion passed from commissioner to commissioner.

"Oh, nothing so glamorous as yourself, I'm sure, sir."

Joe waited, one eyebrow raised.

"PC Plod before the war. Joined up when war was declared. Recruited in Brighton."

"One of Lowther's Lambs?"

"That's right. Royal Sussex Regiment. Eleventh Battalion."

"Lucky to have survived. Not many of the Lambs did."

"Call it luck if you like!" Martin snorted. "We were in that life-wasting diversionary show before the Somme. Richebourg."

"Ouch!" Joe flinched at the name of the bloody encounter.

"I was wounded and sent home. So—I missed Passchendaele. Yes, you could say I was lucky."

"And you recovered sufficiently to step back into your old job." Joe hoped he was feeding Martin the right lines.

"Well, they were desperate. With all good, fit men out at the war, they'd take anything in those days. I worked hard. Jumped into dead men's shoes and kicked about a bit. Drew a veil over certain injuries. Fought my way up through the ranks."

"I expect that, compared with a confrontation with the Sussex promotions board, Richebourg was a doddle?"

Martin gave him a sharp look. "It's been slow and hard going."

"But it won't always be the same, Martin. Lessons have been learned. Wild angry voices have been heard and listened to. One of them mine. No comfort to you at this stage of your career but the police college at Hendon, so long talked of, will open next year. The very best, the sharpest and most dedicated, whatever their backgrounds, will be recruited. We're moving forwards. *You* may not profit from that but your son, if you have a son, could well—"

"I have three daughters and a son. He's called Edmund, like me. No police force for him, Hendon or otherwise. No. All he can think about is aeroplanes. Daft 'apeth wants to be a fighter pilot!" The moustache twitched, signalling a smile, and the solid face dissolved into indulgent affection.

Joe's objection was heartfelt: "Martin, you must speak to him firmly. Dissuade him at all costs! I've never met a flyer yet who was *compos mentis*."

"I'll tell him, sir. But you know what they're like. Have you got a lad yourself then?"

"Sadly no," Joe said. "Not married. Unless we count young Jackie, your escaper. I've been officially assigned care and control until his mother gets here from India. Not quite sure what's expected of me, but I think I ought to start by ensuring you're not planning to put him in manacles or on a treadmill or whatever medieval retribution you still exact down here in the sticks." He smiled while he said it.

"Oh, we've been making progress, sir. Thumbscrews rusting away in the town museum. I think I can say the worst he has to undergo is having his fingerprints taken. Just to confirm the little smudges found on the bannister alongside Rapson's are his. We took samples from a book by the lad's bed but, just to be sure. Now, where would you like to start? I can offer you a view of the body. It's still in the morgue."

Joe silently reminded himself that he was appearing as a concerned uncle. Martin was making it all too easy to fall straight into a professional pattern of behaviour. "What about that tour of the premises you promised? The Rapson Ramble?" he said lightly. "Anything to get out of here! How can you stand it, man? What's that awful stink?"

His expression as he looked around the room gave the lie to his tone of distaste. Dust-laden, cramped, a deliberately insulting choice of working place it might be, but Joe was responding to it with a schoolboy eagerness that had not gone unnoticed by the sharp Inspector. It was a base in a hostile environment, police territory, a bivouac. He noted with approval the shining new telephone freshly installed on a table by the door, notebook and pencil lined up beside it, list of numbers taped onto the wall behind. He took in the row of cardboard boxes along one wall, each one labeled with a painted clue to its contents: *Victim, Staff, Boys, General Evidence.* The blackboard and easel commandeered from a classroom and bearing a hastily chalked message: *Find the bloody weapon!*

"The stink? That could be my rough shag, sir." Martin picked up a pipe from the windowsill and blew down it thoughtfully. "Or it could be a mélange of rotting leather, cat-gut and sweaty socks that's built up over the years. *Cuir de Russie* it's not, but you'll get used to it."

"Will I, though?" Joe asked with a grin. "Not if old Farman has anything to do with it! The moment I swallow my last mouthful of rice pudding, he'll hand me my car keys."

"In that case, better get on, sir. Oh, before we set off I'll just try to get through to HQ in Brighton again. I want to fix up the sniffer dogs. They've got a good pair down there, and we're going to need them if we're to find the knife before the melt."

Joe waited until he replaced the receiver.

"You got that?" Martin asked. "No joy! Damned dogs are out already on a job. Missing child down in Combe Haven. Blacksmith's son wandered off from home last night. I suppose that takes precedence over a missing murder weapon."

"Ah, yes, the weapon," Joe said. "I hear from an overtalkative member of staff that you know who and how. An itinerant knife-grinder seems to be in the frame?"

"Well you heard wrong! He hasn't been arrested. He's a man of no fixed abode. The moment the cell door opens he's off like a shot, and we'll never find him again, so he's in custody pending divulgence of information."

"Helping you with your enquires?"

"Right. That's the idea at any rate. Except he's not being very helpful. Old Rory could have done it, but I'll lay odds he didn't. His contribution to the crime seems to be a peripheral one. He it was who'd just freshly sharpened the knife before a person unknown sank it between Rapson's ribs. Inconveniently, he's come over all shy in police custody and won't utter a word. He's not a gypsy—as far as he doesn't live in a gypsy community—but he swears he doesn't talk English, only Romany when he's in a fix. May be true. I doubt it. He's just waiting for us to get fed up with him and turn him loose."

"Can't you call his bluff—get a local Romany to translate for you?"

Martin put back his head and hooted. "Now I know you're from the Met! A Romany help the police? They don't recognise Old Rory as one of theirs, but they'd never shop him to us. We come last on their list of personae gratae ... somewhere after Old Nick and Judas Iscariot."

Joe smiled. "In the matter of Old Rory's reticence—I think I may just be able to help you. But tell me—if you haven't got the weapon to hand, how on earth do you know it was one of Rory's specials?"

"Cutting edge of forensic science, you could say if you didn't mind a pun, sir. Our Brighton boffins are rather good. The medic who did the PM on the body found some interesting traces around the wound entry point. They can work out how long and how wide the blade is from the profile, but they can also make some interesting deductions from the residue that piles up in front of the mouth of the gash. Too small to see with the naked eye, but they've put it under the microscope. Grinding powder. They've analysed it. Corresponds exactly to the gunk Rory smears all over the blades before he applies them to his grinding wheel."

"So this one went straight from the wheel to the heart without passing through a steak or a cabbage?"

"Exactly. And we know what we're looking for. All the school's kitchen knives were sharpened the day before. Happens every six months when Rory turns up. Does a good job, they say. One missing. Six-inch-blade, chef's knife. Could have been picked up by anyone working in the kitchen or passing by out of hours. It's out of bounds, of course. But it's never locked."

CHAPTER 13

"Well, here we are, Miss Joliffe. It's not grand, but it suits me well enough." There was an edge of challenge in the voice as Miss Harriet Hughes, matron of St. Magnus School, ushered Dorcas and Jackie into her room.

Mindful of the head's briefing, Matron ran an eye over the odd pair. Drummond appeared to be smartly turned out. Fresh clothes, straight parting, handkerchief in pocket. She observed no sign of distress caused by his recent experiences but didn't wonder at it. It would take a blast from Big Bertha to shake the confidence of some of these privileged little persons. He was just a boy who'd put himself by his arrogance into the wrong place at an inconvenient time. And who had heaped further inconvenience on them by running away for protection to—what had the head said?—"a well-connected uncle with a vast potential for trouble-making."

Matron had not been impressed by this. She'd crisply reminded Farman that almost all the boys in his school could claim such a relative—they weren't running an orphanage in Wapping, after all. If you gathered together all the fathers and uncles of the current intake they could probably run an empire, she'd suggested. "Several empires, Matron," Farman had corrected. "That's exactly what they do. It keeps them busy and out of our hair. They entrust us with their offspring and expect to be relieved of all further paternal involvement. No—this uncle is a concern to us for the second of the qualities I mentioned: trouble-making. The man's a *policeman*. Not one of our kind—old buffers shot in at a high level like Sir Renfrew or Lord Buntingforde to head a county force. Men who speak our language, share our patriotic values. I've made enquiries. This one's risen through the ranks, you might say, on account of his record. Well-connected, as I say, but a professional bobby. Worst of both worlds."

"Only if you have something to hide, sir," Matron had said, deliberately to annoy.

She rather wondered why Farman thought he was about to be put under the spotlight. Pompous prat! What misdemeanour did he have on his conscience? Had he been dipping into the school roof fund? To spend on what? Matron reviewed the head's known indulgences. Sweet sherry and first editions of Dickens novels. And his extracurricular activities? An occasional visit, on Wednesdays, to the Odeon in town probably, by himself, to see whatever flick they were projecting. Yet there was no denying that the appearance of this Scotland Yard man was making Farman twitch.

But it was the detective's female companion whom Matron found more intriguing. The Joliffe woman was billed simply as "an associate and representative of the Minister." That fire-cracker, Truelove. If Farman had a crumb of worldly common sense, he'd be keeping an eye on this one.

Perhaps it had occurred to him—"Liaise with her, Matron," he'd advised. "Reassure, soothe, ch—" Matron was quite sure he'd been about to say: "charm" but had hastily edited out this fanciful demand and replaced it with: "chat—er—establish a female relationship. Bear in mind that this lady's eyes and ears could well be in the service of a government minister."

Matron wondered saltily if any other parts of this lady's

anatomy were engaged in ministerial service. It was difficult to imagine any involvement with *political* shenanigans. No, Matron would have guessed that any influence or exploitation in this quarter sprang from a motivation less honourable than whatever the unworldly Farman could conceive of. She was unarguably a pretty little thing. If you liked dark-haired, foreign-looking women. Some men did. With her slim figure, know-it-all dark eyes, and superior air, this one could have managed the Chanel boutique in Regent Street.

Harriet Hughes ran a smoothing hand over her own rich red hair. She might be "matron" by title and she might be approaching forty, but she was not remotely matronly. Her tightly belted navy uniform dress with its white collar and cuffs emphasised a neat waist and bountiful bosom; the dark chestnut hair waved in a controlled way about her head, giving off an intriguing waft of Amami setting lotion. Her features, in contrast, were disappointing, quenched by the glory of the hair. She wore no makeup, as required by an educational establishment, but had taken the trouble to pluck her eyebrows into a fashionable arch.

"I expect you could be doing with a cup of tea after your morning on the road? I have the facilities." Matron pointed to a kettle sitting on a gas ring by the hearth.

"How very pleasant this is," said her guest politely, looking around the room. "I should love to have a cup of tea if it's really no trouble."

Matron lit the gas and reached for the pot and tea caddy.

The boy Drummond sighed and shuffled his feet.

Miss Joliffe launched into a conversation. "We're on the ground floor, here, aren't we? Don't you find that a little inconvenient when your charges are two floors above your head?"

"Not at all. Glad to be out of earshot!" Matron confided. "In any case, I leave repression of noise and high jinks to the duty master. If there's a *medical* emergency—night or day—someone pulls on the bell rope to summon me." She gestured towards an old-fashioned row of bells, each one bearing an ancient name, fixed above the door. "A remnant of the old house. This place was built to be a nobleman's country residence about two hundred years ago. It was turned into a school in Victorian times. Most of the fabric has been made modern and utilitarian. You know—the butler's pantry is now the tuck shop and so on." She smiled. "You find yourself in the old housekeeper's room, which accounts for the bells. I've kept the connections in place for two of them. One is in the head's study, the other one is on the second floor. The dorm prefect and the duty master only have the right to summon me. I have a small bedroom and bathroom adjacent to this room—a suite, I like to call it—and I always leave the door ajar at night when I'm on call."

Miss Joliffe seemed fascinated by these humdrum domestic details. "Ah! The housekeeper's room! The hub of the house. No small burden—the care of a hundred boys," she murmured.

"It's a hundred and twenty. Four dormitories. Plus the two sick rooms, of course. And it's worse in the winter. But compared to my previous posting—I was a nurse at the military hospital in Brighton during the war years—this is a. . . ." Matron remembered the presence of Jackie and edited out the military phrase she had been about to use. "Look, Miss Joliffe, let me deal with young Drummond, and then we can settle down for a proper chat."

Jackie, who was growing increasingly bored, chirped up with a helpful suggestion. "Matron! My form's having library lesson now. It's Silent Reading. My favourite!" he added for Miss Joliffe's benefit. "I'm missing it. Am I allowed to go?"

"The library's just down the corridor on this floor," Matron said. And, seizing on the possibilities: "Silent Reading? If they can't speak to each other, the other pupils can't question Drummond or rag him. Perhaps a good way of getting him back into the routine? Yes, Drummond. You may go. I'll have your bags sent up to the dorm. No illicit contraband in there I hope? No tooth-rotting sherbet fountains? No mind-rotting *Comic Cuts*? Well, as you've spent your time out in police custody, I think I may safely say—off you pop, then!"

Matron's eyebrows arched in amused disbelief to see Dorcas Joliffe sink anxiously to her knees and deliver urgent instructions and advice to the boy. "Great heavens, Miss Joliffe! This is a prep school in Sussex, not an opium den in Limehouse!"

She appeared taken aback by the girl's sharp response. "No stabbings reported in Limehouse this week yet. Can you say as much?" The Joliffe girl watched at the door as the boy scooted down the corridor and entered the library before she added, "He's had a most upsetting experience, he was telling me, and could well be in danger himself. It's no bother to keep an eye on him. Indeed, Sir James suggested that I should."

Matron's slate-green eyes narrowed in suspicion. "Ah, yes! Sir James. The name that opens a thousand doors. Are you by any chance a member of that family, Miss?"

"Not his family—his faculty." The girl grinned. "I say *his*, but he doesn't own the university quite yet. Though he does stump up most of the money that keeps our department afloat. There's not much cash washing about in higher education these days, and a Cinderella subject like psychology needs all the support it can raise."

Harriet Hughes had no time for Cinderellas. "Psychology? How to make a science out of common sense? Say it in Greek!" Her tone was scathing. "Knowledge of the soul. Sounds a teeny bit like hubris to me. Or gobbledegook. I've had too much experience of blood and guts to believe in the soul. I've seen exposed every organ you can imagine—and a dozen more—and never a glimpse of a soul."

"I think you know as well as I do that it's not to be found on a marble slab, Matron. But we may find it in a laboratory one day," the girl said with a smile the Sphinx of Egypt would have envied.

CHAPTER 14

Martin unlocked the door of a room on the first floor of the main building.

"Rapson's study. I thought we'd start here and work our way backwards. Nice little diggings he's got here. Central. Handy. Most of the other masters are out in the Lodge buildings round the back—there's a rear entrance that used to be more important when the place was a gent's res. On the south side—that'll be the way you came in—it's all for show. The 'domestic offices' as the head calls them plus the staff and academic staff quarters are shoved away on the town side. Security nightmare. No thought to protect anyone inside the complex from anyone outside."

"Or vice-versa," Joe said thoughtfully.

"I expect it's never been necessary. No reports of misdemeanours of any kind. I checked the records. One case of arson which was dealt with internally with utmost discretion."

Joe nodded. "I see. Police excluded?"

"That's right. The kid probably got six of the best and his *Woodbines* confiscated. A village lad would have been sent to the Scrubs and birched or put on the next boat to Australia. Nobody seems to lock anything in this place. Except me, of course. I've made the half square mile we'll optimistically refer to as 'the scene of crime' as secure as I can in the circumstances."

Joe peered into the room with appreciation. "Well if ever I tried schoolmastering, I'd hope for a retreat like this," he commented. It was spacious and well lit by two bay windows. It was supplied with a substantial desk and sets of drawers and a filing cabinet. Joe sank into the black leather chair behind the desk and looked about him. "What's behind that door?" he asked, pointing.

"Now wouldn't we all like one of these?" Martin said opening it. "A walk-in filing room. All the storage space you could ever want."

"This chap was—remind me—classics and form master? All this is rather grand isn't it? Why, I wonder, does Rapson come in for such lavish accommodation?"

"I asked. There is a reason. The cupboard you see over there, more of a room really, is where the school records are kept. Rapson found himself chosen—or did he volunteer?—to compile a history of the school last year. He was given this pitch to facilitate his enquiries." He nodded to the telephone on the desk. "Even has his own communications with the real world."

"The desk's a bit untidy," Joe said tentatively.

"Yes. We've logged everything, finger-printed and photoed it. You can touch what you want, sir. The disorder is down to young Drummond. He left a note under a paperweight." He indicated that this was still in position, and Joe leaned over to read it. "Apologises for bunking off and messing up the desk. Bit of a puzzle. Why would he do that? Throwing a tantrum because Rapson failed to arrive to deliver the promised whacking? One reason for calling him back. I look forwards to having a chat with the lad."

"You'll find him a good witness, Martin." Joe decided to confide in the inspector. "Sit down, man. Join me at the desk. Something to tell you. I can explain one little mystery. And hand you another one."

He took Rapson's black notebook from his pocket. "So. . . .

This was removed unwittingly from the room. Jackie still doesn't know he had it in his bag."

Martin fell on the series of photographs, and Joe watched him clear a space and repeat the process of ordering that Marcus had used. The inspector's face grew grim. "I don't like what I'm seeing," he said gruffly. "I can think of no acceptable reason for a master having these in his possession. Can you?" Joe shook his head. "I'm not thinking these are prize-winners—faces from a *victor ludorum* gallery, are you? Look more like last in the sack race, wouldn't you say? Why am I thinking—poor little blighters? We must suppose for a start that they've been got at. By sexual perverts? Is that what we're dealing with? Are these some sort of ghastly trophies? More your sort of Metropolitan scene, sir," Martin said, mustache bristling with distaste. "Not much call for perversion of this nature in Sussex. Brighton, perhaps, but that's London-on-Sea as far as policing's concerned."

Sensing that the Inspector was beginning to flounder, Joe took over. "I agree, it's a possibility which we must consider. And I concede that, sadly, it is a perversion that plagues the capital. Children are harvested, Martin—scooped up off the streets and railway platforms. Bought and sold like apples. Sometimes by their own families. Our Vice Squad closes down one of their ghastly scenes of operation one day, to find it's sprung up the next in a neighbouring street. But I expect you see as clearly as I do the essential difference between these operations and the potential horrors we could have to deal with here?"

"Oh, yes. Class. Wealth. These aren't kids off the street. Someone was paying a vast amount per annum to have them moulded, body and mind, into gentlemen. These polished little pippins don't get shipped off and hawked about on a London costermonger's barrow."

"I agree. It's local. We're looking at something particular to this school. If it's not just a silly schoolmaster's odd fantasy—and

I wouldn't rule that out—it starts and finishes here at St. Magnus."

"And my murder victim seems to have had the key to it," Martin sighed.

"We won't get any further until we get these chaps identified. I'd say they were taken over a period of years. Any ideas?"

"We'll get the oldest member of staff in here to do an identity parade," Martin said. "The puzzle is, Rapson wasn't by any means the oldest established beak. He'd been here six years, that's all. He wouldn't have known most of these personally."

Out in the corridor a bell clanged. Martin looked at his watch. "They're on their break now. The common room's just outside. I'll nip out and collar one of the oldest exhibits. There's a cob-webbed old classics master who looks as though he's been a fixture in these parts since the Prince Regent was down here paddling in the briny. I'll go and ruin his coffee break."

He came back a moment later with a begowned and shriveled figure unwillingly in tow. "Commissioner Sandilands, may I present Mr.—er—Godson?"

"How do you do, Commissioner. Godwit. Classics and Scripture Knowledge." Godwit extended a cold and bony hand, which seized Joe's with surprising energy. "I'm told I can help you with a problem."

"Mr. Godwit, we'd like you to look carefully at the photographs we've laid out on the desk and try to identify these faces which we think belong to old boys of the school."

"Good Lord! Faces from the past!" Godwit put on a pair of gold-rimmed spectacles and examined the exhibits with all the care they could have wished. "I can hand you seven out of the nine," he said after a while. "Who's taking notes?" He rearranged the order of the photographs to his satisfaction. "Numbering from the left and furthest back in time. I'll suggest their intake year.

"Number one: Not known to me.

"Number two: Jefferson. Pre-war. 1910ish.

"Number three: Murgatroyd major . . . 1914. Distinctive, if unfortunate, features. The only son of his mother. His rather . . . elderly . . . mother. She died shortly after her son. Both victims of influenza. Murgatroyd remarried, and there have been a further two boys here after this one. Both successfully completed their spell at St. Magnus. Their father was a most generous benefactor in his day.

"Number four: Hewitt-Jones. 1916. Ghastly little tick! Never thought I'd set eyes on him again.

"Number five: Sorry, not a face I remember, but I'm placing him here because the tie's changed, do you see? So he's postwar.

"Number six: Pettigrew. That's Pettigrew the London grocer. Made a fortune in the war. He had four sons, but I'm happy to say he only sent us the first. Clarence, I believe. Horrid boy! Quite horrid! A fighter. Transferred at the head's request. In other words: expelled. The remaining brothers went elsewhere to trouble others. Let's say 1920.

"Number seven: Peterkin. 1921 or '22. Sad little chap, but clever. Yes, clever. Knew his Herodotus on arrival, I remember. Runaway, I'm afraid. Bullied by the other boys, they said.

"Number eight: Houghton-Cole. 1929. Ah! He went out in a blaze of glory. Set the cowsheds on fire.

"Number nine: Renfrew. Transferred to Templemeadows just last year. We weren't good enough for Papa, apparently. 1932. Will that be all, gentlemen?"

"Just one more thing, sir," Joe said. "Your first impressions of this group. . . . Does any common characteristic strike you? What is it that these boys have in common?"

Godwit fell into puzzled silence. "It's rather hard to tell. It's more a case of what they *don't* have that defines them. None of these has gone down in the annals of the school. I don't remember any one of these making it into a school team. No academic prizes won, either, though I had great hopes of Peterkin. Some didn't stay long. Nothing special about that of course," he added swiftly. "Many of our pupils are from families serving abroad, or moving about the world stage. Boys come and go, you know. And some parents are never satisfied. They must always feel they are getting the very best educational opportunities for their offspring and, if those parents are not blessed with a family tradition of education, they are apt to shuffle their unfortunate children about the country, always seeking better.

"Now, if that's all, gentlemen? It's our coffee time, you know. Young Gosling is preparing a tray for you. I'll tell him to bring it in, shall I?"

"That would be kind of you, sir, and thank you for your help," Martin said politely.

"Gosling, eh?" Martin remarked when the door closed on Godwit. "He seems to have appointed himself some sort of go-between. In the head's pocket, I'd say. Always there at your elbow making helpful noises when you turn around. Creepy bastard! Have you had him up your jumper?"

"Yes, I have." Joe smiled. "It could be just good manners and management of course. But detailed by the headmaster would be my guess, to keep an eye on the interlopers. Make sure we don't wander from the path they've chosen for us."

Joe stopped talking, then passed a finger over his mouth in the soldier's signal for silence. Martin nodded and grinned and looked towards the door.

"Good God, Martin!" Joe's voice rang out. "What the hell are you telling me? That your men have found the sledgehammer that crushed Rapson's skull? And the bloodied handle is covered in fingerprints? And those prints belong to . . . the headmaster?"

"You've got it, sir." Martin's voice was equally loud. "Open-and-shut case. Will you shake out your manacles or shall I oblige? Now, didn't someone say there was coffee on its way?"

He strode to the door and flung it open. An innocently smiling Gosling was a step or two away down the corridor. "Perfect timing, sir," he said. "I was wondering how on earth I could knock with this in my hands. I found you some digestive biscuits—in Langhorne's tin. I hope you like them."

He bustled in, set the tray on a side table, and began to pour out the coffee with the exaggerated ceremony of a Savoy waiter. Joe watched his hands, noting the slight tremble and hearing the clang as he hit the sugar bowl with a spoon. "How are you getting on? One lump or two? Any developments?" Gosling was trying for a casual tone, but his voice emerged an octave higher than its usual pleasant growl, Joe thought.

"No lumps for me, thank you. Just a drop of milk." Joe reached eagerly for his coffee. The real stuff, judging by the aroma.

"Two lumps please," said Martin. "We've hardly got started, and we wouldn't be able to tell you if we had," the Inspector said pleasantly. "All we can say is, we may just have a little surprise for Mr. Farman before the end of the day. That'll be all, thanks, Mr. Gosling. You can leave us to get on."

Left alone again, they grinned at each other.

"Gotcher?" said Martin.

"Oh, I think—gotcher! But what exactly have we got?" Joe wondered. "Further and better particulars required, I believe. I'll get some. Now, shall we proceed?"

"Of course. Look, as you seem to have taken to this room so well, why don't you adopt it as your base? The staff will find it very convenient having you close by, and they'll stop traipsing all the way down to the basement to bother me in the old equipment room. My men can come and go down there without taking their boots off all the time. How long are you staying, by the way? Nobody's told me."

"Possibly because I haven't told anyone. I've set no time limit. The head clearly thinks he's getting rid of me by the end of the day. He doesn't know that I've booked rooms for me and my companion Miss Joliffe down at the old coaching inn in the village."

"The Bells?"

"That's the one."

"Well, that can be the little surprise for the head, in case he asks. Sandilands is taking up residence. Right then, I'll lock the door behind us, and we'll retrace the footsteps of old man Rapson, shall we? Now why, if you'd just been stabbed, would you flee back up here? Wouldn't you try to find Matron? Ex-nurse—she was probably the only one who could help. Have you seen the woman? She could stop a blood flow at ten paces. I'd put myself in her hands any day."

"Telephone?" Joe suggested. "Something he had urgently to deal with . . . hide . . . pick up from his desk? He had an appointment to beat a boy at six, but I don't think that would loom large in the circumstances, do you?"

They moved along the corridor and down the back stairs, now closed to traffic and neatly roped off with warning police notices on display. The hand rail was covered in graphite fingerprinting dust, and smudges of blood were still in place. Joe thought with concern of the small boy and his grisly encounter halfway down as Martin unemotionally pointed out the tiny prints. At the bottom of the stairs was a dried brown patch where the blood had ponded under Rapson's belly.

"He lost a lot of blood. Heart wounds needn't spout much, I know, but the pathologist says he'd suffered more than one blow. Now, we can get him as far as the door and beyond that into the rear yard. By the time we got here, the whole place was covered in snow and it was pitch dark. We lost the trace. Didn't like to do much sweeping—might destroy sign. Thought it better to wait a bit and pray for a thaw. They say there's one on its way."

Joe stood with Martin shivering in the backyard, getting his bearings. Martin produced a plan of the school and handed it to Joe. "They give these out to the new bugs. I've marked the dying man's progress on it in red as far as it goes."

Joe followed and peered into the distance. "He could have been coming from any direction. The rear drive and beyond that, the town—"

"And the two lodges, sir. Where most of the masters have rooms. His fellows," Martin said with emphasis. "Down here in the country, we find people tend to kill each other within their class or social group."

"Oh, we're only human in the capital, Martin—we'll have a go at anybody, but I see what you mean. That's the farmyard, the huddle of buildings over there? A good trysting place?"

"Of a summer evening, perhaps. Not that night, sir."

"Or to the left? What's the row of brick and flint buildings?"

"Maids' quarters. Staff houses. Not bad accommodation, considering. I've seen worse. There's a couple of manservants lodged down there, sharing, and the cottage at the end is where Mrs. Bellefoy lives with her two kids. She was a maid here for years, but she's retired now to look after her son, and her daughter Betty does the maid's work in the school."

"How old is Betty?"

"About twenty. Father never came marching back from the war. Posted missing. He was a farm groom here at the school. Betty's brother's a lot younger. About five." Martin's voice dropped. "And we ought to say—*half* brother. The kid's illegitimate. Mrs. Bellefoy came straight out with it when I interviewed them. Bold as brass. A 'last little fling' she told me. No shame. Her 'little slip-up' she called the lad. Though who she slipped up with she wasn't about to divulge. They don't have an easy life, but they seem to be managing pretty well. You can go and talk to them if you like. But they say they heard and saw nothing out of the ordinary. Except for the lad—he had something to communicate."

"What did he give you?"

"Not much. He's—er—not sure what the word is. He was born not quite right. In head or limbs. And there's a reason for that. She may tell you. Anyhow, while I was talking to them he was listening. He doesn't always catch on, but something got to him. He got all excited and started burbling about a motor car. His ma was a bit embarrassed, but she let him rave on and told me what he was trying to say. He's very keen on cars, apparently. He sits by the road for hours just watching out for them. Gets very excited when he spots a new make. He knows the engine notes and can identify all the village cars and their owners. He was up in his bedroom playing when he heard one in the lane, his ma explained. Opened the window to get a look. He couldn't see it—too dark—but he listened. It came up slowly, stopped and waited a bit, then set off again. Strange car, not a local one. Big engine."

"Did he tell you what time this happened?"

"The lad can't tell the time by the clock, but he remembers the stable bell rang six just after the car left."

"Interesting?"

"Better be! By God, it took some getting! Though I agree—it doesn't sound much."

"A visitor arriving for Rapson?"

"Could be. But then it could just be someone lost in the blizzard and checking the signposts. We've found one or two tire marks, but I think they're all later than the ones we'd be interested in."

"You've got a lot of work done in the short time you've had, inspector," Joe commented.

"And more to do. Mustn't stand about nattering." He handed the keys to Joe. "If I can leave you to find your way back, I'll just nip off to my own HQ and see how my blokes are getting along. There's a sergeant and a PC. It's not much, but they're both good men, you'll find."

"So—we'll go our separate ways for a bit?"

Turning to leave, Martin paused and grinned. "They are separate, aren't they? You'd say the old house is reasserting itself—imposing its original character. Above stairs, below stairs. And never the twain shall meet."

"Except surreptitiously halfway up the back stairs from time to time. Are you about to make a snobbish comment, inspector?"

"Just observing, sir. We do seem to have a different angle of elevation when I compare our vision of the case. Me—I'm nose to the ground, following blood stains through the farm yard to discover who hated a man enough to sink a blade between his ribs."

"While I'm upstairs ordering coffee and swapping stories with Academe, worrying about a set of over-privileged sons of important men. Sons who've gone missing, perhaps. Well, so be it. Let's get on, Inspector. Who knows, in the end we may well meet each other halfway up or down those bloody stairs. But, Martin, something was drawing a mortally wounded man to climb back up them with his last breath, and I want to find out what it was. "

Joe looked at his watch. "I have an hour before my encounter with the meat pie. If you want me, you'll find me rummaging in Rapson's rooms. If I need anything I can always step out and click my fingers. I'm sure a Gosling will come flighting in, saying 'You clicked, sir?'"

He let himself into Rapson's office and made straight for the telephone. He checked that he had a line to the outside and that it didn't pass through an internal exchange before asking the operator for a London number.

"Hello. Sandilands here. Get me your Super, would you? Oh, is he indeed? Look, I don't care if he's french-kissing Wallis Simpson! Drag him to the phone and tell him I'm waiting.

"Ah! Bacchus! Do you need a moment to straighten your tie? Good. Now listen. I'm down in Sussex. Do something for me, and do it fast. Call me back on the number I'm giving you." He read it out. "And here's a name: Gosling. That's right, young goose. George Gosling. See if you've got anything on record? Private investigator perhaps? Could even be a teacher. Oxford, he tells me. Very recently down—he must be about twenty-two. Athletic type. Boxing—that narrows your choices a bit. He's haunting St. Magnus School, Seaford, at the present moment, and he's annoying me. The man's out of place here, and I'd like to know why. I'd be glad of anything you can turn up."

He turned his attention to the contents of the drawers. No disturbance here. A quick search revealed that the right side and the top two on the left contained notes and correspondence concerned with the school. The bottom two on the left held Rapson's private papers, Joe judged. He examined these first and found little of interest. A sheaf of old letters to various correspondents: his mother, who was living in a retirement home in Brighton; one or two old school or army friends. Of more interest was a letter from the local bank manager suggesting to Rapson that he was extracting rather more money from his current account than his salary could sustain, and what steps did he propose? The sums were not breathtaking. Many men received similar letters weekly. Still, Joe had known men murdered for twopence-ha'penny.

He dug about and found a cheque book issued by the bank and began to dredge through the counterfoils. The sums expended were neatly recorded. Apart from monthly withdrawals for—Joe assumed from the small amount—spending money, there was a monthly whack for his mother's accommodation, one or two odd amounts spent at a London tailor's, and a London hotel bill covering the same period of time. Joe twitched with excitement when he found the stub of the cheque that had triggered the manager's concern. Made out to himself for cash only a week ago: a withdrawal of fifty pounds. Joe flipped backwards through the book and found a similar self-payment (cash) the previous month for twenty pounds. And, a month before that, a further twenty. And a monthly twenty in cash each first of the month until he got to the end of the book.

Joe had encountered payment details of this kind before. They usually went towards supporting a betting habit or a mistress or blackmail. He noted the sudden jump in the last month to more than twice the previous amount and remembered that it was always the way of blackmail payments to increase. He'd never known any to peter out. It usually took a death to cancel the arrangement.

He jumped when the phone rang and eagerly picked up the receiver.

"Hopkirk? Good man! What do you mean—right family, wrong species? Good Lord! The cheek! Did they tell you all this willingly? Not important enough to get them hot under the collar, eh? What does it take—mass slaughter of the royal family to get them going? And you were able to do a trade. Tell me about that trade. Well, it's surprising but in its way, reassuring. Have you informed Inspector Jenkins? Leave that to me. I'll ring him myself. I shall enjoy that! He'll be intrigued to know what he thwarted! A ragbag of information, but I'm glad to have it anyway. Gives me the illusion of being back in the driving seat! Tell me— what calibre shot does one use to bring down wildfowl?"

JOE WENT OUT into the corridor and cleared his throat. Gosling was instantly at his side.

"I was just passing on my way to the gym. All games indoors still today. I say, are you looking for someone, sir? I can find you a messenger."

"I coughed, and you answered. Perfect arrangement. Come inside, Mr. Gosling. Take a seat, will you?"

As the young man settled gingerly on the edge of the chair opposite him, Joe caught a glimpse in the anxious brown eyes of the boy he had not so long ago been—uncertain and vulnerable. He decided to take advantage of his uncertainty.

"How long have you been at the school, Gosling?" he asked in a headmasterly voice.

"Not long at all, sir. I came towards the end of the Michaelmas term. I'm a temporary replacement. On supply, as we say, in the trade."

"Ah, yes. The *trade*. Teaching. Would that be the one you're referring to?"

Gosling nodded and swallowed.

Joe affected to consult his notes. "Oxford degree (a good one) in English Lit . . . something of a linguist . . . oarsman . . . boxing blue . . . Army Cadet Force member with a commendation for unarmed combat. The list goes on. What's a star like you doing supplying rugger lessons to ten-year-olds? I'm wondering. One might have expected you to be snatched off the graduation podium, scroll still in hand, mortarboard at a roguish angle, by a talent scout for some grand office of state: the civil service, the military . . . something of that calibre. But you choose instead to hide yourself down here on a remote cliff top."

Joe looked up and fixed Gosling with a frank stare. "Look, young man, you must let me mention your name to a man who would value your attributes. German and ju-jitsu?—he'd know how to use them. He's a man who would spirit you away out of this backwater and back to the metropolis. Name of Masterson." Joe gave him a bland smile. "Colonel Masterson has his offices not that far from my own. In the Cromwell Road."

CHAPTER 15

Gosling shut his eyes and groaned. "Oh, God! Sir, you haven't told Masterson I'm shot to bits already, have you? For heaven's sake! You've only just set foot in the place. What did I do?"

"Calm down, man! I haven't spoken to your boss yet to tell him that your 'cover's blown,' as your mob would probably put it. I have my ways, and I have my contacts. And now you must consider yourself recruited once more, this time to *my* interests. When we've taken a close look at each other's cards, these may well turn out to be the same interests. Who knows? This could actually do you some good, Gosling—or do you prefer 'Drake' like your family name? Just name the wildfowl *du jour* and I'll use it."

"Gosling will do well, sir."

"Good. I like clarity. So, now, tell me what your relationship is with the headmaster."

"An open one, sir. I am—er—in his confidence. I was sent in with his consent to get to the bottom of a problem that has been troubling my department."

"Yes. MI5. Is that what you're calling yourselves these days? Entrusted with the safety of the nation. You're there to protect the rest of us from the machinations of foreign spies on English soil, I had thought. And do we ever need the service! We're all up to our arses in German agents if we're to believe all we're told. Russian Bolsheviks taking a back seat these days and Herr Hitler's patriots swaggering about in full view playing the Bogeyman. Plenty to occupy Masterson in Piccadilly, but what murky business can have attracted his attention to the Sussex coast? Tell me how you're proposing to save the nation from this remote fastness at the southern edge of the land."

Gosling's expression lightened a little, and Joe guessed his shot had gone way off the mark. "Oh, you can forget all that John Buchan stuff—fisticuffs with the Hun and all that! If you have in your mind a picture of Herr Fahrmann and Fraulein Oberschwester standing on a cliff top on a moonless night, torch in hand, signalling to a fleet of German submarines in the Channel—sorry, nothing so melodramatic."

"Hideous scene you conjure up! If it were at all plausible, you'd be needing my Special Branch to tap the villains on the shoulder. Don't forget your little enterprise still ultimately counts on the muscle-power of rough lads in raincoats, all answering to yours truly. MI5 finger them, we arrest them. Frequently we do both. Contrary to the stories you like to put about, we have brains as well as boots. And we use them both." Joe smiled at the cross young face. There was never any harm in reminding these upstarts to stay on their own side of the fence. "Let me know if we can be of help to you with your problem, Gosling," he offered with a tight smile. He glanced at the telephone. "Perhaps I should just ring up your boss and tell him where we've got to. He'll be fascinated to get my update."

"No! No! If you haven't already alerted him, I'd rather you didn't." The boy was once again in evidence as he gulped and blurted out: "He'll be livid, sir!"

"I'm thinking Rapson's murder was an inconvenience for you? Sussex Constabulary and then the Met stamping about your little stakeout scene?"

"Masterson doesn't object to the local man. He knows his place. He knows the boundaries of his investigation. He's less keen on *you* queering his pitch."

"And you were told to contain me?"

"No. Get rid of you." Gosling risked a grin. "'Make sure he's gone by the end of the day.' Those were my orders." He looked at Joe settled comfortably behind the desk, notes and telephone to hand, and he sighed. "Not doing very well so far, am I? Here you are, ensconced—would that be the word?"

Joe winced. "Only if you insist. Got to park my bum somewhere. This'll do."

"Look, sir. I'm not important. I'm a minnow! A raw recruit! I rather think I've been shoved off down here as a sort of test. Or out of the way. I don't think I have the clearance to say anything further, sir. Not even to you. However much you pull rank." The rugged chin lifted in a show of defiance.

"Won't do, Gosling." Joe fished in his pocket and took out the envelope containing the nine photographs. He spread them on the table in what he remembered of Godwit's order. "Now, would your problem be concerning one of these boys?" The steely gleam in his eye conveyed the certainty that he knew the answer.

Taken aback, Gosling spent a moment studying the lineup. Finally he pointed. "That one. Third from the right. Peterkin. John Peterkin. Ran away in his first term at the school. September 1921. But these others? There were stories that boys had gone over the wall ... disappeared ... never been seen again after their time here. We had a couple of names. Are these the ones? Do you know who they are?"

"I've identified seven out of the nine. I don't even know for certain that they disappeared. Or what their current state is."

"Well, yes. They could be alive and well and running India by now."

"Or doing a seven-year stretch in the Scrubs for fraud."

"There's always that," Gosling agreed.

"They could have just gone off to play with Peter Pan and his Lost Boys?"

"Ah! Spirited away by the power of 'wonderful thoughts and fairy dust,' sir?" Gosling shook his head. "Lord! If I've seen that play once, it must be a dozen times! I've got herds of nephews, and what do they all want to see as their Christmas treat? Peter Bloody Pan! Oh, sorry, sir!"

"Quite all right, Gosling. The dear little chap triggers the same reaction in me. When he squeaked the line, *To die will be an awfully big adventure*, he very nearly found his assertion tested out on the spot! I restrained myself from leaping onto the stage and obliging him."

The smile faded from the young man's face as he looked again with concern at the photographs. "I have a bad feeling about all this. A feeling best expressed in gloomy German, I think. *Totenkindergeschichte*."

"Tales of dead children. I hope you're wrong. Let's find out, shall we? If anyone's been setting himself up as some sort of a psychopompos, a guide of souls to the Land of the Dead—a Hermes, or even a playful Peter Pan—we'll have him."

"That would please me a lot, sir." Then, hesitantly: "I say, shall I tell you how I got here?"

"I'd be delighted!"

"It was Alicia Greatorix who made the fuss originally and now, after twelve years, she's making it again. Alicia Peterkin, as she was in her first marriage. She tied the knot with a naval officer at a bad time—early in 1914. She lost her husband at sea that very year. He never set eyes on his son who was born towards the end of it. Little John Peterkin."

Gosling touched the photograph briefly. "His mother was a rich woman, and she brought the child up in a London household by herself. I say by herself, but she had countless maids, nannies and later, tutors, of course. But she was always there, in his presence, devoted to him and ensuring he had the best of everything. A good mother."

"Sounds like an idyllic existence," Joe commented. And, noting the softening of expression on the hard features of his companion, he added, "She would seem to be an impressive lady."

"The existence ended in 1921 when he was old enough to be sent off to school. This school. Mrs. Peterkin had by that time remarried. It's said that her new husband, Greatorix. . . ."

"Hang on a minute. Is this the playboy character I'm thinking of?"

"That very one. A charmer. But a wrong 'un. Everybody could see it but the woman herself. He married her for the money she was expecting to inherit from her very generous father, who was well known to be breaking up fast on the rocks—heart problems. He had made no secret of the fact that his wealth was to go half to his son, Jonas, and half to his daughter, Alicia. He opposed her second marriage, but she went ahead anyway. She presented Greatorix with two sons and her time was so occupied until the moment came when her father truly was at death's door. The old man, just before he breathed his last, changed his will and left the daughter's half of the goodies directly to his grandson, little John Peterkin. To be held in trust for him by his Uncle Jonas until his twenty-first birthday in the usual way."

"Ouch! Greatorix wasn't best pleased to be passed over?"

"No. Turned somersaults to get the will changed and all that. Nothing would work for him. But what with his ravings and the unkind things he had to say about the old man and his stepson who would be rich if these plans came to fruition, while his own two boys had nothing, you can imagine—the penny began to drop with Alicia. He was so angry with his poor little stepson, he sent him off to school out of his sight the moment he was of age."

"A school from which the child promptly went missing."

"Yes. I've been granted sight of the contemporary correspondence relating to the disappearance. The school revealed that the older boys had been bullying John. He was a clever lad, well taught. He turned up here knowing his Latin and Greek already but not prepared to put much effort into sports. You know how well that goes down with some boys! He just disappeared one night, having told the others he'd had enough and had arranged with his mama to be taken away. I've seen the boys' statements gathered by the Sussex men. They're clear and convincing. He went missing in the middle of an autumn night just before half term. Never seen again."

"And had his mother intervened?"

"No. She knew the child was unhappy but presumed he'd soon settle in. The school had an excellent reputation, and the headmaster of the day was much respected. Family man. Ex-clergyman. Her last letter to John—she wrote frequently—was full of love and encouragement and a promise to come down and see him at half-term.

"She pointed out that he wouldn't have run off two days before he was expecting to see her. Reasonably enough. All the searches were made. Not a trace of the boy was ever found. Here or in London.

"Things cooled between the married pair. To such an extent that she began at last to listen to the stories her friends were all too ready to tell her concerning her husband's peccadilloes. The upshot was that she arranged for the fiend to be caught in a hotel room by a squad of private detectives and a photographer and, using the evidence of infidelity, she divorced him. That's when the trouble really started! She was then free legally to accuse the ex-husband openly of organising the lad's disappearance. Even said he'd killed him and buried the body. She bombarded the school and the authorities with letters and demands to reopen the case."

"Successfully?"

"People went through the motions, but nothing new was ever turned up."

"But she didn't give in?"

"No. Twelve years on, and she's still at it. A determined and loyal woman, sir. I have the greatest regard for her. Last year, a cousin of her first husband, Peterkin, was appointed to a senior rank in MI5. She approached him. Not our thing at all—lost children—but this was his cousin's boy. Masterson felt obliged. Well, more than that. He's actually jolly concerned on Alicia's behalf and wants to do what he can. But I'm the best he could spare, sir. I don't, um. . . ." Gosling's head drooped. "I don't think his expectations are high."

"Then he's wrong." Joe spoke quietly but firmly. "This boy would be nineteen by now. A whisker younger than you are. He should be up at Oxford, fresh and keen and translating Homer for the umpteenth time. We'll find him, Gosling. We'll find out what happened to John Peterkin, and I'll listen in when you pick up the phone and tell your boss you've saved his bacon.

"Now let me tell you how I came by this selection of nine boys."

"MAY I SEE it, sir? The black book?"

Joe noted the young officer's eagerness and decided to follow his instinct. He passed the moleskine book across the desk and went to squeeze a last cup of coffee out of the vacuum jug, leaving Gosling to leaf through and come to his own conclusions.

"It's going to take time, isn't it?" Joe said finally. He wasn't sure Gosling had heard him, so deep had he sunk into the contents. "Rapson was making notes—reminders—for himself."

"Yes. What you've got here seems to be a list of dates and initials. The dates are written in Latin. Showing off his prowess with the *calends*, *nones* and *ides*?"

"Or assuming everyone else hasn't a clue and won't understand?

"Tell you something, though. Wonder if you'd noticed, sir—the photographs and the dates don't fit. I mean, they may correspond to some of the Latin squiggles, but there's far more *dates* than there are faces. Nine faces, more than twenty dates. Are we looking at the tip of an iceberg?"

"Frightening thought, Gosling! I can't comment. I haven't had a moment to study the coded bits yet."

"If each of these dates represents, let's say, an outgoing boy . . . a boy leaving before the appointed time—"

"That's a lot of outgoings over the years," Joe murmured, looking over his shoulder. "But then, you said it yourself when we met on the doorstep, Gosling: 'Lots of comings and goings in a place like this.'"

"Exactly. Comings are easily tracked and documented. Goings, well, not so much. Transferred to another school? Which one? Does anyone check that they've arrived? Gone abroad? Any proof? Who would dream of asking for it? Where are the *parents* in all this? Can Alicia Peterkin-Greatorix be the only one who's noticed her son has gone missing?"

"Of course not. I shall have a few phone calls to make after lunch. Using contact details we now have thanks to Rapson's research."

Deep in thought for a moment, Joe eyed Gosling with speculation and decided to give out some information to gain some in return. "Look—masks off. I'm going to explore with you the likely motive for Rapson's interest in small boys. I was going to ask the headmaster outright, but I think I'll get nearer the truth with a worldly young fellow like yourself. I can't be certain—though I've met the man for all of five minutes, so perhaps I'm no judge—that Farman would understand what I'm getting at."

Encouraged by a derisive snort from Gosling, Joe pressed on.

"My first suspicion is that Rapson, solo or with others, has been taking an unhealthy interest—of a sexual nature, I mean—in boys in his care. What are your thoughts?"

Gosling shook his head and laughed. "You couldn't be more wrong! Shall I reveal the contents of an official letter of warning the head sent to Rapson only last week? I checked the wording for him so I know what he said. I expect Rapson destroyed it. Not the sort of thing you'd want to keep in your notecase or tucked into your little black book. But you can check his reply if you like; it's in Farman's file. It says, and I paraphrase: 'Mind your own business, you interfering old twerp.'"

"In response to?"

"A warning to Rapson to keep away from the staff quarters at the rear of the school. And, specifically, to keep his hands off Betty Bellefoy. She's a maid at the school. Very pretty and young, which is unusual. Anyway, her mother had lodged a complaint. Demanded that the headmaster restrict Rapson to barracks or Ma Bellefoy would 'take steps' is how she put it. Farman professed himself puzzled as to what these steps might be, but the family has served the school faithfully for generations and is well known in the neighbourhood. He decided wisely that it would be easier in times like these to replace a single history master rather than a family of retainers. And Rapson is popular with no one, the Bellefoys are liked by all, so he sent a sharp letter of rebuke and defined his restricted area."

"Which he broke out of on the night of his death. I think I must go and meet this formidable lady."

"But it does illustrate the fact that Rapson's urges were not of a kind that would incline him to the maltreatment of young lads. Apart from the occasional whacking."

"I think I must turn around my thoughts to date concerning Rapson," Joe said carefully. "Just chew this over, will you, Gosling? Instead of being a sexual raptor or purveyor of boys to someone at present unknown to us, he could possibly have been one who had noticed and begun to collate—perhaps even inquire into the disappearances. He was writing the history of the school, I understand?"

"God, that's right! He used to bore us stupid with his little anecdotes from the files. Ancient cricket scores . . . casts of school drama performances. . . . No one else found it remotely interesting."

"How on earth did he come to embark on such a task? A personal enthusiasm for the dusty annals of a preparatory school?"

"Not your bag, I'd guess, sir, and decidedly not mine, but *he* did it with—er—relish. In fact, I think he exceeded his brief, if the truth be told. Got carried away. He was initially asked by the head, in response to a parental suggestion—a suggestion backed up by a generous donation to funds—to compile a list of school heroes."

"A list of heroes?"

"It's something schools do these days, sir. In the aftermath. Memories to be kept bright and all that. Example to the new intake. He was tracking down old boys of the school who've won medals for gallantry: the Victoria Cross, Military Cross and all the rest of them. An astonishingly large number of these turned up. Hardly a day passed when he didn't come smugly into the common room announcing: 'Hogweed Minor. Mentioned in dispatches at Omdurman,' or some such. He had all the military service records and was matching them up with the school lists. They're over there in that cupboard."

"Right. We can follow in Rapson's footsteps, then." Joe waved an arm at the filing room. "I've had a preliminary snoop around. I'd say it will take several people weeks to get through it."

"There may be shortcuts we can take, sir. Using the book for a start. If you'll just give me a minute to concentrate. I'm trying to match up Peterkin with his disappearance date. And I think I've got it. Here! Look! At least we can see from this that he hasn't obscured the boys' initials. We've got a J.D.P., plain as day, and a date in . . . hang on a minute . . . *MCMXXI*—that's 1921. Then we've got *pr. Id. Oct.* How's your Latin, sir? When *were* the *Ides* in October? Thirteenth?"

"In October? No. Try the fifteenth."

"*Pridie.* That's the day before the *Ides* which gives us the 14th of October. Spot on! Got him! So we can probably assume the initials are a good guide."

"Yes. I don't think this is a code at all—thankfully! They're just notes to himself. But notes he wanted to keep quiet. No one coming on these unwittingly is going to be seized with an overpowering need to wrestle with them. In his ferreting about, Rapson could have stumbled on some loose threads. And collated them carefully and discreetly here in these pages."

"He had that kind of brain, sir. Never let anything get by. Questioned everything. Tedious."

"Did he give any indication to the other staff that he'd come across something stinky in the school cupboard?"

Gosling frowned and considered. "No. He didn't confide. I was on the lookout for something not quite right with the establishment, following my interest in Peterkin. In fact, I rather directed Rapson towards the Peterkin question. Claimed a family interest. Lord! Perhaps I triggered the whole thing?"

"Isn't that why you were sent here, Gosling? Just doing your job."

"The head had begun to trust me, I think. Or at least to depend on me in a nauseating way." Gosling pulled a face. "Farman may have an imposing physical presence, but underneath the senatorial robes there beats the heart of a pleb and gurgles the stomach of a glutton. The urge to give him a good kicking is overwhelming."

"I'm wondering if we might be contemplating something that could be termed a conspiracy?"

"More than one person involved? Sounds likely. If the head-master weren't such a jelly, he'd be a likely candidate for the frame. Not Rapson—he was a loner. But, sir, the time scale's all wrong for a conspiracy, isn't it?"

"Time? How?"

"The disappearances. We've got this first photo from Edwardian days. Rapson has a date here of *MCMIII*. Eleven years before war broke out. And the most recent is a date last year. There have been three headmasters in that period. Farman was appointed six years ago. Before that there was a Dr. Sutton. Before him, an ancient old bean who retired at the age of eighty. Now what was his name? Oh, where's Rapson when you need him? Streetly-Standish! That's it!"

"Difficult to assign the notion of criminal conspiracy to three generations of headmaster, going back three decades." Joe's voice was full of doubt. "'Welcome to St. Magnus, old boy. Here's the keys to the cocktail cabinet and, while you're at it, you'd better have an open-ended list of boys who won't be coming back. You may wish to add to it.' I can't see it. I think we need to get old Godwit in here again."

Gosling was already on his feet. "He's snoozing in the arm chair in the staff room, sir. I'll fetch him."

Godwit seemed alert enough as he entered and took the seat Gosling held for him. He even seemed pleased to be called on again. "The last three headmasters? I knew them all," he chir-ruped. "A breed in decline, sadly. Streetly-Standish? He was fading somewhat by the time I arrived, but I served for three years under him. Excellent scholar. Though he was not a humanist—the natural sciences were his forte. Strict. Fine leader. Dr. Sutton, his successor? No, I'm perfectly sure he was not known and not related to the previous head. This is not an Oxford college. The heads are chosen by a committee and the most suitable one selected. The position is not passed down. Dr. Sutton also was an excellent headmaster. Differing from the others in that he was, in fact, a family man. Charming wife and three daughters all of whom lived on the premises. Mrs. Sutton doubled as Matron. And the present holder of the post?" Godwit fell silent and marshaled his thoughts. When he was quite ready, out they trooped: "These are straitened times. Many talented men, scholars as well as others, were wasted in the war, of course. The school was lucky to have acquired the services of Mr. Farman. He has been kind to me."

Joe smiled his encouragement and his understanding. "I'm going to repeat a request," he began.

"Ah! You're still looking for the common denominator, Sandilands! And I have, once again, to tell you—there isn't an obvious one. Or even an obscure one. Three different men from three different backgrounds. Different subjects and universities. Different views of life. Different proclivities."

"Their religious beliefs?" Joe asked.

"I use the word again: different. Streetly-Standish was a declared atheist. A very fashionable thing to be in those days, but he didn't impose his views on the school. He was thought modern and innovative even though some of his ideas were a bit ahead of the morality of the time. His successor, Sutton, had been a clergyman. Farman? Who can tell? Overtly, he's Church of England and preaches to us all in the accepted manner. I don't believe these three men knew each other. All they have in common is a stint at the same school. There is nothing else that linked them." Godwit thought hard for a moment. "Except perhaps—" He shook his head, an elusive memory fluttering past him and escaping.

Getting to his feet, he added: "I shall turn this, whatever it is—I'll call it 'your quest'—over in my mind. Or what remains of my mind. I shall not forget. If anything stirs in the depth of this turgid pond of memory, I shall hurry to confide in you or young Gosling here. I take it he carries your seal of approval?"

"You may speak freely to Gosling. We're working together on this. Working to right an ancient wrong." It sounded overly dramatic but expressed Joe's increasing determination to restore the lost boys, if only to memory. The words were received with an approving nod.

A hand as brown and fragile as a dead leaf reached out and tenderly touched the plump little face of John Peterkin. Godwit murmured a few words in ancient Greek, made the sign of the cross over the photograph, and left the room.

Joe turned to Gosling. "When it comes to Greek, I can claim, as with Shakespeare, that I have little Latin and even less—"

Gosling cut short his embarrassment. "Euripides, sir. It's from one of his tragedies. *Alcestis*. We put it on in my second year at Oxford. Outdoors in a meadow on the banks of the Isis. That wonderful summer!" Seeing Joe's puzzled look, he went on with the quiet tact of a courtier. "You'll remember, sir, that, in the play, our hero, Hercules, is trying to snatch back the recently dead Greek princess, Alcestis, from Death?"

Gosling paused to give Joe a chance to say: "Ah, yes, of course. Familiar with the situation, not the injured party. Go on."

"The deceased is the lovely wife of his friend Admetus. He, Admetus, is a bounder and a cad, as all agree. He's destined to die according to a whim of the gods unless some other poor so-and-so can be persuaded to die in his place. His selfish old parents, though tottering at death's door, refuse. The only one to offer is his dutiful wife, Alcestis."

"Far too good for him," Joe remarked. "Wives usually are."

"Her husband—what a shit!—says thank you very much, and the lady prepares herself for death. Tearful farewells to the children and all that going on. In the middle of all this, Hercules, taking a break between two of his labours, turns up for dinner—"

"And senses there's a bit of an atmosphere?"

"Nobody's fool, Hercules! Our hero decides, unlike the caddish husband, that he's not going to let this sacrifice be made, and although by now the lady has actually done the deed and her soul is practically in the clutches of the old boatman, Charon, Hercules piles in with a last-minute, god-defying plan.

"Being a stout-hearted and enterprising lad, he brings it off. After a bit of a dustup." Gosling grinned. "Something of a brawler, Hercules. A dirty fighter. Used his brain as well as his brawn. He sneaked up on Death himself at the key moment of the burial ceremony and got him in a neck-lock. Went one round with the Infernal Lord and won. He rescued the lady from Charon before he could punt her soul across the river to Hades."

"Whence there is no return," Joe muttered.

"That's right. He brought Alcestis home again to her husband, sound in wind and limb."

"I don't like to think how the ensuing conversation went, Gosling! Now, in a good Victorian melodrama of the kind I like, the husband would have killed himself in remorse and Hercules would have gone off with the girl. And she'd have been well pleased with her bargain. Quite a man, Hercules! Your sort of bloke, Gosling?" Joe said, trying to hide his amusement.

"Oh, yes. Half-man, half-god, remember. I'd have liked to have him in my crew! At my back, sir, rowing at bow."

Joe didn't need to ask which of the characters the young man had played on stage and hoped that the attractively pugilistic features had not been obscured by the traditional mask. "No last-minute rescue of Peterkin, in this case, I fear. Not even a decent burial as far as anyone's aware. Did you catch Godwit's words?"

"Yes. Memory not wonderful, but I'll give it a go. At one point the Chorus says something like . . . *Oh, that I had the strength to bring you back to light from the dark of death, rowing back across the sacred river.*"

The words hung between them, ancient, guttural and full of

grief. Joe left a silence before he spoke softly. "I'll echo that sentiment, Gosling. We'll find old Charon and give him a bad time, shall we? We may not return with the bodies, but we can snatch back the souls from oblivion, perhaps."

"We'll take our seats at the oar, sir, and give it ten!"

CHAPTER 16

"Miss Joliffe! I lent you a pair of my twins last year, I believe?" Mr. Farman had placed Dorcas on his left and Joe on his right at the top table for lunch. His comment silenced Joe and the other diners but appeared not to disconcert Dorcas.

"That's quite right, headmaster. I wondered if you'd remember the name. We've not met before but I did send you a letter of thanks, following on my research program at St. Raphael."

"I hope the brothers Simpson were of some use?" His tone was jovial, expansive, and Dorcas replied with equal warmth.

"Oh, invaluable, sir! Twins—I speak of *identical* twins—are very hard to come by. One birth in two hundred and fifty at best, I understand, and they're not always easy to track down."

"And even rarer, I should have thought, in the ranks of the upper classes," Farman commented, nodding sagely.

"I'm wondering, can it be your observation or your research, sir, that leads you to say that?" Dorcas asked innocently.

"Observation. My interest in genetics is not such that I should want to delve any deeper than I needed to into the subject. No, I see for myself, and perhaps others would agree"—he smiled questioningly around the company, gathering support—"that multiple births—litters, one might say—proliferate amongst the lower social orders. I'm sure that if you were to trawl the streets of Seven

Dials you would find vastly more sets of matching faces. Once you had scrubbed off the dirt sufficiently to investigate. I can understand that the material extracted might not be of much use to you from a scientific perspective—the children might have difficulty in communicating. The majority—an alarmingly large majority—of children born in the capital, I understand, do not speak English and certainly do not read and write it."

Joe wondered whether he should snatch the knife from Dorcas's hand as a preventative measure. The idiot Farman had no idea that the girl he was talking to had, herself, gone barefoot and largely uneducated for the first years of her life, excluded by society. She had grown up believing what her grandmother and the village told her: that she was the illegitimate offspring of a gypsy. As the oldest daughter of a loving and charming but feckless father, Dorcas had gallantly helped with the rearing of the children that followed. A tribe in themselves, these included two younger half brothers. Twins. *Their* mother had wearied of the constant hounding by grandmama and, succumbing to bribes and threats, had gone off in the night with her boys, back to her own people. Dorcas's "stepmothers" always ran away. It would be difficult to imagine a more provoking conversational gambit, Joe thought, and he tensed, awaiting the response.

"We take them where we find them, headmaster." Her voice was level, her knife engaged in cutting the hard crust of the meat pie. "Dr. Barnardo's excellent institutions have been very helpful to our department. They rescue hundreds of children from death or exploitation on the streets and allow us access occasionally with our clipboards and our lollipops to question and test them."

"Ah, yes. Sir James was telling me that he takes a certain interest in such establishments." He looked about him to be sure that everyone had noted his intimacy with Sir James. Joe wondered where he had acquired it.

"He contributes financially to their welfare and offers his

personal encouragement and support. He's even been observed to lose to some of the boys at table tennis."

"Sports—as good a way as any to overcome the communication problems."

"And the less fortunate have much to communicate, Mr. Farman. Whatever their language, East End children tell me the same story: that bad diet, infected water, foul air and poverty are wrecking the health of the nation's children."

Looks were exchanged around the table. Eyebrows were raised. Sneers tugged gently at the corners of thin mouths.

Heavy talk for a lunch party. In her inexperience, Dorcas was allowing herself to be led into a serious discussion that could only end in embarrassment. He sensed that with her last comment, the girl had put herself into the open: a fox sighted a field away, a legitimate quarry for the pack, and could now expect a ritual pursuit to the rallying cries of "Bolshy . . . Lefty . . . Red. . . ." And, most unforgiveable by her lights: "Feminist!"

Joe decided to stop the hunt short. "Gentlemen, may I offer you the solution? I'm prescribing second helpings of Sussex steak and kidney pie and weekends of bracing Sussex air for every child born east of Bow Church," he announced.

Surprisingly, murmurs of approval were burbled around the table. "Quite right! Establish a Utopia-on-Sea!"

"The commissioner speaks in jest but—yes! Something must be done to feed the multitude!" an elderly voice said firmly. "How else are we going to get the ranks up to scratch in time for the next war? Eh? Because it's coming, you know! It's coming."

"Most of the 1914 intake were well under 5'4" and dreadfully undernourished," another voice came in, in support. "I remember my batman when he first joined me. Skin and bone. No notion of hygiene."

"'Lord, Thou feedest them with the bread of tears.' Psalms 80. May I remind my colleagues that the Lord will provide?"

Farman leaned to Joe and muttered superfluously, "Doctor Sheale, Divinity."

"Whatever they're fed on, I do note the masses always seem to have the strength to march and riot whenever the fancy takes them" was the lofty contribution of a bluff young man ("Hawkins, History"). "Let's not forget '26! Now there was a damn close-run thing! Wellington would have known what to do about it. Or Napoleon. Gladstone, perhaps. Disraeli even." He sighed. "What has become of our heroes?"

"Nearly all our best men are dead! Carlyle, Tennyson, Browning, George Eliot—and I'm not feeling very well myself." The speaker shook his head and directed an apologetic smile at Dorcas. "Punch '93," he added in a disarming stage whisper.

Inevitably: "Langhorne, English Lit" followed.

Joe didn't conceal his amusement. He laughed out loud. Intrigued by the calculated frivolity of the remark, he noted the name, Langhorne, and looked forwards to an exchange of views with this joker. A man with the smooth, dark looks of an ageing gigolo, enlivened by a splash of intelligence and a twist of irony, he presented an intriguing cocktail, Joe thought fancifully. Not a man you'd share a pint at the pub with. He caught himself searching for a polite formula for asking Langhorne, English Lit, what on earth had propelled a man of his nature into his chosen profession and then remembered that he had a large source to draw on since he'd been asked the same thing himself in a hundred different ways. He caught Dorcas's eye, inviting a smile. When it came, it had the glinting edge of a stiletto.

She'd been escorted to the dining room at the last moment and promptly abandoned by Matron, so Joe had had no opportunity to murmur his usual "Now behave yourself, Dorcas!" Indeed, he didn't think he would have had the nerve to deliver the warning to this composed and superficially congenial young woman. Being the only female in the room, she was the centre of all attention but appeared not to notice it. Sitting amongst the black robes and dusty suits, she glowed in her dark-red woollen two-piece. Joe's were not the only eyes on her; her pretty face and graceful gestures constantly drew sentimental glances from the rows of boys tucking into their pie and mashed potatoes, each remembering a mother or a sister.

The food was unpalatable, the company worse, but at least they didn't dawdle over their plates. These were whisked away by two young men and a pretty girl he assumed to be Betty Bellefoy. The pupils at the long refectory tables had their own routine of scraping and passing down the plates, and the monitors at the ends of the rows staggered to the hatch with the piles. Dr. Sheale said grace, lingeringly, and the high-table party processed out to the common room for coffee.

Mr. Langhorne was instantly at Dorcas's side to lead her in, hand her a cup, and make her laugh. Joe found himself being plucked from the queue for the urn by Farman.

"We just have time for a recuperative cup while the boys have a quarter of an hour's break, and then we're into afternoon school. Now, Sandilands, it will be growing dark in two hours' time. If you're to make the trip back to—Godalming, was it?—you must go to the head of the queue. Come along!"

This was the moment.

"Sir," Joe spoke briskly. "Don't concern yourself. No hurry whatsoever. I shall be staying until the end of the day—and beyond. Arrangements have been made for accommodation in the town. Miss Joliffe and I will return tomorrow morning before start of school. As for young Drummond, you would oblige me by arranging for him to spend the afternoon with Miss Joliffe— and a few chums perhaps—in a secure place on the first floor of the main building. An impromptu drawing class suggests itself. Amongst her many talents, Miss Joliffe, you'll find, is an art enthusiast and perfectly accustomed to teaching young boys. At the end of the day, I shall have a private conversation with my nephew, as a result of which he will either join us down at the inn or stay in school and pick up his normal school timetable."

Farman's face fell and he began to bluster objections. Joe smiled benignly and took no notice. "I should be further obliged if you would fix things so that your Mr. Gosling is available to me in the capacity of aide-de-camp. We will set up headquarters in Mr. Rapson's old study. There's something rotten at the heart of St. Magnus, sir, and I intend to locate and cut out the worm I find wriggling at its core."

"I'VE DONE THE audit, sir. It's all in there. Everything we want and more. It's even clearly labeled and in date order. Alphabetically ordered subsections. I told you Rapson was meticulous." Gosling emerged with cobwebbed hair from the cupboard eager to get on. "What I'd have given to get my hands on this cache! But Rapson guarded his territory like a jealous dragon. I'd no idea that this was here!"

"Did you not? Look, Gosling, I hope you don't mind my commandeering your services like this? I really would prefer to have a sharp lad like you on hand until I've got to the bottom of this."

"Glad to have something useful to do, sir. The charade I've been involved with was getting very tiresome. I've been thinking of doing a bunk myself."

Joe was delighted to channel his energy. "Boring, routine stuff first, Gosling. Worth getting it out of the way. The finances! It strikes me that this place bears all the hallmarks of a well-funded establishment. No tile off the roof, repainted last year, no money spared except in the matter perhaps of school dinners. Are the records—"

"Got them, sir."

"Pull them out and work on them . . . over there on the rug, will you? You may need to spread the sheets out." He pointed to a flat piece of choice Persian rugwork laid out over solid polished floorboards.

"What am I looking for?"

"Sounds obvious, but I think you'll know it when you see it. Unusual amounts of cash in—or out. Don't forget that Rapson could have been paying out blackmail money. The school may have something to hide, too. In fact, I'm pretty certain it has."

"Right-o, sir."

Joe noted with satisfaction that Gosling picked up the black book and set it beside him as he crouched on the floor and began to turn pages. There followed the occasional low whistle and hiss and "Crikey! Can the fives court possibly have cost as much as that?"

Seeing the boy was well settled into his task, Joe picked up the telephone and made a connection with Alfred Jenkins back in Chelsea.

"Alfred? Sandilands here. Just a quick call to tell you—you got him! My men trailed him, managed to arrest him and wring the truth out of him with surprising ease. A charmer by the name of Chisholm. Now—anything to confess, Inspector?"

There was a chortle at the other end that was audible in the room. Gosling had stilled his page scanning activities at the mention of the name, Joe noticed.

Inspector Jenkins stopped laughing and replied concisely and soberly. "Easy enough to arrest. They had grounds after all. I'd expect they found a certain item of lost property in the young gentleman's left coat pocket. An old watch of my father's went missing while Mr. Chisholm was making his delivery. I reported it of course. It had been on top of the chiffonier by the door when he came in to take a look at the railway. Wondered if it was him had made off with it. Well I never! Have they charged him?"

"No. Slippery customer. If he's who I think he is, he's got a rather influential and equally slippery organisation behind him.

They call themselves MI5, and they're all over the place. Mainly under my feet." Joe flashed a warm smile down at Gosling. "Or at my feet. Still, well done, old man! I think he was after not the boy but something Jackie had unawares in his Afghan bag. That's safely here with me too. We'll have a pint in the Dick Turpin when I get back."

Joe replaced the receiver and spoke confidingly to Gosling. "Chisholm? A colleague? If you thought you were the only officer involved with this, it seems you were mistaken." He explained the old inspector's part in the lift-incarceration at the Chelsea apartment.

The account seemed to give the young man a certain satisfaction, Joe thought.

"If he's the chap I'm thinking of, he's not exactly a colleague. Yes, he's one of ours. Employed occasionally in the executive division. A thug. If Drummond was his target, this affair would appear to have escalated in importance." Gosling shuddered. "I'd like to say we wouldn't stoop to such measures, but the dirty washing does get handed over to others sometimes. Out of sight, out of mind. Deniable." He bit his lip, hinting at knowledge that Joe did not have and knew better than to demand.

"I CAN IMAGINE. Right, carry on, Gosling. I'm going to look through those box files of individual school records. Checking first the 'lost boys,' headed by Peterkin. If you want to unravel something, you tug on the end that's sticking out first. Surprising how often that works."

He extracted the seven envelopes belonging to the identified boys and began to leaf through them. "Mind if I talk aloud?"

"No, sir." Gosling seemed surprised to be asked.

"Again, nothing much in common. One or two had health problems. Visits by the local doctor in the night recorded, very properly. A Dr. Carter attended." Joe scratched a note to himself on his pad. "Occasional trip to hospital in Brighton for the more serious cases. Here's a case of blood poisoning from an undeclared wound. . . . Ah! Here are symptoms that are clearly those of tuberculosis, according to Matron's carefully worded note. Not a disease you want to see ripping through a dormitory.

"Right, let's take a look at the fire-raiser. Set fire to the pig sties. Why? Bit young, these lads for enjoying an illicit cigarette, I'd have thought? Oh, my! Thick file. The arson was just the last of his little escapades. Bullying . . . torturing the school cat . . . rudeness . . . swearing at Matron. The lad seems to have been completely out of control and pretty thick with it. His scores on his monthly tests are abnormally low. Letter from the school asking his parents to remove him. No reply filed, but the very next week, he's gone. Just gone." Joe sighed. "I expect his parents took him away and had him locked up somewhere. Fire-raising? That can earn you a place in a mental institution any day. The boy sounds like a walking disaster to me."

They ploughed on in companionable silence, flicking cards, occasionally comparing dates.

Gosling ran a finger along a row of figures. "Got it!"

"I'm glad you've got something; nothing else here is making much sense. Not much *sinister* sense, I'd say. Boys leave because they're ill or naughty or obviously in need of a more rigourous regime than St. Magnus can provide. Nothing wrong with that. No mystery. Apart from young Peterkin. Fit as a flea, bright as a button, good as gold, you'd say. He rather breaks the pattern. Are we going to have to apologise to the school and beat a hasty retreat, Gosling?"

"Hold your horses! Oh, sorry sir! Take a look at these entries in the accounts. Large sums of money—a thousand pounds or more, not the same each time—have been paid into the school's bank account and promptly paid out into a second account I haven't got the sheets for here. Quite often a large building operation follows, with sums drawn back and re-spent."

"These payments, do they correspond with any of our dates of interest?" Joe asked carefully.

"No, they don't. They're all off target. Hang on. . . . They turn up two, three and five weeks later. Ah, I have an exception . . . two exceptions. One's the fire-raiser. His father paid over a large amount the very day the boy went missing."

"For how much?"

"One thousand, five hundred pounds."

"How much does it cost to rebuild a pig sty?"

"I can tell you exactly. It's in the following month's accounts. Work done in fast time by Mr. Green the local builder for . . . one hundred three pounds, ten pence."

"Leaving a generous tip in the offertory box for St. Magnus. Remind me who he was, this Magnus chap—Patron Saint of the Sticky Fingers? 'For your trouble, headmaster'? Hush money? Further information required, I think. And the other?"

"Peterkin, sir. I could have this wrong but—there's an anonymous payment into the school, the week *before* he went missing. Again, it's for a large sum: one thousand pounds."

Joe grew tense. "So, what are you saying?"

"That, at first look, all these disappearances are accompanied within certain loose time limits by considerable payments to the school."

"Through the reigns of three headmasters? Can they have been aware?"

"No way they can't have been aware, sir. They must all have thought it above board."

"So the three heads were all happy to accept the donations— were comfortable enough with them to put them straight into the school accounts, which I see are lodged with perhaps the most prestigious bank in London. Do we interpret them as kind gestures? Some of these fathers may well have been—usually are—alumni of the school themselves. And, wealthy men that they are, they show their gratitude or assuage their embarrassment by making a hefty donation. Some schools couldn't continue in business without such support."

"You're right, sir. My own father made a similar if more modest gesture when I left my prep school, and I never set anything alight." He sighed and sat back on his heels. "Worth going on with this trawl, then, sir?"

"Oh, I think so. Check all the dates we have suspicions of. Just in case."

Gosling continued to rustle his way halfheartedly through the sheets, collating the dates in the black book and ticking off names on a pad he kept close by him.

Narrowing his eyes, Joe went to look over his shoulder. "You've missed one. What's this?" he asked, pointing. "This large sum coming in. Two thousand pounds. Can you trace it to source?"

"No. None of them. You'll need a warrant to get a sight of the bank's details, sir, to get hold of any names. You'll have to go back to London for that. Um, this one did catch my eye but, look, it's outside the dates we've been looking into. It's larger than the others. The kind of sum a rich old codger might leave as a legacy. It can't be connected."

"Everything's connected. What's the date of the entry?" Joe persisted.

"It's very recent. Just a week before Rapson died." Gosling turned a concerned face to Joe. "Now, would someone be paying good money to have Rapson topped, I wonder?"

"Mmm. He was up to no good—I think he was paying out regular sums of his own as blackmail. Could this be linked in some way? But it's all the wrong way round and a sum like that, it's out of the league of bookies, local casino sharks and thugs of that nature. You can hire a top hit man from London to attend to your needs for fifty quid. What kind of service will cost you two thousand? Total massacre of the royal family? What's he been meddling with that earned him a knife in the ribs?"

"And why pay the school? I can't see Farman banking his cheque and rushing out with a freshly sharpened steak knife to earn his fee and then spend it on Persian carpets for the combination room."

Gosling got up and came to look once more at the nine cut-out faces. "I'm not entirely sure why Rapson got his scissors out and did this, sir. This little gallery."

"Aide mémoire?"

"A list would have sufficed. He didn't need to keep their poor little faces close. He was no sentimentalist. He'd caught onto something shady in the disappearances, we're agreed on that much. Could he have been doing a little blackmailing on his own account, do you suppose?"

"Slapping these down on someone's desk and snarling, 'I know your secret, Mr. X!'"

Gosling jumped and looked up sharply. "That would work with me but, sir! I'll tell you something that would really scare the shit out of me if I had something to hide!"

Alarmed by his lieutenant's anxious face, Joe asked quietly, "Tell me."

"These are cut out of large, stiff prints. Can you picture the remaining photograph after Rapson had done his bit of scissorwork? You'd have a normal-looking piece of card portraying twenty or so little boys, and then your eye would light on the gaping hole where a face should be?"

"Good Lord! Imagine getting one of those through the post! *Did* he post them? Where are the outside bits, Gosling?"

"Give me a minute to root about in the store. Bound to be copies in there."

Gosling shot off, and Joe heard him moving boxes about. Finally he emerged, grinning. "Got 'em!"

They fell on the brown envelopes encasing the series of photographs.

"They seem to have kept two copies of each class each year," Joe commented. "So, as a test year, 1921—Peterkin's year—will contain . . . here we are. One copy!"

Gosling had moved on to the back of the file and pulled out a slimmer envelope. And, triumphantly: "Where do you hide a stolen sheep? In with the herd! Here they are—the doctored copies. He hadn't got around to sending them off in the post, apparently."

He pulled out the top one. "Oh, my!"

The sight of the photograph with its calligraphed "St. Magnus Preparatory School" followed by a helpful date was, at first glimpse, prim and ordinary. Then the eye was drawn to the gap in the middle of the second row of boys, the black hole into which a child had sunk. The effect was sinister in the extreme.

"I think I'd get the message, wouldn't you, sir, if I opened this at the breakfast table."

Gosling pulled out all the sheets and riffled through them. "Yes, the dates correspond with the gallery." He began to slide them away.

"A moment! Hand them over!"

Joe took them from him and looked at them more carefully, checking the backs of each for scribbled notes or names and finding none. As he got to the end he looked up. "Gosling! Tell me again—how many faces? Nine? It's nine, isn't it?"

"Yes. Why?"

Joe counted the sheets. "Because there are *ten* sheets here. Ten."

He came around the desk and joined Gosling on his knees, laying down the pile of stiff pieces of card between them. He turned them over until the surface of the last one showed itself.

This was intact. Untouched. No gap signifying disappearance. They stared at the rows of shining faces, unable to speak.

Gosling finally broke the silence. "Sir. You recognise this class, I think?"

"It's year 1932. The current year. Taken last September." Joe pointed with a shaking finger to the familiar fair hair and bright expression in the centre of the back row. "And this is my nephew's class. That's Jack Drummond."

CHAPTER 17

The two men got to their feet.
"Steady on, sir!"

Gosling turned to him and Joe felt his elbow gripped by a large hand.

"He's all right! He's with Miss Joliffe. They're right next door in the old morning room. Remember? You were quite happy to leave him in her care." And, feeling Joe's muscles tense: "I say, would you like me to go and check on Drummond? Sir!"

The response came at once, fast and brutal. With a yell and a thud, Gosling crashed to the floor, knees and chin grinding into the oak floorboards under the pressure of Joe's knee in his back. An iron grip wrenched his right arm upwards, fingers closed around his neck probing for and finding a lethal pressure point. Gasping with terror, he signalled submission, banging frantically on the floor with his free left hand. In all his bouts, this resulted in instant release from a hold, a graceful recovery and an exchange of smiling bows.

The flapping hand was instantly trapped and crushed under the assistant commissioner's left knee, and a voice grated in his ear: "No rules here. You lose consciousness in ten seconds. Where is he?"

"Told you! Next door!"

The pressure increased, and Gosling's forehead clunked onto the floor.

"Clown! I'm not talking about Drummond. Where's young *Spielman?*"

JOE FELT THE resilient young muscles he was restraining turn to marshmallow at the name, but he retained his hold.

"Spielman! Oh my God! No! Under our noses! Let me up! Now! Five hours! He's been gone five hours. He could be any- where." And, desperately: "Stop farting about, sir, and I'll do whatever you want!"

"Sounds like a good offer to me." The light voice came from the doorway. "I'd take it if I were you, Commissioner."

Dorcas was standing in the doorway, Drummond in hand and a quartet of small open-mouthed boys behind her. She turned to her flock. "All's well, you see. The gentlemen are just having a rag. And making far too much noise. I shall speak to them! Go back to your drawing, will you, boys, and I'll join you in a tick. If I'm not back before the tea bell goes in . . . five minutes time . . . you may all go straight down to the dining hall."

Closing the door, Dorcas eyed the two red faces as the com- batants straightened ties and dusted down trousers. Her expres- sion grew fierce. "What a sight for young eyes! What am I to tell them? No use saying you were having a practice bout. They're not stupid. It was quite obvious the commissioner was trying to kill their schoolmaster. It'll be all round the school in no time. You, young man! Gosling, isn't it? What have you done to irritate Joe? Didn't anyone warn you he fights fast and dirty?"

"I'd heard he'd learned tricks in the East," Gosling offered hesitantly, scrambling to his feet. "India, was it?"

Dorcas gurgled. "East India Docks more like. Or The Bucket of Blood in Seven Dials. He's a member of some pretty louche establishments where the pugilist arts are taught and the Marquess of Queensberry has never set foot. You can count yourself lucky he's getting on a bit and losing his edge. Now, when you've had a chance to get your breath back and master your palpitations, Joe, perhaps you'll tell me what provocation gave rise to this murderous attack."

"No bloody time!" Gosling's cry was alarming. "For God's sake! There's a child out there who's been snatched from under our noses. You saw it happen yourself, Miss Joliffe. Spielman. The little kid with the big ears. We all waved him off! He's paid for and on his way."

"What? Calm down, Mr. Gosling. On his way to where? The boy I saw going off happily this morning by Daimler was on his way to London. To the bosom of his family."

"But was he? For God's sake, Sandilands, tell her."

Joe had never spoken more swiftly and to a more receptive audience. Before he had even finished, Dorcas was reaching for the telephone. "Only one way to find out. Give me Spielman's home number. They won't want to talk to a policeman. Thank you. I'll check on him. I expect the little chap is tucking into his warm milk and custard creams. . . . Shush both of you! Ah, am I through to the Embassy? This is St. Magnus School here, where Master Spielman is a pupil. Matron speaking. I was wondering if I could have a word with our young man. It's rather urgent. No? . . . Not yet arrived . . . In that case, may I have a word with one of his parents? Either Mister or Mrs. Spielman."

They waited for an extraordinarily long time.

Finally, as Dorcas was about to give up and break the contact, a voice was heard at the other end.

"Mrs. Spielman? It's Matron here at St. Magnus." Dorcas listened intently to a tumbling of words the men could not distinguish, her face growing very grave. "Please, Mrs. Spielman," she interrupted, "try to calm down. I'm not quite understanding this. Harald is *not* with you in London? Taken ill . . . on the journey. . . . Can you tell me exactly when this happened? This morning? Four hours ago? . . . Hospital? Which hospital?"

The torrent recommenced and Dorcas listened intently until finally: "I'm devastated to hear your news, madam, and I apologise for disturbing you at such a time. I will inform the headmaster who will reply to you later at a less stressful moment."

"Too late. It's too late. Joe, they've got him. He could be dead by now."

"Can't be. What the hell! Between here and London. What on earth happened?"

"That was his mother. She was very distraught. In floods of tears but I managed to understand her. En route for London in the back of the car, he was taken ill. She couldn't bring herself to say the word, but I know what he was suffering from—it was epilepsy. Matron told me herself. She was glad to see the back of him because she was getting scared by the increasing frequency and ferocity of his attacks. The parents had agreed that he could no longer be accommodated at the school. He was recalled to London. Pending transit to Germany. The family is German— well, half: his father. They were planning to get treatment from a German clinic."

"What did the chauffeur do?" Joe asked.

"The best he could. The lady had nothing but praise for *him*. Alarmed by the boy's condition, he saw a sign on the road and the name of a hospital. He instantly drove off the main road and presented himself with the boy as an emergency at the hospital minutes later. Spielman was still alive, he says, when they arrived, and doctors whisked him away into a ward for treatment. The chauffeur telephoned London for instructions, following which he returned to the family home with his story, and the boy's father set out to Sussex to perform his paternal duties. He left central London an hour ago."

"Hold on," Joe said calmly. "I think I need to check all this, but it sounds as though a natural event has occurred and been handled in the best possible way—"

Gosling broke into this soothing speech. "Rot! If you'll take advice from someone you're determined to place on the wrong side of the fence, get in your car and drive while you can." He took Joe's keys from his pocket and threw them onto the desk. "Find this hospital. Get there before Spielman senior. Insist on seeing the boy. Dead or alive, as they say. The payment had been made; Rapson knew a boy was under threat. And now one has disappeared. If you ignore this, Rapson died in vain!"

"Take the keys back," Joe said. "Go down to the garage and bring my car round to the front door. We'll give you five minutes' start. And stay in the driving seat, engine running. Something tells me you're a better driver than I am. And as long as your hands are wrapped around a steering wheel I can keep an eye on them. Dorcas will map-read for you. Dorcas, which hospital are we looking for?"

Dorcas gaped for a moment. "She couldn't say. She didn't know or didn't remember the name. Sorry, Joe. I was trying to—"

"Yes, I heard you. Go on."

"We can rule out Brighton; that's in the opposite direction. We must go north towards London."

"It's probably one of those little cottage hospitals, locals-for-the-use-of, you find scattered around the countryside. Some of them are very good. But which? Did she say how long they'd been on the road before the boy succumbed?"

"Um ... wait a minute ... she said an hour. Not that I'd take that as gospel; she was very upset and not at all clear. You'd say she'd only been told half the story. You know how men can be— 'Watch what you say! Mustn't frighten the horses or the ladies, must we?'"

"The boy left here at ten," Joe said, puzzled by Dorcas's lack of her usual sharpness before he remembered that she was not a motorist and didn't think in terms of miles per hour. "So they were on the road for an hour at the most, probably less. An hour at what speed in the snow, in that car?"

"Thirty, tops," said Gosling. "Say twenty. Twenty to thirty miles north of here on the London road or just off it. Country area, sparsely populated. Big centres to north and south of it supplying serious medical care—you're right, Sandilands. It'll be cottage hospitals at the best. The kind that handle mostly maternity cases or farming accidents. Shouldn't we get hold of a county list and start ringing hospitals in that range?"

"That'll take forever!" Joe was impatient. "And always assuming they're prepared to confide in a stranger over the telephone. You know how discreet the medical trade can be. If we hit on the right one and it turns out to be the wrong one—if you see what I mean—they're going to deny all knowledge anyway. Look, Dorcas, spend a moment cutting out this photograph of Spielman, will you? We may need to use it as identification. We'll take it with us."

"Tempting Fate, Joe? Finishing off Rapson's work for him like that?" Dorcas's voice was subdued. "I'm not sure I want to do this."

"Superstitious nonsense—just get on!"

Dorcas supplied him with the cutout then searched for and found a motoring map in her bag. "It's small scale, but it'll do. How many hospitals can there be off the main London road? Not many, and if the chauffeur saw the sign with a drama going on in the back seat, I'm sure we can find it with three people looking out. I'll find a suitable one and guide you there. Leave it to me."

They listened as Gosling clattered down the staircase and Joe hastily began to collect up documents and put them away. Dorcas hurried to help him.

"Why did you lose your rag with that young man, Joe? Nasty scene. I'm sure he didn't deserve it."

"I don't trust him. He works for the opposition. I wanted to shock an admission out of him, and if you hadn't poked your nose in I might have got it. It's a well-known technique. You'll have noticed that he's younger and stronger than I am and that he's no stranger to the noble art, so—"

"So you used your other advantages? The low cunning and clunking fist I mentioned. But what really provoked you to violence?"

"His pretence of cooperation was irritating me. And I don't forget it was Gosling we came upon shunting little Spielman off in a Daimler."

"We're getting closer."

"What is this? How many layers of the onion have you peeled off me so far? You know I can't be doing with any of that analysis nonsense."

"I think it was the boys, wasn't it? The sudden realisation that Jackie and Spielman might be in danger. That caused the eruption. The translation of pent-up feelings into physical action. Good. I'm relieved to find there's still a heart beating under the stiff navy suiting and the gold frogging. I could phrase that in more scientific terms, half of them German, but I don't want to annoy you."

"No time to be annoyed. One more thing to do before we shoot off into the night. Pass me that note pad, will you?" Joe scribbled on a sheet of paper and tore it off, talking at the same time. "Look, while I get this delivered, I want you to send Jackie straight to Matron to tell her he's staying the night."

"I take it you're thinking he's not in danger anymore?"

Joe sighed. "To be honest, I think another poor lad is on his way to meet old Charon, two obols tucked under his tongue. It's time to fight another bout with the Infernal Lord or whatever Gosling called him. And this is one I'm not certain we can win. Hercules, where are you?"

"No idea what you're maundering on about, but buck up, Joe! I've seen you take on the devil before and win."

"Right. That looks tidy. Nothing more we can do. I expect old Farman will be straight in here the moment our backs are turned, but—what the hell!" Joe tucked the black book into the pocket of his overcoat and grabbed his scarf.

INSPECTOR MARTIN GOT the call just after 3:00 P.M. He pulled on the gumboots he kept by the door and questioned the breathless young constable who was hopping from foot to foot in excitement just outside.

"I said we got it, sir! In the melt. Right in the middle of the yard. The knife. Six inches. Meat knife. Still got blood traces on it. You can cancel the dogs."

"Good lad. Who needs bloodhounds when he's got you and Sergeant Savage on a lead, eh?"

The two men sploshed their way down the path towards the farm buildings and Martin looked up anxiously at the sky. Not much daylight left—an hour at best, he calculated. But it would do. He stopped at the sound of a car engine starting up in one of the old covered horse-stalls that served as the school garage and watched as the Scotland Yard man's Morris belted out backwards, skidded into a three-point turn, and then proceeded more carefully down the route to the front of the school.

"Yard buggering off early," he remarked to the constable. "Will that be London hours he's keeping, do you think?"

The constable nodded and grinned. "Perhaps he's had enough and he's off back to the bright lights for good. Had his snoop around, seen nothing, tucked his swagger stick under his arm, and suddenly—'Carry on, Inspector' is what we hear."

"'Sod off, Inspector' is what I'm hearing," Martin grunted.

"Except we don't hear. Gone without so much as a ta-very-much."

This rapid exit was exactly what Martin had been hoping for. A clear run at a demanding task without the Fancy Pants

Met officer breathing down his neck now lay before him. His departure was only to be expected, and the constable had it right. Of course. So why the dejection he was feeling? Deceived? Let down? Martin reviewed his vocabulary and selected: *Fucked up!* Always a man who could analyse his own feelings and motives, he further decided to condemn his own pride. He'd wanted to show off for this bird. To demonstrate to the Met that he could run a crime scene and come up with the goods. He'd looked forwards to conferring with the commissioner in the matey way the bloke had seemed to favour. All words. Slather. Veneer. Hadn't even the manners to say he was taking off and wish him luck.

Martin sighed. Ah, well. Another entry in the book of experience.

"Sir! Sir!"

Martin turned to see a school steward slithering down the path in his indoor shoes, waving a bit of paper.

"What's up, lad?"

"Message from that visitor. Sandilands. He said it was urgent."

Martin took the folded sheet from him and read:

"Martin! Emergency. Boy missing. Another!

I leave in pursuit. Regroup your office, first light.

Good luck with the sniffers! J.S."

Martin smiled at the crisp officer's phrasing and tucked the note in his pocket. "All's well, constable. And don't fret about the Met. He'll be back to bother us."

CHAPTER 18

Ten miles north and the light was fading fast. The big car boomed on through the gloaming and Joe was glad of the powerful headlights. Glad also of the strong and confident young hands on the wheel. Gosling was a natural driver and—unusually for one his age and capability—silent on the subject. He didn't refer to Joe's modest, workmanlike motorcar as "she." He didn't bother Joe with questions he couldn't answer on mileage, torque or the rattle under the near-side wheel arch. He managed even to avoid a sneering comparison with the Bentley most young men's uncles seemed to own these days.

Dorcas was sitting next to him in the front passenger's seat, a map in one hand and a police hand-torch in the other. She was alert and scanning both sides of the road.

"Not so cold now," Gosling said. "That's a soft southerly blowing in. The thaw's well under way. This lot'll be completely gone by morning."

"Nasty underfoot?"

"Not bad. Slushy rather than slippery, and the gritters have passed this way. Thirty seems safe on this stretch. As long as I don't do anything silly with the brake pedal, we'll be all right. Miss Joliffe? Dorcas? Can you see anything on the map that might be a hospital?"

"No. A way to go yet. I've been studying the map, and I've got my eye on a likely place. Don't worry—I'll tell you in good time to make the turning off. Keep going."

A few minutes later Gosling exclaimed, "There! A sign. Prince Albert's Hospital. Half a mile."

"That's not marked on here," Dorcas objected. "There's no 'H' for hospital." And added vaguely: "A capital 'H' does mean hospital, doesn't it? Not hotel or hostelry?"

"Worth a look," Joe decided. "Turn off, Gosling."

Gosling eased the Morris off the main road and into a still snowbound side road.

"Not such good going, sir, but others have been up here before us, so we'll manage."

"I think you're wasting your time. This has come up far too soon. It can't be the one," was Dorcas's advice.

"Carry on, Gosling," was Joe's.

They rounded a bend, and there it was on a hilltop, silhouetted against the dying orange glow of the western sky. Gosling's foot came off the accelerator, and the car shuddered to a halt.

"Blimey! What do we make of that? We've bolted down the wrong rabbit hole. Surely this isn't what we're looking for?" he said.

"Told you so! Let's get back to the main road. We're wasting time," Dorcas snapped.

"Shush!" Joe said. "It's not the cottage hospital I was expecting. More like a country house hospital! Grand. Extensive grounds."

"'Gothick pile dramatically placed within vestiges of monastic edifice . . . c. 1860,' would the guide book say?"

"Yes. I think so. Mid-Victorian, I'd guess. And, say what you like about Mid-Victorians, when it came to throwing up a crenellation or two, they didn't stint."

"That's not a hospital," said Dorcas firmly. "It's someone's estate."

"She's right. It can't be a hospital, sir."

"If it *is* a hospital, it was put up with a good deal of loving care and pots of money by some doubtless Gradgrinding mill-owner to assuage a guilty conscience. There's one like that on almost every hilltop in this county. Philanthropists trying to outdo each other in the charity stakes. Shall we go on up?"

"Wait a minute!" Gosling said. "What we don't see is ambulances and other hospital vehicles parked at the ready in the grounds. No one coming or going. Who would come out all this way for medical care anyway? You'd go south on the main road to Brighton or north to London. Listen, I don't think this is right." Gosling squirmed in his seat. "Over there, still covered in snow. There's a name plaque of sorts. Give me the torch, Dorcas."

"Here you are. Do you want to borrow a glove, George?"

He dismissed the offer with a grin, got out and, with broad sweeps of his bare hand, cleared the marker and shone the torch full on the golden curlicued letters. In silence they read:

Prince Albert's Hospital for the Mentally Afflicted.

Gosling got back in and said, grumpily, "We've wasted half an hour. Not a hospital at all! It's a mental asylum! A loony bin! The chauffeur would never have brought the boy here. We'd better get back onto the main road and pick up the trail again." He started to turn the key.

"No! Stop!" Joe yelled at him. "It's *exactly* where he might have brought him. And exactly the place where he could have received treatment. Spielman wasn't mentally ill, we know that. But. . . . But. These places have the facilities. . . . Don't they, Dorcas?"

She was finding her words awkward to get out. "I'm afraid they do. Perhaps you didn't know that over ten percent of the patients in the country's asylums are . . . epileptics. And, no, they are not mentally deranged or dangerous by our reasoning but by law are classed as defective, and the asylums have to take them in when they are submitted. A certificate signed by two doctors will do it. If you consult the Schedule of Forms of Insanity you'll find it: 'Diseases of the nervous system.' Epilepsy. K3. Listed alongside sunstroke and syphilis, probably."

"So, a sufferer from epilepsy can be put away in one of these places and kept out of society for the rest of his life and no one will ever question it?" Gosling sounded shocked.

They stared at the darkening façade of the vast building. "A thousand patients, at least, they probably house in there," Dorcas said. "So there's a good chance that a hundred of them are epileptics."

"And now it could be a hundred and one," Gosling's voice was grim. "A coincidence, are we wondering? Look, I have to say Spielman was showing none of the warning signs when he stepped into that Daimler with his book tucked under his arm. He'd had an attack just last week. I'm no expert but, as his games master, I had noticed they occurred at a few weeks' distance from each other."

"Prearranged? Taken away and locked up in a lunatic asylum without his mother's knowledge?" Joe said. "I think we should find out."

Was it the sun sinking lower behind the hills, the raucous calls of rooks returning to their nests in the elms that stood sentinel in the parkland, or a sudden dip in energy that made Joe's heart drop to his boots? The crenellations he had been admiring were no longer stylish but forbidding. "Halt! Who goes there?" they said. Joe searched in vain for a password.

"What are we waiting for?" Gosling said urgently. "Let's see if we've beaten Herr Spielman to it."

MARTIN SANK TO his knees in the slush and stared at the weapon. He took the paper evidence bag the constable was holding out to him, wrote on the outside in indelible pencil, added his signature, and then picked up the knife delicately at the join between blade and shaft with his handkerchief around his fingers.

"On your bike, constable," he said, handing over the bag. "Put this in the messenger bag and take it to the nick. I've told them to expect it by teatime. They'll get it to Brighton tonight, and we might know by tomorrow whose prints are on there. If we're lucky. Oh, and tell the sergeant I'm popping down to Ma Bellefoy's for a cup of tea and a chat, will you?"

His welcome was what he had come to expect over the last few days: warm, even slightly flirtatious, but with an underlying reserve.

The inspector blew into his cup to cool his tea. "The best tea, Clara," he remarked, "and served in the best china." He sipped carefully. "Funny taste. Nice, though. Very pleasant in fact. What is it?"

Clara Bellefoy looked at him in satisfaction over the rim of her matching cup. "These were the last two of a set that got smashed, up at the school. Specials for governors and such-like. They were going to chuck them out, so I asked for them." She allowed herself a tight smile and added: "Not that many perks in being a school-skivvy. Farman gave me a note to prove they weren't nicked. Want to see it?"

Martin waved away the unpleasant suggestion.

"The tea—now that's something you won't get at the Co-op, Inspector. It's called 'Earl Grey,' and the pleasant taste is bergamot. Or so it says on the tin. I only use it for special visitors. And no, I didn't buy it, Mr. Sharp-Eyes! It got given to me—well, to Betty—by the school steward. Unwanted present to the staff from a parent. They didn't like it and told him to pass it on to someone deserving."

"And, naturally your Betty came to mind?"

"Course she did! I'm not stupid! She's on most of those men's minds! The only pretty girl for ten miles around—you'd expect it."

"Still single at—what is she—nineteen? Twenty? What's she waiting for?"

"She's seen the mistakes her mother made, and she's not going to repeat them. The right bloke will come along one day. I'm not losing sleep over it."

"Well, I have to congratulate you, Clara," Martin said with sincerity, glancing meaningfully around the pin-neat parlour. "She's a credit to you. And the little lad—you've done a fine job by him. Where is Harry?"

"Upstairs in his room. He ran off when he heard you coming. Nothing wrong with his hearing. He doesn't like strangers. Usually he goes all shy and can't find the words to speak. Sometimes he gets quarrelsome and finds exactly the wrong ones. When he flies into a temper it can be very embarrassing to hear him. He tries his best to swear, Mr. Martin. I don't know why. I try to teach him right and wrong and good manners but some-times . . . sometimes . . . you'd say he'd got the devil in him. I think he learns those words from the lads who work in the stables. It must be that, because he doesn't go to school, and he hears nothing of the kind at home."

"Is he warm enough up there on his own?"

"Course he is! I always keep a fire going for him in the grate, and he's got a new set of tin cars to play with. It's his retreat. When he's gone off up there I don't bother him. He's all right."

Martin cocked his head to a photograph of Clara's son and daughter, a studio print in a wooden frame sitting on the upright piano. "A fine-looking pair, missis. He's a good-looking little lad. Takes after his ma. Same curly dark hair." He leaned forwards and asked quietly: "What went wrong for him? If you could tell me, there might be something I could suggest . . . some help I could recommend. . . ."

His cup rattled in the saucer as Clara Bellefoy jumped to her feet, her face contorted with anger. "Shut up! Just shut up about my lad, will you! I'm fed up with it! He's what he is. It's his mother's fault, and I'm paying the price. Every day of my life. And I wouldn't want it otherwise. There's nothing anyone else can do for him." She fell silent, biting her lip, and sat down again.

Martin picked up one of her phrases. "You say it's your fault, Clara? How can that be?"

"None of your business."

He persisted. "Most would blame God. Or the defaulting father."

Clara sniffed and reached into the pocket of her pinny for a handkerchief. She blew her nose and then looked with defiance at the policeman. "I've more sense. It's no secret around here, I suppose. Someone will pass the gossip on to you if you keep asking, so I might as well make sure you hear it right. He's illegitimate. There. I told you that before."

"So you did. I didn't throw a fit at the mention of the word then, and I don't on its second airing. Get on, Clara."

"What does a woman do when she needs her job and the cottage that's tied to it, and she finds she's in a certain condition thanks to a man who's gone off? The head could have thrown us into the street, you know, and no one would have blamed him. Well, she tries to get rid of the problem. Village ways. Village remedies. There's always some old crone who thinks she knows what to do. I took advice. Fell out of the apple tree. Several times. And then the kid was born. I think the fall dislodged something. He was born not quite right. Though we didn't know this until he got to two and wasn't walking. Four, and he still couldn't talk. Now six, and we wish he'd never open his mouth. As I said, my fault. My penance. That's the end of it. Why are you here? Not to talk about my zany son!"

"Just to say thank you for the help your son was yesterday. He made quite an effort to tell us about the car in the lane. I appreciated that. And to let you know how we're getting on, missis. A murder was committed a few yards away from your back door—I thought you'd be interested. We've found the weapon."

"What was it?"

"Six-inch knife. Any of yours missing from the kitchen?"

"No. I was here all the time with Harry and Betty when she got home at just after six. No one could have got in and taken one. It's more likely to have been pinched from the school kitchens. They've got dozens up there. Have you counted them?"

"It was all happening around here at six that evening, wasn't it? And I'm still intrigued by that car. It couldn't have been a fancy man arriving for Betty, could it? It's about the time you'd arrive to pick up your lady friend for a showing at the Gaumont. They've got one of those 'Gold Diggers' films on all week."

"No. Betty got back and set about eating her supper straight away. Rabbit stew it was. I like to have her meal on the table ready for her when she gets back. It's long hours she works. We didn't hear the car. We aren't blessed with Harry's ears."

"How surprised would you have been to look outside and see Mr. Rapson moving about on business unknown out there in the courtyard?"

"Very. The week before—not a bit. He'd been a nuisance. Always hanging about trying to talk to Betty. Mucky old tyke!" Clara shuddered. "Bringing her presents and sweet-talking. At his age! Disgusting! I can tell you, Inspector, if I'd attacked him with a knife it wouldn't have been his heart I was aiming for! Well, I couldn't be doing with that. Betty was getting very worried. She's a kind-natured girl and wouldn't have the guts to kick him in a soft spot or even say, 'Boo!' And we need the money she earns at the school to get by. So I decided to do something about it."

"You went to the head?"

"I did! I have to say, Mr. Martin," Clara leaned forwards and spoke confidentially, "he didn't seem very surprised. I think the rumours must be true, don't you?"

"They haven't reached me yet, Clara."

"That he's been seen with . . . you know . . . *town* girls. The floozies who come down here from Brighton for a weekend . . . all marcel waves, cocktails at the roadhouse, cigarettes and *Soir de Paris!* Well, Mr. Farman made no fuss. 'Leave it to me, Clara,' he said. 'I'll deal with it.' And I thought he had. For days we were clear of Rapson. Then you find him knifed to death where he shouldn't have been. In my backyard."

Clara looked searchingly at Martin. "He wouldn't have disobeyed the head for something unimportant. He was up to something, I'll bet. And that car arriving—it must have been connected. A big, posh car, Harry says. We don't know anybody who drives a car like that. Or any car. Nothing to do with us. We didn't want him there at all, not ever, not alive or dead, Inspector. I wish you'd leave us alone. We've got troubles enough."

"AH. THIS DOESN'T get any easier," Gosling remarked lugubriously. "We seem to be faced with a welcoming committee, sir. And the natives don't look particularly friendly."

He parked the car a few yards from the front entrance. No one made a move to get out. Gosling cautiously shut his window. A crowd of grey-robed figures had flooded out through the door and surrounded the car, some peering in through the glass, some tapping on the windscreen. Most were silent with huge inquisitive eyes; a few were chattering excitedly.

"Inmates, I'd guess," said Gosling nervously. "Yes, they're all dressed the same. Big grey capes. So—inmates."

"Patients, you mean," Dorcas said.

She jumped as a hand released the handle of the passenger's door and jerked it open. "Welcome to the Prince Albert, madam, gentlemen," said a cultivated voice.

This was instantly submerged by a babble of noise as comments flowed in country accents:

"There be three on 'em today!"

"Two men is that—and a lady? Where's the fourth? They always come in fours."

"But they were only here last week, wasn't it? That's enough. Send 'em on their way, Francis!"

Joe decided to show himself. He stepped out and walked around the car to confront them. The crowd retreated a pace. There seemed to be about eight of them, all adults, all male.

A voice from the huddle, identifying Joe's bearing as military, called out in a cheeky parody of a sentry: "Halt! Who goes there?"

Dorcas slipped past Joe as he stood, for once in his life, lost for words. "A friend," she announced. "Well, three friends! Who else would you be expecting? We've come to see your superintendent."

"Of course you have!" said the first voice. A hand emerged from the grey folds of his cloak, and Dorcas took it without hesitation and shook it firmly, murmuring her name. "Always welcome. Francis Crabbe. Team leader. Sixth Watch." His eye sought out one man in the crowd and he added: "They're welcome—however frequently they come, Bert. And these are different people." He turned again to Dorcas. "You haven't been here before, madam, have you?"

"Our first visit, Mr. Crabbe, you are quite right."

"Well at least you don't arrive at midnight like the last lot! We never like the midnight visitors much. We try to keep them waiting outside as long as we can," he confided. "But you time your arrival well. The superintendent is just sitting down to tea. Come this way." Francis Crabbe hesitated, then said hurriedly, "Unless of course you want to go off by yourselves and wander about first. That's allowed. Everything's open. Except for the you-know-where," he said confidingly. "You'll need a key for that. But—no secrets here! If you ask the superintendent, he'll be delighted to show you round the cells. But I don't presume to give you a schedule."

"I think we'd just like to see the superintendent first, as you suggest, Mr. Crabbe."

Crabbe walked ahead, chattering with Dorcas along a wide corridor whose tiled floor shone impeccably. Joe noted electric lighting, paintings crowding the walls, tables lining the way, each with a white lace cloth and vase of winter greenery. From behind closed doors as they passed along, Joe picked up a strange melange of sounds: a buzz of conversation, shouts of laughter, the tinkle of a piano very badly played and a crooning voice from a gramophone. The pervading odour was a blend of Wimsol bleach and toast.

Francis Crabbe knocked at a big oak door and put his head round it. Joe heard him say: "There's a party here again, sir. Two gents and a lady. Will you see them now?" and the jovial response: "Why not! Wheel 'em in, Francis! It *is* the Association Hour, after all."

Francis crooked a finger at them, smiled, and retreated back down the corridor with his chattering flock, leaving them to face the superintendent.

A grey-haired, bespectacled man looked up at them with curiosity from the tea table that had been laid in front of a roaring fire. He put down the copy of the *Times* he'd been busy with and came forwards to greet them. In his late fifties and of massive build, he was wearing a thick Orkney fisherman's sweater and a pair of old trousers with leather patches on the knees. He made no apology for his informal getup. "Gerald Chadwick at your service. Dr. Chadwick. New bugs, eh? I'll ask you to sign the book in a moment," he said agreeably. "What about a cup of tea first and a hot mince pie? We're finishing off the last of the Christmas batch. Our own production, of course. Our bakery is second to none. Mrs. Chivers has won the Victoria Sponge prize in the county competition for three years running. And you are. . . ?"

Dorcas again spoke for the three of them while he bustled

about fetching three more cups from a dresser. "Dr. Chadwick, in a second I shall fall upon a mince pie and a cup of tea. There's nothing I should like more. But I will not accept your hospitality under false pretences. We are not the hospital visitors you take us for."

"Oh, really? *Not* from the Lunacy Commission, then? You look like the usual mixed bag of earnest sobersides come to catch us on the hop. Well, I'll settle for crossword addicts. I'm stuck on six across, if you'd care to take a look. Whoever you are, sit down. You must be frozen through." And, as they settled awkwardly in a row on the edge of the sofa opposite: "Why don't you pour, my dear? I expect you're familiar with the gentlemen's requirements. My hands are a bit unsteady these days."

A minute later, apparently unimpressed by the selection of warrant and identity cards he'd been offered and which he'd inspected carefully, he spoke again, his tone light and amused: "Well I never! A detective, a spy and a pretty girl walk into a loony bin. . . . Haven't I seen you before, in a *Punch* cartoon?"

Joe could not summon up a reciprocal smile. "Sir. We are in a hurry. A life—a young life—may be at stake," he said sternly. "I speak to you in my police capacity in requesting—no, let's make that *commanding*—your cooperation in the matter."

Chadwick's bonhomie faded, and pale blue eyes glinted over the half-moon spectacles as he said crisply, "Commissioner, I don't much care to be commanded or even requested by a complete stranger to do anything in my own drawing room. This is the first and only hour of the day when I have been at what passes for rest around here. Don't suppose, will you, that I spend my days with my feet up munching on muffins! At five precisely I shall be at it again, making the first of my evening rounds. Whether you are here or not. If you wish to accompany me, you'll be very welcome to tag along. I don't much mind which one of you is speaking to me and in what capacity—though I'd prefer to deal with the young lady rather than her pet bull terriers. You'll get the same straight answers. So get on with it."

Joe's story was told with a conciseness the superintendent obviously appreciated. He asked one or two sharp, short questions for clarity and then gave his reply: "No. I'll tell you straight up— we do not have the child here. I wish I could produce him, hale and hearty, but I can't. The scenario you describe, it grieves me to say, is distressing but not as far-fetched as you yourselves seem to think. I do see that you are all still struggling with the enormity of such a suspicion. Either natural events have unfolded in just the way you have been told—in which case the boy will turn up, temporarily at least, back on his feet again—or something under-hand has occurred. And you are right to view the prospect with dread. It wouldn't be the first time. Indeed, I commend the speed with which you have reacted."

"You've encountered such a case of kidnap yourself, sir?" Dorcas asked.

He smiled. "Encountered? Say rather dealt with. You see what we are, Miss Joliffe. A community of nearly a thousand patients. Coming and going. . . ."

"Children? Do you have children on the premises?"

"Some. We have groups of adult men and women, segregated for work and sleeping, but a few children too, the majority of whom have family members here. Unaccompanied young derelicts I am relieved to be able to send on to an excellent specialist youth unit elsewhere in the county. I am a medical clinician myself. Theoretical these days, I'm sorry to say. I like to think of Prince Albert's more as hospital than asylum—a place to be cured of your ills and from which you pass out in as short a time as possible. But the state sends me increasing numbers of incurables—victims of nothing more than poverty, mental deficiency, sexual abuse, melancholia, general inadequacy and, yes, epilepsy. We are overwhelmed. We are sinking under the weight. But I do what I can.

"This could be a dust bin, my friends, a stinking receptacle for the dregs of a pullulating society. I won't have that! I run a healing village. Fresh air, hard work—congenial work—and a good, if spare, diet. The patients do most of the work themselves. They have to earn their crust. They work hard. I allow no shirking. In laundry, bakery, market garden and farm. They are the villagers. And in their hours of recreation they do exactly that—they re-create themselves. They paint, they write, they play music. Some even get well!"

He caught himself and smiled. "But I'm launching into my welcome speech and neglecting your business. Your child— Spielman, did you say?—is not here, and if he'd been presented in the circumstances you describe I would first have treated him and secondly have contacted everyone who had an interest: his parents—*both* parents—but also his school even though he had just left it. I would also have notified the local police force. You never know."

"Why did you stress *both* parents, sir?" Dorcas asked.

"A personal experience. In the case of a desperately sick child—mentally unstable or with low intellectual powers or even epilepsy—the strain on the family becomes too great to bear. One parent, usually the father, takes it upon himself to relieve the household of the burden. A scurrilous father or simply one who is a moral coward may make arrangements, unbeknownst to the wife, with a sympathetic local practitioner to 'get him certified' and presented at an establishment like this one. The required number of signatures and acceptances is well regulated. Inspections are made. Nevertheless it is always wise to check rigourously that the consent comes from both parties as well as the medical agent. I take no risks."

"They made less fuss in ancient Sparta," muttered Gosling, disgust in his voice. "Just hung them from a lintel. If they fell off—"

"Yes, they led a simpler life!" the superintendent said. "And in many ways we have made little progress over the centuries, you'd say. It was my uncomfortable lot to trip across one such attempt a few years ago. To my cost. I dealt with it. Now, do you want to be on your way, or would you like to accompany me on my rounds? I can unlock the padded cells for you, but you'll find no occupants. We have nasty electric-shock equipment on the premises, but I'm not sure I could lay hands on it if you asked me to. There are the usual chemical remedies to which we may have recourse in extremis—pacifying drugs and such-like. I use other methods. Restraint is necessary occasionally, but only applied when a patient is in danger of harming himself or herself. That's the rule here."

Seeing them hesitate, he added, "Look, if I were some sort of a Bluebeard keeping wailing children behind locked doors, you could hunt around this building till kingdom come, and you wouldn't come across a child I wanted to hide. It's enormous. Bigger than Buckingham Palace and with twice as many rooms. Hidey holes everywhere, a farm with outbuildings, a stable block, a working well, a dovecote—stocked. Even a folly or two. Some of it I haven't set foot in myself." He paused and fixed Joe with a challenging glare that had an edge of dark humour. "We even have our own cemetery! Hundreds of bodies in it. No one's ever counted. Going back to Saxon times, I shouldn't wonder. Prince Albert's was an abbey centuries ago. Most country hospitals and asylums were. Some graves have marker stones, most are just grassy mounds covering a thousand secrets. But feel free to move about. I'll detail an escort for you. Francis and his merry men will take you wherever you ask to go."

"Thank you, Dr. Chadwick, for your offer and for your under-standing, but I think we'll be on our way."

Murmuring her thanks as they made for the door, Dorcas asked, "Francis Crabbe?"

"He'll be waiting at the door to show you out. Francis is the leader of the watch teams. Everyone has a job or a duty to do. That is his. He has great authority with his fellow patients. An intelligent man with considerable powers of leadership. He makes an excellent deputy."

"I'd noticed. What I didn't observe is any sign of . . . mental disturbance. I was wondering why he was here with you."

The doctor smiled. "He's been here for nearly twenty years and will die here, Miss Joliffe. As you observe, he's as sane as I am. The other patients know that. Though the judge in his case begged to differ. Francis Crabbe was a young beater on a grouse shoot in Norfolk just as the war was looming. Of the anti-war faction, his hot young blood urged him to make a protest. Many pacifists were marching with banners or chaining themselves to railings in Parliament Square in outcry against the unnecessary slaughter the high and mighty were about to thrust us into. Our Francis decided on a more flamboyant gesture. He grabbed a shotgun and drew a bead on one of the shooting party guests. His target was his Majesty, King George. Missed, as you will have noted. Nevertheless, His Honour Justice Bentwood's judgement on the would-be regicide was milder than most had expected and many had hoped for. 'Man's mad!' he declared. 'Can't hang a maniac.' So they sent him to us."

He opened the door. "Ah, Francis! Our guests are in your hands."

THE DOCTOR CAME loping down the corridor after them, catching them as they reached the front door. "Sandilands, you ought to have this. May be all nonsense but, well, child at risk, as you say. One would like to help." His words came fast, his tone was dismissive. "I mentioned an establishment I have close dealings with, a hospital at—I would say 'the cutting edge,' but you would despise me for a punster—of modern treatment in the realms of paediatrics. From surgery to psychiatry. It occurs to me that, in your confessedly garbled account of the morning's events, the child you seek may have fetched up—entirely innocently and in his best interests—at this place. It's further off your route, but its reputation is wide. The director is . . . not a friend, but a colleague. Very highly regarded in the profession. If you want to pursue the matter with him—and I would recommend it as a course of action—I would ask you, out of professional sensibilities, not to mention my name."

He handed Joe a card. "I've scribbled his personal telephone number on the back."

"I shall take your advice, doctor. Thank you very much." Joe slipped the card away in his pocket. "And allow me to hand you something in return. The answer to six across? 'Ancient killer at home at last to a pair of idiots.' Eight letters. Try 'assassin.'"

The doctor shook with laughter. "Idiots in plain view but where, Sandilands, is the home in question? Let me know if you find it!"

CHAPTER 19

The waiter at The Bells handed around menus and Joe and Dorcas looked at them, unseeing, preoccupied.

"All the same, Joe, finishing off a man's crossword like that—it's just not done!"

"Oh? I rather think he invited us to help."

"He was just making polite noises. Burbling a bit."

"Dorcas, I don't think Dr. Chadwick ever burbled anything inconsequential in his life. Every word was weighed. Intriguing man. I do wonder why he spends his afternoons dressed like a rat-catcher, though. Quite put me off my stride."

"Perhaps he'd been catching rats," Dorcas said huffily. "Something you don't seem too keen on yourself. Why didn't you go on, Joe, to the next hospital? Goodness knows where that child may be by now."

"State of the road, darkness, late hour—"

"Oh, you can stop. You won't say it, so I'll do it for you—the child's dead already and was before we started out on our wild goose chase."

"Either that or he's recovered and back with his family. We'll know in the morning, but there's nothing else we can do tonight. Except try to enjoy our supper. Now can we concentrate on the menu?"

"What are you going to have? Not a wide choice at The Bells, I see, in spite of its efforts to turn itself into some sort of a fashionable roadhouse to attract the fast motoring set."

"Yes, it's not exactly the cobwebbed old barn I'd expected—full of yokels in smocks lifting tankards of foaming ale. Much more entertaining! Glad you packed your blue silk."

She looked about her with curiosity and Joe smiled to see the old Dorcas appear briefly. "I've never stayed in a roadhouse before," she confided.

"Glad to hear it! Dens of iniquity. I should be shot for bringing you here."

He noted with approval the dinner dress she'd changed into. It was well cut and discreet. Not one of those backless creations all the women seemed to wear these days. A chap never quite knew where to put his hands anymore when he encountered nothing but flesh down to a partner's waist, and he said as much to his companion.

Dorcas looked around the gathering of dinner dancers. "The lady crossing the floor," she murmured. "Do look, Joe! She's found an entirely new part of her anatomy to put on show."

"Good Lord! It's to be hoped her partner's wearing gloves. Otherwise I may have to step in and arrest them for public indecency."

He looked quickly back at Dorcas and found himself admiring the single strand of pearls, the mascaraed lashes that didn't need the attention, the mouth rouged in red lipstick. Freshly bathed, she smelled of a blend of Pears soap and perfume. He felt suddenly unworthy of the effort the girl had made.

"How's your room?" he enquired politely.

"It'll do." Dorcas leaned to him and confided, "It's got a name on the door. Do they all have one? Mine's the 'Diane de Poitiers.' Mistress to Henry the Second of France. And right next door there's 'Nell Gwyn.' Mistress to Charles the Second of England."

"Heavens! I wonder if they exchange notes over the garden fence." Joe looked anxiously around at the other diners. "Be sure to keep your door locked."

"I will, Grandma."

"Some pretty raffish types in tonight, I'd say. Someone might choose to interpret that nonsense as an invitation to come aboard. And I think I can see what's attracting them to this watering hole. Did you see they're having a dance tomorrow night in the new wing—dance floor sprung, polished, and ready for takeoff to the strains of Santini and his Syncopating Swingers?"

"I'd noticed. How's your dancing, Joe?"

"Energetic. I especially enjoy the South American style. Mothers warn their daughters as they screw in the second earring: '. . . and remember, dear, never tango with Sandilands! You'll stagger off the dance floor with something broken.'"

Dorcas almost raised a smile. "Oh, Lord! Big toe? Bra strap? Back?"

"Not the toes. Never the toes. But there's a judge's daughter in Devon who remains as bent as a hairpin to this day."

The Dorcas of old would have picked this up and run with it, but the mature young woman was, he sensed, too deeply troubled to leap into frivolity with him.

"Well it's either a tango with me tomorrow night with all its terrors or a quiet evening in with Langhorne. He runs the school's Saturday night entertainment for the lads. They have a film show in the school hall. They've got a Laurel and Hardy feature on." Still no smile. He decided to change tack. She'd always enjoyed her food. "You'll have the soup to start, I'd guess."

Dorcas nodded.

"And—don't tell me—the Dover sole to follow?"

She nodded again and made an effort to respond to his warmth. "It's quite like old times staying in an inn together, Joe, working on a case. But people aren't giving us funny looks any more."

Joe stopped a waiter in his tracks and gave their order. He glanced around the dining room. "This lot is too busy staring at each other. Quite a crowd in tonight. Friday? The start of a long weekend. Had you noticed? They're all couples on pleasure bent. And not many are married to each other."

"You'd expect it. Fast train down from London . . . or fast roadster. It's cheaper and more discreet than a hotel in Brighton and in reach of anyone with a Morris. Including us, come to think of it. Do you see the ill-matched pair at the next table?"

"The dry sherry and the gin and tonic?"

"Yes. He's fat and fifty. She's slim and twenty. They've never met before. And they've got their own private detective and photographer in tow. These two professional gentlemen have been parked at the next table where they're moodily comparing the performances of their Wolseley saloon cars over their double whiskies."

This was better! Dorcas had always taken an interest verging on the fantastical in the strangers she came across on her travels.

"Oh lord! How unpleasant! I see what they're at! We're in for a burst of illegal activity after lights out. Let's hope they're discreet."

"Cries of 'Gotcha!' and clicking of shutters! I expect they'll wait until breakfast to stage their little pantomime. That's the tradition with divorce-seekers, you know. The witness and camera man—that's the double Wolseleys—enter along with the scrambled eggs and toast to surprise the guilty party who is discovered, sheets to the chin, in bed with his accommodating lady."

"The chin in question being freshly shaved, anointed with a touch of Penhaligan's best, and the lady fully clothed," Joe commented.

"Ah, you've done this before."

"No. Never tied the knot. But I read the scandal sheets."

"What do you bet, Joe, that our rascally landlord keeps a

special suite always at the ready? Top rate, of course. And heavy tips for the staff."

"All varieties of human life are here at the roadhouse, I'm afraid, as well as motoring enthusiasts. Sorry about this, Dorcas. I was looking forwards to a quiet talk in congenial surrounding. Getting acquainted again. Finding my young friend."

"Don't apologise. My fault. It's the best we could do if I chose to tag along. Not the first time I've fouled up your social and professional life. If I weren't here at all, needing your chaperonage, you could be at this moment a guest of the school, in the spare room at the lodge with the masters. Looking forwards to a ham sandwich and cup of cocoa. And fending off the advances of Mr. Langhorne."

Joe hurriedly turned his gaze from the shining eyes to focus on the rows of bottles at the bar behind her head. Where did she pick up these things? The wretched girl was still not ready to be let out into polite society. He wasn't going to let her get away with an ill-considered comment like that. He cleared his throat. "Langhorne? The chap who was dancing attendance on you at lunch time? Flirting with you over the table? The ally who helped you demolish the headmaster with a few well-chosen quotations?"

"Yes. Good-looking chap."

"That all?"

"Probably. I'm not sure I can admire or trust a man who fights his battles by firing off other men's lines. I'd rather hear his own thoughts."

"Ooh! Hoity toity! It's only a game, Dorcas—played by men, I have to admit, to entertain and confound each other."

"No. I think with Mr. Langhorne it's more than a pretence. It's a glittering outer cover—a defence mechanism."

"Eh?"

"The man's a chocolate box. One of those expensive ones with a pretty picture on the cover, all tied up with silk ribbons, and when you take the lid off you discover it's been empty since last Christmas and there's just one unwanted butterscotch oozing away in a corner."

"Ah! Now I've got it! You describe *me* exactly." Joe rolled his eyes and clutched his heart.

"Don't take it personally. I'm describing most men."

"All the same, Langhorne was paying you flattering attention. Takes some courage to make up to a woman with his colleagues looking on, ready to scoff, you know. I was impressed."

And, pityingly: "It's exactly the reaction he was after, Joe. Consciously or unconsciously. 'There goes Langhorne, chasing the skirts again. Not to be trusted within a mile of a silk stocking.' Don't you see it? He's covering up the fact that he isn't the least bit interested in women. He deceives his fellows; he deceives you. He deceives himself perhaps."

"But he doesn't fool you? A girl with three years of psychology under her belt."

"I think I know real interest when I meet it." This was accompanied by a smile full of regret and mystery.

Joe sighed and decided to ignore this baited hook. "Oh, look behind you! They've got a cocktail bar with leatherette-covered high stools. Care to perch on one and sip a 'Manhattan' while we're waiting for the first course? No? Well, I notice our landlord stocks a wide range of champagnes," he pressed on with a brittle cheeriness. "Fancy a glass of Bollinger, Dorcas?"

"No thanks. Not in the mood."

"Shame! I was hoping to raise a few eyebrows. 'That handsome devil at the corner table,' they'd murmur, `the one with the tiger-clawed forehead and the wolfish grin . . . plying that poor girl with bubbly . . . it's Rudolph Roller, and he's something big in the City. They say he drives a red Royce.' Pause while the table shudders with distaste and then: 'D'you see the unfortunate creature with him? It's Rita Renault, just fished out of the typing pool!'"

"It's no good, Joe; I can't feel celebratory. I can only think there's a small boy out there who may have come to harm. I can't understand why you left quietly like that. Not like you. I'd have expected you to arrest Chadwick, twist his arm, turn the place upside down . . . question the staff . . . at least annoy him by demanding to examine the daybook. Instead of which you complete his crossword with a flourish and stalk off."

"That annoyed him more than anything, if I read him right! But all those options you mention are impossible, or they're dead ends, Dorcas. You heard the man: If he wanted to hide someone in a place like that, you wouldn't find him if you had a battalion and a pack of trained hounds at your back. I believed him. I've learned when to retreat. I'm not Don Quixote to go dashing in like a fool. There are other ways."

"Like handing the investigation to Gosling? You don't like him. You don't trust him."

"I've charged him with parking my car at the school and then doing a bit of telephoning. He's to contact the Spielmans for an update on the situation regarding young Harald, then work his way through Rapson's gallery, checking present whereabouts and, if necessary, availability of death certificates. Routine stuff but, lacking my own men about me, Gosling will have to do. I say this fully realising that he may well be duplicitous. He's also, before he turns in for the night, to set up an interview with the hospital the doctor mentioned."

Joe paused for a moment in thought. "You know what the medical profession is like when it comes to solidarity, Dorcas?"

"They don't shop each other when something's gone wrong."

"I need to check on this pediatrics place. Chadwick had only good things to say about it, but there was just something about his delivery, an oddness. It was presented as an afterthought. But I thought it was rather too casually handed to me."

"I could comment more intelligently if you told me where this hospital is. I probably know of it. The department has contacts with many hospitals. My friends were scattered all around the Home Counties. We compared notes. Let me help you."

Joe handed the card Chadwick had given him to Dorcas and watched her brows lift in surprise.

"You *do* know it?"

"Yes, I do. But it's miles from here. Not on the Seaford–London road at all. To get there, you'd have to travel a further twenty miles north and then branch off to the east and pick up the Tunbridge Wells road. It's a couple of miles south of Edenhurst village."

Joe looked at her steadily. "How do you know this? Have you visited?"

"Yes. Joe, this is the hospital where I did my research last term."

"Ah. The post Truelove wangled for you?"

"I was glad and lucky to have it. It was the plum posting. You must have heard of it? It's always in the papers."

Joe nodded. "The sort of showcase establishment eminent foreign visitors are shown around, I understand. Starry German clinicians especially welcome. Pathé News on hand to record the admiration. Dorcas, how long has it been open, this place?"

"Oh, it's shining new. White brick, plate glass, chrome fittings, the occasional restrained decorative touch. Ah, of course. I see where you're going with this. Five years? At the most. So, of little interest to your enquiry."

Joe smiled with relief. "Nevertheless, I don't neglect a pointer when it's pushed at me by a bloke as clever as I judge Chadwick to be. Just give me an outline if you can, without being too starry eyed."

"It's a research hospital, both surgical and psychiatric. They employ the very best medical staff, and their patients are well-heeled and well-connected. If members of the royal family need a little discreet medical attention, it's where they come. It's out of the public eye, and they receive the most modern treatment. James Truelove is a friend of the director. No, it's a closer relationship than that. Brother-in-law, would he be? I believe he married James's sister. Byam Alexander Bentink. Professor Bentink. He's a consultant, a world authority on epilepsy and other brain mal-functions. A brilliant man."

"So, it's possible that a chauffeur in distress with a suffering child on his hands might have rung his boss from a telephone box or a post office or a road-house with a request for instructions. Perhaps he'd got further on his journey than we had calculated. A knowledgeable parent would have looked at a map and noted that the best option was to drive him to this centre of clinical excellence. Perhaps the boy was already on their books?"

"Entirely possible." Dorcas turned a beaming smile at last on Joe. "We'll find out in the morning. If that's where Harald Spielman's been taken he couldn't be in more professional hands, I know that. Ouf!" She gave an exaggerated gesture of relief. "That's the first gleam of sunshine we've had in this murky case. Do you think I might change my mind and have a glass of cham-pagne now?"

"Of course. But there'll be a price to pay. I mean over and above the five quid the landlord's charging." He summoned a waiter and placed his order. "I want some information. Everywhere I turn I bump into Sir James. He's here there and everywhere. I've only met the bloke once, and he's taken to haunting me. I'm not happy about it. I've made the usual background checks, of course, and I know what he is but I don't know *who* he is. I need to understand him. I want to know as much as you can tell me about him."

Dorcas frowned a frown he had last seen seven years before, and Joe feared she was going to sink into the impenetrable silence that usually followed. Then she came to a decision and spoke dismissively. "You don't want to hear what I have to tell about him, about his integrity, his intelligence, his oratory, his philanthropy, do you?"

Joe shook his head. "No, I'd rather hear he can't fasten his shoelaces yet, slurps his soup and beats his granny. You must have noticed *something*."

The frown became a scowl. "Very well. I'll confide that he drinks the best French brandy and the worst English ale. That he uses *Eucryl* toothpowder, gets his shoes at Lobbs, his haircuts at Trumpers, and always gives his lady friends white roses. You really must stop reading the *Daily Mirror*, Joe. I think of Sir James as the best ancient Athens had to offer in its golden age. Democratic, thoughtful, but with the bounding energy that gets a state rebuilt."

"Good Lord! A sort of modern day Pericles, are you claiming?"

"That's not a bad insight! The citizenry would have gathered round on the Pnyx to listen to James's speeches, all right!"

"Huh! If our old friend Plutarch isn't wrong, Pericles' best speech—the humdinger he delivered from the steps of the Parthenon at the opening ceremony—was written for him by a *woman*!"

"Only a man would be surprised to hear that."

Joe hesitated. Should he risk breaking the news? Surely she knew? He would phrase his next sentence carefully and have his handkerchief at the ready . . . prepare for tears and sobs.

"I was just thinking—if Sir James depends on *Lady* Truelove to pen his *bons mots* for him, Parliament's in for a jolly boring time! His wife, Lavinia, is one of the silliest women in London, I hear."

"Ah, but Pericles' muse was not *Mrs.* Pericles." She spoke with no surprise. He would have said rather with quiet triumph. "The speech-writer you're thinking of was his well-educated and utterly lovely Aspasia. A courtesan. The only class of woman worth knowing in ancient Greece, I would have thought."

"A hetaira? A good-time girl?"

"But well educated and witty, an ideal companion for a politician. I sometimes think we should revive the institution. It would so cheer up the lives of those dull duffers in Parliament."

"To say nothing of their speeches! But no need to encourage the notion, Dorcas. They've been at it on the quiet for years in Westminster."

Her answering smile was the one he most disliked—the enigmatic one. Hinting at possible revelations.

"Here's the champagne, Joe. Oh! Goodness! Veuve Cliquot '26! Have I deserved this?"

He smiled blandly. "No. But it's what I always give my lady friends."

I really must rise above this, Joe thought to himself.

Strangely his comment seemed to please her. Or the gesture. Could it be that she suddenly realised the grapes whose essence had become this vintage had been ripening in the vineyards the last time they'd dined together in France?

A delicate compliment. Joe's own silent toast to the past.

She did remember and reached out to squeeze his hand, murmuring a sentimental reminiscence, when a discreet cough and a whiff of tobacco-infused tweeds at his side distracted Joe's attention. Inspector Martin was standing, looking thoughtful, a solid and lugubrious presence.

"I do beg your pardon for interrupting, but may I have a quiet word, sir?"

Joe made his excuses and followed him to the bar.

"Sorry about that, sir. I hadn't realised how things stood between you and the young lady. . . ."

"*Things* don't stand at all, Martin. She's a colleague, and I've known her for years. It's the surroundings that are disreputable, not us. Can I help you?"

"Yes. Just knocking off. Gosling said I'd find you here. Got your note. But I wondered . . . you said you might be able to make headway with the knife grinder I've still got locked up. I've had him in jug for two days now, and he's due for release unless I come up with something. Do you still want to have a look at him before I cut him loose?"

"Yes. I hadn't forgotten. In fact, I'm arranging it now. I'll meet you—where? Town jail? Tomorrow morning. Seven o'clock too soon for you?" He had given an over-brisk reaction, he realised, in his concern to quell any suspicion that the London copper might be sleeping in with a hangover or worse.

Joe returned to the table. "Now I'll tell you how you can earn your champagne supper. Do you still speak Romany, Dorcas?"

He weathered the outburst of denials: "Years since I spoke it . . . only ever used it as a child with other children . . . never very proficient anyway. . . ." until he received a grudging: "Oh, very well then. Anything to find out who stuck the knife in Rapson."

THEY WERE THE first couple to leave the dining room, followed by the glances of the other diners.

"Early start in the morning. I'd better show you to your room, Dorcas," had been Joe's awkward announcement as they both refused coffee and brandy.

He followed her up two flights of stairs and down a long corridor until she stood, key in hand, in front of a white-painted door bearing a decorated plaque announcing '48 *Diane de Poitiers.*' Joe unlocked the door for her and stepped inside, looking about him.

"Frightful hidey-hole they've given you, Dorcas. Diane de Poitiers indeed! A French king's mistress and owner of the loveliest château in France—I don't think she'd reckon much to this dog kennel. Simply ghastly. Narrow little bed. It won't do. You should have told me. I'll speak to the manager."

"Don't fuss! The maid says they're full tonight. It's really of no concern. I'm used to sleeping on flea-infested blankets under the stars and washing in mountain streams. At least there's a bathroom across the corridor with hot water and good soap."

"Look, they've most unfairly—I can't imagine what they were thinking—given *me* a huge room with not one but two double beds in it, a surprising number of mirrors and an adjoining bathroom with gold taps. Here, take my key. It's number 31. Er, the 'Sir Lancelot suite,' I'm afraid. I can only suppose the architect they employed had a sense of the ridiculous. Use that room, and I'll camp out in here. You'll enjoy the adjustable shower spray. No, really! You're not the only one accustomed to discomfort. I can trump your nights of 'fleas that tease in the High Pyrenees' with four years of rat-infested trenches. But, entertaining though it would be to stand here comparing bites—"

Laughing, Dorcas launched herself at him and folded him in a tight hug. She looked up and kissed his cheek. "Joe, only you would say you couldn't imagine! They weren't expecting Diane to be welcoming a guest this evening, you twerp! This room is just a face-saving token. A retreat in case the lady gets cold feet. Or the gentleman snores. But it would be mean-spirited to refuse such a chivalrous offer. Thank you!" She kissed his other cheek. "I'll beetle off now and spend the night in the arms of—Sir Lancelot, was it? Goodnight, Joe. I'll see you in jail tomorrow."

After an awkward exchange of luggage, padding to and fro along carpeted corridors, Joe took off his shoes and slumped, head spinning, onto his narrow bed. He glared, confused and resentful, at a painting some clown had fixed on the wall opposite the foot of the bed. It was a gilt-framed portrait of the sixteenth century royal courtesan herself, by someone trying for the style of François Clouet. A well-known tribute to the lady, making play with the name she shared with the goddess of the hunt. The eternally virginal and vengeful Diana. Naked save for a pearl necklace round her throat and the oddly erotically placed leather thong of an archer's quiver across one white shoulder, the lovely woman, caught like the goddess Diana at her toilet, stared down at him with hauteur. Tempting, knowing and unattainable, the divine huntress made no attempt to join him. Not even in his dreams.

CHAPTER 20

The station house was tidy, well-ordered and welcoming when Joe arrived with Dorcas at the appointed time. The small number of holding cells—three, and of those, only one occupied—said much for the general peaceableness of the town, Joe calculated.

Before they took a look at the prisoner, Dorcas asked if she could see his belongings. The constable on duty, after a swift exchange of looks with Inspector Martin, pulled down a cardboard storage box from a shelf.

"He's known hereabouts as 'Old Rory.' No one knows his surname. Not much to take the fancy in here, I'm afraid, miss. We removed everything removable including his belt and shoelaces. Well, you never know—wouldn't be the first time."

Dorcas looked quietly at the meagre collection. "No money?"

"Two shillings and threepence, miss. That's kept locked in the duty sergeant's drawer."

"Nothing written. No photos. Nothing personal. Just an old hanky."

"Been tested for blood. It's clean. Well, of blood anyway."

"A half-whittled wooden bird . . . and a blackened old cherry briar pipe. Ah, our bloke's a pipe smoker. He must be missing it."

"He hadn't any baccy left, miss. There's a leather pouch in

there . . . shouldn't touch it . . . we've inspected it, and it's empty."

Dorcas held out a hand. "Inspector, hand me the packet of St. Bruno I see bulging your right pocket."

Narrowing his eyes, Martin did as she asked and was rewarded by a dazzling smile of complicity. "This'll do it." She picked up the pipe and the empty pouch and headed towards the cells.

The accompanying constable returned with the keys, shrugging. "She told me to push off. Seems to know what she's doing, sir."

A rattle of language no one understood followed. An exchange of greetings very likely. Then, surprisingly, exclamations, laughter and chatter.

Joe looked back apologetically at the two Sussex men. "She has the same effect on dogs. Seen it myself," he said, and the three men listened and waited.

"Perhaps I should warn you, Inspector," Joe murmured, "in case you're planning future encounters with Miss Joliffe, that a largely unsupervised upbringing by a bohemian father has equipped the girl with an eccentric view of the world. Not only that, she swears like a trooper. In several languages."

"Sounds like a stimulating companion, sir," Martin replied diplomatically.

"WELL, THERE WE are." Dorcas rejoined them, pulling on her gloves. "Charming man! Irish. Gaelic speaker. Lucky I knew a bit. And he had a bit of Romany, so we managed. He'd like bacon and eggs for breakfast and fish and chips for lunch, and he'll be off at noon which he calculates is the longest time he can manage to stay out of the weather as a guest of the Suffolk Constabulary."

"He spoke willingly, miss?" Martin started to enquire.

"Oh, yes. A man who's gone without his baccy for two days will tell you whatever you want to know. He was using you,

Inspector. Nice warm, quiet billet, cooked food served up at regular intervals, and nothing at all on his conscience to worry him. Well a bit of poaching perhaps. I said you wouldn't hold it against him."

"Did you get him to make a statement?"

"Nothing so formal. If I'd taken a pencil from behind my ear, licked it, and proceeded to make notes he'd have clammed up. But he told me exactly what his movements were on the days you're interested in."

Dorcas listed from memory the clients Old Rory had serviced with the donkey cart mounted grinding stone he lumbered with from village to village. "At the school, he sharpened the six scythes and the grass cutting machine blades and the pruning knives for the gardeners, oiled them, and left them ready for spring, then he did his usual consignment of kitchen knives. He never touched the rest of the cutlery. Two dozen knives ranging from small three-inch vegetable peelers to twelve-inch bread knives. There were four six-inch knives in the bundle. He returned every one to the kitchens.

"After that he again went on his usual rounds and presented himself at the back door of Ma Bellefoy's cottage. At lunch time on the afternoon of Rapson's death, this was. It was just starting to snow, so he put his grinder in the shelter of the old cow sheds. He did her knives twice a year. She has six. Odd ones. None of them a set. Two of them are six-inch meat knives. Both very worn. Getting like tissue paper. Only one more season left in them, Rory says. They're old friends—he knew her when she was up at the school, and he likes to deliver news and gossip as he works. He usually gives her a wooden toy he's made him-self—for her little boy. It wasn't the only thing he delivered. He gave her—or sold her—a rabbit. One he'd poached? He claims it was a wild one from up on the heath. That's what made him unwilling to talk to you. A nasty magistrate could send him to

Australia for poaching, to join his Uncle Tom, who suffered that fate twenty years ago."

Martin shook his head in irritation. "He's living in the past, miss. No one's bothering him for a bit of poaching. There's families around here couldn't keep their ribs apart if they didn't break a few daft rules."

"Then, with the snow threatening, he went off with his donkey into town, where he could shelter and pick up the hotel business the next day. That's where you caught up with him. He hopes you've taken care of his donkey."

"He's all right. Well, that gets us nowhere," Martin grumbled. "Everything agrees with Ma Bellefoy's account. She has a full complement of knives—they're all present and correct. But there's only three six-inch knives in the school kitchens. One missing. And then my constable picks one up out of the snow melt. Two questions: Who took the knife out of the kitchen? And why wasn't it in Rapson's ribs? Well, the weapon's in the labs by now, and we'll have to wait and see what the lads in white coats can come up with. Meanwhile, there's a bit of honest-to-goodness police work the local plod can do."

Martin detained Joe as he was about to start off back for the school. "A moment, sir. Your colleague, Miss Joliffe. . . . I was wondering if she's as good at getting words out of small boys. Ma Bellefoy's little lad is who I have in mind. I'm sure there's things he knows that he's too scared to tell to a big policeman."

"Martin, you must ask her yourself. I'm not her boss."

"I'll do that. It could give us just the leg-up we need."

He smiled at Joe and smoothed his mustache in a comic-opera gesture. "Watch it, Commissioner! We'll be up that staircase while the Yard's still feeling for the light switch."

THERE WERE TWO eager faces waiting for him when Joe reached Rapson's study: Gosling and Godwit.

Godwit spoke at once. "Commissioner, you must attend to my young colleague first. My news can wait. He is due to give a hockey lesson directly. It's a Saturday. I'll return in a moment."

"Five minutes, sir?" Gosling suggested.

"Right, Gosling." Joe settled at the desk. "Spielman. What have you to report?"

"Bugger all, sir. Phone engaged—or off the hook more like—for hours, but I kept trying. Finally I got the butler. Shifty, I thought. Or perhaps just in the dark like yours truly. Didn't want to speak to *me*. What possible business could it be of *mine*? 'Put your headmaster on if you deem it absolutely essential,' and all that going on. You know what butlers are like. I kept at it and managed to get out of him that *he* really hadn't a clue either. The master was still out in deepest Sussex and, after a brief phone call just after five o'clock, the mistress had packed and gone off in the Dodge to join him."

"Five o'clock. Remind me where we were at five o'clock, Gosling."

"Just turning out of the driveway of the asylum, sir. Sir? I hope you don't mind—I thought all this sounded a bit off key. I rang my boss and asked him if there was anything of interest in Spielman Senior's situation. Regarding his professional attachment to the German Embassy or his domestic life. Masterson's going to ring back. I, er, didn't mention your involvement, sir."

"Very wise. We would always want to avoid a lecture on the dangers of fraternization. I hope you got further with the research clinic."

"A little. Again, I can find no trace of young Spielman. The duty matron I spoke to refused to discuss patients or admissions. I threw everything I had at her, including manly charm, but she resisted me. Quoted hospital policy. I might be a scurrilous journalist, after all. Any rogue with tuppence in his pocket can ring them up from a phone box these days, she explained. Their patients value their anonymity. But she did offer to make an appointment for *you*. Three P.M. This afternoon. Professor Bentink will grant you fifteen minutes. That's if you are who you say you are. You must be sure to have your authorisation with you. Sorry, sir. It's the best I could do. They're well within their rights, of course."

"That will do well, Gosling. Anything more of any urgency?"

"No sir. I've really got to dash—fourteen small boys waiting down in the gym for seven-a-side hockey. They're armed with sticks. Lord knows what they're up to! The rest of my report can wait until you've seen old Godwit. Sir—he's always worth hearing."

"Thank you, Gosling. Wheel him in will you?"

Mr. Godwit entered, twitching with excitement. "Ten minutes to go before my class," he said. "I have something to confide."

He declined to take a seat, and they stood together on the rug. "You remember asking me what the three headmasters had in common? I told you nothing. And I still believe nothing. But—"

"The slightest thing, sir, will interest me." Joe was determined to encourage him. "They wore the same stone in their cufflinks. Each had a nanny called Edith. Each was a member of the Society of Druids?"

"No, no, nothing like that at all. But there's one thing they have all done. A rather strange habit. Being so old—bridging the three tenures—I'm the only one who would have noticed and remembered. The first Wednesday of each month, Streetly-Standish used to go off into town—Brighton, I mean. By himself. No one thought anything of it. He never spoke of it. In the school carriage. Horse-drawn, of course, in those days. Oddly, he used to dispense with the services of the groom and drive himself."

"Returning?"

"Always before midnight. Then Dr. Sutton took over, and he did exactly the same thing. Straight after tea on the first Wednesday of every month, a taxi would come to pick him up.

Mrs. Sutton used to wave him off. Clearly no clandestine object
to these excursions. Then our present head, Mr. Farman, took over
seamlessly and—blow me if he didn't keep up the tradition. The
Wednesday taxi comes for him. At exactly the same time. Oh,
sorry. It's not much is it?"

"On the contrary, it's very interesting," Joe said, trying not to
sound disappointed. A monthly trip to Brighton was all too easily
explained, even for a married head. Hadn't Godwit put two and
two together? Obviously too unworldly for such suspicions. "Well,
well! Are we perhaps thinking . . . cinema visit?" he suggested
innocently, having no wish to shock the old classicist.

"The visits of Streetly-Standish predate the arrival of a picture
palace, Sandilands. And he couldn't bear the notion of moving
pictures. A bad influence on the young, he thought. None of the
men were involved with masonry or druidry or any such mumbo
jumbo. Perfectly normal, all three."

"Think back, Mr. Godwit. Their behaviour when they
returned—did they show any signs of, um, weariness, elation,
resolve, mood or behaviour change of any kind?"

Godwit pondered this for a moment. "Ah, yes. Two of those:
elation and resolve. It would take a knowing eye to discern it." He
smiled with quiet triumph. "And a sharp mind to connect events."
He fixed Joe with a watery blue eye. "I don't speak of it, but you
don't strike me as a loose-tongued gentleman, Commissioner?
Thought so. I worked in Intelligence during the war. Too old to
be of any other use, I'm afraid. Cryptography. Connections are
what I've always noted. Like you, Commissioner, I had suspected
post-coital euphoria of a culpable nature, but I eliminated the
unworthy thought. I remember, however, being struck by a more
than usually confident address to the school made by Farman at
the Thursday assembly following one of his Wednesday outings
and groaning inwardly with boredom because the theme he chose
had been a particular favourite with both the previous heads. Of

course, the boys were not to know that—they come and go so quickly."

"The theme, Mr. Godwit?"

"Oh, an entirely innocent piece from. . . now was it Matthew or Luke? The usual stirring stuff headmasters churn out as an exhortation to the boys in their care. Ah! Matthew seven, verse sixteen." He looked challengingly at Joe.

Joe shook his head. "You'll have to remind me, sir."

"It's the grape-picking bit."

Godwit recited from memory in a suddenly firm and mellifluous tone:

"*Ye shall know them by their fruits. Do men gather grapes of thorns, or figs of thistles?*

"*Even so every good tree bringeth forth good fruit; but a corrupt tree bringeth forth evil fruit.*

"*A good tree cannot bring forth evil fruit, neither can a corrupt tree bring forth good fruit.*

"*Every tree that bringeth not forth good fruit is hewn down, and cast into the fire.*

"*Wherefore by their fruits ye shall know them.*"

"Ah, yes. The apple scrumper's license to rob the best trees. I remember quoting bits of that to my father before he gave me a well-earned whacking for scrumping in our neighbour's orchard. He wasn't amused."

"Another Thursday morning favourite of the headmasters was the parable of the sower. Matthew again: chapter thirteen. He seemed to relish the bit about the seeds being scorched in the sun and withering away because they had no root. He finishes with much benignity: '*But others fell into good ground and brought forth fruit, some an hundredfold, some sixtyfold, some thirtyfold.*' Then he tells them they are good little seeds of good stock and he expects them to go forth and multiply. Thank heaven they're all too young to fall in with his exhortations."

"Mmm ... that chimes well with the views he was expressing to Miss Joliffe over lunch. He seems to have dismissed three quarters of the population of the capital as seed sown on stony ground, I'm afraid. Any mention of Sodom and Gomorrah? Noah and his Ark, perhaps?"

Godwit beamed. "*Rem acu tetigisti*, Sandilands! I thought you'd get there."

"It's a fascinating insight you hand me, Mr. Godwit. I shall go and confer with my local colleague and seek his opinion. If you have any further thoughts, I shall be pleased to hear them."

Joe closed the door as the old man left, and he stood, head bent, collecting his thoughts. He battled hard to ward off the swooping attack of the direst suspicions, gulping, chewing dry lips, breathing deeply, calling on common sense to come to his rescue. But panic was getting the better of him. When his knees began to twitch, he did what he had learned to do on the battlefield—he took action.

He raced downstairs to the equipment room and burst in on Inspector Martin, who was briefing his sergeant.

"Martin! I need your help, man! I need some local knowledge. Could you possibly find out, using the telephone, what social, political or other meetings are held in Brighton on the first Wednesday of each month? And have been held there for at least ... oh ... thirty years. It may be the key to this whole business. Rapson's murder, the boys' disappearance. They're all linked. It's not upstairs and downstairs—it's all the same thing."

Chilled by the set face and sharp tone, Martin dismissed his sergeant and listened to Joe's brief account of fears he hurried to admit were unreasoning. The inspector responded in his measured, countryman's voice: "Sit down. You're not mad, just careful and damned suspicious. Like me. Help yourself to a cup of tea from my flask and listen in while I phone. I'll try first Mabel in the city library. I'm sure she'll have a list of gatherings. I warn you it'll be a long and probably surprising one. Brighton's a busy place, and there's a lot of foreigners, loose-livers and eccentrics about with time on their hands."

Martin was put through to Mabel and spent an inordinately long time in badinage, Joe thought, squirming in his seat. But it seemed to pave the way for action. "Good girl!" said Martin when he'd finally conveyed his request. "Two pages of foolscap, eh? Well, go ahead. I'll weed 'em out. I'm taking notes, and I'll be repeating them for the benefit of my team who is here with me and hanging on your words. Now, just avoid any children's hamster breeding clubs and ladies' knitting circles and the like. I'm interested in hobbies, occupations, interests for middle-aged men, and it has to be on a Wednesday."

"After teatime," Joe supplied.

Martin got busy with his pencil, repeating out loud anything that might be pertinent to Joe's enquiry, however odd.

"Ballroom dancing lessons available every day of the week, eh? On the Wednesday: tango chez Alphonse, Viennese at the Pavilion, Scottish in the Palm Court.

"That's more like it—cercle français at the high school, every Wednesday.

"German language lessons, every week day with Miss Gunter at her own residence. No, don't bother just now. We can always come back.

"Begonia propagation?" He glanced at Joe, who shook his head. "No, Mabel. Flower and dog breeding not a priority.

"Poetry lovers, Tuesdays? Nice to know they're still alive, but they don't concern us.

"Ah! Cinema, of course. Two picture palaces, three showings every day. Look again, Mabel. Anything special about a Wednesday? Ooh, er! That's news to me! Not listed, eh? I'm not surprised. Hang on, I'm making a note of that and, no, I won't ask how you came by the knowledge. I don't want to spoil our relationship." He turned, grinning, to Joe. "I think we've got something! Saucy French films on at ten in the evening. On Wednesdays. Coincides with the midweek soccer fixtures so fellers can lie to their wives about getting home at midnight in a state of excitement!

"Liberal club . . . no, that's a Thursday. Try the Conservative club, Mabel. Fridays. Young Cons, Sundays." He sighed and waited while Mabel ran through her list.

"What, Mabel? Say that again, love. I don't think you're pronouncing that quite right. Ah, got you! That's 'g' as in 'ginger,' not as in 'gaga.'" He scratched on his pad, suddenly pensive. "Wednesdays? Six o'clock. Monthly. Well-advertised. Well, it would be. No expense spared. Mabel, give me the address, my angel. . . . Well, where else, eh? Nothing but the poshest accommodation for those gents. But sadly, another dead end. No, I think we can file them with the poodle fanciers and the Salvation Army! Not much interest to us. . . . We're looking out for do-badders, not do-gooders. Ah, well. . . . Thanks, love. Look, keep that list to hand, will you? And especially that gen on the continental art movies. Most interesting, that. Look, keep all this to yourself, will you? There's a good girl! And stand by. I may need to consult you again."

He took his leave and replaced the receiver, puzzled and grave. "Stout lass, Mabel, but a bit of a chatterbox. Seemed best to rake over the trail, sir. Send her down the wrong rabbit hole. That last bit of info may give you something to chew over." He held out his pad and showed the last entry to Joe.

Joe read, swallowed, and looked back at Martin. "Oh, my God!" he whispered. "I think the Yard's found the bloody light switch!"

"And I don't much like what it's illuminating, Commissioner." Martin got to his feet in alarm. "I'll tell you straight where I stand! Me, I'd have shut the buggers down years ago!" He held up a hand to deflect argument or criticism. "There's not many would agree with me, I know. An unfashionable point of view . . . not modern . . . not smart . . . and perhaps I'm talking to someone who knows better?"

He waited for, but did not seem to be surprised to receive, a denying shake of the head from Joe.

"This lot. . . ." the inspector hesitated to use the name he'd written in his book.

"Let's call them the 'ginger-with-a-g' group, shall we?"

". . . go all the way to the top. Untouchable. Society's darlings. If you go poking a stick into this select anthill, you know who'll come buzzing out? Churchill, H. G. Wells, George Bernard Shaw, Marie Stopes, a Huxley, a bishop or two, a royal or three, practically all the scientific establishment, the *Times* leader writer, and a dozen peers of the realm. Up? Down? North? South? Where the hell do you go with this?"

The inspector gave a cheerless laugh. "Sandilands DSO v. Britannia Inc. If I were you, I'd put on a false moustache and a tin hat and beat it to the Riviera before they can train their big guns on you."

"Too late for that," Joe said. "I've heard the creak of the ranging handle. But don't be concerned, Martin. A bit of fancy footwork will keep me out of their crosshairs."

Martin looked at him pityingly. "Those were probably old Rapson's last words."

"Rapson didn't have a clear conscience plus a small army of policemen working to save his skin. I can start by getting a full list of members. Then we know who we're dealing with. Special Branch will have one. How many of them do you suppose there are, Martin? Not just the Southeastern Chapter—over the country as a whole?"

"Fewer than a thousand, probably. Two hundred of those south of the Thames? It's hardly the Women's Institute. They're choosy about who they take on the books, but they don't hide from public view."

"No. They rather flaunt themselves—call themselves an 'Education Society,' if you please! Still, if they're in the open, it'll make our enquiry a bit easier."

Martin grimaced. "It's their best defence—their public image, their well-known names. Look, tell me, sir, if you had any sort of a case against a . . . what shall I call it? A conspiracy? A cabal? A ring of murdering excuses for humanity? Where would you ever find evidence for it? I say 'you' not 'we' because this is way out of my league."

"But not your *county*, Martin. *You* are the man with the hand-cuffs. The comfortless answer to your question is: *We* find *our* evidence in a hospital graveyard under unmarked stones, as like as not," said Joe dully.

"Better book the dogs, then," said Martin.

CHAPTER 21

Joe had asked to see Jackie Drummond in the morning break. Rather than meet him in Rapson's study, with its bad memories, he elected to walk with him along the corridor to Matron's office, where he'd arranged for Dorcas to be waiting. Matron was on duty in the tuck shop and not likely to return for half an hour.

The boy seemed perfectly calm and pleased to see them again but, by his slight reticence, Joe recognised that the school was drawing him back again into its routine and ethos.

"Uncle Joe! Dorcas!" he said cheerfully. "I hope you had a good night at The Bells? Mummy and Daddy didn't care for it much."

"*Now* you tell us! Not wonderful, I agree. Though Dorcas had gold taps in her bathroom. And I did enjoy an early-morning swim in their pool."

Greetings over, Joe told him that the local inspector was certainly not looking for Jackie in connection with the killing.

"No, it didn't seem like he was when he interviewed me yesterday, sir."

"Martin interviewed you? Without me being present? Or Dorcas?"

"It was more like a chaps' chat, sir. I told him everything, just as you said I ought, and he said thank you very much, my uncle must be proud of me, and I was at liberty to go. I'm at liberty, Uncle Joe!" He savoured the words. "Glad that's all over!"

"Yes, so am I, Jackie." He managed to avoid catching Dorcas's eye. "And I *am* proud of you, my boy! I wish we'd known each other earlier. So much to talk about. But the first thing is—what are we going to do with you now? Your mother will be here in three weeks' time, and of course she will decide what's best for you. I have some ideas myself, and I shall put them before her. But *you*, Jackie, tell me what you're minded to do with yourself."

Jackie looked down at his feet. "Honestly, sir, it's not as bad as I thought it might be. The other boys haven't ragged me. Not one bit. The dorm prefect, that's Lloyd 2, moved me up next to him and told the others I was a toff who'd stood up to Rapson, and he'd got no more than he deserved. Not really sure what a 'toff' is, but I think it's not a bad thing to be. Funny though. Didn't think I would, but I rather miss Spielman. I'd have liked to tell him what I'd been up to. He'd have made a story of it. I suppose that must have made him my friend, do you think? Can you have a friend and not know it?'"

To Joe's alarm, Jackie's voice quavered and his lips began to tremble. With a small cry of compassion, Dorcas dashed forwards, put her arms about him and hugged him close. Jackie didn't seem to object. Without releasing him, she whispered in his ear, "Of course you can! A story takes two—one to tell it and one to listen. A pair. He was thrilled when you gave him *Treasure Island*, and he'll always keep it—with your name and now his on the inside page. That's a good link. When people ask, he'll say, 'Drummond? Oh, Drummond! My first friend. Remember him well! Tell you a story about *him*!' Spielman thought of you as his friend. It's just taken you a bit longer to catch on, clot! Remember him, Jackie, and what it felt like to know someone you'd smack a bully in the watch chain to protect, and go out and make another one. You can start with Lloyd 2—he sounds a discerning lad."

After what Joe judged to be a ridiculously long hug, Jackie finally broke away, grinned, and announced, "In that case I think I should like to stay on here at St. Magnus. Just as long as Rappo's not coming back to get me. It's a lot better with Mr. Gosling in charge of us. He never whacks!"

Arrangements in place, Jackie dashed off to play indoor hockey, leaving Joe and Dorcas staring at each other.

"Now what was all that about? Was it wise, all that spoiling? Not a good idea for a boy to get dependent on female attention in a place like this."

"What do *you* know? Jackie's from a loving family who show their affection readily. He's used to being grabbed and hugged. And it's more than a good idea, it's essential! It's a crime against nature to send little squirts like that away from their mothers!"

"He's nearly ten, Dorcas. A lad that age revels in the company of his fellows. The pack instinct, don't you know. If he'd been born a Spartan, he'd have killed his first man by now."

"Look, Joe, I've been involved with . . . witnessed . . . some pretty groundbreaking experiments. I shouldn't be telling you because it's very hush-hush, and the piracy that goes on in the experimental psychology world you wouldn't believe!"

Joe was alarmed. This was out of character for Dorcas. She loved to gossip, but she was never indiscreet. She had her own secrets and knew how to keep those of others. But he sensed in her an excitement, the troubled excitement of someone who has something unpleasant to convey. He listened.

"Monkeys are the nearest living relative of Man's—thanks to Darwin everyone knows that. I looked in on some work being done in the laboratory with baby monkeys, work designed to find out what are the essentials in the normal development of human infants, whom they much resemble. Fascinating stuff! Food and physical closeness quite simply are the two most vital things and the greater of these is physical closeness. Hugs, Joe!

A monkey infant will forego food in favour of a hug. If you deprive it of its mother, it will seek its comfort from an inanimate piece of fur—or even a bit of old cloth—in preference to food when it's made to choose. They're very like humans in their responses."

"Oh, I don't know. Given a choice between Hector the Horse and a sticky bun, *I'd* have gone for the bun every time." Joe thought he'd keep it light. He was not comfortable with the direction of this conversation.

Dorcas sighed in exasperation. "Can't you be serious?"

"Very well. 'Made to choose,' you say? I'm not sure I want to contemplate the method by which they made their infernal discoveries. Or why anyone thought it necessary to bother."

Dorcas looked sad and shifty, he thought, at the same time. "No. I know what you mean. And it was most unpleasant to hear the protests and screaming that went on when the mothers had their babies taken from them. But an essential part of the process of course."

Gently he said, "A torment for you as well as the monkeys. You didn't have to put yourself through this sort of experience to understand yourself and your origins, Dorcas. I'm sure it's a bad idea to have a *personal* motive for scientific enquiry. And I was always there to help you. Standing by—your own piece of substitute fur. I could have talked to you, helped you to digest it all and reconcile yourself to your parentage. And your upbringing. I'm the only one who's aware of all the ramifications of your family tree. I know more about you than your father does, if you think about it. And I'm a good explainer."

This was received with a sad smile. She reached up and briefly stroked his cheek. "You're part of my problem, Joe, but you can't see it."

"I'm damned sure I could come up with some better answers than a few screaming monkeys! What knowledge that's of any use to man or beast did they expect to give to the world by applying this torment? They're no better in my book than medieval torturers—worse! *They* applied their foul techniques to extract information and confession. These modern Torquemadas in lab coats do it to insert their own dubious theories and hear them confirmed back to them by the screams of innocent creatures. And the real cruelty is they've no sure idea when they start what the information they seek may be or what they can possibly do with it when they have it. They perform their grotesque experiments on the off chance their fancies will prove to have substance. Tell me the creatures didn't suffer in vain."

After a moment: "I can't. They did. The experiment was abandoned."

"Ah. Someone saw the light of reason."

"Not even. It was heard that an American laboratory was working on the same ideas. And they were six months ahead."

"What a waste of time, lives and money!"

"Can you say that? I'd no idea you had a Luddite streak in you, Joe. Others may uncover some truth we ought all to have knowledge of."

"At best, what earth-shaking results might those sad monkeys have revealed?"

"Deep truths about attachment . . . nurturing." Her voice lost some of its certainty. "We were starting to learn that, deprived of their real mothers, the babies were capable of transferring their affections to an inanimate scrap of fabric if that's all that was on offer. If they were then further deprived of even that comfort, they went quite mad. I hated to see those poor creatures clinging on to scraps of woolly cloth thinking it was their mother. When they pulled them off they cried so, Joe, and twitched and grasped with their little hands. They have hands, you know, not paws."

Joe took one of Dorcas's hands and held it steadily until the clenched fingers relaxed. "I can't say we've ever discussed the creatures before, but I know about monkeys. I admire them. I've watched them for hours in India. They're revered in that country. Any man maltreating one of the tribe of Hanuman the monkey god would be beaten with sticks by an angry crowd—probably led by me if I was on hand. Though everyone knows the roving bands are a darned nuisance—messy, thieving rogues and not always kind to each other, I may say. But I'll share with you the fruits of my monkey-watching, Dorcas. Monkeys are a tree-dwelling breed. The babies spend their earliest days aloft, swinging about in the branches, hanging on to their mother's fur. Let go, ungrasp the handful of fur for one second, and they fall and crash to the ground and die. A good grasp is more important to their survival in the short term than mother's milk. Of course they scream when they're torn from what they sense to be their hold on life! It must feel like an attack of vertigo, but much, much worse. What chumps your scientists are!"

Dorcas waited for him to simmer down. "Now you see why I've never discussed it with you. Has anyone ever told you what an ugly brute you are when you're angry?"

"Not many live to mention it."

"Ah. I'm having a lucky escape."

"Well, it sounds a revolting procedure to me, Dorcas. Knowing your attitude to animals I'm surprised that you didn't set the whole monkey tribe free in Regent's Park and burn the laboratory down."

"I thought about it. But there was no park on hand. This was going on at the research clinic I told you about. St. Raphael. In the end I walked out in a cowardly way. It's hard for a lowly student to decide she knows better than a doctor of philosophy talking German in a white lab coat. And they'd have known it was me. I think they may even have guessed who put something sticky in his lab boots."

"All this nonsense about nature and nurture—I'm not sure it's a good thing for you to be wrapping yourself up in. The last time we spoke—seven years ago, do you remember?—you said you were going to make a study of it, the better to understand yourself. Has it helped? I thought I heard you giving a smart reply to Langhorne when he was whispering Shakespeare into your left ear over the coffee urn."

"*'A devil, a born devil, on whose nature nurture can never stick.'* It's from *The Tempest*, and the devil being insulted is Caliban. Langhorne was just testing me out. And enjoying the jinglejangle of the words. I don't think he really understood what he was saying. He's got a mind like a thesaurus. Mention 'nurture,' and it falls open at the letter 'n.' When I started to talk to him about inheritance and environment and the interdependence of the two influences, with references to genetic input, quantitative and qualitative relevance of seed and soil to final product, his eyes glazed over.

"Yes, like that, Joe. You can unglaze now if you wish. Time, I think, to go and interview the Bellefoy child. The inspector said if we went after eleven, we'd find Betty there too. She gets off early on a Saturday."

THE CHILD, HARRY, was sitting curled up like a baby on Betty's knee when they arrived. Far too big for such a perch, he spilled over in an ungainly way. When he saw Joe and Dorcas come in he struggled to get up and flee, but Betty held on to him tightly and whispered in his ear. She put down the alphabet book they'd been studying and said in a country voice that managed to be bright and yet soft at the same time, "Harry's doing well with his letters, sir, miss. I won't ask him to show you because he's too shy, but he's a dab hand at M for motor car and O for orange. He can even draw them with a pencil."

"May I see?" Dorcas took the book and opened it. "See there, Harry . . . that's D for dog, but it's also D for Dorcas. That's my name. Can you find me H for Harry?"

Betty quietly turned the pages, and the child pointed excitedly at H for house and mumbled his name.

"Well done! That's right! Why don't you show me your motor cars, Harry? I hear you've got a terrific collection. May I have a look?"

"Off you go, Harry," Betty said. "The inspector told us you might like to see them and talk about them. Harry's got them all lined up ready in his bedroom if you'd like to go along with him, miss."

"Where's your mother this morning, Betty?" Joe asked when they had clumped upstairs.

"It's a Saturday. When I get back down from the school she always goes off into town and does the shopping. Sometimes she goes to the pictures—there's usually a matinee on. It's bad enough working up at that place, sir, but it's worse being cooped up here with Harry, day in, day out. I try to relieve her when I can. Cup of tea? We've got Earl Grey if you can stomach it."

Betty got up and made her way across the sparsely furnished room towards the small outshot housing the kitchen. Joe watched her. Small, neat-waisted with an abundance of dark, curly hair and a shy under-the-lashes way of looking up at a man. Yet she remained unmarried, and Joe wondered what was wrong with the men of Seaford that they hadn't snapped up this pearl. Could it be her slight limp? Hardly likely, but Joe could see no other flaw.

"I love Earl Grey," he called after her. "Let me help you."

"Gerraway with you! A gentleman in the kitchen! I wouldn't know where to put myself!"

"I fend for myself in London, Betty. I'm an ace with a teapot. And I won't get under your feet."

Five minutes later Joe emerged from the kitchen carrying the tea tray and having inspected the range of kitchen knives to his satisfaction.

They drank their tea, smiling to hear the sounds of toy motor cars revving up and brakes squealing, grunting and laughter from upstairs. Joe plunged into a conversation about the relative merits of James Cagney and Paul Muni. Neither appealed much to Betty, who disliked gangster movies. Clark Gable—now that was more like it. But she especially liked perky blondes like Jean Harlow and Carole Lombard, who talked back and got their own way. They shared a view of Greta Garbo: two yards of pump water, according to Betty; overrated and moody, according to Joe.

Dorcas came back down to the parlour at last, full of praise for Harry's motoring knowledge.

"Oh, he sits by the roadside up on the turnpike for hours, miss. He clocks every car going up to London or coming down to The Bells. A lot of the drivers know him and give him a wave. He knows all the makes. He can do a good impression of the noises their engines make, did Mum tell you?"

"He identified it for me just now," Dorcas said, ignoring a warning frown from Joe. "He picked it out of his lineup of models and showed me. Making the matching big-car noise. It was a Talbot. He's seen it before on the road. He said I could bring it down to show you, Joe. And here it is."

She held out a tin replica of an elegant car with grey and black paintwork.

"What model is it?" Joe asked. "It usually tells you underneath."

Dorcas read out: "1926 Talbot 18/55. It's one of those with the spare wheel over the driver's side running board. Big cars—you can get seven passengers in there, and they have a reputation for being fast. Plush inside, too. I rode in one once. It has grey velvet upholstery, I remember, and little silver holders to put your nosegays in."

"May I see it?" Joe took it from her hand and peered at it, then he placed it carefully on the table. "Do you recognise the type, Betty?"

Betty gave him a shy smile. "Oh, sir, I don't know one car from another—except for a Model T Ford, perhaps. A lad I know in town—his dad's got one of those. Lends it to Tom at the weekends sometimes." She blushed and bit her lip. "But that one—no. Looks expensive to me. I wouldn't be giving a car like that a second look. Harry may have seen one on the main road."

"I expect so. Well, thank you so much for your hospitality and your information, Betty. Must be getting back. Many phone calls to make before lunch."

"DID YOU NOTICE the marks, Joe?"

"I did. The child had done them himself, I think."

"Yes, in indelible pencil. He'd scratched off whatever it said originally on the number plate and put his own letters on. Two of them: 'O' and another 'O.' Not much is it?"

"Considering he can only do two letters anyway, it's next to nothing!"

"But—number plates—I wonder. Boys set much store by them, you know, Joe. I noticed other cars had had their plates painted over by an adult hand. They were the familiar cars he knows in the village. He showed me. There was a Morris, a Ford and a Riley. All with authentic Sussex numbers filled in. That Talbot means something to him. He kept pointing to it and making a noise. He was so earnest I took out a pencil and drew the letters in my notebook to show I'd got it. That calmed him down. They may be part of the registration of a car he's seen on the road."

"I'll grasp at anything. I'll pass this over to Cottingham when I get back to the telephone. He can get on to records. He'll thank me for that on a Saturday!"

They walked back along the path bordering the muddy court-yard that linked the Bellefoys' cottage with the school buildings and stopped for a moment to look at the police flag marking the spot in the centre of the sodden grass where the knife had been found.

"Now, what would Rapson have been doing crossing an open area already under snow?" Joe wondered. "Wherever he was heading, he'd have stuck to the path."

"Someone could have thrown it. Pulled it out and chucked it as far away as possible into the snow. From here." Dorcas demonstrated. "Now, why do that?"

"I think you know. Leave a knife in the wound, and provenance can easily be established. If you have to get rid of it in a hurry, throw it into a snowdrift. Seems to have worked. It took Martin's men two—or is it three?—days to find it."

"Tell you something else, Joe. Bit odd. Betty is the only wage earner in that household, isn't she?"

"The only one, yes. The cottage is a tied one, of course, so they pay no rent. All the same it must be hard to manage. They seem to do all right."

"Careful management and no frills, that's evident. The women don't indulge themselves but—you must have noticed—they *do* indulge that boy. His set of cars, Joe, was rather special. The box it came in was still there being used as a garage. By mail order from the Gamages catalogue. I remember Orlando making a fuss about the cost when my brother asked for a tin car. Just one. Harry has thirty. They're really collectors' models and must have cost a month of Betty's wages.

"But there's more. His room was kitted out in—oh, not extravagant—but good-quality furnishings. His bed is a sort of heavy-duty large-sized cot with sides you can put up. Perhaps he falls out of bed still? Specially made to order, I'd say, supplied by Heals on the Tottenham Court Road. And, tucked up in this splendid little bed, there's a teddy bear. Not just any bear, one of those new continental ones by Steiff. Soft carpet. Thick curtains, good fire going and a full coal scuttle. The rest of the house—well, you saw for yourself—is on the edge of poverty."

"With all that cosseting and attention, I'm thinking young Harry is one lucky little monkey!"

"Yes, I'd say they spend every penny they have on that boy."

"Penny? Would you say—penny?" Joe asked thoughtfully.

CHAPTER 22

"Immediately after surgery? Will that do? I finish at twelve noon. Do you know where to find me? High Street, the double-fronted Georgian next to the iron-monger's. I look forwards to meeting you, Assistant Commissioner Sandilands."

Dr. Carter put down the receiver and muttered, "Curse you!" In truth, he'd just said goodbye to the last of his patients for the day, but he needed some time to think about things. So. It had come to this. Was there any point in arguing, remonstrating, self-justification? Yes, there bloody well was! He felt no guilt. Whatever he'd done, he'd done it out of principle. For easement in a harsh world. To improve the lot of the unfortunates who were powerless to do it for themselves. But how had the buggers arrived at his name? Who had mentioned it in connection with the removals?

Inspector Martin, the local man, was a good chap—he'd understand if the circumstances and the benefits were explained to him. Might even be persuaded to look the other way. Perhaps he should have taken the officer into his confidence earlier? Involved him? But then, individual placeholders came and went, the office remained and was never more congenial than the man occupying it. That had been his reasoning. And now he had this Sandilands buzzing round. The man who'd just been on the phone was an unknown quantity. Metropolitan CID officer. He'd throw the book at him without a qualm. Or make Martin do it. By the time the coppers had trawled through the records they'd have enough to get him struck off the medical register at the very least.

Sighing, he went to his filing cabinet, extracted one file, checked the name on the spine, and grimaced. Who'd have thought this innocent would have brought about his downfall? He placed it on his desk. It would be a mistake to make them search for it. Everything aboveboard—that was the tone to take.

Donald Carter poured himself a much-needed tumbler of whisky and waited.

"YOU DON'T OBJECT if I bring my colleague Inspector Martin, do you, doctor? I believe you two know each other?"

"We do! Always a pleasure, Martin. Assistant Commissioner, how do you do?" Dr. Carter shook the firm hand offered him and pulled up another chair. "Sit down, both of you, and tell me how I can help you."

"By revealing the contents of one—or two, possibly three—of your files. Patients' records. Inspector Martin has obtained the requisite authorisation from the local magistrate. A search warrant, Carter." Sandilands slid a folded document on to the desk. The doctor's eyes, reading upside down, took in the chiseled script of the headed sheet: *His Majesty's Metropolitan Police.* He gulped. "We could, using this, look into anything in here that takes our fancy." The icy grey eyes surveyed the room, calculating and commanding and taking it all, lock stock and filing cabinet, under his authority.

Sandilands waited for the doctor's nod and his murmured: "I understand that," then he turned a less stern gaze on Carter. "But I'd much rather do this neatly and quickly by dipping into your *mental* filing cabinet. You agree?" he suggested.

The doctor nodded again and put a hand on the file sitting at the ready on the desk before him. "I may need to check dates and so on, but I'm ready to speak to you."

"The Bellefoy family up at the school—"

"The Bellefoys?"

"Yes, all three of them. Tell us a little about young Harry and his problems."

"Oh, very well. He's five years old. I don't need to check his birthdate because I was present at the event, and it was Christmas Day 1927. I registered his mother as Clara Bellefoy and his father: unknown.

"The child was born slightly prematurely, and possibly this affected his development, both physical and mental. He's quite a strong boy but somehow badly wired up. Clumsy. Uncoordinated. He was late to crawl and late to walk. But his mother and sister take such good care of him his condition improves by leaps and bounds. They spoil him of course. I've had to speak to them. Not that they take any notice. Harry's mentally defective, you'll have realised if you've seen him. You have? Poor speech and reasoning. I've had him tested, and he's two years behind on the scale we use. But again—those women are working wonders."

The policemen had listened quietly, giving nothing away.

"And Betty Bellefoy? If I were to look, what, I wonder, would your file reveal about any broken limbs in December 1927?" This question came from Inspector Martin. The CID man blinked, pursed his lips, and kept silent.

Ah. Well, it had been worth a try. Seeing no way out of this, the doctor got up and went to his cabinet. "Here you are. Bellefoy, Elizabeth. Born 1913."

"In your own words, doctor," Martin encouraged. "It's all right, man. It's only us. The boy's in no trouble. We've got a puzzle that needs clearing up, that's all."

"You'll find Betty suffered a broken ankle falling out of an apple tree—the Bath Beauty at the bottom of their garden, on . . . December 24th, 1927. Multiple fracture—it was the devil to set. That what you want?"

"So—not Clara at all? It wasn't Clara who threw herself out of the tree to dislodge an unwanted child from the womb?"

"No, it was little Betty. And not the first time she'd tried. I suppose it was the extra weight this time that did it."

The doctor's head went up, he sniffed, tooted into a large handkerchief, and glared back at them.

"I was called in. They'd hidden the pregnancy under layers of pinnies, as women do, and the girl had gone on skivvying at the school, condition unnoticed. They were planning to deliver the child in secrecy if it couldn't be got rid of, but what with the ankle and all and Betty in double agony, Clara gave in and summoned me. The poor child, in her pregnant state, must have been exposed every day of her hard life to the sight of the man who'd brought it about. The man who, the previous March, had raped her. She was only just fourteen, gentlemen."

"And Betty's baby became officially Clara's," Martin said heavily. "Wouldn't be the first time that's happened. If a mother's young enough not to stretch belief beyond bounds, she'll sometimes take the blame. 'Afterthoughts' they're sometimes called, these children. It happens that an auntie takes a child in with nothing said. It's better than the alternative: the orphanage. Or the loony bin. But it's the criminal father I'd like to get my hands on, doctor. Did the Bellefoy women ever tell you his name?"

"No. They never did. Just 'a man at the school.' It could have been anyone from the headmaster—well, perhaps not him—down to one of the school stewards. Randy lot, some of those boys. Get up to all sorts of mischief in the summertime with the girls from the village. Those old cart sheds are nothing but an invitation to cider-fueled bucolic debauchery."

"And young Betty had got involved with some lad who'd not known when to stop?"

"That sort of scene. Not in the least unusual—it's the way most marriages start, officer, and no one bats an eyelid. I think

Clara had some scheme of her own that she didn't want me to be a party to. 'Just leave it to me, doctor,' she'd say. 'I know what I'm doing, and you can be sure it'll be the best for Harry.' She's a determined woman. Resourceful. And she loves that child dearly."

Dr. Carter fell into deep thought and was left untroubled by the pair of police officers while he pondered.

"I say—could these questions have anything to do with the murder that's taken place up at the school just the other day?"

Martin replied. "We believe they are connected, doctor."

"If they are, then you must have guessed the identity of the father and possibly the reason for his killing? Oh, no! How sickening! I don't want to contemplate such a horror! Him? That man? Rapson? Surely not! There are rumours that he.... Oh, that can't be! But if it is—"

The officers looked steadily at Carter, allowing him time to absorb the unpleasant idea. When he could stop spluttering, he said urgently, "Look, you're powerful men! Can't you do something to avert another tragedy? Because that's what you'll bring about. You'll wreck three lives."

The doctor took off his spectacles and gave them the full force of his earnest blue eyes. The midday sun, stealing at an angle through the window behind him, lit up his bald head and gave him the authority of an avenging angel.

"If we could, we would, doctor."

Carter believed Sandilands. The Met man's expression was no longer flinty but conveyed a great sadness.

"But meting out justice is not our role, you know. We seek out the truth. Others judge their fellow men. May I ask if you could stand by in support if the worst occurs?"

"Of course. Of course."

Sandilands picked up and pocketed his warrant to indicate that the interview was over.

Martin paused at the door as they were leaving and loosed a

Parthian arrow. "Doctor. One last thing. Are you by any chance a member of the Eugenic Education Society? Wednesday meetings once a month in Brighton?"

After a short silence the doctor asked, "Why do you ask? Strange question and surely none of your business?"

"We have reason to believe it most definitely is our business, doctor," Sandilands took over. "I'll come clean with you. We're inquiring into the behaviour and movements of certain members of this society in connection with a crime—a series of crimes— against young people. We believe that Rapson is one thread sticking out of the Gordian knot. Help us to give it a tug, will you?"

"Whatever next? And to answer your question, I am most certainly not a member. Many physicians are involved—I am aware of that—and I would probably have made better advancement in my career had I been a member but—no. And no! I am in favour of life and humanity in whatever natural form they present themselves. And, gentlemen, a word of advice from me: Always mistrust a word that begins with *eu*."

"Yew, doctor?" Martin asked.

"Ancient Greek: *eu*. It means *good, well, fine*. And it most often signals a lie or deception is coming. The word 'euphemism' says it all! 'Speak fair.' Use a sweet word to express an unpalatable idea. A spoonful of poisoned honey! So—those scourges of Mankind, the Furies, became the 'Eumenides.' 'The Kindly Ones.' An instrument to rival the bagpipes in unpleasant sound is a 'euphonium.' A 'eulogy' is a fine-sounding speech, usually about a dead person and usually lies. Eugene—the well-bred boy—is the cousin who poked me in the eye with a stick when we were boys. And 'eugenics,' my friends, is the new-fangled science of breeding fine offspring. By calculated selection of the parents."

"You see something wrong in that aim, doctor?" Sandilands asked.

"For a start it's not a science as it claims to be, nor ever can be. Eugenics . . . genetics . . . all bogus."

"Bogus?" Sandilands picked him up on this. "Must I tell my niece she's wasted three years of her life studying genetics as an element of her course at London University?"

The doctor gave him a level glance. "You might well mention it. The proponents of this quasi-science have made use of Bateson's work, that he has termed 'genetics' and that he, in turn, has devised after the pea-planting experiments of a Moravian monk. Interesting stuff—yes, interesting, and it must be pursued—but it won't bear the weight of a complete social upheaval such as they are planning. Enforced sterilisation of the unfit is on the books."

"There's a Sterilisation Bill going through Parliament as we speak, I understand," the London man remembered.

"The movement's gathering pace! The United States, Australia, Germany, Scandinavian countries, all have leapt on this infernal bandwagon and are going downhill faster than we are. Are we cart horses to be selected or discarded to produce ever more acceptable generations of children?

"Eugenics! Hah! The name's a made-up word. It is in itself a euphemism for a very nasty notion. Selective breeding and its obverse—selective culling. Eugenics—sounds innocent enough. Fine breeding. Until you realise that it involves compulsion and the denial of human rights culminating in the knife and the lethal chamber. It's the children of the future who are everything to the eugenists. Children who do not exist, who may never exist, are shaping our laws in Parliament as you observe, Commissioner. Surgeons are sharpening their scalpels. In some of the American states they're using them! Vasectomy and salpingectomy are being practised, in themselves dangerous procedures. Many thousands have already suffered. The presently living are being sacrificed for an army of phantom children of the future."

Carter paused for breath, aware that the vehemence of his outburst had startled the two officers.

Martin spoke gravely, shaking his head portentously: "That can't be right! 'What's posterity ever done for me?' I've often heard it asked."

The doctor and the assistant commissioner burst into laughter, a release from the tension of the last five minutes.

"And there you have your best riposte to the eugenists!" Sandilands said. "Laughter! A good British guffaw."

"THAT SHORT INTERVIEW raised more questions than it answered," Joe commented as they hurried back up the hill to the school.

"Oh, I'm not sure I'd say that," Martin said comfortably. "It solved a murder case. I know who, why and how as a result of the doctor's information and insights. Just a question of gathering in the evidence from the laboratory, pulling all the threads together, and then I'll be in a position to make an arrest. Can't say I'm looking forwards to that very much. As far as I'm concerned, Rapson got what was coming to him. But I'm wondering, why at that particular moment?"

He thought for a moment, then spoke aloud for the first time the name at the forefront of their minds. "Clara. She'd had five years to think about it and had done nothing, not even complained to the headmaster, that his new form master had raped her daughter and got her into trouble."

"Do you think Farman has any idea?"

"No. I don't. And if Clara's capable of snatching up a knife and stabbing a man—three times, they're saying—on a snowy night in her own backyard, there's more to it than just a sudden urge to avenge her daughter for a six-year-old offence. Clara's a planner, I'd have judged."

"I took a peek at the knives when I barged into the kitchen.

Two, as old Rory said. But not a pair. Only one was worn thin. The second wasn't new, but it wasn't well worn either. A replacement?"

"I think so. The other thin one ended up in Rapson. I've not had the lab report back yet. Some prints may have survived two nights under snow."

"But you're right, Martin. Something triggered it. Clara's snatching up the nearest kitchen knife, I mean. I bet we can trace it back with a bit of imagination and fevered speculation. Calm me down if you think I go too far. I think Rapson was being blackmailed by Clara. 'I'll go to the head and tell him if you don't cough up.' Blackmail's too strong a word, perhaps, but you know what I mean."

"Dues being exacted," Martin corrected.

"Better. His cheque book shows he was paying out a sum of money—in cash—every month. What's the betting that's been going into caring for Harry? Possibly putting away a little something towards his future? Clara strikes me as being a calculating and careful type of woman. That household is frugal but well-ordered. But just before he was stabbed, Rapson withdrew vastly more than the usual amount. Why? Was it intended for the Bellefoys? Blood money?"

"Close the women's mouths with a wad of bank notes and have the lad taken away? But where to? That car the boy heard, it was coming for *him*! A Talbot, you tell me. Does that signify?"

"I'm waiting to hear back from London. They can trace the registration numbers of all the cars in the country. My super is on to it. But it's a Saturday. . . ."

"There's more to this than just the Rapson murder, isn't there? You hinted as much from the beginning. It's linked in with *your* enquiry."

"Yes. Rapson isn't exactly the key to a very nasty business, but he's the signpost. Think of it this way, Martin: If you came across something in the course of your researches into the history of the school, a pattern of disappearances, unaccounted for, suspicious in different ways. . . ."

"And you had all the time in the world to ferret about and all the documents you needed to hand, a telephone . . . the authority of the school behind you. . . ."

"You might find out what was going on and who was directing operations—much more easily than coppers like us ringing up on the off chance. Boys for different reasons are being spirited away from the school and into the blue yonder. Never seen again."

"This is a notion that has an appeal—we now know—for Rapson! He himself has an unwanted, defective and expensive offspring round his neck. I think the victim of blackmail became himself a blackmailer. Instead of rushing to the police, he confronted the villains he uncovered and made them an offer: 'Extend your services to me as a personal favour for not blowing the gaff. I have another little job for you.'"

"What a fool!"

"Not the brightest. He took on a cold and clinical organisation who deal in death."

"Death, sir? You'd go that far? I was thinking on the lines of segregation or sterilisation. The loony bin or the snip. Possibly both?"

"There was one *eu* word the doctor didn't utter. The second part of it is another Greek word: *thanatos. Death.* An easy death. Let's call them a Euthanasian Society. I think these birds went along with Rapson as far as sending the car after dark to make the pickup. But something went wrong. The child escapes, or is never presented, or was never going to be taken, the car takes off into the night, and Rapson staggers back, dying of knife wounds. Having got his comeuppance?"

"We need to look again at that courtyard when the snow's finally disappeared." Martin's voice suddenly held a ray of hope.

"Who knows what tale it may be able to tell us if we look in the right places, sir. This organisation—I like the sound of that. Several people involved, are we thinking?"

"Almost certainly. Rapson, I'm sure, must have worked out that if there is such an organisation in place, it very likely features the headmaster. Farman. The man who attends the meetings of the Eugenics Education Society. The man who has no time for anyone of less than human perfection."

"Unless it's himself, of course. Farman! You'd be looking at him a long time before you thought of Adonis! I can't see it, sir. Eugenist by conviction, I'll grant you that, but cold-blooded murderer? Naw! He'd preach 'em to death, but I doubt he'd lay a finger on one. I can't see him shoving a child off a cliff one dark night."

"Nor can I, Martin. I think he's just a cog in a much greater machine. He's an enabler—does the word exist? Oh, Lord! I find myself trying to avoid euphemisms after Carter's little pep talk! He's a sort of Charon. Not killing the children himself but ferr—oh, my God!"

Joe stood, unable to move, mind racing.

"You all right sir? You look as though you've seen a ghost."

"I have." Joe shuddered. "A ghastly, grey-garbed, pitiless figure. Charon. Do you know what the headmaster's name is in German? A horrible coincidence? I'm not superstitious or particularly credulous, Martin, but this makes my blood run cold. It was Gosling who said it—as a joke. 'Herr Fahrmann,' he called him. *Fahrmann*. In German that's *the Ferryman*."

"By God! Funny that! Makes you think. I wonder where he's stashed all those obols he's collected for punting the kids across to the Underworld?"

"That's a very copper-ish thought!" Joe grinned. His smile faded quickly. "But I'll replace it with something more sober—I fear we have one lost soul still adrift on the river."

"Maybe *two*, sir. Did you notice that file Carter had on his desk at the ready when we went in?"

"I did. I thought he was going to refer to it, but he didn't."

"He was surprised when you opened up with the Bellefoys. That wasn't what he was prepared for."

"Did you catch the name on the file, Martin? Weston? Means nothing to me."

"Means something to *me*! I put a sergeant in charge of it. That blacksmith's son who went missing Tuesday. Jem Weston's lad, Walter. Now, why was the doc expecting to be grilled about little Walter? I'll get hold of my sergeant. I was going to call him off the inquiry, but I'll leave it open a bit longer. Take responsibility myself."

"Another thread, Martin? Give it a tug! Use your local clout!"

"Ah, yes, thinking of local clout, sir, did I hear you say I'd managed to twist a magistrate's arm to sign one of your search warrants—and all before breakfast? I don't remember bursting in on old Brigadier Murchison as he buttered his toast. How come?"

Joe passed the headed sheet over to his colleague. "Forged, of course. I always carry one. One day some bugger will twig, insist on studying the small print and challenge the signature, and then I'll have to do a bit of fast thinking, but it's held good so far! Now, race you to the telephone!"

CHAPTER 23

Gosling was hopping from foot to foot at the bottom of the back stairs as they clattered in, Joe a few yards ahead of the inspector.

He launched straight into his message. "Masterson's reported back, sir!" He looked warily at Martin.

"Go ahead. Martin needs to know. Our cases have become one, Gosling."

"Very well. The Spielmans are on the move! Herr S. has signed off at the Embassy. Masterson thinks his role there was temporary, cooked up or clandestine. Anyway, short-lived. According to Messrs. Thomas Cook, he's booked a passage back to Berlin with his wife and son. Three tickets. They take the boat train and arrive in Dover to catch the morning ferry. That's tomorrow morning, sir. Masterson is arranging for one of our operatives to watch them from the station. But, sir, watch is all we can do. You do realise that a man in his position has diplomatic immunity? Officially, he can come and go by any conveyance without question. No way we can hassle him."

"Where are they now?"

"Gone to ground! They've checked in at a small hotel near the station. Two of them. They don't yet have their son with them, sir."

"Awaiting delivery from wherever he's spent the last two days, are we thinking? But in what condition? Did you get any hints from the other parents of the disappeared, Gosling? Any luck?"

"Not much." He held out a notebook. "I didn't ring Alicia, of course. I know her responses, and I don't want to raise her hopes. She starts every conversation with the same words: 'Have you found him yet?'"

"She must know her son is dead, surely?" Joe asked gently. He had noted Gosling's tendresse for the mother of the missing Peterkin. Another little monkey hanging onto a furry substitute?

"Oh, yes. She's nobody's fool. She wants simply to know the truth and, at best, to bury her son."

The three men settled into Martin's ground-floor headquarters to continue their meeting. Joe rapidly filled Martin in on the background to the nine missing boys, and Martin took some pleasure in telling Gosling of the information they had dug out on the Eugenist Society.

Gosling looked anxiously at his watch and then at Joe. "Remember our appointment at the clinic, sir. I'll make this brief and give you my notes to look at while I drive."

Gosling launched into his resumé.

"Nil returns first. Eliminate the dead wood.

"Number one—still not a clue as to ID.

"Number two. Jefferson 1910. No good. Last male member died in the war. I got hold of a granny. Sharp memory though. Young Douglas died of the influenza. His death certificate is in the family archives. And will the school kindly stop pestering them now, she added."

"Ah! A footprint! Rapson was here before us."

"Number three. Murgatroyd. Major. Again—dead of the flu. Streetly-Standish had done his best, but to no avail. I asked about the minor Murgatroyds. Thriving, both of them, thank you. The mother—that's the second Mrs. M.—answered. Blessing in disguise. Their father died six years ago and the second son, hale and hearty and the apple of his mother's eye, has inherited the title. Poor dear Lascelles! He would never have been able to carry the burden of the estate. Not quite all there, you know."

"You manage to get *some* information over and above what's strictly necessary to answer your questions, Gosling?" Joe said, amused.

"It's the way I ask them, sir. Mothers—most of them—like to talk about their sons, dead or alive.

"Number four. Hewitt-Jones. The tick, sir. I got his father. None of our bloody business. What the hell was I expecting? What sort of a ghoul pokes about into children's deaths? Did I seriously expect to be granted a view of the death certificate? Pish! Tush! The rest was unrepeatable, sir.

"Number five. I managed to put a name to this one. Harrison. Tuberculosis. Father confirms he was shipped off to Switzerland but died there. Again, certificate available for inspection if I can be bothered.

"Number six. Pettigrew. The London grocer's son. Father hardly remembered the lad's name. Oh, yes, Clarence. Unmanageable boy. Could never have run the firm. It was decided to transfer him to another school, but before this could be effected, he died."

"Don't tell me? Of the flu?"

"No. His body was fished out of the river, ten miles from St. Magnus. Assumed to have run off in a temper. He was very headstrong. Death certificate available for inspection, the father told me. It's a chorus line, sir! Death by drowning, two doctors' signatures on the document. And, suspiciously—Was I the interfering rogue who'd pestered his wife a month ago?

"Number seven. Peterkin, sir.

"Number eight. Houghton-Cole. The arsonist. Parents not at home. I got the butler. Expelled from the school and died of the measles shortly after. The body had been cremated, he added—with a touch of satisfaction, I thought.

"Number nine. Renfrew. Transferred to Templemeadows. I rang them first. Not on the roll, never has been. Parents have gone abroad. Still trying on that one, sir."

Joe clutched the sides of his head in a rare moment of despair. "There's a grim, unthinkable pattern coming out of all this, don't you think, Gosling? Do you see it? And a refrain. Do you hear it?"

"More clearly than you perhaps, sir. 'Blessing in disguise.' 'All for the best.' I've heard their lying voices on the telephone. Go ahead—say it, sir."

"Enough of these boys to arouse my suspicion had a background of inadequacy of some kind. Physically, mentally below parental expectations or—as with Peterkin—simply in the way of financial gain. You repeat for me the phrases of excuse. Justification: 'He could never have run the family business . . . his brighter, younger brother has succeeded (thank God!)' My worst fear—and I long for you to tell me I'm being ridiculous, Gosling—is that some—not all—of these parents are guilty of procuring the deaths of their own offspring for what they would probably call eugenic reasons. Bad apples . . . defective genetic systems . . . should be eliminated."

"But how do they come to know a ferry service to oblivion exists? That it has its port of departure here at St. Magnus?"

"The membership list. How many of these parents or guardians are members, I wonder? We shall see."

"God! Can't you imagine it?" Gosling exclaimed. "The conversation between leather armchairs at the club . . . whisky in hand . . . 'I say, that's quite a problem you have there, old man.'" He was suddenly speaking with the bluff tones of a man twice his age. "'Quite understand. You're not the first it's happened to, you know. Oh, no. Other names would surprise you, but—lips are sealed, of course. There are remedies, however, for those brave enough to avail themselves of them. Steps to be taken—that *ought* to be taken for the sake of Family, Society and Empire. Indeed, it would be unforgivable to neglect to take the steps. Merely doing one's duty.'"

"They might add at a practical level—and never forget, Gosling, that these are intensely practical people we are dealing with—that the matter can safely be taken out of the family's hands if the problem is committed to the care of such and such a school. There would be peripheral expenses to meet, of course. Nothing out of the ordinary. This is an ethical and prophylactic service after all, not remotely venal."

Martin absorbed all this and expressed a shared despair: "But there's nothing there that we can go with. No foothold! It's good work Gosling's done, but what have we got? Documented deaths. Tied up, signed for, obols in mouth, and gone across the river."

Gosling was silent for a moment. Then: "Oh, come on, sir! Let's unleash Hercules! One last sprint for the finish, eh? I reckon we can get to this clinic in less than two hours. An hour if I put my foot down. We can't leave this last stone unturned. And worth upending, I'd say. One medico fingering another—that's always worth a look. For Alicia Peterkin?"

"For Alicia," Joe agreed. "Come on then, and as we go I'll fill in more details of Rapson's dirty past. See you later, Martin. Have the kettle on for five o'clock."

He threw the keys to Gosling.

WHEN THEY ARRIVED at the car they were greeted by a cry of relief. "Where've you been? I thought I was going to have to do this by myself."

"Out, Dorcas! Go back. You're not wanted on voyage."

"James would want me to be here. I know the place. It knows me."

"You think that's an advantage? I've balanced your familiarity against the fact that—if my fanciful deductions prove halfway accurate—we're in for trouble. And I don't mean a bout of fisti-cuffs between gents. I mean violence, possibly guns. We may be challenging men who have careers, reputations—lives—at stake. They are ruthless and won't think twice about engineering the swift disappearance of anyone who threatens them. That includes you. Whatever would I say to Sir James?" Joe had aimed for light, but he heard waspish. "Off you go. I'll tell you all about it over dinner."

"Just as well I packed my Smith & Wesson with the ham sandwiches, then. I've got a flask of coffee and some of cook's flapjack too. I've been raiding the kitchens. They'll let you have anything if you say it's for that lovely Mr. Gosling: 'Sweet boy, far too good for them.' I'll feed you as we go because I know you haven't had any lunch."

Gosling licked his lips. "Flapjack, sir!"

"A sop for Cerberus? A low trick, Dorcas! As I seem to be lumbered with the pair of you, I'd better tell you what transpired at the doctor's earlier. Missing boys seem to be turning into some-thing of epidemic proportions in the county."

JOE LET OUT a low whistle of appreciation as they rounded a bend and were offered a glimpse of the clinic they were seeking through a copse of tall elms.

"Saint Raphael Clinic," a brass plate announced on one of the gateposts at the bottom of the drive.

"Raphael is the patron saint of healing," Dorcas supplied. "And, of course, an archangel."

"I'm more interested in the architect," Joe said. "This is very good. Walter Gropius, are we thinking, rather than Edwin Lutyens? But—clinic—isn't that a bit modest? This is a vast building. How old, Dorcas. Any idea?"

"Five years at the most. It's way ahead of its time, don't you think?"

Joe exchanged looks with Gosling. "Five years? That all? Ah! We had hoped for something a little older. Thirty years perhaps. At least."

"Well, if it's old you want, try the village. Edenhurst. It's full of ancient and lovely things. There's a row of almshouses. St. Raphael Sanctuaries for the deserving and aged poor or something like that. They keep a dozen old ladies there, rent free. Under the terms of the original foundation."

"Original foundation? What was that?"

"No trace left. They bulldozed what was here to make room for what you see now. There was a hospital of sorts—all red brick and gloom, you can imagine. That had, in turn, replaced an earlier medieval building."

"Burial ground? Any vestiges?"

"Yes, if you look over there to the east. It's hidden by the line of the private wing. It was flattened and grassed over when the work was going on—too bothersome to excavate, I'd say. And, farther off yet, there's—cleverly camouflaged by a change of brick colour against the hillside behind—the essential part of a hospital that everyone wants to ignore: the incinerator."

"For disposing of unwanted material," Gosling said tersely. "Amputated limbs . . . laboratory animals . . . small boys."

"The whole complex belonged to the Anglo-Saxon church that originally occupied the site," Dorcas went on with deliberate calm. "There was once a church on this site. A large and very famous one. Famous especially for its sanctuary. Close enough to London, where all the villains were, then as now, it was the place criminals fled to, to hang on the sanctuary knocker. The sheriff's men couldn't touch them. It's said hundreds of villains found safety inside the walls. But of course they were trapped. The moment they put a nose outside, they were bagged."

"Let's hope the villains aren't still hanging about," Joe said.

"The knocker is. The lion's head sanctuary knocker. It's huge. It's been passed down from building to building I expect. They've mounted it on the present front door. Not at all in keeping with the modern lines, and I'll bet the architect had something to say! But the gesture's in keeping with tradition, and that's what people really want to see."

Gosling, with ten minutes to go before their appointment, was driving slowly, allowing time to look at the buildings. Gleaming rosily in the westering sun, the white brick managed to look at once welcoming, pure, and spare. Large plate glass windows caught and reflected back a golden light, wide and innocent as smiling eyes. The low-lying building sat easily against the undulating landscape of the North Downs, its straight lines contrasting with but not challenging the natural beauty that sheltered it. Two wings came forwards, ushering the visitor to a well-defined front entrance. A service road continued on around the back, Joe guessed, to the usual offices and hard-standing for ambulances and other vehicles, out of sight and not spoiling the uncluttered impact of the main building.

As they watched, a group of nurses came out and began to walk down the drive. Rosy cheeked and neat in their navy uniforms and capes, they chattered and laughed and waved amiably at the passengers in the Morris. Gosling pulled over to one side to allow a delivery van to pass them. As it swished by they read in a florid cartouche painted on the side: *Ernest Honeydew. Grocer. Purveyor of the cream of Sussex provender to the Gentry since 1813.*

Joe laughed. "Is that what they fed you on, Dorcas? Cream of provender?"

"Yes! It was very good. The students ate the same food as the private patients. I've never had lamb chops and lobster like it."

"Well, the Prince Albert it's not!" Gosling said. "All grow your own on the home farm. And, as Langhorne isn't here to oblige, I'll have to say it myself:

There's nothing ill can dwell in such a temple.
If the ill spirit have so fair a house
Good things will strive to dwell within it.

The Tempest, sir. Though I think Miranda was talking of a man she fancied rather than a building."

"But the one often reflects the other, don't you find?" Joe said. "There's a man's taste behind every brick laid, every window positioned. I wonder who we're to meet at the centre of this perfection? A Caliban—a born devil, thing of darkness—or an Ariel, who does his spiriting gently?" Joe mused.

"Just park the car with its nose facing outwards, will you, George?" Dorcas said impatiently. "And, Joe, will you check my pistol for me? I think I loaded it right but—better safe, eh?"

She pushed her battered leather student's satchel over to him.

"My God! There's a gun loose in here! A heavy one. Dorcas, that's insane! I don't even carry one myself these days. And certainly not out of a holster. Where did you get it? Do you even have a license for it?"

"Oh, stop fussing! I was given this by someone who is concerned for my safety. Who rather disapproves of the dubious places I frequent. In a professional capacity, of course. I like having it, and I know how to use it. I'm a good shot. I put the catch on, didn't I? I just get cold feet at the last moment—you know that uneasy feeling—did I turn the gas tap off? Did I remember to put the bullets in? Give it back!"

"Gosling? You? Do you have anything to declare? I like to know where the shots may be coming from, particularly when the troops firing them are standing behind me."

"They don't trust me with firearms yet. I only have my fists, sir."

"Then keep them in your pocket. There, that's safe," Joe said, handing the satchel back with reluctance. "You may hang on to it—provided you promise me it stays in the bag, and the bag stays on your shoulder! I'd keep it myself if I had somewhere to stow it. I don't want to go in bulging in unnatural places like a federal agent."

"Very well. You know where it is. Just ask if you need to borrow it."

"And, Gosling, leave that black briefcase of yours behind. We need our hands free. We don't want to be taken for tax inspectors."

Dorcas gave Joe a tender look. "Fusspots! Behaving like a pair of great crested grebes! *Übersprungshandlung.* That's what you're both demonstrating. Birds who can't decide whether to attack or flee sometimes just go away and peck grass. You don't want to get on and do the next thing so you find other trivial things to distract you. Gentlemen, if you're ready?"

CHAPTER 24

Gosling darted out ahead. "Let me do the knocker, sir!"
Joe hung back and watched him reach out a hand to
pat the shining brass head of the lion that managed to return his
wide grin despite the heavy ring in its mouth. "Well done, old
son! Glad you were there over the years. And glad you've survived,"
Gosling muttered with gruff affection, then he seized the ring
and banged.

"You know—I think I've been wrong about that boy," Joe
admitted.

"You may excuse yourself for that. I'd guess Gosling has been
wrong about himself," Dorcas said mysteriously. "For many a year."
She stuck a head through the window and called out a bit of
advice: "George, we usually use the electric bell."

"No," said Joe, "Let him ask for sanctuary in the time-hon-
oured manner. I'm all in favour of taking out a bit of insurance—
you never know."

They were expected, at least. A stately dame in crisp uniform
and a very fancy white starched and pleated head dress was
waiting behind the door. She flung it wide and stood back to
admit them.

"Melinda Mallinson. Matron. Do come in! I rather expected
you'd be bang on time. A.C. Sandilands and Mr. Gosling. And—

of course—our Miss Joliffe! How lovely to see you again, Dorcas. Not much time! Follow me, please."

She turned and gave them a bracing smile. "Try to keep up now! Nuns and nurses—always on the trot!"

Joe hoped he'd be able to find his way back out of this maze of corridors unaided if it came to it, but he couldn't be certain. As they scurried along he registered left and right turns, noted markers on walls and doors, using locating techniques taught him by an old jungle hand. This place with its myriad rooms, all with activities going on behind closed doors, made the hairs stand on the back of his neck as the trees of the Indian forests had done. Unknown territory. Hostile. Be wary!

A door was flung open as they passed, and a mother holding two children by the hand emerged, smiling and calling good-byes to the young doctor who held the door open for her. "Yes, Robin. Didn't I say we could go home on the bus if you were good boys? Come along, Benjamin. It's this way."

Joe calmed himself.

"Here we are. You're very punctual. Shall I send along a cup of tea? Would this be too early?"

"Thank you, no, Matron. We're not expecting to linger."

Matron leaned to them confidingly. "Thank you for saying that. Most understanding! I ought to tell you that the professor has an evening engagement up in London. He's addressing the Royal Scientific Society, and he really must catch the four thirty train from Tunbridge."

Professor Byam Alexander Bentink was as welcoming as his staff.

He came forwards to shake their hands as Matron performed the introductions. "Sandilands . . . Gosling . . . and—oh, no! Keep her off!" His hands went up in mock protest as he made a heavily playful show of catching sight of Dorcas, who had been hanging back.

"Miss Joliffe I know already—to my cost. Back to haunt us, Joliffe? I thought they'd given you the sack!"

Joe could not take offence at the rudeness on her behalf since the stranger making the comments appeared disarmingly amused by them. His appearance was reassuringly familiar. Joe had been taking orders from men who looked like this all his fighting life: men in their element astride cavalry chargers, atop war elephants, teeth to the wind on the bridge of a battle cruiser. Here was a tall, spare man of middle years with wide shoulders from which hung a starched white laboratory coat. Carelessness or a statement? Joe would have taken it off before greeting guests. The broad features looked like nothing so much as a relief map of the Trossachs, Joe thought, admiring. Nothing understated here. Ridges and valleys wound their way through a weather-beaten landscape occasionally enlivened by an outcrop of bristling mustache and matching eyebrow. The eyes were as deep and as grey as Loch Katrine. A thick hedge of dark hair streaked with grey framed the whole impressive countenance. Forceful and confident.

"If this man decides to tell me I'm barking mad, I shall have to believe him," Joe concluded. He would have guessed a Scot like himself but for the very English name and the very St. James's accent.

"Not at all, professor," Dorcas said demurely.

Only Joe would have known from her first words that she disliked Professor Bentink.

"A sense of humour prevailed, I'm glad to say, and I was forgiven," she said lightly. "'Student prankster' I believe my record shows for the world to see. But not sacked at all."

"Mmm. Do I detect the influence of my tender-hearted brother-in-law? I think I do! Pulling strings again! James was ever susceptible to a pretty face!"

A second insult. Joe's fists clenched, and he opened his mouth to go on the attack but, intercepting a warning shake of the head from Dorcas, closed it again.

Gosling, however, was off the leash and running free. "Well! Lucky old St. Raphael to have enjoyed the services of an attractive researcher, eh?" he said cheerily. "I've been trying to recruit Miss Joliffe myself—tempt her into taking on a permanent post with my own firm. Intelligence, diligence and a university education will always get you our attention. Add beauty and spirit to the mix, and she's a dead cert."

Bentink turned his gaze on the earnest young face. He couldn't have been more surprised if the doorknob had spoken. "Your firm? And what *is* this business of yours, young man, may I ask?"

"It's *The* Firm, professor. And our business is the Defence of the Realm."

The capital letters were audible.

Joe stifled his astonishment.

Bentink broke into a broad smile. "Indeed? Well, well! I'm delighted to hear that our aims coincide." He dropped his voice a little. "Though I would advise caution, young man. Reticence. I'm sure we ought neither of us to be talking of the projects nearest to our heart. This little pitcher," he pointed at Dorcas with joking reproof, "has big ears. And a lively tongue. There'd be a fluttering and a tutting in the bureaux at Oliver House, Cromwell Road, if they could hear you declaring yourself so openly in her presence. Your Director Kell would appreciate it, I'm sure, if I were to send her to wait in the next room."

"It's all right, sir. Miss Joliffe has been processed, sworn, and signed and all that," Gosling lied with confidence. "You could say she's one of us. Though she's still in training and has yet to commit herself to a permanent position. It's rather like becoming a nun, sir. There's always an escape clause."

Bentink listened to this nonsense, not in the least taken in by it.

"If you say so. Tell me: Brigadier Glancy—settled in at the Irish desk, has he?"

"No, sir," Gosling said, patiently playing the game, "I've never heard of him. There is a new man in the post you mention, but I'm not at liberty to mention his name."

"Can we get down to business" Joe said sternly, "after that shower of shibboleths? We all know who we are."

Bentink appeared to capitulate. He smiled and spread his hands to indicate the chairs set out in front of his desk. "Sit down, all of you, and we'll continue with the entertainment, though quite what form this should take I'm not certain. Do I get out the cards? Propose you for membership of my club? Suggest a dram or two of my excellent Islay whisky?"

When he had them settled in a row in front of him, too like an audience for Joe's comfort, he went on more crisply: "I'm assuming from Mr. Gosling's reticence-shattering admission that we're all in each other's confidence and may speak freely. An enterprise like mine is investigative, experimental, controversial, and—quite rightly—comes in for the usual government supervision. And I expect that's what you are imposing on me now. Checking I'm not swapping secrets of mind-control with the Russkies, eh? Tedious, time-wasting nonsense, but one learns to accommodate it. But, Scotland Yard involvement? This is a new departure. I'd like to know why Sandilands is here."

"A courtesy call, professor," said Joe amiably. "You will have observed no squad cars, no secretary. . . . I don't even bring a notebook. I feel I ought to apologise for our lack of political clout or motivation. I'll come straight to our problem. A child went missing in the wilds of Sussex yesterday morning. A sick child. An epileptic child. In transit from his school on the south coast to his home in London, he was conveyed to a hospital whose identity we do not know, and he's not been seen since. Much turbulence and anxiety at both the school and the family home.

Inevitably, 'Who do we know at the Yard?' is the question on everyone's lips. And the answer, predictably: Commissioner Trenchard. My boss asked me to investigate."

"Ah. And sleuth that you are, you pounce on the word 'epilepsy' and pop round to see me?"

"In a nutshell, sir."

"True, the condition was, at one time, a special study of mine, though I am involved with larger subjects these days. His name? . . . Spielman? No. I'm almost certain—not on our books. But wait."

He opened the door to an adjoining room and called into it: "Miss Stevens! Check a patient name for me, will you? Spielman." He spelled it out with an eye on Joe, who nodded confirmation.

A moment later his secretary appeared in the doorway holding a file. "Sorry, sir, no one of that name. This is the nearest I could get."

She held out a file discreetly, the name hidden from view. Bentink, with a gesture that said he had nothing to hide, took it and read out loud: "Speerman. Ah. A miss is as good as a mile. Sorry, gentlemen."

The secretary reclaimed the file and withdrew.

"I have a photograph," Joe said. He reached into his breast pocket and took out the ten cut-outs, selecting the picture of Spielman.

Bentink took it from him and looked at it without much interest. "No. I have never encountered this child." He looked with slightly more curiosity at the remaining photographs in Joe's hand.

Joe began to lay them out in front of Bentink. He was suddenly stricken with embarrassment to see the crudely cut shapes, which were beginning to curl up on themselves like brandy snaps sitting incongruously on the sleek ebony surface of the desk. An automatic gesture from Bentink revealed that he was having the same reaction—he put out a pad of three manicured fingers and flattened the one nearest to him. Joe flinched to see the small face obliterated.

Bentink caught Joe's hesitation. "Odd things the Yard has in its pockets! What are you showing me? A new parlour game? Spot the Criminal of the Future? That's easy! *He* is. Number six."

Bentink poked a finger at one of the faces, pushing Pettigrew, the grocer's son, out of line. "Hard to judge at this age, of course, before the features are sufficiently developed but—speaking purely as a participant in a parlour game—I'd keep an eye on this little thug, Sandilands! A client in the making, if ever I saw one.

"Number three—a tragedy—is a mongoloid type," he rattled on, enjoying himself. "They don't have much of a hold on life, you know. A goner by now? This snap wasn't taken yesterday.

"Number five is ill. Possibly tubercular? I'd have him seen to.

"Number eight—troubled face. Haunted. He's not seeing what we see. Has he—what's your phrase?—got form, commissioner?"

"Arsonist," Joe said, and the response seemed to please the professor.

"Quite a rogues' gallery. Wouldn't breed from any of 'em—apart from number seven, who looks perfectly normal."

"Lucky you're taking this as a game," Joe said with asperity, "or I'd have to think that, in your eyes, the last-century views of Cesare Lambroso still held good. The bony forehead, the large jaw, the prominent eye ridges: sure signs of a born-in-the-bone criminality." He allowed his gaze for the briefest moment to skate across Bentink's uncompromising features.

The professor almost smiled. "I think Charles Goring refuted all that," he replied easily. "But you would know more than I on that subject. Never forget, Sandilands, you and I both have this in common with Socrates: We're neither of us oil paintings. Could both scare the horses if the light was right. But you, I'd judge, were at least *born* attractive. Fate clearly took a scalpel to those handsome features, but by then you'd learned that appearance is related to self-worth and behaviour. Handsome is as handsome does. I often note that."

"In fairy tales, perhaps," Joe mused. "Not necessarily in the street or the laboratory."

"Certainly not in Parliament. And that's a pity. We must be forwards-looking, Sandilands, if we're to maintain our position in the world. To be the best, we must breed the best."

He cut himself short, sat back, and fixed Joe with a suddenly weary look. He waved a hand over the photographs. "Interesting, but—in answer to your question—I haven't bumped off any of these boys."

"I don't believe I asked that question."

"Oh, come on! Met Officers don't carry around photographs of boys who are alive and well and toasting crumpets for tea this Saturday afternoon. They're missing, presumed dead, and you're investigating. I'm sorry, but I can't help you."

He slid the pictures roughly into a pile like cards with Spielman on top. "This boy. The most recent? Epileptic? Sad. Had the child been brought to us here, we would have been able to treat him, I'm sure. But—'lost,' you say? An 'unknown' hospital? I find this difficult to understand. An odd set of circumstances, wouldn't you say?"

"Yes, and imposed by the vagaries of the English weather. February. Telephone lines down, roads blocked. The boy's family is about to return to Germany, and they're finding their plans disrupted. Various people have involved themselves in lending a hand. You see before you a selection of those Good Samaritans."

"A German family, you say . . . Spielman. . . ."

"Diplomatic service."

"Not just any child, then. Embassy involved? Guaranteed to whip up a froth. I begin to see why they've got you chasing about the countryside, Sandilands. Our German cousins are exercising an ever stronger influence over our top brass. Hah! Gosling! I know you're understaffed in the Cromwell Road, but you're also blinkered. Focused on the Red Menace and the Green, Russia and Ireland. Have I at last got through to your superiors with the suggestion that they give more attention to the old enemy? Germany! I was over there last year with a delegation, on a professional visit. Cozying up, breathing admiration, swearing eternal friendship, meeting their top scientists. Not being classed as a top scientist myself, I was paired with a policeman. A certain Rudolph Diels. Heard of him? No? You'd better do some homework, then. Because you *will* hear of him. Impressive fellow! Young and vigorous, gallantly scarred face of a duellist, and head of the Prussian Political Police. We had a long conversation about the work he is commissioning from men like me—from my German confrères, that is."

"Work for which the National Socialist government sees a need?" Joe asked.

"Ah, yes. All spies cozily together as we are, I suppose I may divulge these things. Just a few days into his new office—the thirtieth of January, wasn't it, the election victory? Mere days! Chancellor Hitler is sweeping through government. Heads are rolling. Resignations being tendered, appointments being made. That's probably what your Spielman is up to. Been recalled to do his patriotic duty at the side of his new master. And we see changes already in the university psychology departments. Jews—or those who merely have a Jewish wife—who have been at the forefront of research are packing up and coming to England or crossing the Atlantic. Before any lecture can begin in the universities—you'll find this hard to believe—the academic giving it is now required, on pain of instant dismissal, to salute and say the words 'Heil Hitler!'"

He gave a low rumbling laugh. "Just imagine! If I were to

stand before a hundred students in a London lecture theatre, raise my right hand, and proclaim 'All hail MacDonald!'"

"The outcome would be much the same, professor," Joe said easily. "You'd lose your post. But the charge in England would be one of imbecility."

"And well deserved!" Bentink agreed. "But over there—you know how it is. You've fought these fellows. Highly efficient, but soldier ants. No sense of the ridiculous."

"Not all, sir," Joe murmured. "Not all."

"Oh, yes. If it's exceptions you look for, look no further than the director (for the present moment!) of the Berlin Psychological Institute. Wolfgang Köhler is finding all this saluting rubbish a bit hard to comply with. He performs the action but with all the eager anticipation of a vegetarian who's just been served with a juicy steak. But most have accepted the situation—politics and leanings in a country that has never been democratic are less compelling when large grants are on offer to any prepared to stick their arms in the air and make a Roman salute."

He sighed and shook his shaggy head. "It seems what we have now is a *Ganzheitpsychologie*. The larger unity, the nation—the *Volk*, if you like—overrides the interests and rights of the individual. The plan is to put German applied psychology to the service of the National Socialist government, which values it."

"A science-backed Nazi ideology," Joe murmured. "Interesting. You are well informed, professor."

"And shall be even better informed when I return from the Dresden conference in April." He gave Gosling a knowing look. "Confidential exchanges over the port with your top brass on the cards, young Gosling? I think so. As Miss Joliffe will confirm, the Prussians are more generously funded, less heavily supervised by government, and more adventurous in their approach. Imaginative, ruthless and productive—they are most impressive. And they are not our friends. No matter what the *Times* leader writers tell us."

Puzzled as to where he was going with this, Joe picked up an odd point that had intrigued him. "You are not regarded as a top-ranking scientist, you say?"

"Not quite yet. And certainly not in our own country. Psychology? What's that? Ask a selection of people in Piccadilly, and one third will say it's to do with the spirit world, one third will say it's to do with sex, and the remaining third will say it's a load of bollocks. Ask the same question on the *Kurfürstendamm*, and they'll tell you it's a practical science that will solve the nation's problems."

He was wasting their time deliberately with the useless generalities of a man propping up the bar at his local pub. In five minutes he'd look at his watch and claim he had to bustle off to his next appointment, so sorry not to have been of more help. Joe decided to push things along.

"The headmaster at the school—St. Magnus—from which the boy Spielman disappeared sends his regards, by the way. And he hopes you found some benefit in the use of the twins he sent you for research last term."

Bentink bowed his head briefly in automatic acknowledgement but seemed not to remember the name.

"Mr. Farman is the headmaster. I believe you know him from your mutual membership of the Eugenic Society?"

Bentink's brow furrowed. "Ah—the Brighton chapter? Yes, now you come to mention it. Farman. Got him! He takes the stage occasionally. Corpulent old windbag. But a true and tenacious spirit, I have to say."

"One of a strong series. The two previous headmasters were equally supportive of the eugenic cause, I understand."

"It passes down the generations. The young absorb knowledge and resolve at their father's knee. Nature *and* nurture in harmony. Supporting each other. Fatuous to argue about which is the more influential. Miss Joliffe will tell you. Good genes, good family are the lifeblood of this country, Sandilands, but we must never disregard the effect of a good upbringing working with them. My father was a guiding light in the Eugenic Education Society, as it was called originally. My brother-in-law James's father also. He was a contemporary of Galton, you know, and one of the founder members. You could say we were a eugenic family. Tribe, even, since we make a point of making strong bonds with each other's family."

He paused to allow this to sink in, his face stiff with pride.

"*Good wombs have borne bad sons*, Shakespeare tells us," Gosling remarked annoyingly. "Really, he's said it all, hasn't he? Who needs psychology when we have the wisdom of the Bard to guide and inform?"

Bentink waited with a pained expression for the interruption to be over, then he bent a keen look on Joe. "Many of your own profession, Sandilands, are eugenists, if not in practice, at least in spirit. But then you, a policeman, would consider yourself to be in the front rank of the struggle against degeneracy. And so you are! Hats off to you! Your profession has our support and our sympathy. London—the Great Wen!—with its pullulating underclasses, is consuming ever more of the country's resources. Most unfairly. The willing, the able and the well-bred of our country are struggling to fund the feckless and the incapable. A sparrow feeding a cuckoo! The crime rate rises at the very time when the London bobby himself is challenged to riposte. I hear it is ever more difficult to recruit men of a certain stature—physical and moral—to combat this fast-breeding, self-propagating slime. No consolation, but they find they have much the same problems to confront in Germany.

"The difference between our approaches being that *they* take it seriously and are prepared for—indeed, are already engaged in—taking practical steps to combat the threat."

He got to his feet. "And now, gentlemen, I leave you to make a tour of inspection if that would amuse you. Take Matron along if you wish. Alternatively, take Miss Joliffe—she knows the building inside out, inquisitive little creature that she is. You may go about wherever you please."

Joe spoke ritual words of departure. ". . . and thank you for taking the time to see us, professor," he said politely. "We'll leave you now to practice your salute."

There was a tense moment as Ben Lomond crashed into Ben Levi in the craggy expanse of the face. Bentink managed to turn his frown into a benign smile as they left.

"Lord, Dorcas!" Joe whispered. "Whatever did you put in that man's boots?"

"I know one of the lab technicians. I asked him to get me a particularly obnoxious sample of monkey diarrhea."

CHAPTER 25

They walked disconsolately down corridors, occasionally peering into rooms that appeared to be unoccupied, ducking out of busy wards with murmured apologies to the duty nurses, preoccupied and getting nowhere with their token inspection.

"Sir, could you work out what that bloke's point of view was? After all that chat, I couldn't say whether he approves of the Nazi new boys or hates their guts," Gosling said when they reached a deserted corridor.

"I was wondering if he knows himself. Many people are ambivalent. I'd say he started out by making vaguely antagonistic noises to draw a reaction from us. To find out where we stand. Was he reassured by the stiffness of our upper lips, Gosling? By our flamboyantly patriotic professions? Possibly. But I think it was his own instinct for glory-seeking and empire-building that swept him into a revelation, towards the end, of something much nastier. Well, nasty by my lights. Admiration for the new regime? Fascination?"

"You don't know the half of it!" Dorcas said. "It's obsession! It's my belief he won't return from Dresden! Your crack about the saluting really shook him. I think he's heard the siren song of prestige and unlicensed power."

"We came here for Spielman, not to put Bentink's psyche under the microscope," Joe reminded them.

"We may not know what we're looking for, but we ought to make a serious start and stop casting about like a pack of masterless hounds," was Gosling's suggestion.

"Just one more ward," Joe advised. "Keep your heads down. We've still got company! And we do know what we're looking for. We're looking for the Lethal Chamber," he said grimly.

"Don't be mealy mouthed! The Killing Room, in blunt old Anglo-Saxon," Dorcas said. "We won't find it anywhere close to these scenes of well-regulated medical care."

"Where's she taking us, sir?" Gosling wanted to know as they left the Edith Cavell Ward and their pace along the corridor accelerated.

Dorcas stopped, looking about her, and spoke urgently to them. "We've been given free rein, so he's very confident we'll find nothing. But I'm not wandering into this maze completely clueless. Think of the architecture—flat roof, so nothing over our heads. Modern, so no archaic features like cellars and basements. It'll be on the ground floor with easy access to the rear for entry and disposal. Away from public and patient areas. Only one way to go. The animal research lab. No casual enquirer would go into that menagerie out of choice."

MINUTES LATER THEY stood surveying cages and operating benches in a very long room, empty and scrubbed clean. White tiles and chrome pipes gleamed. The air was redolent of pine-scented disinfectant.

"Nothing here," Gosling said, running a careful eye around the walls. "All activity abandoned, you'd say. A dead end."

He jumped, startled, to find a green-coated technician had appeared at his side.

After a soft cry of recognition, Dorcas seized the stranger by the sleeve and drew him forwards. "George, Joe, this is someone I know. It's Adam. He's one of the animal stewards. He cares for the creatures in their main quarters in the village and presents them here in the holding cages ready for experimentation and . . . clears up afterward."

"Miss Joliffe!" The red-haired boy could not have been more than seventeen. He had eyes only for Dorcas, and his pale, sharp features flooded with relief. "I saw you come. My letter? You got it?"

"I did, Adam. That's why we're here. Thank you. Wheels in motion. These two gentlemen are inspectors from London. They'll know what to do. Not much time. What have you to show us?"

"We should be all right. I watched the boss take off in his Rolls for the station a quarter of an hour ago. You were tracked as far as Cavell Ward. Then Matron decided you were a waste of time, gave up, and went for a cuppa." He looked anxiously behind him. "Or else she passed on the baton."

"I don't believe we were followed this far," Joe said.

Adam gave an uneasy grin. "Don't be too sure. You didn't see *me*. Nobody sees a bloke in a green coat pushing a trolley. And I'm one of a dozen. So prepare for a swift bailout. There's a back exit. You needn't cross Matron again."

"This is where the boss torments baby animals?" Joe said, looking about him at the cheerless cages with dismay.

"Sir!" Adam turned an anxious look on him. "That's bad enough, but it's worse than that. Tell him, Miss Joliffe!"

"Yes, Miss Joliffe," Joe said invitingly, turning to her with a politely enquiring expression. "You've got our attention! Something you've been working towards for quite a while. Perhaps you'll tell us why you've lured us to this charming spot?"

"I told you about the experiment that was abandoned. There were six of us students present to witness the torment. You can't imagine what an inferno of pain and screams this room was!

Afterward, three of the students went away to write up notes, and three of us stayed behind."

"It took courage, sir," said Adam stoutly. "I was proud to hear them speak out!"

"We faced up to the professor and demolished—at the time we thought we were demolishing—his experiment in no uncertain terms. We gave him what for, Joe."

"Ouch! And his response?"

"He demolished *us*. All three of us. Sacked us on the spot. 'Leave the hospital at once!' What's more, he told us we lacked the qualities to be students of psychology in his university and he was going to have the Chancellor strike us off."

"But you didn't leave it there?"

"No. I went straight to Sir James and told him everything. He listened. He laughed at me and explained that no laws of any kind had been broken and that his brother-in-law had a point. This was a scientific field of enquiry. He thought I was being overemotional, but he was sympathetic. He talked to people, and the upshot was that all three of us were quietly reinstated. We never came back here, of course."

"Until today."

"Adam had seen the whole grisly scene, and afterward he helped me."

"With information, sir. And I warned her as how there were other things—worse things—no students ever clapped eyes on, and she gave me her address at the university."

"Three weeks ago I got a note from Adam. I rushed round to James to show him, and he was shocked. He'd suspected his brother-in-law was capable and probably culpable of unpleasant behaviour—"

"Hold it there, Dorcas. Why suspected? Who had alerted him? Did you ask yourself? Bentink doesn't go about with A for Arsehole branded on his forehead."

"He didn't say, but I believed him when he said he'd no idea how far it went. He could hardly take on Bentink, the most respected psychologist in the country and a director of a prestigious hospital with royal funding. The British Establishment will do anything to avoid a hint of a scandal. You know that, Joe; you're a part of it. You and Gosling, both. James thought the best plan was to attack this . . . this . . . cancer with a scalpel. He spoke with Commissioner Trenchard, and they decided to get the evidence—clandestinely if necessary—then face him with his iniquity and force him into a discreet resignation at the least, the gun and the brandy on the terrace with MI5 to witness it at best."

"Heavens!" Joe said. "What on earth did you put in your letter, Adam? That resulted in *me*—an honest copper—being shoved down this rat hole like a ferret?"

White-faced and earnest, the boy squared up to him. "I need this job, sir. I don't go getting into mischief lightly. The animals, I get too fond of 'em. I know that, and I can hide it—master it, needs must. If *I* weren't here, looking out for them, there's those who aren't too particular. But what I can't stomach is the children, sir."

"Children?" Gosling exclaimed in disgust. "They allow children to come down here? What are they thinking of? It's not a zoo!"

"You haven't understood, sir!" Adam's anguish was hobbling his tongue. He struggled to force out: "Animals are not good enough for his purposes, it seems. He's moved on to humans. Children."

"He's not the first, Joe. There are rumours that Pavlov himself was not content to experiment with dogs. He worked on children."

"Pavlov? But he's Russian! This isn't bloody Russia!"

"Come and have a look next door, sir. That's where it all goes on."

Adam went to the far side of the room and produced a key from his pocket. He slid aside a chrome panel to reveal a keyhole.

"Ah. The Locked Door! A touch of the Gothick at last in this monument to modernity!" Gosling's light remark covered his fear and incredulity, Joe thought.

The space beyond proved to be a suite of three rooms. The two smaller ones were study and filing space for documents. The largest was evidently the operating theatre, though Joe struggled to find a different word, a word to encompass the horrors he sensed had occurred in this grotesque space.

"It's very white." Gosling was finding his powers of expression strained as Adam switched on blinding high-wattage lights.

"There's a reason for that, sir," Adam said.

A central, shaped couch at working height, clearly an operating table, was covered in some shiny white material that Joe had never seen before. He noted sockets in the walls on either side providing current for the electric wires that dangled from a peg. A range of fluids in laboratory glass containers were ranged neatly on the shelves of a bureau, and a copious sink and draining board occupied one corner. Hospital? Research laboratory? Torture chamber? It could have been any or all of these.

"This is where he brought them, sir. The gyspy children."

"Gypsies?"

"Don't expect that would be reported in the capital, but here in Sussex it was. Just once." Adam spoke roughly. "The gypsies have been complaining that children have disappeared from their camps. Makes a change! They're always being accused of stealing country children. T'other way round it makes you think there's something to it. Anyway—I know as there is. I told Miss Joliffe. And now you've come. I'll leave you to do what you have to do and go and keep an eye out."

Joe looked back uneasily, checking their line of retreat. "Wait! Bentink must have help. Apart from Matron, I mean. An operation so well organised depends on manpower. Manpower that stays vigilant and doesn't knock off at teatime. Who's still in the building, Adam?"

"The two medics he's hand in glove with are off for the weekend. But the heavies he uses are still on duty. There's only two, but they're big 'uns. The Trusties. Well paid. London blokes. Don't mix with the rest of us. Hobnailed boots but not thick heads. No, they're sharp lads as well as rough. They restrain the animals and the kids that get hysterical until someone can get the needle in."

"Where are they?"

"They were detailed to be on watch out there by the cages. Right now. Making sure you didn't get any further. I gave 'em a message. Nicked a sheet or two of the prof's writing paper last week in case of emergency, and I scribbled a note. Pretended I'd rushed it back from the car for him. An afterthought before he shot off. They don't read too well, either of 'em. Told them they were to go and stand guard in the graveyard over the fresh plots. They went but they won't stay out there freezing for long. Better get on—they'll be back."

"And looking for you, Adam?" Joe asked.

"I'm scarpering. Picking up my old ma and going off to an auntie's in London."

"And then?" Joe handed him a card. "Give me a ring next week and we'll talk."

"Get on, Joe!" Dorcas urged. "You know what's gone on here. Sterilisation. Death to order. Death by experimental methods, even. You've seen it now. Let's get out."

"No, wait!" Joe was peremptory. "I can't use this! There's absolutely no proof here that what you claim has happened, has indeed happened. It could be simply a dentist's chair or equipment for the treatment of epileptic patients. Easy to account for. Speaking professionally, I can't take this any further. Unprofessionally, that's a different matter, and I shall put the boot in but as it stands. . . ."

"Proof? I can get you proof!" Adam was impatient and sweating with fear in the cold room. "See that little window over there? He filmed the experiments through it. That's why he needs the big lights and the white paint. If you go next door into the filing room you'll find there are reels still on the bottom shelf. Not labelled so I can't help you there."

Dorcas was swiftly on her knees working her way along a shelf of boxed film reels. "No names. No dates. Just numbers. I'm going to take the last two in the sequence. Experiments gather momentum and refinement. The last in a series is what you want. It's a lucky dip, but here goes. They'll just fit into my satchel if I move the pistol over a bit."

Somewhere a door banged shut, and the sound was followed by absolute silence.

Desperate to leave now, they made for the door.

A sudden clang of metal on metal broke the silence. A signal. It was followed seconds later by a crescendo of noise as a steel stick was bounced from bar to bar along the cages, coming towards them. A bass accompaniment of nailed boots swelled the sound, clattering along the tiled floor of the monkey lab. They stopped, frozen for a moment in flight. Instinct took over. Dorcas pushed Adam behind her and ranged up behind Joe and Gosling who, without a word spoken, stepped out into the larger room, presenting a solid front to whoever was surging onward down the darkened laboratory.

"Well, what have we here?" A Cockney voice. "I can see you, Adam, yer carroty little runt! Hiding behind the skirt. Having a party are yer? Yer forgot to invite us."

Joe looked with dismay at the guardians of this foul place. Adam's description had not gone far enough. Over six feet tall and burly, both men wore not a reassuringly crisp lab coat but the coarse leather jerkin of a gunnery sergeant—or a London thug. They had the sleek muscled bulk and pitiless eyes of wild boar. Big boots and showy red neckerchiefs announced that they meant business. As did the short metal truncheon the spokesman held in one hand.

He smirked at Joe and Gosling and smacked the weapon suggestively into the palm of his other hand in a gesture he'd surely seen in a gangster movie. "Well, well! Two smart-arses caught abusing the boss's hospitality! These men are intruders, Jonas. Did anyone warn you they were expected? Naw! Me neither! Show 'em how we welcome intruders, shall we?"

The man talked too much. Bored, belligerent show-offs whose moment had come at last, they were going to savour it. But it was their eyes, supercilious and mocking, that chilled Joe. These men were confident in their place and their position. Like bull mastiffs, they obeyed one master. And that master was not on hand to call them off. The pack instinct would take over. He'd encountered London thugs before; once they'd downed their prey they kicked their heads in. They owed no allegiance to law and order; they would be deaf to an upper-class voice. Useless to try to talk his way out of this encounter. Bluster or reason, either one would go unheard. He wondered if Gosling had come to the same conclusion. Better be certain.

"Give it ten, Hercules," he muttered sideways.

He was spurred on by the click of a safety catch behind him.

Presenting a broad smile to the two slowly advancing thugs, Joe held up his left hand, waggling his Scotland Yard warrant card showily in front of their eyes.

"Ever seen one of these, eh?"

His right hand chopped sideways into the nearest man's neck before he'd finished speaking. His left, dropping the warrant, slammed upwards into the wrist that was already raising the cosh, and the metal bar continued on its trajectory, shooting upwards out of the man's grasp and clanging to the floor behind him. Joe followed with a fist to the undefended jaw to slake his own anger and then threw his weight onto the slumping body with the determination of a hound bringing down the heavier boar. He forced the man to the ground and applied more judicious pressure until the grunting stopped.

Gosling's left hook on the other man's jaw was a satisfying cruncher but not a disabling blow against a taller and heavier opponent. He needed to duck and dodge two swipes from an over-confident meaty fist before a second blow from his left put the man down to join his pal on the floor. He stepped back, looking slightly surprised.

"Do we need to do anything further with these louts, sir? Um. . . ." He glanced around him at the stark surroundings. "In the matter of restraining, I mean? A bit of rope, perhaps?"

Adam managed a grin. "With all these cages about? Naw!" He waved the key. "Shove the buggers in there," he said. "In the ops room. It's soundproofed. I'll lock 'em in. There's no way out. They'll be there until the prof gets back from London. Could be midnight. Could be tomorrow morning."

Joe had already grasped the ankles of the thug he'd knocked out and started to pull.

Before they left by a back service entrance, Dorcas dropped a kiss on Adam's forehead. "Bless you, Adam. Come with us, we'll take you to your mother's—and don't worry! Joe will see nothing bad happens to you. He's not a ferret at all. More of a warhorse. He'll pound Bentink under his hooves."

Joe groaned. Living up to Dorcas's expectations had always taken the stuffing out of him. "I've done quite enough pounding for one day," he said. "Gosling? Are you fit to drive? Hands survived, have they? Thank God for that! Dorcas, I think this would be a good moment to break out the flapjack."

CHAPTER 26

They made for the ground floor headquarters on return to St. Magnus.

Martin was still at work by the light of several electric lamps he'd requisitioned and set about the room. The radiators seemed to have been invigorated, and a warm tobacco-scented fug greeted them. The inspector had taken further steps to give a more professional air to the dingy place: A map of the county had gone up, stuck onto a blackboard on wheels: a rank of correspondence trays occupied the surface of a large table jammed in between a decaying vaulting horse and a rack of rotting tennis raquets. A second table in the centre of the room bore, surprisingly, a white cloth, four place settings, a flagon of cider, and a large cottage loaf with a pat of farm butter alongside on a breadboard.

Inspector Martin looked at his watch. With a gesture, he invited them to take a seat at the table.

"Right on cue. You made good time. Lots of information to exchange. Thought we'd do it over supper or after supper. Not sure how you lot are fixed, it being a Saturday. I thought perhaps the commissioner and Miss Joliffe might have stopped off at The Bells for an American cocktail or two. But just in case, I took the liberty of—Ah! There we are! Right on time."

He hurried to the door to open it for a school steward who came in, red in the face and panting, laden with paper parcels.

"Well done, lad! No, keep the change. I hope these are still hot?"

"Piping, sir! I went on my bike. And I made sure old Arnie gave me this lot fresh out of the fryer. I said yes to salt and vinegar—hope that was all right."

"Haddock and chips from the local chippie," Martin announced, depositing a package on each plate.

"Glad I signed out of school supper. It's bread and cheese on a Saturday. Staff all out cutting a rug somewhere." Gosling's eyes gleamed. "I say, I do hope you can eat haddock and chips, Dorcas?"

His nice manners obliged him to ask, and if the girl said no, Joe knew that poor hungry Gosling would forgo his steaming plate of fried fish to go in search of something she *would* like to eat. But Joe knew the boy's supper was safe. The old Dorcas would have rejected the suggestion of a delicate palate and regaled him with stomach-turning tales of hedgehogs baked in clay and offal sausages. Joe, with silent approval, heard her say simply, "Certainly can! I'm a student—fish and chips is a treat. Gosh, these look good! Cider, everyone?"

By unspoken agreement, no one mentioned the case until the last chip had been eaten, the last crisp morsel of batter crunched. Dorcas and Gosling swiftly cleared away the debris of the meal, refilling the glasses with cider. Then three pairs of eyes turned on Martin.

"I hope your day was as fruitful as mine," he said, producing envelopes and documents from his briefcase and piling them on the table in front of him. "Rapson, first. Murder of. We have our killer. Or two killers. Or none. You can take your pick.

"There was enough light left and enough snow gone to get out onto the grass in the courtyard after you left. The killing patch. I could read it like a book! Pool of blood still there marking the spot where the knife had gone in—and been pulled out—but footprints as well. The ground was soggy enough before the snow fell to take an imprint, and once the covering was gone, all was revealed. Here, take a look at this."

Martin slid a sheet of graph paper across the table. A meticulously recorded scene-of-crime plan in various coloured inks plotted the movements of three people.

"Key: Red's for Rapson. Blue's for the child. Black for the killer," Martin explained. "We'll start with the boy. Harry. Coming dark. He'd been out on the turnpike clocking the cars as usual when it came on to snow. Or something spooked him."

"Like a gent in a big Talbot saying, 'Get into my car, little boy, and we'll go for a ride'?"

Martin nodded. "We see running footsteps straight across the yard, you see. It could be that he knew he was late and he'd get into trouble with Clara." Martin shrugged. "At all events, running. And here," he pointed to a red mark, "is where we could say 'Enter villain.' Rapson. What's he doing down here? Gone to liaise with the driver of the car he'd ordered up? Harry makes a run for it, and Rapson pursues. Look, his steps overlap. And the spacing indicates a man in a hurry, allowing for short legs and corpulence. Just after six, are we thinking? The car had come for Harry and was waiting in the lane. But Rapson never caught the lad to put him in it. See here? These black prints? Woman's size four shoes. Never overlap the child's. They ran straight past each other. Black squares up to Red, toe to toe, and Red gets a knife stuck into him. Someone pulls it out, releasing a gush of blood. Rapson's steps then go staggering off back into the school building and the woman's return to the cottage."

"Blood traces on Clara's clothes? Shoes?"

"None. The women had cleaned up. Probably ended up in the school incinerator next morning. They had plenty of time."

"Shoe size confirms Clara's presence?" Joe asked.

"Both women size four. But this is the real clincher." Martin passed a Sussex Constabulary laboratory report over. "Blood test on the knife. Rapson's type A, plus—and the boys were quick to spot this—a different blood completely."

"Two victims?" Gosling asked in astonishment.

"Yes. But the second sample wasn't human. Animal. To be precise, a rabbit. That's the nearest they can come to it. Rabbit blood."

"Clara had a rabbit from Old Rory," Joe remembered.

"And she cut it up that afternoon and stewed it for Betty's supper. When she saw the danger—perhaps the lad was screaming for help—she picked up the nearest tool and went out to see to it."

"Her prints were on the handle?" Joe asked.

"No. Only Rapson's. Smudges under his, but nothing identifiable."

"You've charged Clara?"

"Not yet. There's a problem."

Joe frowned, seeing the inspector's unease.

"She confessed to it. I put the scenario to her with the evidence, and she hung her head and said yes she'd done it. Bloody old Rapson had been bulldozing them into taking steps to send Harry off to some place he could be taken care of and forgotten. What man would ever want to marry Betty if the truth came out? he asked her. He threatened Clara that it certainly would if she didn't comply. Rotter! I could knife him myself! Anyway, it was a hands up to it from Clara. She'd heard young Harry yelling and run out with the knife exactly as I've explained and stuck it in Rapson three times. He stood there, upright and snorting but not dead. At this point, Clara fled in horror. Looking back, she saw him pull out the knife and then throw it to the ground—they will do that!—and stagger off to the back entrance.

"At that moment Betty gets back a few minutes late from

school because she's been held up waiting on young Drummond. She takes it all in and helps clean up. They decide to leave the knife, thinking the bad weather will destroy the prints, but anyhow, Rapson's were the last ones on there. She goes back to the school kitchen and nicks one of the meat knives and puts it in its slot in their own kitchen. Harry is sent to bed and told nothing's happened. He's to say, if anyone asks, that he's been up there playing with his cars."

"Clear as day. What's your problem, Martin?"

"Trouble is, Betty confessed as well. And blow me if she doesn't make it sound convincing. The women are covering for each other. Deliberately, to spread confusion?"

"Or because they appear genuinely to believe the other one did it?" Joe offered. "The inference is that it must therefore be the work of a third party. I've seen that happen. And, I can tell you, it works. If the accused really aren't certain, the jury is even less so, and an acquittal usually follows."

"According to Betty, as she was getting back from school, she saw Rapson chasing Harry, ducked into the kitchen, and snatched the first knife that came to hand—from the draining board—and stopped him in his tracks. Three stabs, and she pulls it out. Rapson amazes her by not keeling over but standing his ground. She wipes the knife on her skirt and shoves it in his hand. He drops it and stumbles off. But then Betty goes one further. Modern lass. Reads the papers. Listens to gossip. Clued up, you'd say. She accuses Rapson, who's no longer here to defend himself, of—" Martin glanced at Dorcas and, seeing something in her expression, braced up. "Of paedophilia. Interfering with young boys. Says she'll stand up in court and speak out. Says she was only defending her little brother from a sex-crazed monster."

"Look, one doesn't want to pose as barrister for the prosecution, but isn't there a little matter of Rapson's—er—well-signalled proclivities? A certain tendency to pursue members of

the opposite sex, Betty in particular? The headmaster's intervention and all that?" Joe said tentatively.

"The lass has got that covered," Martin announced with ill-
disguised pride. "She's going to say as how that was all a sham, a
pretence. Haunting her was an excuse to get close to the lad. You
can imagine the effect of that delivered from the witness box. A
girl whose honour has been doubly betrayed. Every male breast
in the jury will be swelling with indignation."

"Tell me, Martin, how do you predict that defence will go
down at the Sussex assizes?"

Martin smiled. "On previous performance, I'd say the judge
and jury will decide for self-defence or justified homicide or both.
The twelve good men and true will all be local. And young Betty
in the box would tug at your heartstrings. You can imagine. They'll
ask for Rapson to be dug up to stand a charge of something—
anything."

Martin was ill at ease in spite of his positive forecast. Dorcas
and Gosling turned glowering looks on Joe.

The voice Joe heard breaking into the strained silence—wily,
manipulative, authoritative—was that of Sir George, his mentor
in India. Surely not his own?

"Allow me, Martin, to put an alternative scenario before you.
We have here, in Rapson, a man who—and his bank manager will
confirm this—had been for some years the subject of blackmail.
His bank was becoming alarmed and had resorted to issuing
warnings. Can we guess at the subject of the blackmail? An
unhealthy interest in small boys? His career would never survive
the revelation that was threatened. The blackmailer was most
probably a man in his own immediate surroundings. Someone
close to him? A professional colleague? A combination of guilt
and fear and suspicion screw his emotions to a height and, perhaps
with the trigger of the scheduled beating of a small boy in the
offing, Rapson cracks under the strain and decides to do the

honourable thing and end it all. He snatches up a knife from the school kitchens as he passes through on his way out of the school and goes off to find some space in the courtyard where he won't make a mess on the carpet. A space where he can be viewed from the cottage making his statement—'See what you women have driven me to!' And he stabs himself in the heart.

"Now, the Romans were adept at this type of exit, and perhaps they were his inspiration—historian and classical scholar that he was. But it is in fact remarkably difficult to summon up the strength to do it. His attempt is not immediately fatal. In great pain and instantly regretting his action—as many suicide victims do—he tears the knife from the wound and, rapidly shedding blood, starts off back to the school to find medical help. Are we surprised that only one set of prints was found on the knife—Rapson's own?"

"The rabbit blood, sir?" Gosling was eager to hammer down every nail in this creaking construction. And at once he answered his own question. "Old Rory! He'd just handled all the knives, and he'd been killing and gutting rabbits. Cross-contamination!"

Joe nodded. "Well, what do you think of that, inspector?"

Martin cleared his throat. "I think it's the most brazen, duplicitous pack of lies I've ever heard spoken. Shame on you, commissioner! Do you know, I think if we were just to lose Old Rory's statement and advise the women to keep their traps shut, we could get away with it. He's never going to turn up in a court of law as witness anyroad."

Joe smiled. "Well, think about it. No rush. What other revelations do you have in that pile of documents?"

"This came for you. Special motorbike messenger from Whitehall."

Another brown envelope crossed the table. "You'll see it's been opened. I notice you had it addressed to Assistant Commissioner Sandilands and Inspector Martin. Very thoughtful. So I had a peek. Oh, my! Lists of members of the Eugenic Society. Two. Countrywide and a selection for the southeast."

Joe fell on it and skimmed his way down the alphabetical list, grunting with surprise and exclaiming as one famous name after another caught his eye. "Confirmation. Farman's here. Also Bentink. There's our link."

"Anyone else we know?"

"I'm afraid so. There's Dr. Chadwick, father and son, many notables listed as 'Mayor' of this, 'Alderman' of that, physicians aplenty—but I'm wasting time. Gosling, give me the names of the missing boys in alphabetical order if you can remember them."

Gosling snapped to and recited the names:

"Jefferson."

"Here."

"Hewitt-Jones."

"Listed."

"Houghton-Cole."

"Present."

"Murgatroyd."

"Three of those—we'll have to check initials."

"Pettigrew."

"Here."

"Renfrew."

"Here."

"And your last, Gosling?"

"For Peterkin, look under Greatorix, sir. The stepfather."

"Yes, he's here."

Joe broke the deep silence. "Gentlemen, I think we've got the buggers. Time to roll them all up."

"Did you make an arrest at the clinic, sir?" Martin enquired.

"No. Hard nut to crack, St. Raphael's Clinic. Shall I tell him?" Joe asked the others unnecessarily.

Martin listened without interrupting the tale. And finally:

"But you've got it with you? The evidence? These films?" he asked eagerly.

"Yes. We'll have to take a peek at them in London. I'll get them back to the Yard and give them a good going over."

"It can't wait. Spielman's still out there. It's a Saturday." Gosling looked at his watch. "Seven o'clock. School hall! Quick! It's Langhorne's weekly treat—Laurel and Hardy will be just finishing. The film show for the boys. If you can get up there before he starts pulling the plugs we could have an after-hours command performance. I know how to work one of those projectors. I've filled in for Langhorne once or twice."

Joe was already tearing out of the door.

CHAPTER 27

The school hall still smelled, not unpleasantly, of small boys who'd recently been laughing their socks off and sucking on aniseed balls and peppermints. When the last child had gone with much giggling and pretend fighting from the room to the upper floors to prepare for bed, a puzzled Langhorne had been politely dismissed also and his expensive equipment requisitioned. When asked why he should leave his pride and joy in the hands of a doubtful quartet who arrived after hours carrying their own film reel, not even Joe could think of a convincing explanation. Langhorne had, in the end, withdrawn with a theatrical show of raised eyebrows and mutterings about "a very ancient and fish-like smell" that he declared himself able to detect.

The moment he'd gone, Dorcas busied about checking that the blackout curtains were doing their work at the windows and that no one could peer in from the outside.

She settled down at the end of the row next to Gosling, who'd stationed himself beside the projector. No one suggested she might like to leave. Gosling's nimble hands threaded the film, adjusted buttons and screws, repositioned the screen, and refocussed. Then, at last, he pronounced himself ready to start on the film. He'd loaded up the one Dorcas had advised—the most recent, according to its number.

Martin turned off the house lights, and the metal wheels creaked into life.

Flashes of white light and unintelligible symbols followed on the screen, and suddenly the film had started. Eerily silent. Harsh black and white with little grey. Breath was drawn in audibly as a scene they recognised appeared on the screen.

The white room at St. Raphael clinic came up. Overlying it along the bottom, a strip of numbers gave the date and time. A fortnight previously, Joe calculated. The clock in the background behind the operating couch was given close focus. Twelve noon confirmed the time given. It seemed important to the filmmaker. Without a break, a physician entered.

Joe peered eagerly at the gowned figure, seeking an identity, trying to turn it into Bentink, but the cap and mask hid the features. Physicians still lagged behind police forensic staff when it came to the wearing of protective gloves, Joe had noticed. The hands on view and the eyes were those of a middle-aged man, but that was as much as he could make out. The white clothing against the white walls gave him an insubstantial, ghostlike appearance.

The doctor was escorting a child. A boy. He was wearing a white hospital smock and looking anxious. Dark hair, dark eyes, unknown to the audience. A second surgeon, similarly attired, appeared and, one on either side of the table, they caught and fixed the boy's arms to the sides. Wires were produced, and these were applied to the child's temples.

To Joe's horror, the boy began to twitch and writhe and try to free himself. It was a moment before he realised that the boy had entered into an epileptic fit. The fit started at five minutes after 12:00, and the film was interrupted at 12:10.

A blip in the film indicated that a splicing had occurred. A second scene with the strap 'London' and the same date and time appeared. The same layout but a different room. A clock gave the same time. A second boy, so like the first they must have been identical twins, came in, and the procedure was repeated. But on this second boy, no wires were applied. He lay looking uncomfortable and scared as the minutes crawled by. At 12:07, the twitching began. Though not as intense as the first boy's, it seemed to be a mirror image.

It was Joe who leapt to his feet and snapped out a command to a very willing Gosling to switch the bloody thing off.

Dorcas ran to put on the lights, and they sat, in a huddled group, shaking with anger and distress.

Finally: "Will someone please tell me what we've just seen?" Joe gritted out the words.

With an effort at calm, Dorcas tried. "An experiment. Those were identical twins. Very valuable to Bentink's research. I'd say they are the rarest of the rare—a pair of epileptic twins. He was trying to show that they are so closely linked by their genetic make-up that inducing a fit in one of them by the application of an electric current will produce a reciprocal and simultaneous reaction in the twin separated by fifty miles."

Joe deliberately damped down emotion. "Could it possibly have been faked?"

Dorcas took her time in replying. "Not the exploitation. But the results? Yes. I can see how he could have arrived at this demonstration. And, Joe, I believe that's what it is. The fact that it's filmed—it gives the experiment the aura of a stage illusionist's trickery. But the pain and the terror, they are real. One, at least, of those boys may not have survived. And God knows what further horrors are on the other reels. There were ten altogether."

"Who are these boys, I'm wondering? Patients?"

"No. They are—were—gypsies."

"Dark, I agree, but how can you be certain?" Joe thought he already knew the answer but waited for her confirmation.

"It may be silent, but I could read the lips of the first boy. He was calling out in Romany. For his mother."

She could do no more. Dorcas covered her face with her hands, and her shoulders began to heave uncontrollably. It was Gosling who flung both arms about her with a cry of concern and murmured into her hair. Joe was swiftly at her side with a large handkerchief, and from somewhere Martin summoned up a glass of tepid water.

Martin's down-to-earth voice brought a measure of calm. "I can get a print of the lad's face off that, no problem. Take it to the encampments and show it around. Then the East Sussex boys can move in and do their job." He was on his feet ready for action. "I'll have that bloody place turned inside out and dug up. I'll string the bugger up! I'll kick him till he squeals! Bloody toff! Why does he think he can treat those lads like animals? Gypsies? Worth less than nothing to him. Would he do the same stuff to a kid of his own class? Applying electric currents like that—it can kill."

"Well, there you have it, Martin," Joe said. "Spielman? Renfrew? Peterkin? All the lost boys we know of? Perhaps those we can only guess at? Have they passed through his pitiless hands? Does he draw a line? From monkeys to sons of ambassadors and statesmen—has he any boundary? I think we should enquire with this ammunition in our knapsacks. A dawn raid, are you thinking? Can you activate a colleague in East Sussex? If we're going to do this, it must be watertight."

"Leave all that to me. The force'll be ready. And we'll be glad to see you there, assistant commissioner."

THE TELEPHONE WAS ringing as they approached the equipment room. Gosling sprinted ahead and caught it before it rang off.

"Hold a moment, will you?" he said as they entered. "I'm going to repeat that for interested parties who need to know. The Spielmans are now in Dover. They're waiting to catch the earliest ferry in the morning. . . . Not possible to detain them. . . .

Diplomatic immunity in force. Herr Spielman going to take up an important post in the new Parliament in Berlin. We feared as much. But why Dover? Have you wondered? Surely Harwich to the Hook of Holland is their most direct way to Germany? . . . Extra baggage arrived? What extra baggage? Describe it, please. Thank you. I'll let you know. Hold a moment."

He turned to Joe, ashen-faced. "Well, that explains Dover. They've just had a little local delivery. It's more bad news, I'm afraid, sir. They've registered, as well as their many trunks and suitcases that came from London with them, an extra unit. It arrived late this evening by local lorry and is awaiting stowage on the boat when it loads up. It's a coffin, sir. A child's coffin."

Inspector Martin crackled with fury. "Give me the bloody phone!" He snatched the receiver from Gosling. "Now listen here, you, whoever you are! Bloody good work keeping track of these buggers! Well done, lads! And stay up behind them, but— hear this—they are murderers. They've had their own son killed, and that's his corpse in the coffin on the quayside. He was, until two days ago, a pupil at a school on my patch, and I'm investigating his disappearance. Inspector Martin here, Sussex Constabulary.

"You may not feel able to touch these birds, but *I'm* going to ruffle their feathers! I'm going to take a bar to that coffin. Get hold of the shipping details for me, will you? I need to know where it's come from, who signed for it, and by what route it came.

"Now, Dover. That's two hours' drive maximum from here along the coast road. I'm getting my best men and a police pathologist over there. They'll be there by ten. Just ensure that nobody touches that box or tries to move it even an inch. I'm going to break into it first and answer questions later."

A few frenzied minutes of dialing later, Martin was through to his own brigade and rapping out orders. "Dr. Soames? He's a good man. Is he available? Is he up for a bit of body-snatching? Start him now in your fastest motor. Ring me back here if there's a problem."

After more sweating minutes of organisation, Martin faced Joe. "Can I leave the clinic to you and my colleague tomorrow morning? I'm off to Dover. I'm expecting to find in that coffin the body of little Spielman. I'm expecting his death to be fully certified by the correct authorities. He'll have died of an epileptic fit. Of course. But I'm going to ask Dr. Soames to check everything including the skin under his hair where I'm pretty sure we'll find traces of electric terminals being applied. After our little film show I think I know where to look."

"Inspector," Dorcas spoke hesitantly. "For what it's worth, I talked to Mrs. Spielman on the telephone when Harald went missing. I don't think she's involved. I'm sure she has no idea that her husband's been up to devilry of this kind."

"Good. That may be the only ammunition I have. If I can't arrest him, I shall at least make sure his wife hears the truth. It's not much, but I shall play it for all it's worth. I'll make him squirm!" he finished viciously.

Martin stormed out of the room, whistling up his sergeant and his constable as he went.

"That's what happens when you rouse one of Lowther's Lambs!" said Joe. "Formidable enemies! Shouldn't want to face one myself."

"Nor me, sir," Gosling said. "But I'll tell you who I should like to face up to again, in the changed circumstances. Bentink. If you don't mind, I'd like to come along tomorrow."

"I shall be pleased to know you're there, Gosling. This is not going to be an easy one to crack. Time for—not the fists, but the low cunning, I think. But—and I'm sure we'll both agree on this—not the place, the time or the situation for Miss Joliffe. Though an evil thought creeps in. I'll tell you who it *is* just the right time for! Pass me that phone. I'm going to do something I never thought I'd stoop to!"

He asked the operator for a London number and while he waited for the connection, muttered, "What's the time? . . . Oh, well, they tell me Fleet Street never sleeps. . . . Ah! That the *Daily Mirror*? Put your editor on, would you? This is Scotland Yard here."

And, a moment later, "Let's be fair! What was the name of that local rag? *Sussex Advertiser*? They reported the news of the gypsy children's disappearances. They deserve our notice. I'll issue an invitation to the unmasking."

CHAPTER 28

"They'll be there mob-handed and in position by nine. Best I can do," had been the result of Martin's calls to the chief constable of the Sussex Police. "It *is* a Sunday. Still, there's a squad of a dozen officers glad of the overtime. Four hounds promised and possibly the old man himself will turn up after morning service. Good luck with it. You're to liaise with the superintendent you'll find there."

And here they were, some minutes before the appointed hour, liaising. Superintendent Crawshaw and his men had listened intently to Joe's briefing, dismay, incredulity and resolve flitting, one after the other, across their stolid features.

"So, you want us to get busy with the dogs straight up, in the cemetery, sir?" the sergeant asked doubtfully.

"Yes. We're not tiptoeing in. We have the warrants. There shouldn't be much in the way of patients arriving—it being a Sunday—but any members of the public arriving for appointments are welcome to witness the police presence. It's surprising what a degree of panic a few bloodhounds can stir up when they're observed, nose to the sward in a graveyard! Get the men to yell and the dogs to howl. Put on a blood-chilling performance."

"Sir, there's a couple of journalists hanging about. Do you want me to. . . ?"

"No, Super. They're here at my invitation. Give 'em free rein to roam. When you've organised the dogs I'd like one of your officers—make it two, hard men—to arrest Matron when she sticks her nose out to question the noise and isolate her from the remainder of the activities. Charge: aiding and abetting a felony. Vague enough for the moment."

Crawshaw pursed his lips but called forwards two officers and gave instructions.

"Apart from that extraction, Super, the rest of the hospital is to go about its usual business. I won't be held responsible for affecting the normal medical procedures. Now, we'll execute the plans as discussed, shall we? I'll take three of your men and go with Mr. Gosling and Miss Joliffe to confront the director. When we're ready to arrest him and his medical staff, I'll put them in your hands. There may also be two London roughs, the muscle he uses."

"Glad we brought the big van, sir."

They waited until a squawking, spluttering Matron had been whisked away. Then they set off down Joe's remembered route to Bentink's office.

He burst without knocking into an empty room. Joe swallowed his disappointment and made use of the opportunity to order the constables to remove and log the contents of the desk, including diaries and appointment books. He was running an eye over the filing cabinets when a cool voice spoke from the open door.

"Back so soon, Sandilands? And you bring your minions with you? Would you kindly ask them to release my staff? I could do with a cup of coffee. Start behaving yourself, and I'll get one for you. I've just got back down from town with a headache, and I find my hospital being turned into a funfair by the Keystone Kops. There must be an explanation. Are you filming this? Should I smile for the cameras?"

The men stood back and looked uncomfortable. Joe wasn't surprised. Bentink without his white medical coat was even more impressive. At ease in his dove-grey Sunday morning Savile Row suit, he strolled into the disturbed space that had been his office, put his furled umbrella in its stand and his hat on a hook, and took command.

"You can save your coffee for the Chief Constable, Bentink. He will be joining us in time to wave you farewell as you are taken from here in the police van to Tunbridge Wells jail, where you will answer the charges we have against you."

"Charges? What have you in mind?"

"Kidnapping, torture and murder of minors. Children. Children pilfered from local gypsy families. In addition, you will, while our guest, help us with inquiries we are currently pursuing into the disappearances of certain pupils from a school or schools in the county of Sussex."

Bentink gave a theatrical shudder. "Really, Sandilands! Being a policeman is having a terrible effect on your powers of expression. Stop mangling the English language, man!"

The men looked up mutinously. Keystone Kops? Minions and manglers of the language? This didn't go down well with Sussex men. The sergeant took a menacing step closer to Joe in support. Joe was glad to note the instinctive response.

Bentink smiled and sank down into his leather Bauhaus chair, sleek and powerful as the man himself. "Sandilands, you must let me pass you the number of an excellent alienist in London. Your mental confusion is becoming an embarrassment to all. These are charges that, in their seriousness, would be alarming were they not so ridiculous. I am a medical man. Of some distinction, I might add. I have sworn my Hippocratic oath, and I abide by it. I do not torture children. And what on earth makes you suppose I would soil my hands by contact with gypsies?" He turned a look of quizzical appeal on the constables. "Local men, I see. Men who understand our local problems. They come into daily conflict with these people. Worthless, illiterate, law-breaking rogues, they'll tell you if you ask."

In his arrogance he had gone too far.

The sergeant inflated his impressive chest and spoke up. "Sir. They may be gypsies. But they're our gypsies as long as they're on our patch. A child is a child. And they've been going missing. Six so far. As we know of. We're going to find out where they are, what's happened to them, and chuck the book at the unhuman what's responsible. This is England, sir, and we won't have it."

Suddenly Bentink had had enough. He got to his feet. "What have you done with my telephone? I am about to ring the Minister for Reform. Sir James will enlighten you as to the way we handle things in England. Gentlemen—if any here deserve that appellation—prepare to have your arses kicked."

"When you get him," Joe said, handing him the instrument, "tell him the police have, on celluloid, yards and yards of filmed evidence of you and your henchmen tormenting, in illegal experiments, kidnapped children. You, sir, though masked throughout the proceedings, are identifiable by a ring of particularly flamboyant style. A ring I observe you are even now wearing. Sergeant, may I ask you to look closely and note this ring? It might be a good idea to bag and label it before it disappears."

When this awkward procedure was completed Joe asked: "Now, would you like me to put on a showing of the filmic material in question for these other gentlemen of the law? We could go along to your viewing room. Or would you prefer your brother-in-law to be present at the premier performance?"

Joe was struck by a thought that the overpowering presence of Bentink had put from his mind: the man, sinking back into his chair, had no idea that his Lethal Chamber had been invaded. He'd been shocked out of his complacency to hear that Joe knew of the films. "Good Lord! Your men are still locked up where I

left them—in your killing room. They've been there since yesterday afternoon when we helped ourselves to the evidence. Oh,
well, if they haven't made use of the facilities and done each other
in yet, they may be in just the right mood to spill whatever beans
they have relating to you and your grisly operations."

He turned to give an order to the sergeant. "Go with Miss
Joliffe, she knows the way. But don't let her near the thugs—she'd
do them irreparable damage. Pick up four lusty blokes to accompany you and two pairs of cuffs. Leave one officer with me, will
you?"

Left alone with Sandilands, Gosling and one policeman,
Bentink maintained a truculent silence. Not overly concerned. Joe
decided to annoy him. "Constable, I think we'll take the precau-
tion of cuffing this one as well. He won't outrun us, but the
waiting pressmen will expect it. They've screwed in their flash-
bulbs, and they're ready for a show."

At this, Bentink raised a terrible face suffused with rage and
hatred. Joe prepared to weather a frenzied outburst. But the voice,
when it came, was controlled. He spoke with quiet force: "For the
last time, I tell you, Sandilands: I have had nothing to do with
your missing boys. I beg you to use your skills and resources to
establish that. I am not a common criminal. Do you imagine I
would involve myself with the offspring of Englishmen of quality?
Men of breeding and background? Men of value to society like
you, like me? Look elsewhere. And do it quickly before the world
discovers what a fool you are."

Joe reminded himself that the monster Caliban had at times
spoken the most persuasive verse, conjuring up *sounds and sweet
airs that give delight and hurt not.*

He stopped his ears and held out the handcuffs.

"RING, SIR?" GOSLING muttered to Joe as they accompanied Bentink out into the sunlight. "What was all that about?

He had one on this morning, but I can't say I noticed one on the film."

"I could have sworn I saw one," Joe said vaguely. "Ah, well—he seemed to *think* we did."

CHAPTER 29

With two recent burials revealed already in the old cemetery, one or two incriminating pieces of evidence taken away in bags from the incinerator, and the remainder of the film cases in the capable hands of the Sussex force, Joe decided they could beat a retreat. Superintendent Crawshaw was too energetically busy, too preoccupied with his plethora of evidence to argue when they said they were leaving. Joe realised that, despite his London input, this had become a local case. The children were, as the sergeant had heartily said, 'on our patch.' They would be avenged.

The others? The lost boys? Joe feared they would never be recovered. Apart of course from poor Spielman, who was still in transit. Joe was looking forwards to discovering what Martin had achieved with his crowbar and his pathologist. The inspector's swift actions would be noted by the top brass and Joe, for one, would not be surprised to be addressing the Sussex man as Superintendent Martin before the year was out. The bills of lading and the death certificate he probably had right now in his hands would hammer the last nail in Bentink's coffin.

Unless the shadowy government agencies could come up with some Houdini-like escape trick at the last moment. Joe was a realist and determined always that the last person to be deceived would be himself. His career was hanging by a thread. He knew he'd vastly overinterpreted his instructions. "Creep about," he'd been told. "Watch and discover. Report back." No one had authorised him to go about insulting and slapping cuffs on one of the most influential men in the land. "The husband of the sister of the next prime minister but one," sounded laughable, but Joe understood how that world worked. Ramsay MacDonald, son of a Scottish parlour maid, might well be prime minister, but the reins of real power were in other, more ruthless hands. Hands that would not falter when it came to signing Joe's dismissal document.

He looked at the cheerful faces of his two young companions. Unaware, self-congratulatory, happy with their achievement. They had no idea.

But they were right in their innocent beliefs. The police force was the servant of the state and its countrymen. The Sussex bobbies had seen that clearly. "They're *our* gypsies." Any soul living within their jurisdiction had an unquestioned right to life and liberty. The Force did not exist to protect the interests of individual members of the government, and he would maintain that to the last.

But, at least, with the source of the euthanasian-eugenic organisation—Joe stopped himself and mentally substituted *murdering machine*—cut off at its source, he felt Gosling would be able to confirm Alicia Peterkin's fears at last. She could pray for her boy without the hobble of unfounded hope. And there would be no more disappearances. There just remained Farman to be dealt with. Joe was looking forwards to sinking his boat.

The glorious weather, if not reflecting, at least improved their mood. Sunlight sparkled on the remaining flashes of snow, and the earth, thankful for the soaking, was greening over. Snowdrops gallantly shrugged off the drifts and stood to attention, promising an early spring.

"At the risk of being accused of—what was it? Something in German for pecking grass?—may I point out," Gosling said as they sped along, "that we're passing very close to the Prince Albert? As it was that good old bird—Chadwick?—who set us off on this trail and put Bentink in the bag, what about calling in for a cup of tea and saying thank you? We needn't divulge much. I don't think it would be necessary. I'd say he was very clued up—in everything but his crossword, of course. And it's always nice to know you've been helpful."

"It would be the polite thing to do," Joe agreed.

"I'd like to see Francis Crabbe again," said Dorcas.

And Francis Crabbe, when they pulled up at the asylum ten minutes later, was pleased to see Dorcas.

Out came the hand from under the grey cloak, and he flung back his hood to reveal a lined and lean but handsome face, marred by a very amateur short haircut. A face Joe remembered seeing a thousand times in the trenches. A face under duress but determinedly happy. A face he'd have chosen himself without a second thought to be his lieutenant.

"You came back!" Francis exclaimed. "Glad you did!" And, surprisingly: "Good timing! Chadwick's not at home. He's gone off to visit his old dad in Brighton, this being a Sunday afternoon. It's what he always does. But I know he'd want to give you a cup of tea. Come in. Come in!"

Francis dismissed his accompanying crew. "No, lads, you can go straight into the hall, now. I'll stay alert."

He turned to his guests. "It's the Sunday knees-up. Can't work on a Sabbath, so we might as well play, the boss says. Talent show. Music Hall Memories, sing-along, that sort of stuff. Most remember the songs they knew before they came here, and we have a gramophone to learn the words from. It's the best bit of the week. Crikey, can you hear them!"

They could indeed hear many voices raised in song as they

passed the great hall. Gosling and Dorcas came to a standstill, bright eyed, singing along with an old Victorian music-hall song:

Father's got the sack from the waterworks
For smoking of his old cherry-briar;
Father's got the sack from the waterworks

They belted out the punch-line along with the full-throated roar from the congregation:

'Cos he might set the waterworks on fire!

Francis turned to Joe, and Joe was touched to see the man had a tear in his eye. "Did Kipling ever write anything so English? Dickens? Naw! It took some unknown Londoner to do it, and he did it in one line."

"You're right. It's perfection. Says it all, really. It says why we pass our laws and why we choose to obey them or laugh them out of court. It's what we fight for," Joe said quietly.

"And why we win," Francis nodded. "Now, that cup of tea?" He led them on, humming to himself.

Settled in the superintendent's parlour, they chatted politely to Francis, who was warming his backside in a proprietorial way before the fire, until the tea he'd rung for appeared on a tray in the hands of one of the inmates. She served them, bobbed to Francis, and withdrew without raising an eyebrow.

"So Chadwick's visiting his father, you say. A doctor also, I understand? He must be getting on a bit, the old feller?" Joe asked while the tea was being poured.

"Over eighty. He was superintendent here before the present Chadwick. Ruled with a rod of iron, the old man did. Ran a tight ship."

"Tell me, Francis: If this enterprise were a ship, what would be your role on it?"

"Chief engineer. I don't set the course, but I keep it running."

The easy conversation came to a halt when they'd been allowed their second sip of tea. The bald question came out of the blue.

"Sir, do you think I'm mad?"

Joe answered. "I'd say you are one of the sanest men I've ever met. But then I've never seen you drunk on a Saturday night. I might change my mind."

"Mmm. . . . The boss says any man who says he feels like a tree or looks like a tree is sane and probably just a bad poet. Any man who says he *is* a tree is mad. So I'm wary about saying out-right that . . . I am sane. It's all relative anyway to the subject and the man investigating him. There are degrees of insanity as there are degrees of physical illness. I make something of a study of them. Well placed, you might say. I was the village schoolmaster and an anti-war firebrand before I decided to save the world from a blood-crazed establishment."

Francis hesitated, then took courage and spoke firmly: "The maddest man in this whole institution is Chadwick. The superin-tendent. The only difference between him and the inmates is that he has the key. I know it's an old joke. This is the one time it's true."

Joe broke in. "Francis, listen. We're not government inspectors. We're not qualified to even hold up our end in a conversation about psychology or psychiatry or mental illness, let alone give an opinion on a specific case."

Francis said urgently, "But the lady is!" He turned appealing eyes on Dorcas, and his words came in short bursts. "You told me . . . when you came . . . that you studied . . . psychology. I thought you'd at least listen. None of the other toffee-nosed old hens who visit could give a monkey's, but you—"

Dorcas took the slopping tea cup from his hand and placed it carefully in the saucer. She kept hold of the hand. "I am lis-tening, Francis. If our conversation is over their heads, these two noodles can just go back to the hall and join in the singsong."

"No! No! He's a *policeman*, isn't he—the big one? I need him to listen. It's not about me, miss! I don't count for anything. I'm not trying to talk myself out of here. It's the children! No one will ever hear me out when I try to tell them about the children. 'He's raving,' they say and report me to Chadwick. Then I get a beating and lose privileges for a month."

Joe put down his cup and said carefully: "Go on, Francis. We're all listening to you."

"It's always after dark. They arrive. The Specials. Not like the ordinary admissions. They're taken up to the you-know-where, and they don't come out alive. Whatever they do—him and his gorillas—it's quick at least. I think it's electricity, but they have bottles of stuff up there as well."

Joe could hardly breathe. He caught Gosling's shocked face. He was aware of an urgency in Francis Crabbe, whose eyes went constantly to the mantel clock, and he forced himself to question swiftly, "How frequent, Francis—these arrivals?"

"Irregular. Once or twice a year. One year it was three times. I've written them all down in a book. He's no idea I have it."

"Good Lord!" Joe said faintly. "Can we get into this room?"

"No. He's got the key."

"But Francis, you mentioned it when we came last time, said it was open to view and did we want to take a look," Dorcas said.

"I wanted you to ask to see it! Make trouble for him. I always have a try when there's a woman in the inspection group."

"Why does he keep you on, Francis, thorn under his saddle that you are?" Gosling asked gently.

"He needs me to run the place. I keep the lid on and the wheels oiled. I try to see justice is done in a place that is outside the realms of justice. I protect the inmates from him and I protect him from the inmates. Rome survived its mad emperors, but it wouldn't have got far without its tribunes of the people. I've made myself indispensable."

"Well, as a policeman I could demand to view the premises," said Joe. "We'll wait. But we'll need more evidence of wrong-doing." Joe was thinking aloud, still stunned by Crabbe's revelation. His mind was running on the likelihood that all physical traces of those passing through would have been destroyed with oiled efficiency. The room would have been cleaned and belongings incinerated.

"Proof? I've got proof!" Francis was suddenly gleeful. He looked at the clock again. "Not much time. He'll be back early today—he's gone in the fast car."

"Remind me, Francis, what kind of car does your boss drive?"

"He's taken the Talbot today, sir. It's a big grey one."

"Do you know its number?"

"It's a Sussex registration: BP4200," he said impatiently.

Gosling shot a look at Joe, eyebrows raised in alarm. "Well run, little Harry," he murmured.

"Look, you gentlemen stay here just in case. I'll take the lady to the library. It's just a few yards down the corridor."

With a quick nod of reassurance for Joe, Dorcas got up, patted her satchel, and set off with her guide.

"HERE YOU ARE, miss."

Francis ushered her into an empty room. It was evidently well used. Tables and chairs were available for the browsers, even a couple of armchairs. The walls were lined with full bookshelves, and there were further piles on a table under the window. Dorcas reminded herself that this establishment was the size of a large village and she might expect to find a facility of commensurate size. One wall that caught her attention was devoted to books suitable for children to read, many of them ABCs and nursery rhymes.

"No, miss. It's over here." Francis made off to the far wall and began to search in the adult section under the letter S. "If you want to hide something, hide it in plain sight. That's not bad advice. And there's nowhere much you can hide something in a place like this."

He ran an eye along the row and tugged on the spine of a book until it was protruding an inch beyond the others. He stood back.

Dorcas peered more closely and uttered a soft cry. "I know this book," she said. "And I know its two previous owners. Take it out, Francis, and open it up at the first page inside."

Francis took *Treasure Island* down and did as Dorcas asked.

"There's two names here. Jack Drummond—crossed out. And under that, Harald Spielman, miss."

Hardly able to get the words out, Dorcas whispered, "How did you manage to get hold of it?"

"A lad arrived in daylight. Unusual that. Last week. He wasn't fetched. He was dropped off by a Daimler. The chauffeur left him with me at the front door and buzzed off, cussing about the weather. The boy didn't know what was going on. Thought he'd been taken to London, I think. Looking about him, impressed by the size of the building. He handed me this book because it was too big for his pocket. And he'd read it before, anyway. 'You may have it, my good man,' he told me. I put it away in the pocket of my cloak. I know a fine story when I see one. We can always use spare copies in the library. Then I saw the names. First time I've ever got hold of a name, miss."

Francis was eager to leave. "Can you put it away? In your bag?"

"Of course." Dorcas swung her satchel in front of her and undid the buckles. She held the flap up, and Francis Crabbe carefully turned the big book on its side to slide it in, spine first. She was alarmed to see his eye light up as he caught sight of the Smith & Wesson. The eye, she remembered, of a man sent here for misuse of a firearm. A countryman familiar with rifles and shotguns.

Francis caught her wariness and smiled. "Never realised psychology was such a dangerous pursuit, Miss Dorcas. Come on! Let's get back."

They were halfway back to the parlour when Dorcas remembered what Joe had told her. Something so essential she stopped and tugged Francis by his sleeve. "Wait a minute. There's another boy. I have to find him or find out what became of him." And by a huge feat of memory she came up with a name: "Walter Weston, he's called."

Francis pursed his lips, unwilling, it seemed to reply. Then: "The blacksmith's son, would that be? Local lad? Fair hair? Big lad for his age?"

"That's the one. He went missing at the same time as Harald Spielman."

Francis looked up and down the corridor and listened. "We may have time. Look, follow me and run if you can. What have you got on your feet?"

Dorcas lifted up a leg and showed him her low-heeled serviceable boot.

"They'll do. It's still a bit sticky in the graveyard."

CHAPTER 30

Joe poked the fire. Gosling poured more tea and helped himself to a second slice of jam sponge.

The clock chimed the half hour.

The clock chimed the three quarter hour.

"That's enough!" Joe snapped. "What kind of trusting idiots are we? To sit here and be made fools of by that maniac? He's probably taken Dorcas hostage and forced his way out of the house. He's got her into one of the boss's stable of motor cars and they're halfway to Brighton by now."

"Calm down, sir," Gosling advised. "You know the girl better than I do, I think, so you ought to know she just wouldn't allow any such nonsense. All the same...."

They raced to the door together.

"THERE'S THE OLD graveyard, miss."

He pointed to a collection of ancient headstones leaning at drunken angles to each other, confidingly close, passing on gossip. Some stones were flat on the ground, some at the height of a low drawing room table.

"It's a favourite place for the little girls to come and play. A safe place. They don't understand the significance. They can get away from the adults here and the rougher lads. They use the tombstones to play house."

"In this weather?"

"In any weather. They're well wrapped up. Mrs. Dunne wouldn't let them out otherwise. They're enjoying the sunshine. See there!" Francis pointed. "They're having a pretend tea party. We'll have to interrupt their game."

Dorcas noticed he was still looking about him anxiously. His finger directed her towards a tombstone. Sitting on top of it were three little girls in bonnets and scarves, holding rag dolls and chattering happily.

When they came face to face with the little group, one of them took off the bonnet, revealing a shock of short fair hair and a cross face. The child addressed Francis. "Have you brought Dr. Carter, sir? He said he'd come and see me today."

Astonished, Dorcas sank to her knees in front of the child. "Walter? Are you Walter?"

"Yes, missis. An' I want to see Dr. Carter and my Mum."

"He's coming, lad. He's coming. The doc always keeps his word." Francis turned to Dorcas and led her a discreet distance away. "Walter, as you see, is a little boy who doesn't at all mind playing with girls. They make something of a pet of him. He's very gentle and," he whispered, "not quite all there. He's a regular admission," Francis explained. "Signed for and supervised. His family doctor is his sponsor. Along with his mother. She signed the papers and forged the father's signature. That was just a cross anyway. Verified by the doctor probably. Now he'll be in trouble, I expect. I hope not. He's a good bloke."

"Walter's *mother* committed him? This little poppet?" Dorcas was aghast.

"There were problems at home. The father is a big-fisted man with a short temper who feels duty-bound to toughen up his soft son. The household is going through straitened times, with the work drying up. Not so many horses about these days, and money's short. Tensions in the family. Little Walter was bearing the brunt of all this. His mother feared for the boy's life and took the drastic step of sending him away without his father's knowledge. Chadwick was unwilling at first to take the boy under such circumstances. He'd done it before and got into trouble for it. I advised him otherwise on account of the good Dr. Carter has done us many a favour. And knows some of our secrets.

"So here he is. I see to it that he's having as happy a time as is possible in this place. Young Jessica here is trying to teach him to read. Walter's a bit bewildered, but at least he's alive. He's not had the snip yet, they've—"

Dorcas could not keep the horror out of her voice as she interrupted. "Snip? What do you mean, Francis?"

He looked at her with the eyes of a clapped-out horse on its way to the knacker's yard, pained and accepting. "It's routine, Miss Joliffe. We've all had it. He says the state supports and encourages it. Can't be doing with any hanky-panky leading to procreation of more idiots, can we? Too many of us already."

"But, Francis, it's not legal! Every time they put forwards a bill, it's defeated in Parliament."

Francis breathed in deeply and looked about him in despair. "How would we know? What could we do?" And, suddenly focussing his gaze: "Oh, my God!"

His eyes, constantly sweeping the horizon, had suddenly fixed. His voice rapped out: "Children—quick march! Run and report to Mrs. Dunne. Now! Go!"

The three picked up their dolls and fled.

Picking his way towards them, two hundred yards distant, came the figure of Superintendent Chadwick.

Dorcas shuffled close to Francis Crabbe. "Any use running for it? He's between us and the car. And we couldn't take off without Joe."

Francis grimaced. "I've nowhere to run anyway. What do you think he could do to harm you, posh folk that you are?"

"It's life and death, Francis. If he knows that we've found out about the killings, he'll know that he'll be swinging at a rope's end within six months."

"Don't be too sure of that. I'd like to see justice done, but he's a clever man. Mad, as I've told you, and bad, as you've learned, but clever. Monomaniac like Napoleon. Running his own little kingdom. He *enjoys* having power of life and death over everyone. Here he comes, all smiles and a cosh—or is it a gun this time?— in his pocket. He'll talk his way out of this. He'll have made his plans. I know his mind. He'll be planning a little motoring accident for you. 'On these slippery roads, can one wonder? The young driver was clearly going too fast on that tight bend, that killer loop just outside Seaford,' is what they'll say. There's no way out of this. Well . . . perhaps one. . . ."

Advancing on them at a fast trot, one hand still in his right pocket, Dorcas noted, the menacing figure grew larger.

JOE SEIZED A grey-cloaked figure, shook him, and shouted his demand. He released him on hearing the spluttering reply.

"The graveyard! They've gone to the bloody graveyard!"

They burst out of the front entrance to see Chadwick's Talbot parked, engine still steaming, but no sign of the superintendent.

"Bugger *him*," said Joe. "Let's find *them*! Graveyard—which way?"

Turning the corner they caught sight, silhouetted against the declining sun, of Chadwick making at a fast pace towards the collection of headstones that marked the cemetery. As they watched, three small figures hitched up their skirts and ran from the scene. Chadwick forged on. He broke into a trot. Straight towards Dorcas and Francis Crabbe, who seemed, like frightened rabbits, to be huddling close for comfort and backing slowly away.

Joe couldn't hear the exchange of words as they hurled themselves across the squelching turf but his eyes, wide with horror, took in the scene that seemed to happen in slow motion in front of him.

THE WORDS EXCHANGED were short and crude.

"Judas!" yelled Chadwick, coming to a halt a few feet away.

"Murdering swine!" Francis Crabbe shouted back, holding his ground. His voice was firm, even exultant, but the arm he passed protectively around Dorcas's shoulder was trembling.

The two men stood a few feet apart, raw emotion pulsing between them. A lifetime of unspoken words dammed up on each side, and there was no time to deliver them.

"End of the road, Crabbe! And you have three others on your conscience now. They'll have to go with you. If you'd kept your trap shut—but you never learned anything profitable in your useless life, did you?"

"I learned this much!" screamed Francis. "From your Bible classes!" He held out a staying hand and thundered in a priestly voice: "'I find then a law, that, when I would do good, evil is present with me.'"

"I'll put it on your tombstone," Chadwick jeered. "An epitaph!"

With a speed that took Dorcas by surprise, Francis plunged a hand into her satchel and came up with her gun.

No warning, no bargaining. One shot. With a look of surprise, Chadwick buckled at the knees and slumped to the ground, a red hole between the staring eyes.

Joe panted up with Gosling at his side. Gently he took the gun from Crabbe's grasp and put the safety catch on. His next act was to seize a shivering Dorcas in a tight and wordless hug.

Tactfully, Gosling went to check the body, which was lying collapsed backwards over a tombstone.

"A bit slow on the draw." With a toe he pushed a Browning revolver away from Chadwick's hand. "He's a goner, sir."

"Hit by a Smith and Wesson at point blank range, he would be," Joe said, back in control again. "I don't need to ask why, but I wish you'd left him for us to deal with, Crabbe."

"Couldn't be certain he'd not get away with it. He always has. This was the only sure way. I've had mad fantasies about this for years, sir," he admitted with a shaky grin. "Look at it this way—if *I* hadn't shot, Miss Dorcas would have. I could feel her hands twitching. Right now she'd be in all kinds of bother. I'm not sure she's the kind of lady who'd get over killing a man, even a monster like that. She might have had to stand trial. Wouldn't want that. Anyway, I'm mad. Officially mad. What are they going to do? Send me to a loony bin?"

Francis Crabbe smiled a smile of pure reason.

"Christ Almighty, Crabbe! I believe you've just set the water-works on fire," said Joe, admiring.

CHAPTER 31

They met for the last time in the equipment room, sitting at the table while whistling coppers cleared the place of documents and evidence boxes.

Joe looked around him with the familiar blend of regret, anxiety and triumph that always accompanied the closing of a case. Anxiety was winning the struggle for his attention. He grimaced. "Tin hat and a one-way ticket to the Riviera, I think you suggested earlier, Martin? Advice we might need to take, all four of us."

"You've knocked the top off a beehive, Sandilands. And it's *you* they're all buzzing after. But I'll tell you, if anyone needs watching it's that professor we've got under lock and key in Tunbridge. I warn you, he's got all sorts of mischief planned for *you* when we let him loose."

"Let him loose? Why would you do that?"

"He seems confident he'll get bail. Seems to think you'll know why. Pity we couldn't get him for the St. Magnus murders. I thought when the lid came off the Spielman coffin, we'd have it sewn up. Oh, it was all tickety-boo on the surface; death well documented and accounted for. All aboveboard. Nasty scene," Martin confided. "Spielman blustering and claiming immunity, Madame Spielman shrieking and distraught. But—alerted—our doc confirmed suspicious death, signs of electrodes applied under the hair."

The inspector looked steadily across at Joe. "He's a good bloke, that one. Came straight out and said if he hadn't been warned to look for something a bit fishy, he'd have passed the body straight through. No question. Then we looked more carefully at the documents. And the bottom fell out of our theory. Two unknown medical signatures on the death certificate—both bona fide doctors used regularly by Chadwick. No, neither of 'em Dr. Carter. He's well in the clear on the eugenics racket. And then we tracked the delivery van back to the Prince Albert."

He paused to puff his pipe into life. "That was a bad hour you put us through, commissioner. You were out there on the road. We were busting a gut to get hold of you and warn you. Leaving messages here there and everywhere. The school, The Bells, the RAC patrol boys. Ringing and ringing. But you'd disappeared . . . gone off the dial. Blimey, I'd have—" He glanced at Dorcas and censored the soldier's phrase which had been on the tip of his tongue, "—been extremely concerned had I know you were driving straight into that snake pit!"

"We were shitting bricks too, inspector," Dorcas said.

"So, you're all off this afternoon, leaving me carrying the can?" Martin concluded with affected grumpiness.

"Not all. Gosling's staying on here for a bit."

"Liaising with the new headmaster when he gets here," Gosling said. "Calming things down. Providing some continuity."

Martin expressed the hope that when the interviews took place, somebody would have the sense to check whether the applicant's featured on the Eugenic Society list. He suggested a little blackballing might be advisable. "You know, Farman really thought we were making a silly fuss. Tried to make out he didn't know he was sending those poor boys off to their deaths—they were just onward bound to further specialised treatment at the parents' request. Huh! He's got his lawyers quite convinced he's been misunderstood! Deluded or what?"

"Self-deluded," Dorcas suggested. "The very best kind of liar. Like his Matron. She was just doing what the headmaster asked her to do, of course. Packing the boys' trunks and waving them off."

"Matron aided and abetted, but I'm pretty sure she wasn't privy to the hideous truth. Didn't know because she didn't ask. Well rewarded. Money closes more than mouths, it closes minds. She claims that, insofar as she had any thoughts at all, she reckoned all that discreet leaving by the back door after dark was designed to avoid any disturbance to the other boys."

Martin sighed. "Very persuasive lady. Runs rings round the men. She'll move on unscathed. But not unchecked."

"From a London perspective, Farman has been quite useless when it comes to rolling up the conspiracy. They were too smart to give away names and contacts. He received his orders by telephone. Not always the same voice. And he, in turn, rang up the Prince Albert. Chadwick & Son, your friendly family undertaking business, established 1895. Purveyors of bespoke death through two generations."

"Christ! Why? Chadwick and Bentink—*two* butchers operating in my county? Why?" Inspector Martin's outburst voiced everyone's horror and disbelief. They listened in hope of enlightenment to a carefully delivered explanation by Dorcas, who was the only one prepared to take a shot at it, though Joe noted with understanding that her voice lacked its usual confidence.

They nodded in agreement with her suggestion that eugenics was a two-sided coin. One side urged the improvement of the quality of the population by breeding selectively from worthy stock, which would appear to be Bentink's philosophy, the other side urged and attempted to licence the removal of undesirable elements, preventing them from reproducing their faulty genetic makeup. An approach put into practice by Chadwick. The two faces, each unaware of the other, shone out from a freshly minted but utterly counterfeit coin.

"Any chance these devils were working in concert, sir?" Martin asked.

"No sign of it. I think they operated totally independently of each other, though it's clear that at least Chadwick had some suspicion of what Bentink was up to. Both were members of the Eugenist Society through the generations. They were at least each *aware* of the other's existence and, perhaps, proclivities. And what did our fine, idealistic Utopians do when push came to shove? Chadwick betrayed Bentink, just handed us his card. Simple as that. Distraction. Laying off the blame."

"And successfully," Dorcas said. "We fell for it. Well, no. It was my fault. I was only too pleased to seize the chance to hurry you along to the St. Raphael clinic, which I had decided deserved an investigation."

"Don't blame yourself," said Martin. "If ever a place needed a light shining on it, that one did! Bentink is now busy blaming everyone he can think of and calling in favours from the greatest in the land. Think on!" the Inspector warned. "With all the discretion that bloke has guaranteed over the years for god-knows-what delicate conditions amongst the high and mighty, some of them will be only too ready to hear his pleas. The embarrassing secrets he must hold in his files! These birds'll go to a lot of trouble to squash a revelation of anything from syphilis to face lifts."

"Does this make us lose our faith in humanity?" Gosling wondered out loud.

"Always," said Joe. "If we have any humanity in *us*. But then I find, in most cases, there's usually someone quite unexpected lurking ready to pick up the torch and shine it around. I'm thinking of Adam and Francis Crabbe. Men who know what's right and go straight for it with no regard for their own safety and no thought of reward."

"Reward? Farman was rather partial to a bit of that. I've applied to get a look at his bank statements. Should be interesting," Martin said. "The money trail? Did you get a line on that?"

"The cheques came anonymously from a very reputable London bank, numbered account. I wouldn't be surprised to find it was a holding account bulging with donations from a eugenic faction."

Joe thanked Martin for all that he'd done at the Sussex end of the operation. "On the bright side, we leave you well placed for promotion on the satisfactory outcome of all this, Martin. No, it was well done, and I shall say so!" he added seriously. "If anyone's prepared to listen to that bungler Sandilands when I get back to the Yard."

Martin's opinion was that the hardest part of the task awaited Joe back in London. "You'll never get to the spider at the centre of all this. Contacts will be cut, doors will bang shut. The establishment will close ranks on you. Too many reputations at stake."

"My own as well," Joe admitted.

He sketched out his plans for further action on his return to London. The nine lost boys were lost no longer. Eight at least had been brought back into the light, and Joe was determined that they would be acknowledged. The parents who still remained would be confronted with whatever evidence he could get together. He realised it was too late for a lawful conclusion for most of these cases, whose trails had led to a cold gravestone at the best, but he would do what he could.

This was not a task he could delegate to one of his superintendents. Any such enquiry would spread poison, invite recrimination, risk unbalancing the status quo. It was a course of action that would wreck a police career. It was for his shoulders alone.

For the last time, Joe laid out the nine faces on the table top, and Martin, Dorcas and Gosling silently studied them.

"Farewell ceremony, sir?" Martin asked.

"*Ave atque vale*, I think Godwit would say. No sooner greeted than bidden farewell. But no longer lost," Joe said. "Thanks to Hercules here." He grinned at Gosling. "And thanks to Edwin Rapson. I've had some strange guides through my cases but never one as unlikely as Rapson: murder victim, rapist, blackmailer and would-be killer of his own flesh and blood! But it's the thread of his researches that led us through the labyrinth."

"You keep saying that, Joe," Dorcas said. "Threads, knots, webs, mazes. Have you got to the middle yet? This spider Inspector Martin conjures up?"

"No." Joe shook his head. "But I know I'm close. These lads will lead me to him. It's not over yet."

Gosling seemed to take this as a cue. "Sir!" he said, putting up a hand in his excitement to catch Joe's attention. He reached out and with the gesture they'd become accustomed to, he moved the sepia print, the oldest boy who still remained nameless, to the left of the lineup. "Sir. I think I know who this is." He took a brown file envelope from his briefcase. "Found it an hour ago. Out of place. Deliberately misplaced? Rapson ferreting about?"

Gosling, with Joe's encouragement, had battled on with his research into Rapson's little black book and a meticulous examination of the lower strata of the school records. Unwilling to let even one soul make the final journey unknown and unmourned, Joe guessed.

"There were three candidates with the same initials over two years, but I think I've got him, sir. The ninth boy." He frowned for a moment and added: "Or should I say, the *first* boy? It's this boy's death that may have paved the way for all the others."

He placed the file with quiet triumph on the table.

Dorcas and Martin looked at the name with interest, but it

was Joe who reacted strongly. He recoiled with the startled disgust and fear he might have shown if Gosling had flung a snake in front of him.

"Gosling!" Joe cleared his throat, trying for control. "This name. Have you established a connection?"

"Oh, they're connected all right! Five or six more on the school rolls down the decades. Dedicated alumni, you might say. Keen and supportive. Generous donations. And they have," he paused, choosing his words, "a certain presence in the upper circles of the present government. Am I right?"

This was confirmed by Martin's low whistle. "Gawd 'elp us!" he muttered, and he reached into his pocket for the list he carried about with him. "Here he is. Listed. Eugenic Education Society, Mayfair branch."

Martin eyed Joe with a blend of amusement and pity. "Better seek an appointment with the prime minister, Sandilands."

THEY SAT ON in silent contemplation of the task and barely noticed the hesitant tap on the door.

When it was repeated, Martin called, "Come in!"

It creaked open to reveal the small figure of Jackie Drummond.

"Oh, hello, old son! Come and join us," Martin said cheerfully. Trembling with some emotion and clearly awed by the assembly of adults at the table, Jackie nevertheless shot into the room and ran to Joe's side.

"Here! What's up, old man?" Joe asked with concern. He took the boy by the shoulders and held him steadily for a moment. "Jackie, what's the matter?"

"They told me you'd gone! They said you'd left and gone back to London, Uncle Joe. Without telling me."

"No, no! What rubbish! We're both here, Dorcas and I, as you see. We are leaving and pretty soon, but not without saying goodbye. Never!" Defiantly, he gave the boy a hug. Gosling and

Martin looked aside tactfully, but Dorcas grinned. "Besides, we haven't had our talk yet. You could well be coming with us back to Aunt Lydia's if that's what you want. This isn't the only school in the country. I've found a rather wonderful one in the north where they have a forwards-looking headmaster, the pupils choose their lessons according to their own interests and there's no whacking allowed. We might manage to persuade your mother to send you there instead."

Recovering fast, Jackie spoke up. "It's not that, Uncle Joe. It's all right here." He flashed a shy glance at Gosling. "And I reckon if Mr. Gosling can stick it, I can. No, I wanted to say, when Mummy arrives, she'll want to see you. I wondered if, with Easter coming up, she could bring me to Auntie Lydia's and we could all have a talk."

Dorcas came around the table and took his hand. "Excellent idea, Jackie!" she said. "There's a great deal of talking to be done. I'll bake a few extra hot cross buns. Can't wait to meet—Nancy, is it? Now, push off, old thing, and leave us to get on with our packing up. We'll see you again before we go. Perhaps—as there's no headmaster to say no—we can sneak you out for supper at the roadhouse this evening? What about it?"

CHAPTER 32

APRIL 1933. SURREY.

"Dorcas! Come here and help me test out the hammock!"
Joe stood back and checked his handiwork. He enjoyed
a bit of estate work at the change of the seasons: repairing the
fences, cutting the grass on the croquet lawn, assembling the
garden furniture. Lazy old Marcus could never be bothered even
to give the instruction to the men to do it.

He'd changed into a pair of rough gardening trousers and an
Aran lifeboatman's sweater so old he remembered his father
wearing it. He knew what Gosling would have said he looked
like: a ratcatcher.

"Oh, hello, Joe. Look at you! Now I know it's true—Lydia's
story that you're descended from Ragnar Hairy-Breeches, Man
of the Borders. Does she know you've been busy doing this? It's
only just spring, you know."

"It's sunny, isn't it? Go and fetch a woolly if you're not up to
braving the elements. I've decided I'm not going to waste another
day of my life. There may not be much of it left, professionally
speaking. I've got two weeks leave while they decide what to do
with me, the bluebells are thick on the ground—my favourite
flowers—and just breathe in that wild garlic! I'm enjoying every
moment of it. I'm anticipating summer."

Joe settled down on the hammock and patted the space by his side. "Come on. Jump up. You can do it."

Dorcas looked at him doubtfully. "You never used to let me sit with you."

"You're much bigger now. The balance will be better."

Dorcas settled herself awkwardly into the space he'd left.

"I thought you'd be needing a bit of company," she said. "I was watching your face when you said good-bye to Jackie after lunch. You looked like a father waving his oldest son off to school for the first time. You know, the tears bouncing off the stiff upper lip. You got fond of him, I think. Well, we all did. I know how you must feel. I've lost people."

"More than your fair share, Dorcas." Joe smiled. "But then, you've found some too. And, speaking of your latest acquisition, was that your Truelove on the phone just now? That's the third time today."

"Not funny, Joe. And it was the second. James is not 'my true-love,' so you can forget the nasty jibes. Married man, as you know."

Joe rolled his eyes. "Since when was that an obstacle to skulduggery? I've decided to speak to Orlando. It's time your father told him he was aware of nefarious intentions towards his daughter and warned him off."

Dorcas groaned. "Not horsewhips and club steps?"

"Yes. And I shall hold his coat while he does it."

"And a very silly pair you'd look."

Dorcas wriggled and hitched herself closer. In a voice that was almost a whisper, she asked: "Would you really like to know how things are between me and James? You're never going to ask me, are you?"

Joe shook his head.

"He's attractive, friendly, funny, and he likes female companionship. He likes me. He wants to take things further. I'm considering it."

"That all?"

"All I'm prepared to say to you."

"And is that what he had to say just now? I wondered what had put that secret smile on your face."

"No. James had some good news he wanted me to pass on to you. He's been given a new department."

"I think I can guess which."

"Education. With Aidan Anderson under investigation, not to say a threat of imprisonment, James is taking over. Since you stormed into London, flinging accusations and handcuffs about and generally tearing down the pillars of the Temple, there have been resignations and reshuffling in several departments of state. Starting, of course, with the spider at the centre of the lethal network: Aidan Anderson, alumnus of St. Magnus, member of the Eugenic Society and minister in the Education Department."

"I was pleased to corner him and rip his mask off. And I don't regret it, whatever happens. Dorcas, there was no family resemblance, was there? I didn't miss that, did I? Between the minister and his cousin? Our first lost boy, the study in sepia?"

"No. I couldn't see one either. As boys, they must have known each other, Joe. They were at St. Magnus at exactly the same time: between 1895 and 1900. But there were no features in the photograph you could possibly have identified."

"But Aidan thrived and went on to Oxford and a political career. Arthur sickened and sank under a debilitating nervous illness. Precisely what we'll never know. Was it unintentional, that first disappearance? It could have been, you know. Or was the child put down? Whichever one, the idea of a convenient disappearance with the blessing of a eugenist philosophy was planted, one must assume, by that occurrence. And the notion of a cull in the name of eugenics passed on down the generations."

"Well, Aidan now finds himself culled. James has been given

his department, and he's incorporating Reform into it, so I suppose he's doubled his empire. Well, he deserves it. He's kind and
clever. I told you so."

"It rather depends on who he's trying to make up to at the
time. If you were to ask his brother-in-law Bentink's opinion on
Sir James, the response would be unrepeatable. It might include
the words 'traitor,' 'conspirator,' 'bolshy police-poodle,' 'marriage-
wrecker'. . . ."

"The first three, fair enough. But James wasn't to know that
his sister would begin divorce proceedings."

"And leave her husband in the lurch? She made her mind up
pretty quickly to stay in London when he slipped bail and headed
for the continent. Don't imagine I'm unaware that strings were
pulled and officials looked the other way. I'm quite certain you
were in there from the beginning, aiding and abetting, if the truth
were known."

"Does it matter? Bentink's out of the country and can do no
more harm."

"Rubbish! I can't imagine what evil the man's perpetrating in
the name of science over there where his views and methods are
supported and encouraged."

Dorcas was squirming with excitement. "I can! James told me
just now. It's why his sister decided to pull the plugs on the beast."

"I'll try not to glaze over while you tell me. But I don't expect
I shall understand a word."

"Oh, you will! You of all people," she said. Then added quickly:
"The word is a made-up one. Bits of Greek. You'll work out the
subject of his new scientific enthusiasm when you hear it. It's . . .
um. . . ." She took a run at it: ". . . *eutelegenesis*. You won't find it in
a dictionary. Or even in a scientific paper yet. It's one of those
fashionable words scientists murmur to each other."

"Not another *eu* word! Lord! This one sounds even more
dastardly than the rest. Let me think. *Tele*—that's 'at a distance,'

as in 'telephone,' so we've got 'good breeding at a distance.' Sounds like something a stockbreeder might have need of. I mean transporting bull's—er—essence, in a glass jar a hundred miles to a suitable recipient. No! Dorcas! Tell me I've misunderstood."

"You probably haven't. 'Artificial insemination,' an animal breeder would have called it when it was invented in seventeen hundred and something. Some wise men are beginning to say: We can breed the very best in plants and animals—why do we ignore the needs of humanity? The brightest and best of our men are not remarkable for their fecundity. Bentink actually calculated that fewer than a hundred babies are being born to men of calibre in this country every year. I do wonder what sources he used! He estimates that, given the right number of women prepared to oblige—and Joe, they are coming forwards!—he could increase this tenfold. Already there are five hundred on the waiting list in England and two thousand in the United States. In three or four generations we would be looking at a race of supermen. They say."

"My God! I've never heard such tripe! Who are these silly women? What do they think's on offer? They'd sign up for a Rupert Brooke or a Douglas Fairbanks, and that's understandable, but when I look around at our brightest and best brains, what do I see? I see the ugly bodies, the unattractive features that seem to be part of Mother Nature's sly deal. To use Bentink's own words: 'You wouldn't want to breed from them.' Anyway, what man would be so arrogant as to volunteer his seed anyway?"

Dorcas snorted. "Well, Bentink for a start! It was at this revelation that the relationship with *Mrs.* Bentink began to curdle. Imagine—walking in the park and seeing dozens of baby Bentinks out in their prams!"

"No bonnet big enough!"

"James says his sister was only too glad when he ducked off to Germany, where they take him seriously. Well worth the loss of the bail money."

"No waterworks over there, I expect." Joe sighed. "You know, I'd give a lot to hear Francis Crabbe's views on—what was it? No, I won't say the misbegotten word, and I hope never to hear it again. Though perhaps I might share the thought with Francis next time I visit. Just the sort of nonsense he'll appreciate."

Deep in thought, they sat on in companionable silence interrupted only by a loud cuckoo in the hedge.

"She's arrived early this year," Joe commented.

"I've never seen the point of cuckoos. One of Nature's barmier ideas," Dorcas said. "Laying her eggs in some poor unsuspecting sparrow's nest."

A minute later: "I was thinking of Jackie. I know Nancy's his mother but—"

"But what?"

"She's the most awful cow. Lydia thinks so too, I know, though she's much too loyal to say so."

"Sad to hear you say that. I loved her once." He'd been meaning to tell her, try to explain how it had happened but hadn't known how to phrase it and here he was blurting it out in four words without warning.

Dorcas appeared unmoved. "Thought so. Well, she didn't love you. Too self-centred. Nancy gets what Nancy wants, I imagine. Sensible woman, though. She combined scooping up Jackie with extending her stay with her sisters and booking into the hospital in Brighton. Had you any idea she was six months pregnant?"

"No. It makes a lot of sense. Childbirth can be tricky in India. Much better to get it over with while she's in England."

The conversation was proving more painful than Joe had anticipated, and the hammock had been a bad idea. They always were. But he ploughed on. "I never knew her very well. I feel I know her husband, Andrew, much better. He's very like me, you know."

Dorcas nodded.

"I didn't, for instance, know that Nancy had had a second child, two years after Jackie was born. A girl. She died when only a few hours old. Nancy's determined that this time things will go better. She claims she's rather elderly for childbirth anyway. What an idea! I thought she was looking quite splendid."

He was remembering the walk he'd taken along the cliffs with Nancy when the storms had subsided. Jackie had repeated his decision to continue at St. Magnus, again citing the example of Mr. Gosling.

When he'd relayed this to Gosling, instead of the shout of scoffing laughter he expected, the young man had gone silent for a moment, then admitted he felt he wasn't cut out for the Service. He'd even thought about—and pleaded with Joe to talk him out of it—staying on and doing a bit of schoolmastering. Much to be done, and he thought he could do it better than the men who were presently at the school. With Farman in clink and a new head on the horizon, perhaps St. Magnus would be a different kettle of fish. Joe would not even try to talk him out of it.

Nancy had chattered on about Jackie and the school, about their friends in India and had repeated warm messages from Andrew. She'd left it until the last moments before the walk ended to say what he really wanted to hear. "I'm so sorry, Joe. I thought you'd have forgotten. If you'd ever realised. But it was bad of me. I should have told you in case you were concerned. He's not your son, you know. He's Andrew's. My doctor told me that this does happen. A childless woman has an affair and soon after, a baby is born. But a careful study of the dates reveals the unbelievable has happened. One of Nature's little jokes? When she goes on to produce further children, there can be no more doubt. The husband is the father."

And into his stunned silence: "Jack thinks the world of you, Joe. We'd all be very happy if you would consider visiting him at the weekends. For manly pursuits—you know, swimming, riding, shooting. The stuff an English gent has to know."

Joe had fled back to Lydia's and drunk a bottle of whisky. He made a raging and drunken vow that if he ever saw Nancy Drummond again he'd push her off a cliff. Marcus had caught his glass as he dropped it and agreed to help him do just that.

And, well into April in the Easter holidays—under pressure from Jackie, Nancy admitted with a tinkling laugh—she'd accepted Lydia's invitation to bring her son to spend part of the holiday with them.

The few days had felt more like a month with Dorcas about the place, dark eyes seeing more than they should. Still, he'd had a good time teaching Jackie to ride and play badminton. Sod the woman, he'd be a devoted uncle. Not difficult.

Dorcas gave him time with his thoughts then said quietly, "Jackie is your son, Joe, isn't he?"

"No. He's not. I had thought so. I mean, there was every chance that he *was*, but Nancy explained exactly why he couldn't be."

Painfully, awkwardly, he gave her Nancy's account.

Dorcas considered it and came to a decision. "Then she's mistaken or deliberately deceitful. I'd guess deceitful. She tricked you *into* paternity, why shouldn't she be tricking you *out* of it? One sees why—she wouldn't want you to have any claims on the boy. And you can't argue with her, of course you can't. But you need to know."

"I have to believe what the lad's mother tells me!"

"No, you don't," said Dorcas stolidly. "She's a lying hussy, I thought we'd established that. Anyway, there's proof she can't suppress. A proof from Nature, and I'd trust Nature before Nancy Drummond."

"What are you talking about, Dorcas? You know nothing of this."

"I use my eyes and my common sense. Have you ever noticed how Jackie, when he's worried—and that's been quite frequently over the past weeks—has a gesture he can't suppress? Not that it would occur to him to try. He smooths down his left eyebrow with the knuckles of his left hand. Like this. It's a self-soothing gesture."

"I'd noticed. When he's agitated. Yes. Doesn't every boy?"

"No, they don't! The only other person I've seen doing that is you, Joe."

"Me?"

"It's so automatic you don't even notice. I used to think it was because your brow wound was itching, but it wasn't. You do it when you're upset." She turned his troubled face towards her and peered at him.

"Like now. Go on, Joe, you know you're longing to do it." Her lips curved into a teasing smile. She was so close he could smell peppermint toothpaste on her breath.

"I beg your pardon?"

"Scratch your eyebrow. You're as tense as a bowstring, but you can't release the tension because I'm sitting on your left hand."

"You don't think the two might be connected?"

"You can't use the right. The family trait doesn't allow for that. I think it has most probably a genetic origin, passed down the generations like blue eyes or pigeon toes."

Joe swallowed, closing his mind to the shaft of hope that stabbed suddenly through him. "I don't believe a word of it. That's the sort of mumbo-jumbo that gets psychology a bad name. But it's strange, he felt like my son. Didn't look the least little bit like me, but I think I knew, and Nancy's denial didn't make me sad and disappointed. It made me want to wring her neck."

The thought seemed to cheer Dorcas. She patted his arm encouragingly. "Glad to see that specter from the past howling off back into the woodwork. But look, Joe, no need to indulge in whimsicality. Do a bit of detective work! Women always think men know nothing about the cycle of generation and pregnancy and birth—"

"There's a reason for that."

"Well, it's time you found out. Science is on the march, and you must keep in step. Dates, Joe! I can't possibly help with this but I'm sure you kept a diary of some kind in 1922. Blushing? I see you did! Well, just work out the date, ask Jack the date of his birthday, and I can tell you whether you can be excluded from the equation—or not. It's not everything but. . . ."

"I know about collecting evidence." Joe smiled. "Never investigated myself before, but I'll do what you suggest."

"Poor Joe. You must be in turmoil—family pressures on one side, heavy court cases looming on the other, the enquiry coming up, and political storms brewing. You don't know which way to look. I expect you've called me out here for a good reason."

"A reason?"

"Yes. Time, I think, for a bit of distraction. Like the great crested grebes. When it all gets too much, just ignore it, and go off and find some seeds to peck. Stop fidgeting!"

She put up a hand and turned his face towards her. The dark eyes were shining with an emotion he'd never encountered before. Joe still hesitated to put a name on it, but whatever it was, it was undisguised, unveiled, unchallenging and totally hypnotic.

"You won't yell for help, will you, if I put my arms round you, hug you close and give you a proper kiss?" she asked.

"Great heavens, Dorcas! Do you know how? Are you sure you want to? I have to ask."

"Yes, I do, and yes, I do, and no you most certainly don't. I've been meaning to for years. Now, don't be such a weed! Lie back, take a deep breath, and think of England in springtime."

Joe took a deep breath, several deep breaths, but remained sitting upright.

"No. Sorry, Dorcas. I can't. High jinks in a contraption like this at my age? It could all end in shrieks of laughter. Look, I sent the men off to repair the barn roof. If you'll take a stroll with me down to that patch of ancient woodland, you can whisper in my ear, and I'll consider any indecent suggestions you care to make in perfect seclusion."

"Ah! You know a bank whereon the wild thyme blows?"

"Wild garlic anyway. It's growing very thickly this year. They say its scent is very invigorating."

He stepped down and lifted her from the hammock. He held her tightly and kissed the top of her head. "Sorry, Dorcas. It's taken me rather a long time to see it. I'm still struggling with the idea that you might love me. It's a very strange thing, but I begin to understand when I look at it with the Bard's eyes—as young Gosling would say:

> *So we grew together*
> *Like to a double cherry, seeming parted,*
> *But yet an union in partition:*
> *Two lovely berries moulded on one stem.*

He grinned. "Well, one lovely berry, anyway. The other's a bit bashed about."

"Joe, can we leave the bards out of this? I like a man who does his courting in his own words. Or no words at all."